W9-BZW-010

"Here is a novel that sets the species down in its proper plain place: talking animal. Late Bloomer to the Big Window. Robin McLean is unafraid of the grand scale, wary of the luxury of mercy. I read *Pity the Beast* ravenously, stunned by its savage and glorious turns."

NOY HOLLAND, AUTHOR OF *BIRD*

"Like any Western worth its salt, *Pity the Beast* abounds in fiction's elementals: muck and dirt and dust; flies and fire and shit; spirits both mythical and distilled; and, of course, fucking. McLean is a writer of the hardscrabble sacred and well-perfumed profane, and her grotesques cry out from their place there on the page. Behold, the heiress to Cormac McCarthy—her pen to the old man's throat, her prose blood-speckled and sun-splattered and all her own."

HAL HLAVINKA,
COMMUNITY BOOKSTORE, BROOKLYN

PITY
THE
BEAST

ROBIN MCLEAN

SHEFFIELD – LONDON – NEW YORK

First published in 2021 by And Other Stories
Sheffield – London – New York
www.andotherstories.org

1 3 5 7 9 10 8 6 4 2

ISBN: 9781913505141
eBook ISBN: 9781913505158

Editor: Jeremy M. Davies; Copy-editor: Jane Haxby; Proofreader: Sarah Terry; Typeset in
Albertan Pro and Syntax by Tetragon, London; Cover Design: Anna Morrison; Printed
and bound on acid-free, age-resistant Munken Premium by CPI Limited, Croydon, UK.

And Other Stories gratefully acknowledge that our work is supported
using public funding by Arts Council England.

Supported using public funding by
**ARTS COUNCIL
ENGLAND**

CONTENTS

For Cindy, to keep a promise.
For Marsh, who stayed behind.
For Margaret, always.

Entreat me not to leave you,
Or to turn back from following after you;
For wherever you go, I will go;
And wherever you lodge, I will lodge;
Your people shall be my people,
And your God, my God.
Where you die, I will die,
And there will I be buried.
The Lord do so to me, and more also,
If anything but death parts you and me.

RUTH 1:16—17

ONE

Percheron

Once, here, on this high plain, there were only Horse, Bear, Rhino. No words to put to things, no call to put them. But today? Ginny and Dan in the barn, and words like this: "You fucked me over. You fuckin' fucked me over."

Ginny behind the heaving mare said, "Her water's broke. I broke it."

"He was fucking her while you were fucking him and thereby fucking me over," said Dan. "Now that foal's too big for her."

She swatted flies. Her hat was filthy from mucking. Her coveralls were unzipped to her waist. One arm hung free folded to the knee, the other was stuffed inside itself. Her flannel shirt was rolled up her elbow. The dust filled the doorway like the bees and flies.

"That foal will turn her inside out," Dan said. "That foal will bust her."

"No one knows how things go."

"How they go, how they go," he said. "Look at her belly." He spit and stirred the dirt with his boot. "Behold the suffering of an innocent creature."

Ginny spat too. "Behold?" she said. And: "I've got things to do."

Out at dawn, Ginny was in the barn as midwife. Dan saw to the cows. Most of the herd already speckled the south field to the east, burned two weeks back and quickly regreened. The cows ate the grass. Dan was a punctual rancher. He'd slapped them through the gate with his stick, one black, one white, then a tricolor bull calf. The calf turned his head and paused at the ongoing ruckus in the barn: a hoof to a stall and a bucket kicked over. "Easy, easy," Ginny cooed.

The calf ran on to mingle with the herd in the boulders and grass, grazing, shitting, swinging tails. They would cut off his balls in a week. Dan listened to the barn, which was red and peeling, the shed too, the corners a quarter-century off-plumb. When the hoof kicked the stall again, the gutter shook to the loft that yawned black, empty of hay. The cat slipped out of a raccoon's hole. Morning is the very best time for reproductive suffering. This is well-known.

Seven horses—a little cavvy—swayed likewise, in their own time, out into the corral. The palomino first, the chestnut last behind the cob, the gang in the middle biting on each other's necks. They bunched at the fence and sniffed new air. The little mare followed, a pony, small-framed to begin with, bought at the cannery auction and never fully past the effects of starvation. She lumbered between the crossties, stepped out past Ginny after the herd. She was a mixed breed, brown, with her big belly swinging. Any fool could see Shaw's Percheron had got her. What's monogamy to a horse, after all? A rare discipline in the animal kingdom. For millions of years, grazing on these same fields, the primal inhabitants of the Great Plains spared it not a thought. Fretting over infidelity about as much as Horse, Rhino, Sabertooth concerned themselves with the continental plates pushing patient below the earth. In millennia since, we've learned that both the earth and a good fuck can turn around and get you killed if you're not keeping a close eye. But what's the earth to a horse, after all?

"How could you do it?" Dan said to the barn wall. "You fucked me over." Ten years married. Ten years in love before that. A young man still.

"Settle down now," Ginny was saying, following the mare out into breaking day. "I can't help you if you kick me."

Dan caught a fly in his palm. He would tell Ginny about the fly, a private joke. The yard will fill with flies when the sun gets in, *easy easy*, soon, a few hours, but the Mormora Mountains still cast their long blue shadow and these flies were young, cold, dumb from smoke. The last calves shouldered through the gate. Another black, another white, then the acorn calves, more heifers, not impatient or impolite. Dan slapped their rumps and they romped and kicked across the field to find their mothers. The haze sat on the ground waiting for a breeze. He should forget about the fly.

"We'll get that foal out of you," Ginny was saying. "I promise."

Now the horses. Pacing and pawing. The little mare after. Dan turned the first seven out to the south field, the cob going first this time, the chestnut last again, always last, the Old Man, and Dan closed the gate after them. The mare hung her head over the top rail. She watched the herd break free into morning, trotting then halting, drifting by boulders, tossing heads, flicking tails. The young ones galloped the sidehill to the creek. He ran his hands across the mare's belly, withers

13

to stifles, which bulged under her great weight. He listened at the enormous bulge.

"Still two heartbeats," Ginny said.

"I'll burn Shaw's house down if this comes out badly."

"You're not some caveman."

The mare wanted out the south gate. Dan offered the north. She acquiesced, bobbed out of the corral, and he followed. "Maybe I am," he said. "You should hear them in town. For days, nothing else. You and Shaw." He nodded toward the oak. "You should've closed his gate. You're smart. Should've covered your tracks. Protected us."

The mare headed up the north field, the last field to be burned, just yesterday. The ground still smelled strong, black-stubble char the quarter mile up to the old oak. Dan followed.

"I'm sorry," Ginny called after him.

"I'd like to be a caveman," he called back. "I'd like to try it."

"I've said sorry a hundred times." His back was lean and dry and split in the middle.

"Say it again anyway."

"I'm sorry I did it."

He bent, rubbed his knees that were always sore now. "I don't feel better."

"I'm sorry."

"I've loved you right, haven't I?"

"Yes you have."

"What's he got?"

"I don't know."

"I've been good to you, haven't I?"

"Don't know why," she called. "It felt good. I couldn't stop it."

14

He held his head. "You should hear them talk and talk."

"Forget them. It's only us."

"Only us?" His grin was wrong. He turned back uphill after the mare, who was on a beeline. He walked with long fast strides, three miles an hour uphill. He'd clocked it. He liked a straight line as well as any. If he stayed to the line past the oak, he'd jump Shaw's fence, which ran the knob above Shaw's house and barn, and keep going up Hinton's Hill to Barryman's Quarry, two more hours along the ridge to the base of the Mormoras where the land was too broken up for grazing.

"She's headed for shade," he called back. "Come on. I'll need you."

They made a parade of three up the quarter mile. An oak was a rarity in the region, the seed no doubt delivered in the excrement of birds. "Hurry the fuck up," he said, but calmer now, praise be.

"I'm hurrying the fuck up," she said in a matching tone, but hung back in body and mind near the outer range of his mutterings.

What's the earth to a horse? A place to place the hoof, a cradle of grass, a prop to rest his nose while ripping grass out by the roots. And the Herd would have had no interest in eons. Seasons maybe, days maybe, the change of the wind certainly, the daylight hours on their pelts. No interest in geysers. In salt licks, maybe. Horse was a watcher, a minder of his own business, with eyes screwed in on the side of his tin-can skull, peripheral observer, yes, but what of those objects right in front of his nose? Expert in grass and wind, in the locations where rodents bored their holes, since such pits will break a forelock with one misstep. And then Horse would be left by his Herd. And then Wolf would come.

"Can't fucking trust anyone," Dan was saying, flaring again. "Least of all, it seems, our fucking wives and mothers."

"I'm no mother. What do mothers have to do with it?"

"Mothers start it."

He listed the usual local bad examples since the past is ever useful for lecturing.

Twelve million years back, we're talking, with Horse grazing in the walnut's shade with his clan, his wives bossing him, giving in to him or not while offspring and rivals stood off on distant hills watching for changes in the Herd and wind, for any mistake. Bear rumbling farther off, waiting for the same thing, digging a root to chew, ever hungry, ever exiled for his fearsome looks, and ever more fearsome keeping his own company. The Herd swished their tails at Bear's scent, also to express the desire to mate, also to say hello to the morning sun on their withers, also to deter Fly, though Fly is never deterred for long, will survive all catastrophe, since he thrives on debacle and disaster: internal bleeding, contagion, volcanic eruptions. What creature doesn't seek blood? What creature doesn't keep flesh on with flesh? Bear eats Foal. Foal blood soaks the soil where the grass will grow deep green and thick. Mare will feast in that very place, grief forgotten when her hunger is satisfied.

"Though Ella's fine," he was saying. "As mothers go. To be fucking fair."

"Fuck yeah," Ginny said sweetly. "Be fucking fair to fucking Ella who's fucking the fuck fine," since she had limits too and

16

could out-cuss Dan eight days a week and sometimes you have to kill fire with fire.

Sabertooth crouched. Rhino and Camel ripped branches for berries that blackened their tongues. Earth dervished on the business of planets. The eruption was merely due. When it came, Horse chewed on, blinked, as the sky thrilled black and tall for a thousand miles. Buzzard spied the tower-cloud coming, tipped her wings and flew fast south across many rivers and fat bodies of land, but wings fatigue and clouds do not. The air was full of tiny shards, microscopic glass, and these snowed down on all. Chickadee fell first, the most fragile webbing in the lungs, then Crane, who had flown straight through the cloud thinking oh, it is only a cloud, fell with his throat full, legs a tangled mound of ash. Rat keeled over from a bird's nest he'd been raiding, an egg escaping from his paws when he fell, no mother to meet Chick when he hatched, no heat, no worm or regurgitated grub. In the few hours he lived, Chick thought the world was a gray and silent place and he its only inhabitant, his kingdom, all he would ever know, and he ruled it from high in his branch, good and fair to all. To him his life was long and full of interest, but for the chill on his naked bumpy skin and the unexplained pain in his belly, his eyes scanning the sky, his mouth panting open with vague expectation.

"Saul's a goddamned lucky man," Dan was saying.

"Hell, yes. Since Ella's a fucking peach."

Badger fell from a limb, Dog from a cliff, floated downriver.

For Horse, the pain was exquisite, long and thirsty. The Herd marched slow to the water hole. Mud was cool on their hooves, the only soothing possible. They nuzzled the foals, a small comfort for lives so short. Breathing was hard, got harder, more shards in each inhalation, more blood. Weeks went by. Bones decayed as the Herd swayed and waited, organs swelled and pressed into organs that pressed and overlapped and crushed each other, no other place to go, one side wins, the other subsides. It was one of those rare conjunctions of scale, when nature, for reasons of its own, takes time out from the routine of hatching life to make good and sure that a few beloved offspring have been well and truly annihilated.

"Ella, Ella," he was saying, so—

Rhino was last to collapse, the biggest lungs, the grandest capillaries. From a distance his belly was a smooth round boulder.

"Why me?" he was saying.

The sun came up anyway. Tomorrows are blind and ruthless. With them came humans, rabbits, sweet grass. Then new, strange humans in wagons. Wives already with child, walking with sticks beside the wheels; tins of meat riding under the canvas. The new folk drank from creeks. They saw painted faces in the bushes, feathers and spearheads, and kept their powder dry. Men circled the wagons with the women and children safe in the middle. They drove off the natives, ate the rabbits, chased bison through reeds for meat and tanning. Dan knew the story of westward struggle like everyone, and as he trudged up to the oak in failure, he tried now to gather strength from it, from success, from the men before who'd sweated through troubles, dug wells with picks and shovels a few seasons on when there was time for "leisure," since a creek was fine for running water. They made gates for their oxen with split trees, ate their oxen when starved. Wives died left and right. Oxen died. The men married sisters off trains from Baltimore who thought they'd come out to see the new babies.

"Cheer up," she said. "You can always get yourself some other wife. Pick of the litter."

Dan doubled over and she passed him by. He took up the rear.

"Life moves in mysterious fucking ways," he said, or asked.

"No it doesn't," Ginny said without turning. "It's all happened ten million million times before this, ten billion times fifty."

"Not this exactly."

"Nothin' new under the sun."

"You're fucking wrong."

"No I'm not and you know it."

The old folk planted eastern corn that sometimes grew, scrawny and mealy. Potatoes were best against western birds but the elk and bison liked them. Sluices turned mills till drought. Plows broke against hidden rocks. Blades were ordered from St. Louis. They came in three months. Blades and sisters arriving by train. The men built barns and doors of rough-sawn. It was always sunshine, terrible sun, Indians in every crack and crevice, scheming. Girls made wildflower crowns and waited for eastern boys. In other times, in other places, cheating wives fed volcanoes. Fornication versus copulation is a delicate point anywhere, something to do with pleasure or sin? But these mountains were sedimentary, or lacked calderas. For somewhere to chuck a faithless wife you'd need to go south, the Yellowstone region or farther. But wait, didn't volcanoes want virgins? Virginia, *I do take Virginia,* for ovulation, ejaculation, insemination, fertilization. Who decided those words should rhyme?

"What in hell are you on about?" Ginny said. Then, "Quit this muttering and march on up."

She was pointing at the poor little mare up at the big old oak that didn't belong here, that shouldn't have set down roots here, not by rights or nature, and the sight of the mare's suffering moved Dan to action. He rose and walked but talked on still.

No volcanoes here, maybe, but plenty of carbon and flame, plenty of fire worship. Dawn-risers, field burners, Dan's people, his valley. They burned their fields from low to high, whole families in long pants and steel-toed boots, up and across, up and across, rubbing their eyes from neighbors' smoke. The valley was wide and dry. The Mormora Mountains east, black cliffs without foothills, mile-high curtains for keeping out witnesses. Keeping out the sun, too, till long after daybreak.

"Fucking's the crux," he said. "Fucking's the beginning. Fucking's the end."

"Amen."

"I do love saying it."

"Say it all you need to."

From the oak, all the valley spooled out. Fields burned across its rises and falls. The inheritors of the plain—just specks from here, skittering at the ends of plumes—carried hoes, rakes, and gas cans from their barns to their lowest fences. Ginny and Dan didn't need to see it close. Far off was fine. Their neighbors uncoiled the hose, paid it out across hard pack, turned spigots on full. The water sputtered then flowed before the weed burners were lit. Last year's grass was dry and matted. Burned fast and hot with the smallest puff of breeze. The first hills, each year, are a quarter burned before the sun tops the Saint's Head. Neighbors wave shovels and rakes across creeks to neighbors who wave shovels and rakes. For a hundred years now they've marched up and across the fields herding fires. Up and across toward the knobs of knobby hills. For a hundred more they will stamp the flames with their boots on top, then walk down again and start another, till the valley smolders black. Kids will always jump the fire lines. Parents will forever scold—such tedious work—and hot as hell even in morning. These people will drink from hoses and creeks as smoke rises between hills, mixing with sticky spring shoots and new buds, dung on skin, gritty teeth gritty. Tongues and lips will spit as a plane flies over. The plane is counting fires all over the region, this flight from Elkins to Romeo. The commissioner's report is due Monday, saying, "Burning two weeks near St. Cecilia, mostly small livestock operations, sheep, cattle, and a few equestrian. Two hundred to two thousand acres is average. It will soon be too hot, dry, and foolish for burning. Heat lightning will soon decide ignition: spike down after midnight, skimming west to east over hills and hills, farms and ranches, forking down from time to time to touch off neglected fields, a barn roof dried for decades, an unfortunate home, then exit, the innocent culprit, twenty thousand feet above the highest ridges, off across the Reservations."

"Except that no goddamned commissioner talks like that," she said.

The people wave their hoses at the plane. Water arches in sun, nozzles glint. Always the same: their eyes water.

They dab sweaty wrists. The plane dips its wings, a friendly stranger. The lines of fire are pretty and memorable. This is modern aviation. The plane banks toward the Saint's Head Ridge, aims for the Gunsight.

"Quiet, I'm thinking," Dan said and shaded his eyes. "How's about I bash him with a baseball bat."

"You don't own a baseball bat."

"I'll poison his well."

"You've never been mean."

"I'm mean now."

On the hills smoke still skimmed the ground. Only lazy ranchers burned this late in the day. Here was an oak that could still remember the settlers' wagons. Arms out and tired in the air. The mare fell in its shade like a sack.

"Get her off that root," Ginny said.

Dan sat on a low branch. "She doesn't feel that root. That root is nothing."

"Comfort isn't nothing." Ginny tried rocking the mare then sat with her.

"Don't talk to me about comfort."

They waited for the foal, nothing else to do. A bell rang down at Shaw's. The villainous Percheron made an appearance at Shaw's fence. Ginny's hand was up inside the mare's back end.

"Almost crowned." She wiped her hand on her pants. "Come on, darlin'. Come on out."

"Grab a leg."

"Not yet." The sun went on rising and the morning shadow shrunk. Dan threw rocks at the stud, but his aim was poor. The Percheron only flicked his tail.

"Sure, throw rocks if it makes you feel better."

"Nothing makes me feel better."

The Percheron kicked the gate. The new steel clanged, coped and fitted, full welds, new J-bolt hinges, all busted in where a truck had rammed it. HORSES KEEP THIS GATE CLOSED hung on the top rail. The stallion was gray and enormous, eighteen hands, a ton and then some.

"Percherons were bred for war," Dan said.

"Cut it out. Concentrate."

She pulled her flannel shirt off to a T-shirt. Her hand went back up the mare.

"The French beat the Arabs. Took their horses back to France. Bred them to free French stock. A thousand years." The gate clanged.

"Task at hand, Dan."

The mare arched. The stud's molars were noisy from thirty paces, chewing last year's dried-up mats, since Shaw's people, way back, were from Chicago and they did not burn their fields in Chicago.

"This foal's residual from war and theft," he said. "What do you think of that?"

"I could use a hand."

"Grab a leg and pull."

"Where's this blood from?" It was her hand she was talking to.

The head came, then the neck. It was a private time. Dan cut a stick and whipped the air. "A Percheron's the second-biggest horse. Shires win first, largest on the planet. Clydesdales win third. Clydesdale people bicker. Percherons hold all the records. That's undisputed."

23

"Shut up," she said. "Get over here."

The mare pawed the air. Dan fanned the flies from her face. The Percheron grazed and grazed. What are life and death to a horse, after all? Unworthy of comment is what.

The foal fell out, gray and enormous. The mare nuzzled its gray ears folded back, licked the face and spindle legs tucked up to the muzzle, tucked down and still. The foal came to them warm but was getting cold. Dan dragged it downwind by one back hoof. He dropped the foal on the far side of the oak in the sun. The mare gave up sniffing and laid her head on stubble. Her belly rose and fell.

"Better think of getting up," Ginny said and slid her hand inside the halter, didn't tug, not yet. Tripped to the fence and sat, her face in her knees, in the meantime. Peeled her coveralls off to jeans, flung the coveralls. A young woman still. The Percheron nibbled her hair from over the fence with his big lips. She shoved his face. The wind was hot. Dan walked down to the barn and returned with a shovel. He dug a hole. Ginny raked the afterbirth in. She pried a stone.

"A stone's just for show," he said. "Only slows the coyotes."

"They won't bother," she said. "Plenty of food this time of year."

He set the stone over the hole. Sat back down on his branch. All this was once a tide of stone, rockslides from the Mormoras. Imagine the tumble. The new piles and gorges. How strange the new mountain must have looked after the slide! The little gorges later filled by wind, leaves, and dust, then covered over with roots and sod until even the tallest rocks were buried to their chins: *Here Lies a Stone Big as Your Barn. I Will Crush Your Barn at the Resurrection.*

24

"It's incurable," he said.

"Silence is the only cure for the incurable."

They urged the mare up, to no avail. They watched the cows and horses below, the fires blurring the neighbors' hills, Milton's and Johnson's, Baltazar's and Cortez's, the Mestizo cluster, though intermarried now, mixed with Bolts, Blakes, and Native clans who'd lightened up and gone to Congress, come back disgusted. Shaws. A plane with pontoons was bound behind the Saint's Head, to lakes you couldn't walk to on the Old Swede's Trail. Dan thinking *grin and bear it*, sisters again, weddings. "In storms or raids," he said, "they pushed the oxen in their own cabin doors, shoveled dung out their tiny windows, dried it, stacked it, burned it in winter for baking."

"Ah uh," Ginny said.

"It flavored the skin," he said. "Washed at quiet pools."

He looked at his wife, thought of women who'd turned their chins from side to side between mossy rocks, their mirrors drowned in Nebraska rivers behind their swimming oxen. Squares of glass twirling away toward the Mississippi, tumbling south, sharpened by stones, till they slit some poor stomach open at the Gulf of Mexico. He liked the thought. For lip paint, berries. It made the women rosy. Good thing those pioneer men weren't too choosy.

"She'll have to stand soon," Dan said of the mare.

"She'll stand."

"Or it'll be two for the pit instead of one."

"Give her time to get herself collected."

They dragged the foal to the cow pit. The foal was light, two hooves each down the slope to the corral, around the barn. The backhoe stood at the edge. They swung the foal like a hammock, one, two, three. It cartwheeled down to join new dead calves, also chicks that had frozen and a fox Dan had shot. The walnut shaded the cow pit. They shoveled in lime.

"We'll need more lime," he said.

"I ordered it yesterday."

"That foal was pretty." He powdered the foal lightly. "Might've won a ribbon." A butterfly skipped so close they heard its clicking muscles and screws. "So many wouldn't believe one can," Dan said.

"Can what?"

"Hear a butterfly."

A little brown with white trim and hardly worth notice. It flew through a lime cloud. They coughed and covered their faces with sleeves and skin.

"It would be easier if you'd died too," he said next.

"Well I didn't."

"Like a splinter. Like a tapeworm. It's going to bust out of me."

"Don't let it."

"I might feel better if I hit you. It might relieve me."

"Do it then," she said. He balled his fist. "Get it over with."

He slapped the top of her head, but was too upset to aim right. He picked up the shovel, but she took it from him. She threw it in the cow pit. "Enough already."

They sat on the edge despite the stink. "Am I a good man? Or not?"

"You're a good man in a bad mood."

"I'd like to feel better. How can I accomplish that?"

"How should I know?"

"We have to be careful. We have to think."

"I agree. We need clear thinking."

He moved closer. "You should be more affectionate. That's one thing."

"I know it."

"You should put your hands on me. Like you did him." He wrapped his legs around her legs, his arms around her middle. He sniffed her neck. "For peace again."

"Soon," she said. "Give me time."

The butterfly dropped down to the pit. He rocked her on the edge and she let him.

"A horse has the largest eye of any land mammal."

"You've told me."

"People think lions, people think elephants. People overflow with mistakes and blunders."

"I know, I know." She pried his arms off. But gentle. "Let's get on back."

They stood and brushed themselves off. The butterfly roamed the high dirt walls between landings on a rump, then a forehead, then an ear with a tag beginning to rot where it sipped, then a hoof to a lip to a sunny flank to a scrotal sac until the lime burned its pinhead feet. It skipped off to cool them. Elsewhere, the planes landed too, spun down the ends of runways, tied down, refueled. Others dropped into blue lakes and scattered ducks, fishing lines off pontoons, rolled cuffs, sunburnt knees, toes swinging cool as bait.

They walked together from the cow pit, stiffly, arm in arm.

Word travels fast over hills and creeks. Saul and Ella were first to arrive in a plume of dust.

"Sister to the rescue," said Dan.

Their truck nosed in at the rusted saw blade on the barn. Ginny didn't care to see them walk up the slope with a cooler between them. They also brought a hacksaw, a bag of chips, rum and Coke in an old milk bottle. Saul screwed the top off, drank, passed it.

"Poor gal," Saul said. Leaned the hacksaw against the oak. Ella passed the chips. The Percheron's harem of grays had joined him at the fence. They grazed and watched the show.

"Son of a bitch," Saul said. "Gigantic stud."

Ginny finished the bottle to backwash. The mare seemed to be sleeping with eyes open.

"Still," Saul said. "Screwing is part of nature. Foals, etc."

"True fact," Dan said. "We all want to screw."

Ginny flung the bottle.

"Just look at the size of him," Ella said. "Imagine that thing getting on you."

"Why are you here?" Ginny said.

"How 'bout a truce," Dan said. "Just today."

"We don't need help," Ginny said.

"I asked them over," said Dan.

"It's private."

"They're offering. They're family."

"Grannie never turned down help," Ella said.

"Grannie's dead," Ginny said. "Seems like a while now."

Saul popped a top with his ring. Beer foamed over his hand. He licked his fingers.

"A cock like that," Ella said. "Split any mare wide open."

"Seems you've put some real thought into it," said Ginny.

Saul got a kick out of that, but a look from Ella stopped his laugh. "In dogs, this would never have happened," he said.

"The bitch size fixes the size of the pups. A teacup bitch bred to a Saint Bernard stud will produce a teacup Saint Bernard. No trouble with the pelvis."

"We need to get her up," Dan said.

"A horse who won't stand dies quick," Ella said.

"In a few hours, even," Saul said.

"She'll get up," said Ginny.

"Why don't you go find Shaw?" said Ella. "Why don't you run along?"

"Will you shut your everlasting trap?" Ginny said.

"We're here for the horse," Ella said.

"What we need is a plan, not catfights," Saul said. "This is red-light stuff."

"Let's get her up," Ginny said. "Then you two can get on home."

Now it was time to tug on the halter, push her rump, rub her shoulder, speak into her ears. Dan tapped her with his whip, but gentle, then quit. The sun baked the blackened ground. The men unbuttoned and unpeeled to skin. The women rolled their jeans up. The roofs in town were pebbles. The stadium was a horseshoe. Crowd noise came from time to time.

"I wonder who's winning," Ella said.

"Sedalia will win," Saul said. "Our ropers are better, but our riders are worse."

"Who cares about roping?" Dan said. "Get her legs under her."

"Come on, girl," Ginny said. "Get on up."

They urged, tugged, rocked her. "Son of a bitch," Saul said.

"Lift her, goddamn it," said Ella.

Saul ran down to make calls. The mare lay still. Another truck arrived in dust and parked at the barn under the saw blade. New arrivals climbed the hill with bottles in their free hands.

"I say it's colic," said one. He showed his pistol. "For the worst-case scenario."

He set it in the crotch of the tree while Dan opened more beers with his ring, same as Saul. They talked cows and caliber for starters, then quick about the lawsuit on the Reservation, land claims the Indians were making, ridiculous, then sharpening hand tools—tips and turmoil over hoof clippers—an upcoming cannery auction, woodlots and a box truck with Canadian tags at a car lot in Romeo, looked like a find, kids off to college and empty nests, Shaw leaving town. Ginny sat by the mare and picked at her boot heels.

"How'd your place burn?" Saul asked.

"Fast and hot, thank God." They chewed ice. "Colic for sure."

"This ain't colic," said the third man, who borrowed a knife to slice buns that had just arrived.

"I've seen this before," Saul said. "The foal presses the nerve during hard labor. Nerve goes numb."

"Happens in all mammals," said the neighbor with the pocketknife.

"That's not it," said the neighbor with the pistol.

"Get the weight off the nerve," Saul said. "Stand her up and pressure's off it."

"Her intestines are inflamed," said the pistol.

"They're tangled with the female organs," said pocketknife.

"She's tired," Ginny said. "That's all."

"Can't be tired if she wants to live," Ella said. "If she's weak she's dead."

"Broken record," Ginny said.

"If we could jack her up somehow," Saul said.

"Hoist her," Dan said.

"This horse is grieving," said pocketknife.

"Horses don't grieve," said a man with a cold.

"Of course they grieve," Saul said.

Now here was a neighbor on a white horse carrying a metal detector. The Percheron led his mares away.

"Shaw left yesterday," the latest guy said.

"She's thinking of going after him," Ella said.

"Screw you again and again," Ginny said.

"She's not going," said Dan. "She's staying."

"If she doesn't," said metal detector, "St. Cecilia is ruined forever for potlucks and bake sales. How will we stand it?"

Ella spun on the man. "Everything's a joke to you."

"Let's get this mare standing," Ginny said.

"We weren't talking to you," Ella said.

"But here I am," said Ginny, face-to-face with her sister.

"Should've gone with him. She deserves more than a slap."

"Too many years of you," Ginny said. "Dull, Ella, dull."

"Dull's fine. I've earned dull. Proud of dull. Dull's honest. If what you are's exciting, probably best go be exciting somewhere else."

"Hold up," Saul said. "That's Dan's decision to make."

"No one wants you here anymore," Ella said. "Go catch Shaw. Make a love nest in Pollings or Cheyenne."

"Hold up," Dan said. "I haven't decided."

"My ranch," Ginny said. "Get off."

"Your ranch," Ella said. She shouldered past Ginny, not a shove exactly, then circled back to the mare, her sister shaking and red.

"That's what I mean," Saul said. "That right there."

The men sipped and smiled. The mare nosed an empty cup.

"This girl needs a bucketful pronto!" Saul called. Kids sprinted down to the well.

"Get on home," Ginny said, collecting herself. "Me and Dan can handle this."

But Dan kicked soot. "I think we need 'em."

"Come on," Saul said. "Relax. It's good we're here."

Soon both Ella and Ginny were down on their knees with the still mare. Ginny's face was filthy and dark while the sun lit Ella's through the leaves in patches. It was a sweet face about to turn old. Lines were only now forming. Saul sucked a piece of straw. They tied ropes around the mare. The flies circled. More neighbors were arriving from across the creek and calling out, "Hey!" They tottered over via boulders, drew up bigger across the sidehill. Ella doled out cups.

"Anyone bring a pistol?" one new arrival said after looking the mare over.

They carried two beams for levers from the barn, dropped them at the mare.

"A Percheron must be black or gray," Saul was saying, "to hold papers in America. Strong and compliant despite his size. He was bred for plows and wagons."

"I never knew the name," said a neighbor just arrived by bike.

"Long before the motorized truck or tractor," Saul said, "the Percheron and its ilk powered our farms and nation."

"Good days," said pocketknife.

They sat on the beams. They cooled their mouths with Fireball. They worked the first beam under the mare's hind end to lift her. The mare did not kick or care.

"Careful," Dan said. "She's tender."

"This is foolish," said bike.

Then the second beam. "On three," Dan said. They levered her. The mare rose a few inches, tumbled, and a water bucket was knocked and spilled all over.

"Failure," Saul said. "First try."

"I have better things to do," said metal detector. He untied his horse and led him away, left the metal detector with a girl who begged, told her to drop it by when done with it. They rolled the beams aside, sat and drank some more. Watched the world, talked of dead cows, lime, and butterflies. The Indian School running out of money, which doesn't grow on trees, and how a good life comes from hard work, of course, of course. Cheaters and beggars never prosper. They drew schemes in the dirt with sticks, levers, and lifts, erased with hands and heels. "That's a good design," Saul said. They catnapped. "Five minutes will do me." Three went to town for spicy mustard, for more beer, gin. More trucks pulled in. "How long does it take for a horse to die?"

"It all depends," Saul said, mostly awake.

Smoke rose high. The haze leveled near Saint's Head Ridge. Dan checked the pulse at the mare's back leg. Ginny yelled that she was going for more water. The Percheron nibbled Dan's hat and he pushed the joker's snout away. He watched Ginny downhill with bucket swinging. On the old ranch, running water was a girl sprinting with a bucket.

"Two girls," Ella insisted.

She dawdled with tadpoles. Knew every flower. The cabin was made log by log, a two-man saw over piles of sawdust. Draw the knife to strip the bark, watch your fingers, boy. Roll them, scribe them, thump them into place. Mortise and tendon to joists and purlins, block and tackle, tripod and arm. A chisel makes the cleanest notch. Crank the drill for holes, then pound the spikes in. An earthquake won't sunder these corners though the house may sway. Cut the sod. Size it. Tin will come later. Indians watch the house from the hill. They climb that young oak, crouch in the limbs and crotches. Steal a dog, a horse, a girl. What's one white man to do? But from Indians there were admirable tricks to learn. They raised their drinks. If the girls were bad enough, for example, if one was handy with a needle, if stones were sewn in a hem just right, if the pond was deep.

"The trouble with women is they have no restraint," Dan said from the fence post. Ginny stood far below, a girl again with the bucket swinging from a fine strong arm.

"She's still pretty," Saul said, and the other men nodded.

Ella looked down at her sister. Refilled the cups without comment.

They watched Ginny to the corral gate, Ginny's boots through the powder, mixing her tracks with horse tracks and every other creature's. Sun was high now. She sopped her brow with her sleeve.

"Men always liked her," Dan said.

"I'd cut off his balls, drop them in quicksand," said the neighbor with the pistol.

34

"Waiting in the weeds like that," said the neighbor with the pocketknife.

"Liars and cheaters prevail," said a portly neighbor arrived on a dun gelding with a maul over his shoulder. "Survival of the fittest."

"That's depressing," Saul said.

"But true," said Ella.

"She's a big girl," said pistol, fiddling with the hacksaw. Saul said leave it be.

They were happy and peaceful as the breeze pushed smoke around the sidehills.

"She says she'll never do it again," Dan said.

"Cheaters don't stop," said pistol. "Once they've tasted it."

The mare rocked as if to stand, huffed and kicked. Ginny at the wellhead, to the pump, up and down, up and down.

"Shaw liked that part."

Dan kicked a tire driven up and parked for tailgate seating.

The gush from the well splattered her boots, one bare ankle then two. The bucket tipped. She bent to drink then left wet footprints over to her grandmother's porch. Three stone steps. Her hand shielded her eyes. Her boots sat beside her.

"Almost seems like she can hear us talking," Saul said.

"Too far," Ella said.

Dan lay on the ground, his hands behind his head, the fingers interlocked.

"Anyway," said the maul. "There's no such thing as quicksand. Quicksand's a lie."

"'Course there's quicksand," said pocketknife.

"Bad news is we're nearly out of ice," Ella said.

"That tree might be the trick," said pistol.

They all looked up into the oak, circled it, pointed up into its branches.

"I'll run down," Saul said. "Find a pulley and rope."

When the rodeo team arrived, they were still in uniform, pale blue with navy piping, bolos ripped loose and white hats with blue. Saul set them to untangling rope. They found a good tarp in the barn for a sling. They folded it and worked it under the mare's belly.

"Be careful," Ginny said, still steaming, but bending to the task. "She's had a day."

They followed Saul's directions: sewed the rope through grommets along her spine, snugged the rope to the spine and made loops on each end. Threw the rope to a scrawny rodeo kid on the first good limb. His hat was too big for him. He caught the rope and dropped it back down, then dropped down himself to take his place along the line.

"Listen up," Dan said. "Saul has some words."

"Dear Friends," Saul said, stepping forward. "Bow your heads." And they did. "Almighty God, Great Spirit, Universe, Whoever You are. Please do bless us and this fine ranch since we all need help sometimes. Lord, Your Honor, Jehovah: help us do right for this beast of the field, this poor angel, in her day of grief and trouble and throughout this frightful life. Amen."

"Amen."

"Are we ready?" Dan called.

They heaved like sailors. The rope went taut. The loops, the grommets lifted over the little mare's spine, the mare lifted. Her head swung. Dirt fell away. She was heavy. The mare whinnied and bucked as they dug in with boots and hips, pulled the rope fist after fist. The rope squeaked on bark. The branch strained and sagged. "Almost got her!" Her hooves lifted off the grass. "A few more inches." When she dangled well, the line strained and the people held. They leaned on the rope and waited for instructions.

"Ease her back down to her feet," said Saul. "See if she'll put weight on them."

"I can't hold," someone said and dropped off the rope.

"Careful!" The mare dangled to the tips of her hooves. "Is she standing?"

When her knees buckled, her hooves tucked under.

"Pull back! She can't stand!"

They dug their heels in, leaned.

"Haul back!" The branch strained. Legs pressed. Their boots tore into the dirt.

"Haul back!" Puffing, sweating. The rope bit into their palms and forearms. The rope moaned. The mare moaned. Some little kid started crying.

"How's crying going to help her?"

They pulled and got her up again then tied the rope off to the oak's trunk.

"Let her dangle," Saul said. "Get circulation to the legs."

Some went for gloves. Some massaged her forelock and knobby knees. The breeze turned the mare in a circle too slow to see. The branch bounced. Her head hung as if she might graze. The people walked to the creek to dip their hands. They drank water on their knees and beer on boulders. The kids found the pistol in the crotch and set empties on fence posts for shooting practice. The bottles sprayed Shaw's grass.

When the owner confiscated the pistol, the kids threw rocks. They talked of babies and croup and climbing roses and a star bronc rider from Sedalia who ran off to join the army. Some said he was queer, but that was impossible, a joke. The Percheron had retreated to a clump of trees. Dan massaged the mare's stifles and said sweet things. Ginny brushed her with a curry comb from the tack room. They consulted a horse book. The tall girls braided her mane and counted boys. When Dan offered Ginny a paper cup, she said, "This isn't a party," and slapped it. The tall girls heard the whole thing, told the tall boys and boys told others, so the slap of the cup passed here and there, until everyone later claimed to have witnessed it. Another plane. They fixed the rock ring for a fire later. Ella said she'd wanted to be a teacher, Saul a pilot of a spaceship.

"Astronaut, you mean."

"No sir, a pilot."

Ella said it reminded her of a story: once there was a berry picker who strayed from the clearing, ended with a bear for a husband. She'd been warned not to wander far.

"She didn't listen?" the kids said.

"It wasn't her nature to listen." Ella winked.

"Screw you," Ginny said and kicked dirt at her sister. The kids were fascinated.

Ella brushed off her boots. "She didn't care for compliance, this picker," she said. "No fun."

She winked again, which was when Ginny stepped in and slapped her, which was when capillaries busted in Ella's nose. It gushed red and she hunched, then Saul got Ginny around the middle, started in at hauling her off, then Dan intervened. "I got this." He peeled Saul's arms off and dragged his wife to calm her at the tree. She didn't calm, but Ella did. Saul handed her a hanky. She dabbed. The white cotton was soon dotted red.

"Gather in," Ella said. "I'm not finished telling it."

The same crybaby howled at her description of the berry picker's wedding to the bear, the animals on the guest list, the buffet line, who sat with who, the minister a turtle in a bow tie, ha ha ha.

"You Samaritans can shove off anytime," Ginny said, losing steam with each repetition. Now the words were dull and no one heard them. Some strolled down to the cow pit. They came back up with egg salad in a white bowl with blue flowers. Afternoon lazed on. From time to time they lowered the mare to try her.

"Can't quite yet," Saul said. "Pull her back again." He conferred with Dan.

Some went away to check their cows. Dust followed trucks down the road.

"I admire you," said a pretty widow to Dan, the horse book in her lap. She sat on a blanket with her three kids, her husband dead from melanoma. "Sticking with things."

He stared at her a long time. He turned a page, leaning across.

"Good people keep trying," he said, and blushed. "They move on."

Friends stopped by who had moved away, just in town for a 4-H dinner or for a mother who was dead, trucks loaded with rocking chairs. Stopped by to say hi. Heard what happened to him. They whispered, Ginny in the distance, slapped his back.

"I once had a horse that loved a tuna sandwich," said an old man.

"Horses are vegetarians," said the pretty widow.

Dan smiled at the woman. She smiled back. She held herself beautifully in grief.

"I scoff at your book," said the old man.

The pretty widow closed it, and the old man went home with his cane. He died a week later. He had a good life, they would say, then forget him, forgot him now, talked of sweet grass and killing gophers with dynamite as the widow read captions to Dan: "A Percheron must have command and gravity, attractiveness and elegance. Ideal for modern times. Born of desert and war, then enslaved. Oh, gray chargers. Oh proud African, noble residue of calamity!"

"What's residue?" the pretty widow's kids asked. "What's calamity?"

Ginny stalked over with a little spit on her lip that took too much time to wipe away, saying it was "something big and terrible," and the widow's pretty kids asked Dan if he would play sheriff with them. They pointed at the barn, the loft, the weather vane with the cock. He left the pretty widow, romping downhill with the gang; "Tallest of the posse," she laughed. He hunted after the seven-toed cat with them. A red dog chased them, all in fun. Saul didn't mind him going. The pretty widow continued reading horse captions to the crowd, turning the pages with a grin that dimmed only when Ginny paced fuming into her periphery, saying, "it's a show, it's a big damn show," from Lipizzaners and Morgans, nearly to the Zweibrücker, every caption in the book, when the branch snapped.

Trucks drove up the hill with lumber for Plan B. The chain-saw sliced the broken branch. They bucked it as the sun dropped west and made a pile. The women shaded the mare with a blanket over sticks planted around her as a lean-to. The men worked on tailgates. Their forearms were thick and sure and drove the nails in one swing. Dan waved goodbye to the widow.

"There's always a solution," Saul said, watching her go.

He and Dan clinked bottles. They sang "Erie Canal" and "Yellow Ribbon." Sawdust stuck to skin. Hotdogs burned. The fire cooled when they dug up, hauled over, and flung on Shaw's old punky fence posts from the weeds along the new steel ones. Shaw wouldn't miss them. Who cared if he did? Saul tallied lumber. Dan drew lines for the next design. Ginny sat apart with the mare. Ella wore a crown of tiny flowers her daughter had made, her eldest, who taught her two younger siblings how. They'd all just arrived with Saul's dippy cousin. The men worked fast. The sun was drooping.

"What you need is a box of snakes," said the scrawny rodeo kid. "Drop it in his tack room."

"The potato barn," said a neighbor with a ratchet. "That's where Dan caught 'em. Shaw and Ginny."

"Shaw doesn't have a potato barn," said the neighbor with a sledgehammer.

They banged hard and cut. Wood chips flew.

"We'll double up the legs and cross braces," Dan said.

"This rig will hold three of her," Saul said to the worried kids.

"We'll need bigger bolts," said ratchet.

Dan headed to the shed. They watched him go.

"If she were my wife," said chainsaw, "I'd poison his feed."

"Why punish the animals?" Saul said.

"I'd run him though with a pike," said the rodeo kid.

"Tie him to a chair," said pistol. "Drop him in the Gunsight."

"And pollute the Gunsight?" said the rodeo kid. "No thank you, sir."

"What's a pike?" Saul said, winking, passing a bottle of Fireball.

"God, you're ignorant," said ratchet.

"I'd say it's a private matter," said the neighbor with the maul in his coveralls. The dun had huge haunches to hold his weight. "Stay out of it."

"Look here, a diplomat," said the rodeo kid, skinny, a fast talker.

"This here's the modern world," said the maul.

Kids offered green apples in quarters but the mare refused. Ginny said, "Git."

"Bad apples run in families," Ella said. "In ours it runs in the dark-haired line." She was tipsy. She passed cornbread muffins and told it: "Way back in sod-roof times, an Indian Spy occasionally came to this farm. Had his way with the mistress. Grannie told me all about it."

"Never heard of no Indian Spy," Saul said.

"Why would you?"

"Indian blood," said pistol of Ginny, out of earshot. "Look at those features."

"His orders came from the chief," Ella said. "Kill the man or worse."

"Steal the wife," said a neighbor with an ax.

"This Indian tied his horse in the cottonwoods by the creek so the dog didn't bark. He crouched behind rock after rock and skulked in to survey and plan, silent as shadow, his face painted up invisible. When the dog barked, he dodged between the wagon and outhouse, slipped around to the ox tied in a hole in the hill above that creek. They had no barn yet."

"Where's that cave?" said the rodeo kid.

"Rockslide," Ella said. "Gone now."

Saul shook his head. The Mormora cliffs were purple. Dan arrived with cotter pins and sat on the tailgate to listen.

"Her man off toiling in the fields," Ella said. "This Indian circumnavigates the woodpile, spying on the porch every minute. This wife, you see, was nearly always alone."

Dan sat on the tailgate.

"What she look like?" said the rodeo kid.

"Fine slim hands, an apron tight around her waist. She was shapely and clever with eyes in the back of her head. She could feel the Indian before she saw him. 'I have knives aplenty!' she called in her native tongue. 'Good for slicing the throats of pigs and cows, and savages such as you!'" Everyone laughed. "She had Ginny's lines about the mouth. I've seen the pictures."

"I've never seen pictures from that far back," Saul said.

"A handsome Indian?" said a neighbor with a chisel.

"I'm guessing angled and tall," said the neighbor using Saul's hacksaw. "Half-clothed and pretty. How problems start. Beauty."

"She was lonely," Ella said. "He was handsome enough. Striking."

"Where'd she screw the Indian Spy?" asked the rodeo kid.

"The cave with the oxen, the cabin floor," she said.

"The tack room," said the rodeo kid.

"Cuckold is the word they used then," she said.

"An outdated term," said pistol.

"Hand me the block and tackle," said the maul. "We're losing light."

The sun dropped west over the Judas Range. They bolted the legs of their latest contraption, pried and shimmed and drank until they stumbled. They talked death: arsenic vs. heart attack. Murder for revenge vs. conviction by jury. Hanging vs. electric chair vs. lethal injection, the latest thing so sure not to last. Bullets vs. knives and how many paces for each? Old-fashioned was best. Your asps vs. your cobras. Poison vs. scalping vs. smallpox vs. how best to drown a man in the Gunsight. "Rocks tied to boots," Dan said. "A deep lake is efficacious," and they agreed.

"Effi-what?"

They agreed Dan was just showing off.

"Horny bastard! Horny bastard!" kids screamed at the Percheron, then forgot him.

"Was she ever even pretty?" said a girl with a braid.

"Who cares?" said the boy touching her thighs. "I say we hunt for cows."

It was easy. They lay in the south field happy and full. The day was nearly evening, and they counted clouds, gauging altitude, which were clouds and which were smoke, guessing depth of snowpack on the peaks: Mount McBolding, Big Stamp, Why Not Valley.

"What a life we have!" they called. "What a place!"

"To think we might have been born in some stinkin' city!"

They were filthy with soot and sweat but might have kissed each other with joy. Their design was complete and standing—a giant wooden sawhorse twenty feet tall with legs double-braced at the knees and a sawed-off king post for the backbone. The block and tackle dropped from the belly. The rope swayed. They stood between the legs of the now enormous contraption.

"Let's rig her," Dan said.

They walked it leg by leg over the mare. The rope dropped to her sling.

"Gather in," Saul said, swaying from heat, drink, worry. "Bow your heads to any god we agree to." They did. "Dear Friends, may the Deities protect us, bless us—this beast— over whom He gave us dominion—responsibility—us small and humble—all of us—the ignorant but—this land that humbles us—sorrowful life—" He forgot the rest of it. "Amen."

They caught hold of the rope. They heaved like sailors. The first chill of the evening, they didn't feel it. The mare was lighter from the block and tackle. Only five men were needed, Dan, Saul, and three others. The rope went taut. The grommets lifted.

"Whoa!"

They tied the rope off at the oak against the orange-pink sky that Dan claimed was the purest kind of falsehood, a mere optical illusion conjured by particulate drift from fires billowing a hundred miles west, while Saul called bull crap on him. Weren't all sunsets illusion, after all? Light filtered through dust from somewhere? Sometime?

"Why the hell nitpick, friend?"

Others joined the debate around the Contraption's high legs that drivers down on the highway saw rise on the hill as a huge, flat-backed, headless creature, withers in the branches of a lone tree.

"The prettiest sunset in all the world!" people called.

"Thank God for pink, orange, and red!"

"Thank God for good neighbors and family!"

"For this magnificent land!"

"For this life for just one hour!"

"She looks strange," said the girl with the metal detector.

"Like a puppet," said a bronc rider sitting close to her.

Dan waved Ginny over from her examination of the contraption's leg. He held her wrist up. "We've really done something here today! Me and Ginny thank you!"

They didn't look at Ginny. "You'd do it for us!"

Evening. The faintest line of pink. At the oak on the hill, kids rubbed their eyes, needed baths.

"Will she live? Can we stay?"

Engines turned over. A few headlights lit the house backing out. Some sat unattended and lit the mare. Her legs made tall shadows that tangled up the slope to Shaw's fence and across it. They sat by the fire, flung in logs from the bucked-up pile. Their eyes were red, their faces aged to eighty.

Once, a college man came and set some machine atop the Saint's Head to measure the wind. Wanted to compare the wind in the Mormoras to places back east. Yankee pride. Mount Such-and-Such has the highest winds ever recorded by man.

"I remember that fool," Dan said.

A helicopter dropped the latest equipment at the peak on a calm day. A crack crew. PhDs. "Screwed the contraption right into the rock."

"I remember," Dan said. "The first breeze in November pushed it off."

"Should be jailed for stupidity."

"What about that Indian?" said the neighbor with the maul. "We never heard the end of him. Did the old man ever catch him? Did he get away with his crimes?"

"They always get caught," Ella said.

"What Indian?" Ginny said.

"Quiet," Dan said. He dragged a pine limb from a tailgate. The needles exploded when he threw it on. Some of his guests rolled off their logs at the sudden heat.

"Shaw's an Indian word," said the neighbor with the bag of bolts. "Shaw, squaw, Choctaw, Chippewa."

"Screwing an Indian," said the rodeo kid. "Must be something."

"Simple and quick," said the neighbor with the bag of bolts. "Undressing is done in seconds. A few ties of leather."

"Ha."

"She'd have buttons though," said pistol. "Gals back then had slews of buttons. Buttons might slow him."

"Naw. Slow him? He's got his blade."

"One go, bottom to top up her blouse along them buttons."

"Then no more buttons."

"She's got needle and thread."

"Sew the buttons back on later."

"Needle and thread can fix most anything."

"But not all."

"Some things can't be fixed."

"Needle and thread can't fix not nearly hardly everything though."

"You're all drunk," Ginny said.

"Quiet," Dan said. "She's telling it."

"He caught them in the barn," Ella said. "Buttons on the planking. Pearly buttons everywhere. In the cracks between the boards. She'll never find them all."

"Nipples big and brown as pancakes," said the neighbor with the bag of bolts.

"I wish I'd seen it," Saul said, laughing, rubbing his hands together.

"Nipples hard and sharp as granite cliffs in the ice-cold sea," said pistol.

"I wish I'd seen it," Saul said, not laughing.

"There's no planking in a cave," said the rodeo kid. "You said their barn was a cave. The floor would be stone."

"What cave?" Ginny said.

"Get it right," said the rodeo kid.

"Caves everywhere," Saul said.

"The barn was a barn," said bag of bolts. "Stop disturbin' my picture."

"What is this?" Ginny asked.

"Shut up," Dan said. "She's telling. We're listening." He drank the last of a can and he crushed it. He pitched it into the fire and it sizzled.

"How'd he catch 'em?" said the rodeo kid. "The sneaky love-birds."

"A peephole," Ella said.

"Bull crap," Ginny said.

"A chink in the board and batten," Dan said. "They never heard him coming."

"In the bushes?" Saul said.

"The bushes at the chink," Dan said. "Peering in."

"What'd she look like?" said bag of bolts.

"Her lips were painted," Dan said. "Red as berries."

"You've all gone crazy." Ginny was up, backing off, watching faces.

"What's she doing now?" said bag of bolts.

"Her arms over her head like a bonnet," Dan said.

"Pushing against the wall," said bag of bolts. "She's getting her angle right."

They stared in the fire. "The bonnet falls on the hard pack?" said the rodeo kid.

"The planking," said bolts.

"Her hair is loose," Dan said.

"I love a bonnet," Saul said.

"With his hands in her hair," Dan said.

"Yes," Saul said, his face tight with seeing it. "That too."

"Pounding and thumping," Dan said. "The old leather cushions."

"That old couch in the tack room," Ella said.

"No," Ginny said. "Fairy tales."

"The couch between his trophies and sink," Ella said. "His wall of bridles."

"Bits, crops, and saddle soap," Dan said.

"What can you see from that peephole?" said the kid. "One eye or two?"

"The groping and sucking," Dan said.

"Wait," Ginny said.

"Shut up," said Ella. "He's telling it."

"Are they screwing yet?" said the kid.

"Ha ha ha," said bolts.

"Are they screwing yet?" said the kid.

"'Course they're screwing," said the maul.

"He said groping and sucking," Ella said.

"Dripping and moaning," said Dan.

"Yes, Jesus, yes," said bag of bolts.

"Like rabbits?" said the kid.

"Like buffalo, *boom boom*," said bolts.

"Not rabbits," said Dan. "Not quick like rabbits."

"What then?" said the kid.

"Tell it," Ella said.

"Slow and deep," Dan said. "A bigger animal."

"A cow? A horse?" said the kid.

"Yes, Jesus, yes," said bolts.

"Quiet down," Saul said. "I can't see with all this jabber."

The fire stared out at the black land, one gold eye in the universe. The mare's fuss in her sling. The rodeo kid unbuttoned his collar; below that he was all snaps. Ginny stood with a stick at the edge of the dark.

"Look at her face now," Ella said.

"We're lookin' hard," the maul said.

Dan stared in at the flame, showed his teeth, seeing without looking.

"What's her face mean?" said the kid.

"Her face," said pistol, "is sin."

"Not sin," said Dan. His eyes were slits and wet.

"What's her face mean?" said the kid.

"Her face is just firelight," Saul said, staring into it.

"My ranch," Ginny said, slicing air with her stick. "I told you and—"

"Shut up," said the kid. "We're never leaving here."

"Her face is lust," said Ella.

"Not lust," Dan said.

"Worse than lust," said bolts. "Better."

"Her hands down his backside," said ax.

"Yes," Dan said. "Better than lust."

"Tell us," said the kid.

Dan's mouth getting ready for words, but no words.

"Tell us," Ella said. "We're all old friends."

"Her hands on his face," Dan said.

"I'd kill him with my hands," said bolts.

"But what's it mean?" said the kid. "The hands?"

"You'll grow up soon," Ella said. "You'll know."

"Tell me," said the kid.

"It means she loves the Indian," Saul said. "That's all it means."

The valley was a great black bowl with a few lights. The kid unsnapped his first pearly snap, then the second and third. The sky was clear but for a thunderhead. Heat lightning is a misnomer. There is always thunder. Its sound dissolves over distance obstructed by mountains or hills or the curve of earth. The cloud's anvil is the highest peak outlined in silver when the moon drops behind it, still less than a quarter, waxing, friction between ice and water, the positive and negative at thirty-five thousand feet, though seventy-eight thousand feet is the current record, nearly outer space. The kid's shirt was open to his belt. His skin steamed from the too-close flame. The party rubbed hands on knees, crossed and resettled their legs, and a boot kicked a log and the fire sparked and flared and resettled. They fed it with broken shovel handles and rakes and twisted beams, which burned fast and bright and twisted more and split and dropped in half and popped and moaned.

"His house is dark," said the rodeo kid half naked at the fence.

"How dark," Dan said.

"Not even a porch light."

Dan walked to the fence, set his hand low around to Ginny's spine. A soft hand.

The stars sketched Shaw's roofs and corners. Dan snatched Ginny's stick away. She sprung for it, but he was too fast. He hauled back, speared the stick toward the barn, a javelin.

"Look what they're doing," Ginny said low to him, a whisper. He took her hands in his as he'd done before so often, once when they'd married in the square, *Till death do us part? Yes*, since her Grannie hated church weddings and his uncle sat on the church steps watching, Cattlemen's Hall in case of rain, too hot to go in, *No one needs us. Okay, let's go*, fingers entwined as they'd sprinted, only him in white, between the slant-parked trucks through the alley to the backlot.

"You blaming them?"

"I'm saying think," she said.

"They'd die for me."

He shoved her toward the fire. She shoved him back. It was a good show now, he with her arm, then she pulled her arm free and she tried to kick him, missed, nearly fell, small laughter, a wild beastie. She broke to the fence again, shoved the fence, kicked it, turned to all, her back against the fence.

"I didn't love him," she said. Only the fire crackled. "But I loved every minute of it."

"I've had enough talk," Dan said.

He stalked to the fire and they made way for him. He kicked a log and it rolled from the flames and he plucked it up, the cold end. He waved it, some signal to a faraway hill. It glowed redder with the wind it made. Then he started to spin with the log. He turned and turned with the log at arm's length, a wing, faster, then faster.

"Will you look at that."

Then the glow was a red orbit around the invisible center where Dan had been, a crazy red spinning ring. The ring walked away from the fire. Up the slope. Closer and closer to Shaw's fence, spinning and tilting, redder and thinner around the black center till it hovered at the crest of the hill, till Ginny's face and Shaw's steel posts were tinted red by it and outlined by sky, till the ring stopped and tipped, as if to aim or think or test the air. Dan's voice said, "Here she comes," and the ring jumped into sky, end over end, an arc of light over Shaw's fence—red over black in the retina, a meteor, self-propelled, innocent, since there was no hand inside the center to launch it. The meteor landed, bounced, rolled, a log again. The old grass flared.

"That'll torch him," said the rodeo kid, hanging on Shaw's fence. The grass across the fence smoldered then caught. Breeze took it, knocked the fire flat, widened it.

She'd moved. She was hunkered on a rock in the dark when he came for her. She fought noisy as his free hand rummaged her hair and yanked her, tried to kiss her, but lips met jaw and teeth. They watched his hands search for better purchase—the back of her head, low behind the ears, a shelf of bone and soft beneath. The head is just a small thing. The neck is weak. He kissed her mouth. They cheered and grumbled.

"Funny-looking," said the rodeo kid, staring, as if he'd never seen a kiss.

"Now he's fixing things," said pistol.

Dan dragged her behind the tree, success determined by weight and muscle mass, though she fought like a cat. The rodeo kid in the tree reported.

"Does she like that or not?" said the kid.

All that noise.

"She's got a rock," the kid said. "She's smashed him with it, smashed him good."

The sound of the rut and rasping.

"Listen to that," he said. "Now he has the rock. The rock is his now. Now he's flung the rock off. Now he's choking her." Boots twisted in the dirt from the sounds in the dark. "She's simmered down," the kid said. "She's sleeping now, some such. A little murmuring." Then all was quiet behind the tree.

"I'd like a turn," said pistol.

"Ask him," said Ella.

When Dan came from behind the tree, he wasn't walking straight, his pants at his knees, his hand on his bloody face.

"Her rock," said the rodeo kid. "She smashed him in the face with that mother of a rock."

Dan leaned against the tree. His back rubbed the bark as if it was itching. Someone handed him a beer. The glass was green in the firelight and cold and dripping from the cooler. He pressed the end of the bottle over his face.

"How bad's that eye?" Ella said.

His fingers quivered around the bottle. His lips moved.

"Men have lived fine without eyes," Saul said. "Soldiers. Sailors."

"I'll check her," said pistol and he crept around the tree. He wasn't noisy or long about it. Sledgehammer followed. He was slow and messy and after went to the creek to clean himself. Maul passed up the chance.

"Truth is I never liked it," he said. They nodded, knowing it about him, but he craned his neck to see anyway.

Ella looped an arm under Saul's knee. She sat below him against the log at the fire. Dan slid down the tree. The bottle fell away and he covered his face with his hands. His boots sprawled out crooked. The rodeo kid's turn was next and quick, since he'd never done it. He whooped in the dark after. He'd left his big hat by the fire. He didn't need his hat right now.

"Will you take a turn?" said Ella.

Saul drank and he handed Ella the bottle and she drank and handed it back to him.

"Boy, do you hate her," he said.

Ella flung her head back, laughed, open-mouthed to eat everything. She wasn't herself at all and, too, she'd expanded into some new skin that fit her.

"My little darlin'," Saul said. "I shouldn't."

She took his hands and stood him up. He staggered off.

The rodeo kid climbed to his limb. "I don't think he's managing."

"Drunk," said Ella. "He'll get it right in a minute."

The rodeo kid had some torch now that danced on Saul's bare hind-end, which jerked and jumped between Ginny's legs, which lay stupid and tired. Dan slumped by the tree, listening. Ella's hands moved in the firelight like knitting a sock.

"What a night," she said, voice breaking the silence up. "What a day."

"Shaw's fire's ripping well," said the rodeo kid. He dropped from the tree.

"They'll see it in town soon," said pistol. "Send trucks out."

"No one's looking," said Ella.

The rodeo kid's shirt hung on a fence post. He found a cooled-off log, smeared his hands on the charred end, smeared his face, arms, his neck and chest still smooth and hairless. He ran around the fire whooping. "Look, I'm the Indian!"

"Where'd he come from?" Ella said, shaking her head as they watched him run and dart while Shaw's fire fattened, ate the hill.

"Someone better run," Dan said. "Let those horses out."

The rodeo kid ran. He jumped the fence in his jeans and boots. The National Rodeo once came in to St. Cecilia, the crowd, the bleachers, they remembered. The steer wrestler is always the biggest man on the team, always over six feet tall and always single-syllabled: Kane or Buck or Shaw. It's a race against the clock, not the steer. Take him down in four seconds flat, fastest time wins. That time the prize steer was trucked in from Rapid City, Julio or Ramos. Famous for size and havoc. Saul was coaching roping in Carlyn so didn't see any of it: the sisters on the hot steel bench above the chute together, a clean jump from the horse but the steer veered left. Shaw was gored, dragged all over the ring, clown chasing, helicoptered down south with a speared liver.

"Ten minutes more and Shaw'd've been dead," said Maul.

"None of this trouble," Dan said against the tree.

"Good old times," Ella said, glancing back for Saul.

"What will happen?" said Maul.

"Nothing will happen," Ella said. "The house won't catch. The shed will."

They fed the fire with cups, cans. When this old oak fell over they'd buck it, split it, stack it in a pile. Pry the stump, snap the roots from this stony ground. Burn the root ball on a Saturday night. After that, there'd be no shade in the north field.

The rodeo kid reappeared panting hard. He led the Percheron and the mares. The kid opened the gate. The horses ran through. The kid closed the gate and ran behind the tree.

"When you die, you're dead," Saul was saying from the dark. "Make no mistake."

"She dead?" the kid asked.

"A *coward dies a thousand times*," Maul said.

"She dead or what?" the kid said.

"I said get home," Saul said.

A scuffle in the dark, then the kid appeared, scooped up the hat and was gone in a streak downhill toward the barn, looking behind him, a wild smeary face.

"I could use a hand," Saul said, when the footsteps faded out. Dan slipped around the tree, left Ella on the fire side, listening.

"Check her," Ella said. She leaned her head against the tree, listened to their silent jibber-jabber. The wind died down then blew again, bellowed the fire across the fence, warming the air. The mare's rope squeaked with heat and pleasant smoke. Wood popped and snapped. Neither fire was close to going out.

"Walk her to the pit," she said. "Take one arm each."

When the deputy came it was full dark. The others had drifted home. He parked with the fire trucks at Shaw's. Gadgets hung off his belt. He felt the mare's legs with hesitant and inexpert hands. "It's not her legs," Dan said. His teeth were hazy red. His lip was split.

"This horse gonna make it?" said the deputy, staring at Dan. "Where's Ginny?"

"She was feeling poorly," Ella said. "I've not seen her."

"Which is it?" said the deputy.

"Maybe she's with Shaw," Saul said. "I guess Shaw's left town."

"What happened to your face," said the deputy. Dan turned his face into the shadow.

"A spat is all," Ella said. "I checked his eye. His eye is fine."

"The sky is gone," Dan said. "Only branches shelter us from the universe."

"Anyone know a poem?" Maul said. "Something cheerful?" No one answered. "Listen, my children and you shall hear of the midnight ride of Paul Revere . . . " He took a drink. "Can't remember it. My brain's askew."

58

"One if by land and two if by sea," said the deputy. "A signal light."

A bat flew through the branches. A cricket. "We go on faith alone," said Saul.

"Who does?" said the deputy.

Ella walked Dan an ice cube then returned to Saul. "Never would've dreamed this up," Dan said, rocking on a root.

"How could you?" Saul said. "Why would you?"

No hint of going. The deputy stood flat-footed at the edge of light, the glint of his badge, his clean shiny face. The mare was forgotten, just a stranger of a different species.

"More of a nightmare," said the deputy with a quick smile. "I reckon."

"You're new," Saul said.

"Only new here," said the deputy.

"Where you from?"

"Outside Casper."

"We have friends in Casper. You don't sound like Casper."

"Everyone's in costume," Maul said. "Everyone's a fraud."

"Speak for yourself," Saul said.

"We should have him over," Ella said. "Him and the sheriff, an old friend."

"Always ready and willing to eat," said the deputy. "You see lightning tonight?"

"Too drunk to recall it," Saul laughed, and the deputy laughed too.

"Something started that fire at Shaw's," he said.

"Something always does."

"You okay, bud?" said the deputy.

"I'm not your bud," Dan said.

The deputy stepped out of the light. He hunted all around the tree. He called Ginny's name out.

"Those are brand-new boots he's wearing," Dan said. "Not a spot on the leather."

"I saw his boots," Saul said.

"There's always lightning somewhere," said Saul. "One hundred strikes to the earth every second. Billions of volts, miraculous power of destruction that gives life to all. Sometimes blessings are hard to comprehend. We resist what we can't see and explain with feeble senses."

The deputy reappeared. His hat was squarish. He set his hand on the crown and peered below. The porch light glinted on Ginny's truck by the water tank. Town was a twinkle place. Headlights crawled up the big hill south out of town to everywhere else. He set his perfect clean hand on the mare's back.

"Better mosey on back to town," he said. "File my report."

"Your report," Saul said.

"Yessir."

"Mosey back to headquarters," Maul said. "Back to HQ."

"Yessir."

"Why don't you send a letter home to Mom while you're at it," Saul said, cheerfully. "All mothers like news from prodigal sons lost out west."

"To Casper," the deputy said too quickly.

"I'm just joshin' ya," Saul said.

"I send her postcards," said the deputy. "Not letters."

"Right-o," Saul said. "Mamas like postcards too. Scanty though they are. Don't mamas like them, Ella?"

"'Course they do. Postcard's a fine idea."

"Well then," the deputy said. "Tell Ginny hi."

"We sure will," Ella said.

"Much obliged," he said. "Ma'am."

"Much obliged *to you*," she said.

"What's funny?" he said.

"Nothing's funny," Ella said.

He left through Shaw's gate, calling back, "She'll need some shade tomorrow."

It was true, they conceded, after his goodbyes. The sawhorse would stand in full sun. The rig must be moved. Ella was overcome with sleep. Saul folded his coat over her. They'd move the mare in the morning. Dan would offer the mare an apple. The mare would take it.

"What she needs is wheels," Saul said.

"The backhoe," Dan said.

They staggered down to the cow pit again. They revved up the backhoe and drove it up. The tires imprinted the ground to be seen tomorrow. They let the engine run while they lowered the mare, fist over fist. She lay in a heap as they cut her free. They walked the sawhorse away leg by leg. It was difficult. They stood in the headlights. They'd break the contraption up someday, burn it some fine night. Dan looped the knots of the rope on the teeth of the bucket. "No mistakes this time." Saul hopped into the cab. Dan gave a thumbs up. Saul pulled the lever. "We should've thought of the backhoe first," Dan called over engine noise.

"I'm happy to see you improving," Saul called.

The bucket rose, the mare rose, her legs dangled, the hooves almost brushing. The backhoe rumbled into gear and drove her into future shade.

"We'll have to keep moving her as the sun shifts."

"Of course."

Her spirits would improve by the hour. They'd feed her and bathe her with sponges, keep her company. They talked of buying acreage and women in Winnipeg since city ladies don't let themselves go. They'd hauled up lawn chairs, a card table, tongs for cooking.

"She'll be better soon," Saul said. The fat sliver moon sat in the west and sank away.

"I'm encouraged," Dan said, a cloth tied over his bad eye.

They shut off the engine to conserve fuel. Refueling would not be easy. They would rev the engine three times a day. They would move her with the sun into fine cool shade. They would haul buckets from the well. They would drink water together. At nights, there would be blankets and tarps for spitting rain and a well-built fire heaped and stacked to last. They would brush away the flies as needed. The cows would soon graze the north field too, which would green up quickly. They would frolic and play. Any cow would buck for such sweet new grass.

"Howdy" Mom—9 months. Sorry about no Adios—
Wish you were here though you'd hate it—Can't
believe the stars/air—Postcard's Iowa—CORN—
Who knew how "great" the Great Plains are? You
didn't—I'm a Lawman now, a Silver Badge—Giddy—
Like Matt Dillon in GUNSMOKE. Yep. Working
graveyard shift tonight, thought it high time to drop
you a line, Mr. Prodigal! I'm on a big case now. Foul
play. I can sniff it. Hot on the trail ... Sunrise is pretty.
I'll drop this in the box on lil' ol' Main Street. Say
hello to Marvin (if it's still Marvin)—News: I think
I might lasso me a new girlfriend soon. A real wild
thing, a cowgirl, getting a divorce (just once but you
can relate anyway). Look! Pen's run out—

Well, I do hope you paid close attention to those messages from our sponsors during the break, buckaroos, because they've got some fine products your parents could surely use in the old homestead. But now let's settle back in to our exciting serial, *The Long Trail of the Rodeo Kid* (based on a hair-raising true story!). If you're only now tuning in, you'd best saddle up and hold tight, 'cause this week's episode finds your hero and mine, the Rodeo Kid, in one heck of a thrilling and terribly terrible mess.

It's dawn again, and here we are in an average barnyard after a raucous party outside a small western town by a river. The air is chilled, dewy, smoky, crystalline, lots of words like that. A tree stands on the hill in the nearer distance cluttered by large debris, bulky, alien, geometric. We won't ask. It's no matter. That's the past and we're the future comin'. The sky's dry between ridges of two distant ranges, east and west. The western range seems smaller but this is just a trick of backdrop to indicate "farther." The eastern range looms, however, so big behind the hill that it seems an actor in the show, and the sky, so flat and uniform this time of day, it is surely blue paint brushed on. The birds, both wild and domestic, dart, fly, and call for seed, gathering at feeders in town and at the barn door where they know it's hidden. The hawks wheel in blue as expected, their small heads clicking tiny readjustments.

The Kid stands in the dusty ranch yard, his fists at the navy piping of dirty pants. He wears no shirt. He lost it in the confusion before our commercial break. His face is filthy, his chest and arms likewise. He's been sleeping in the barn. Found his hat dangling from his thumb. He lifts the hat and looks it over. His eyes are blue as the sky, as sapphire shining in the sun, too rare a color to play an Indian. His day as the Indian is done. He is young. He is both thrilled and disappointed. He walks to the well, bows to it. There is soap in a tin cup. He sets his arm to work at pumping and he cleans himself of Indian.

He drips when he stands. No towel. He spins to take things in: the tree and the three stone steps to the porch. The propane tank. The clothesline fallen on the berry bushes out back, a pair of socks, old graying pegs. We zoom in and out on cottonwoods that sprang from the seeds of the trees who hid the Indian Spy, the Original. They fill the space between dirt and sky.

The boy yawns. He's been a child, a puppet. The strings are broke now. His privates still tingle. His eyes are full.

If the boy could do both, stand in the barnyard at the wellhead and also watch himself standing in the barnyard at the wellhead, sit in the loft and in the yard also, for example, watching himself thinking of the Indian Spy spying in the cottonwood, he would divide himself in just this way. This is the world no one speaks about. He's been waiting for it a long time, felt it coming when he was younger, now it's arrived in a wave. He shakes with affirmation.

For all his scrubbing the grime and soot still streaks down his chest, staining his waistband where his body dips inside it. Only his face and palms got clean. He can see this from the window in the barn loft. He's hungry too. He bends and rubs his innocent, clean hands in the dirt again, smears gray on the knees of his rodeo pants, up his thighs. He has calluses already.

Enter the hens. They peck around him. They're an audience, like us, but they're in the show too. Their coop door hangs open. No one thought of the hens last night, their safety from foxes, dogs. The Kid notes it, so we note it.

But someone remembered the horses at least. We can all agree there's a big difference between horses and hens. The Kid hears the horses shifting under his feet in their stalls as he sits in the loft watching himself at the door to the coop. This is tremendous fun.

He is addled. He knows it. There's something terrible and wonderful about addled, a requirement of growing up. A red dog chases the flock below. *The* red dog.

They scatter around his other self, the Kid, down in the yard, hens squawking, flapping and pretending they can fly. They divide around him, too tall and too slim even for a cowboy, as creek water will divide around a rock. The Kid is the rock. All else is the water. This is knowing he is alive now. He is an actor now. He will fill in. His body.

A cat waits behind a chicken with black-blue wings. The cat keeps low, is big-pawed, believes he's a sabertooth.

There's a truck parked at the main gate, really an old telephone pole on a black forged hinge. The gate is down. Over the gate is an archway of welded pipes, tall enough for deliveries by truck—feed, pallets—and for moving cattle in or out. A brand hangs down from the middle: V4. If the boy were to float above the gate on wings, he'd sit on a pipe, examining the couple sleeping in the truck. Saul is in the bed, slapping at bugs without waking. Ella is in the front passenger seat. The window is cracked for air. She's restless. Feels the boy hovering over the hood.

He flies to the tree on the hill where Dan is sleeping unsoundly by the mare who's still awake, of course, blinking in her sling. The ranch is quiet except for the cattle lowing, moving up and down in the fields. The scene is vast and serene. Yes, the little town, below, over there.

A roof is nothing. A boy is something. He flies back to himself in the barn loft. He rests his wings.

His face is beautiful despite the smudgy blue shadows under his eyes. He's tired, of course. What a night! The creature in its cocoon, at its metamorphosis, is never at rest. He sets his hat on hay gray from winter. He must clean his pants, but the dirt, too, is wonderful. It matches the smudges on his skin. All is wonderful, his handsome jaw, his icy eyes in penetrating squints, the bits of straw strewn attractively through his tousled hair.

He crawls to the north window above the cow pit. There is movement in the pit, metamorphosis there too. The woman has rejoined the living as the cock crows.

She's climbing across calves and a stiff gray foal, a human shape made of muck shifting through muck. She has a plan. She is dragging bodies to the bodies. She is building a set of steps with corpses. This is a good idea, the Kid grants it, but he still isn't impressed. Anyone would've come up with it if they woke up in that kind of grave. And here she's climbing the steps, steady as she can. She reaches the lip. She's out. She lies on the turf at the lip of the pit, a wet, stinking, drowned skunk. She stares up into the walnut. Her eyes shift to the window of the loft. The Kid makes himself scarce.

She crawls toward the barn. A horse head hangs out a stall. It nickers at her, nibbles. A loving scene of love when she reaches it, then the head disappears into shadow. She zips her pants. She is Eve rising from the clay this time around, Genesis revised. Her left eye is awful to see. Her lips are swollen. She is hideous, red, chapped, caked with fetid pit rot.

At the barn wall, she crouches, keeps low. She's heard a howl on the hill. An animal cry, she must think, its gut ripped open, but no, turns out it's only Dan dreaming. She crawls. The Kid can smell her thinking, taste her confusion. She will crawl to the northwest corner. She turns once, feeling him behind her, inches away, but he's gone in a blink behind the stack of pallets. The morning is a blue fog. She stifles a cough. He stifles one too. She wipes her nose and he does the same. He sees the top of her head from the west window now; also looks at her crotch from the cat's favorite hole. Her head is round like a melon from every angle. Her crotch reeks. She can feel the air moving but she can't explain it. Anyone looking then would see him, but only the birds do, and they fly past at the business of birds. They, he knows, in their rudimentary stage of evolution, have no opinions. The barn wood catches the shoulder of the woman's flannel shirt. Tragedy is a matter of opinion and tone. His mind is rich and full. His mind, he now knows, can make anything.

Her shirttail is riding up; the skin on her back is showing. She is bruised about the kidneys. She crawls around a rusty gutter. Her spine is horizontal to the earth. A brick from above could break her back. He lets the brick alone. He has mercy on her, poor thing. On the west wall, her jeans' ass is in full view. She crushes an anthill with her giantess knee. The pit is behind her now. The pit is the past. He tells her this with his mind. She gives no indication of understanding. Instead, she passes a stick of old siding hanging off the barn. A sixteen-penny nail has sprung away from the barn on one end. She pries it free. She shoves the stick under her arm and crawls on through thick vegetation, drags under branches and thorns, sucks her finger. From the corner she can spy on the whole yard. A chicken struts up and struts on.

There is a hand over the tailgate. The tailgate drops. Saul rolls out. There is weeping ongoing on the hill. Saul cups his hands to call. Ella speaks out the window, the mealy words of married people. The boy will marry too someday. A big wedding with ribbons and cake. Saul goes in the house and comes out of the house with the shotgun. The truck's engine turns over. The brake lights flicker. The gate swings open and closed again. The truck accelerates toward the main road. Dust swirls. They'll be back soon. The note on the counter says as much. The woman stands at the barn. A horse whinnies, a cock crows, a cow lows in the misery of a too-full milk sack. The boy slides down the conveyor, meets himself on stone porch steps. The woman watches him sit. She'd thought she was totally alone. This is the biggest mistake humans make. Animals never make it. The Rodeo Kid is disappointed in the Dead Woman, frankly.

She staggers to the well, the chickens follow. She kneels, sets the stick-with-nail down by the wellhead, pumps and pumps. She drinks from the tin cup, spits, flings the cup, lowers her mouth direct to the spigot. She drops her pants and washes though the boy is staring. He is eating a green apple. There's a whole bag of them in the kitchen. Saul's note is in his hand. The Rodeo Kid crumples it and stuffs the torn paper in his mouth, swallows the note with a bite of apple. She grins at his joke, so the boy guesses the Dead Woman is feeling more like herself. She's not angry yet. She understands the world has left her.

She retrieves the stick with the nail. She approaches the Rodeo Kid, stick dangling from two fingers. She's limping, maybe not dead but suddenly old. He finishes his apple. Her eyes ask him if it was good. Yes, his eyes say. The apple was juicy and the skin had tiny white spots, promising crispness and freshness, though it was no doubt imported from the southern hemisphere. There will be no crisp apples in the north for months. The woman stands before him in the dirt. Her right eye is swollen shut. The stick is in her right hand. The boy tosses the apple core at a flowerpot, making a dull ring.

A moan from the hill. Horse or man. If the Kid looked away to the hill, at the noise, it would change everything. He doesn't look. He sits on the top step. She's eye to eye with the Rodeo Kid. She is very ugly now, a cow. Her face is destroyed with bruising. Tits sag under flannel. Her teeth are crooked and black. The boy never noticed it before. She is the personification of something. She takes another step. A smile again splits her split face. He stands. This makes him much, much taller than she on the top step. He says peace with his hands, says stop with his pout, but her swing is good and fast.

The nail gets him in the thigh, not deep. He doesn't howl. She whips the stick-nail into another swing of impressive force and speed. He ducks but his cheek is grazed. She's on the top step now, and the Kid has to wonder whether all her crawling and limping was an act. He's backed against the door, under the shade of the porch. She has him pinned with her weapon across his neck, her face in his face speaking vicious and ugly. He has her arms locked, the nail at his face. Maybe he could pry the stick free and turn it on her. Instead he breaks away, ducks under. Blood spills down his cheek, smears across it. Another backswing, another miss as he jumps. She's slowing down. She's expended her energy. She'd be nearly comical if you had time to stop and watch. The boy is quicksilver now, gone, young legs pumping. He somersaults under the gate, runs through the truck's settling dust, looking back, falling to one hand, skinning it, more blood for his trouble. He's a black speck on the distant road. He cuts into the woods and doubles back.

The woman drags her bloody stick into the house and closes the door. She ransacks the place. The curtains quiver in the parlor. The hens flap on the porch at the noise. The brass chandelier swings. The cat's head ticktocks staring in from the window box. The woman leaves with a pack on a shoulder, a knife in her hand, an umbrella under the other arm. She wears good walking boots with wide rubber treads, no heel, no leather sole. Only a little limp. She wrenches a small ax at the splitting stump, rips the clothesline down all the way on her detour to the barn, shoves branches aside with umbrella and ax.

Meanwhile, back up the hill with the mare, Dan sprawls beside the branch naked but for a rag about his head, dreaming of a different world, hovering spaceships, women who obey.

And meanwhile, back at the barn, the cob doesn't want the bit but takes it. The rooster hasn't quit. The woman tastes manure on her tongue. The panniers are badly packed. She leads the cob up the north fence line shared with Bowman.

And likewise meanwhile, speak of the devil, this neighbor is enjoying a little dawn target practice. A set of bottles sits on fence posts. Bowman wears earmuffs. His jeans are black and creased. The pistol makes his body longer, one leg in front. The bottles fly. Early rising's no trouble for Bowman. Last night he turned in at ten. His mind and body are perfectly fresh. Bang. Each shell costs a dollar. He's got plenty. His little son runs to set new bottles. Bang bang bang, a Ruger. The woman's stopped the cob to watch the shooting show. Bowman is a local talent. The bottles are mostly brown. Some are Fireball red, but they fly like the rest. The son waves at her with a stiff arm. Bowman stands down. They both stare at her. An eagle drifts over with widespread wings. The son hands the rifle to Bowman, taking the pistol in return. Bowman shoulders the rifle. Bang. Feathers rock down. The rifle follows the bird and levels horizontal, turns. The crosshairs hover on the escapee's forehead, a violation of the Golden Rule of Shooting Practice. She tugs the cob.

Cut to the crotch of the tree, where the obedient children replaced the pistol, and then cut to the pistol. Ginny fires one bullet into the mare's temple. Dan, the sleeping beauty, snoozes through that too.

At Barryman's Quarry she leaves the cob to graze. The house dangles on the quarry's edge. She slips past cordwood stacked for ten winters, up the front porch and in. She emerges with a 30-30 lever action saddle rifle, exact same weapon over every mantle on our show. The rifle is theft, it's true, but one can hardly go to the mountains without a rifle. The Kid will need one himself.

She rides one knee over the horn, not quite sidesaddle. The cob bobs with energy, a quick walk then a trot then a canter. Annoyed, she lifts her knee over, despite discomfort, rides proper now. Our hero has no trouble following her at first. He doesn't approve of stealing but concedes the theft of the rifle was a difficult case: all a cowboy does is justified if he must do it. This is fact. Though, he wonders, does this also apply to Indian Spies?

Barryman might even forgive the stolen rifle. Barryman is a cowboy himself, after all. They're all cowboys here except for the Indians. Consider too that Barryman's door was unlocked, as good as saying Come on in. The porch light burnin' bright all night, clearly indicating Feel free. Moths nearly killing themselves against the bulb! What of that, folks? And Barryman's house was exactly on the way. Such an ostentatious domicile, the biggest house in town. The quarry made Barryman rich. Which is why everyone hates Barryman. So let's call the rifle hers, pardners. 'Least till we meet a cowboy who's got himself a stronger claim.

      ∝ —— ∝

Dan loves the past, but he dreams of the future. Screaming in his sleep under the tree, what did he see? What did he forget as soon as the pain in his head woke him up?

Some sci-fi scientist behind a sheet of glass, writing some kind of report. Not that deputy's. What did it say? You could just about make out

FINAL ARBOREAL CENSUS
2179, May (under the arch of a flame-gold sky)
SPECIES: *Callitropsis nootkatensis*
LOCATION: West Sea

It was nearly ready for transmission back to Central Cedar Lab: "On the Carpathian Peninsula on the West Sea six varieties of cedar are fully restored, three others at 93.34%."

But the point, to the yeoman on the wing watching her superior at work, was that he was *writing*. Pen and paper were historical fiction to her. That, in olden times, the hand had dragged *a stick of ink* across processed wood pulp to record data, the implement woven in the fingers. Also carbon sticks or chalk. But the act was hardly *dragging*, she saw now. The pen *glided* in the cedar scientist's hand, forming graceful blue-black loops. Who had taught the old man this quaint, extinct craft? Some even-more-aged person? Who'd learned it in turn from someone long dead?

CEDAR SCIENTIST'S NOTE: *Stupendous dramatic display of local megafauna during inspection on beach: (wild mustangs) colt (black) and filly (brown in estrus) divided by blowdown.*

YEOMAN'S NOTE: *blowdown: Trees piled like pick-up sticks.* (She *writes* on the wing with the corner of her big sponge. The letters dry and disappear.)

74

These were the best transcriptions the yeoman could manage from the scientist's ornate scrawl, seen upside down through a window she was meant to be cleaning. They were two strangers separated by the craft's thin shell. Windows were the most menial work on any restoration ship, but she preferred a wing, if truth be told, which it wasn't, because who ever asked what a yeoman liked? Other than the wind? So noisy. But, truth be told, she lounged on this wing whenever she could, to see his pen *skate* along, to see what he said he saw. She worked this wing when at port for census, on cloud hovers for repairs (though she tied down for these), or even at R&R, since the cedar scientist rarely left the ship.

She had a sponge and bucket on the hump of the wing. Salt was stubborn.

She washed the window with big sweeps of her arm.

She heard screaming somewhere. Probably just the wind again.

The cedar scientist's scribble about horses filled his page, a feathery absorbent material, no longer wood pulp, certainly not animal skin pounded thin. Staff would transpose his ink to Plain Print, feed it into Central Brain. Who was his transposer? The yeoman was jealous of whoever it was.

The cedar scientist was near retirement—last trip to the West Sea. He was hurrying, it appeared, to sign off on the nearly complete restoration of formerly indigenous cedar (another success, after controversy, the yeoman had heard at mess). But if the cedar scientist was giddy in his work today—*giddy?* an old person's word; the yeoman puzzled at its arrival in her mind—it was due to this other miracle before them: the dramatic equine display on the beach. Horse Love impeded by Fallen Wood (blowdown).

In her mind the colt and filly were Romeo and Julie, a foggy combination and not quite right yet, and the yeoman would have called the female "chestnut" more than brown. Damn but the window streaks were persistent! And that wind! Always bringing more!

She needed a squeegee but none had been requisitioned. Salt was tough. The cedar scientist had no idea she was there, though they were barely a meter apart. And such a bright sharp day.

HIS NOTE: *Colt enraged with frustration. Blowdown extending from tree line well into surf. Filly eats berries, bushes caught in tangled forest matter. Mule release will complicate!*

HER NOTE: *blowdown: A fence between male and female.*

She'd nearly forgotten the mule in cargo, the big feller. She'd slipped down into the hold, fed him chips and sandwich crusts. An off-load ramp would soon appear for their new, experimental cargo.

HIS NOTE: *A graying flag above and behind the trees on the beach. Black once.*

HER NOTE: *flag: a bit of cloth on a stick, ugly skull-face with an X below.*

And then: *The winds here can scream like a human man.*

TWO

Bear

In the pit the lime had burned her face. Oh, beautiful slime. Covered with, encased, engorged by. They had tossed her on the calf, some calves, so many dead calves. She could hear them up by the tree with the mare. They would run out of beer. They would sleep by the fire thinking *Our work is done, not clean and neat, not fair in every stinkin' way, but clean and neat is for city people.* She comprehended it. She even sympathized, part of her. She deserved it and didn't and did. The pit was deep, cut from the earth with the sharp steel teeth of the bucket forged in a steel mill in Pittsburgh or Akron. How had it come to be there, the bucket? The calves were bony. Nature makes it so. Many can die. Reproduction makes up for it. Reproduction too is natural. She licked her tongue across her lips. Spit on her cuff, rubbed the cuff across her face. Her face burned. Why, she was hardly dead at all. But she would never be lovely again, never beautiful. No men would chase her. She would chase no men. Then she was laughing. She was never beautiful. She was just herself.

❧ —— ❧

"A place just like here," said Maul, chasing her, gesticulating at the canyons of the Old Swede's Trail. He'd stopped to rework a diamond hitch. "I flew them in the war."

"Which war was that?" Saul asked.

"Did you hear how the cowboy got stampeded?" Bowman said, interrupting.

"How did he?" Saul said, not noticing.

"Tightening the nuts on his mustang."

"Ha."

Morning. Second day of the search party. Saul and Bowman rode ahead to another joke, and Maul remounted his dun, though couldn't stop his motormouth.

They followed the cob's stout hoofprints that vanished over rock and reappeared as deep gouges and half-moon scuffs or less. The tracks had swerved into the Mormoras at the first cairn of the Old Swede's Trail then ascended the black cleft at a steep uphill, passing to port of the second cairn a quarter mile on, to starboard of the next, and so on. No tricks or evasion, the rider's filthy fingers perhaps woven through the cob's mane, the filthy face perhaps burrowed down in coarse hair, sleeping it off, perhaps, not steering the ship at all, perhaps dreaming of the pit since what else could the rider dream? Rooster crowing again, the cock, the herd lowing in the south field fending for itself as animals had done from the beginning of time, crawling over the dead again, across dead, all dead, fingers plunged down in the bowels of a pig, the lady parts, morning coming, because the rider was not dead yet, no, still not dead. And now Ella, too, passed each cairn, but very much upright, perfectly orderly and fair, wide awake, last rider in the pack train for many next rocky miles.

The Old Swede had stacked rocks for the cairns to look like small squat stone men, not stone women, with two piles to form the men's legs, space left for a crotch, then a big flat rock on its side for hips, then a rock standing on end for the shapeless torso, another on its side for shoulders broad enough to carry the weight of the world as all men's shoulders must, and necks selected with a divot for setting the round, nearly perfect, pea-brain heads.

"What's the delay this time?" Ella called to the front, but only Dan just ahead on the chestnut spoke back, saying nothing of importance.

Their hats were light in color with wide brims, turned up at the sides to shed the sun or rain down your back. Ella's was wider than the rest, held tight with a string under her chin. She sat straight on her horse, a pinto, a pretty young one, wild despite recent gelding.

"I said she's gainin' ground!" Ella called. "Goddamnit!"

Again, no one but Dan turned to reply and again she didn't listen. She'd turned down his volume by degrees since the morning after when he'd first appeared at the burn barrel in Grannie's yard with a flowered sash about his head. Saul had looked away. Ella hadn't. It is woman's task to see all. To take all on board. She'd twisted his volume knob a little lower when his sash mutated to a black eye patch, a notch lower still at the stone corral the first night where he'd started up refusing blankets. Wanted the blue tarp only for sleeping garb. Rocks for pillows.

When the sheriff didn't show—but who would have called him?—Dan headed down the oak's slope with his bundle of sinful rags, past that Blasted Contraption to the corral fence, climbed it, his naked legs in boots, jumped it, left the corral gate hanging open, a beeline to the house, through the mudroom and parlor, some tornado had hit, no time to study it, beelined to Grannie's powder room. Soap sat in a dish shaped like a swan, stopped the drain, ran warm water, hot, filled the sink to the rim, submerged his swollen face causing overflow, pink, a goodly deluge to the innocent mat. He blinked out water. Stared. One eye was swollen shut, a slit. He lathered soap. He held his right lid open with glistening shaking fingers, tips and knuckles doing all the work. His body parts fought each other, a war over open or shut, the eye. Fingers prevailed in the end. He tipped his head back, dripped soap in the slit, howled, kicked the wall above the baseboard heater. Heater rattled cacophonous, an old model. He pounded the wall around the mirror with both fists. The mirror fell across the sink, did not break yet, but water splashed the poor mat again. It could take no more, this mat. He repeated with the slit, fingers and soap, added clean water from the tap, bent over, repeated, the sink overflowing until the slit was clean as the day it was born. Hydrogen peroxide, a nearly full brown bottle, was behind the door where the mirror had been. He trickled it onto the slit, wept it out, kicked the toilet off its bolts and its lid slipped off and cracked in two. The mirror shattered on the mat this time. He found the sewing kit in the left bottom drawer and threaded the largest needle, a difficult and slow procedure. His hands. He knelt on the mat to look down into a shard, the best angle. His knees turned warm in an instant on the mat and glass. He tacked the lid closed over the slit with the first stitch. Blue thread. The needle entered his upper lid, a dive. It quivered silver and red as it punctured into the blue-black folds. Horrible. It felt good to do this. Correct to sew it. He was a baby once, like everyone, perfect, no pain at all until that birth tunnel crushed him, yes, expanding next, as planned, grew and became a man and then-now was crushed again. That's the promise of birth, dark then light. No need to howl, *shush my baby*. Men have lived without eyes, pirates and soldiers. Thread was needed, a little soap, on battlefields, in ditches, on the high seas, among the stars. Scars bridge over gashes and slits and pits of all kinds.

No one witnessed "The Sewing of the Eye." So was it true?

To the others, his eye was pure speculation now. There was no eye. Only the patch.

Ella had always wanted a paint. Now she had him. He was chocolate brown islands in a creamy sea. Black eyes. His hooves were petite and split-colored, same as the mane and tail dripping off him. His forelocks were black and wild. The tack was black leather and silver. He was beefy and slender both. Real truth is contradiction, yes and no at the same time. Saul had given her the colt halter-trained only, schooled him up to riding with great care and concern. He was a good husband, all in all. She'd bought the tack without telling him. It was the last of the money after Ginny bought her out. They'd bought the new truck first, red, five years of scratches now. They'd sold Grannie's truck to a young couple who didn't care about rust yet. The couple took the old goat too, part of the bargain for the truck, a friendly one with short bristly hair. The woman was charmed by his strange eyes and insisted. Ella still missed the goat sometimes. An animal can be more friend than a friend. He used to stare in the window at cards being played behind the curtain, trying to figure the meaning, why the quick movements of those magical human hands? Hearts and spades? The kids watching TV, braiding hair.

"Hey!" she called. "Ever heard of giddyap!"

The goat would wonder why he couldn't come in. Ella had no answer for the goat. It had to do with power, she knew, since speech belongs to humans only, words to name things, to place value, to conquer. For the goat, birdseed would be gold. Gold would be dirt. So the man comes in the door. The goat stays out.

"God help me!"

He wouldn't, and the men weren't listening. Saul would repeat what he'd been repeating. "Going fast as we can, darlin'. Accuracy in trackin' takes time."

Same answer since the morning after, since her peachy heels and matching church dress, since that burn barrel. Imagine thinking she'd make it to church! She spurred the paint at her own foolishness. He bucked and she spurred him. She blocked the dress out of her mind, and the burn barrel too, blocked it. Blocked naked Dan staring deep into its flame, a dead man risen from the grave to torch his outfit, the fancy sash across his face. She blocked the sash, the eye, the man. She blocked the church door she'd never entered that Sunday morning, already an age ago. Blocked the church.

She blocked her sister and the pit.

The goat's horns grew in funny. One was floppy and fell off at three inches. The other grew up properly, then U-turned, aimed into his blocky brain. Saul fixed it. Held the goat down, fingers across the rock-hard brow. His horizontal pupils were turned vertical under Saul's big hand. The cord snaked across the yard. The electric buzz was entirely alien; the goat couldn't escape it. Couldn't escape Saul. He looked up at the trees seeking salvation. The saw spit bits of horn into the snap peas. His tiny tail wagged throughout the catastrophe. What choice but to trust? He danced about the yard after, blood flying across green grass, dust, and sun as he shook his head, then lay in the cool weeds, thinking.

They were stopped again at the bottom of a bluff. *Slow as slow as slow*, Ella wrote in her little saddlebag notebook.

"On what kind of chase can you *write* in a book!" It was not a question. *Slow as molasses chase. Molasses.* She'd packed a squeeze bottle of it so put a line through the word.

"For fuck's sake!" she tried later and the four men turned, unaccustomed to that degree of vulgarity from her.

"That's right, fuck! Fuck's the operative word here!"

They rode on when her fit was done.

Slow as a glacier but too hot for glaciers so she blocked them.

She considered going home. Her three kids. She could not block them. In the dubious care of Saul's cousin. How many miles till they missed her? She pulled back on her reins. The paint objected but obeyed, turned, pawed, watched the ten mules climb, *slow as mules in a pack string on an uphill slope.*

Saul and Bowman were finally going up and over the bluff after some other delay involving rope rope rope. *The natural leaders.* Bowman: the neighbor across Dan's fence line, Mr.

Tall-Lean with chiseled jaw, the man taking all their money. His boy was staying at Dan's with the cows. Their fiasco was a Bowman family windfall. *Slow as . . .*

The very front pages of her little book were full with lists, ever crossed out, ever growing. Still, most of the book remained divinely empty, an open range of pages to be arrived at and filled, though not the last page, which was already jammed with tiny words, a "mule thought," numbered as *the first*, though mules don't—as goes the common wisdom—tend to think or count. Her own handwriting too, very small.

She'd blocked the mule thought this morning in the tent and did so again now.

The bluff was not big but steep . . . *a pillbox of dust.*

Halfway up was Maul. The keeper of the animals, the mule man, the neighbor with the maul—that eager *voyeur of the normal,* that *hovering damned creature* who'd played choirboy at the tree trunk, a satellite watching as the fuckers fucked. *Not his type.* No. Merely a *salivator* at the grunters, a peeper at Dan's crotch and that rodeo kid without a shirt.

Maul dropped down from his meaty dun. He waddled up, staggered, scrambled ahead on fat-legged fours in the dust to the front of the first pack string, five mules in each. He urged the line with patience, kindness even, that he'd not shown to that poor poor woman, Ella's sister. He called down at Dan. Waved his hat. It was not contradiction. Thinking was made for inversions, perversions, residue of events. The mind contracts around paradox like a pearl. In the end, though, it would be Ella's actions Ginny would judge one day. And God would no doubt take her side.

One little gray tried to pass the jenny and all was forgot.

"Watch that gray making a move on the jenny!" Maul called down at Dan. "Watch that jenny! She's smarter than you!" Maul's coveralls could fit three of Dan. *Poor Dun*, she might write, but did not. "Those mules will blow up!" he called, and Dan shook his head and Maul quoted some old book, "*Hell is empty and, by God, all the devils are here!*"

"They're not blowing up," Dan called with venom.

He walked his chestnut. Urged the first string with a stick to the last ass and swishing tail. He led the second string with a rope to the second jenny, a buckskin. The chestnut had gray showing on his muzzle. The black patch over Dan's eye flashed at particular angles. The mules swayed and lumbered uphill with careful steps when what was needed was speed.

Ella preferred last in line. The last rider can see all.

The day was hot and the canyon walls cooked them. Birds floated up in columns, no need for wings. No clouds. Dust swirled around the mules' bellies. Their hooves obliterated any trace of the cob's tracks. They were packed high with gear for a week.

"This is how the world is, my darling," Ella told the paint.

One glove rested on his neck. Her wrists were narrow bands of sunburn despite best efforts. The paint waited, but fussed in protest. She understood, but he had to learn. He danced on his back legs. His energy would find its place very soon. But to wait was in his best interest. He didn't see it yet. He was a child-horse still. Rebellion was natural, and therefore good, both to feel it and to quell it. Every young thing has its time, then the boom is lowered. Let the boom wait. *You are young*, she thought. To exert himself was still such pleasure. He would amaze himself with the power of himself.

The bluff would fall away under him eaten by his hooves. Gravity was nothing to him. Friction was nothing. The whip was nothing. It had been an aggravating day already. So little sleep in that old tent with Saul's snores after standing First Watch only stoppable by a hard elbow to the ribs.

She gave into curiosity, opened the little diary to the last page.

Mule Thought #1 (collective): The Itch. When it was close by the mules leaned into bark, when they chanced some bark, when given time to spend with bark and the bark was rough and old and good and the bits of dried-out mule skin were evicted by the bark, along with the bark, the pressure of the big mule body pressing into those tiny cliffs and crevasses, a tiny vertical world of tree trunk, the huge animals made *so needy* by that itch—nearly defeated by the small. A recalcitrant mule gets a bullet in the brain—a mule that stops forward progress does too. It is a rule, nearly a fact. The bark seemed so inert to some, seemingly truly *dead to some*, the opposite of *free*. Freedom was a worthy thought for mules and men, but the bullet in the brain intruded, stopped the thought, and the line of thought was sliced through.

Closed it, locked it, slid the book away in the saddlebag.

"Who's been writin' in my book," she called, but without energy, not loud enough to be of note, then "Invasion of privacy," even less so.

"Haw! Head 'em up!" Maul was whipping a mule.

She tightened her legs around the paint. Poor boy. Resentment and frustration were made by God too, like serpents and beetles and dung. The first string was on the summit of the bluff now inching over.

"She's in fuck-all Minnesota!" she called.

"Probably only to fuck-all South Dakota!" Maul called back easy-like, and she whipped the paint who stormed at the insult but not enough to disturb her hat.

The first string disappeared over the bluff's summit one by one. They might have fallen off a cliff. There are chasms everywhere. Ella couldn't hold him back now. She heeled his ribs to cover this fact and he blasted up the bluff and her hat flew back over her braids, her first in years. She'd let her oldest girl braid the braids. Ten years old. Her hand reached back but the hat wagged free and she forgot it. The paint passed the second pack string, surged to the summit, and she hauled back on him there, where he bucked and turned angry. Her children would love to see this: Queen of the Mountain.

From above she saw the creek and Saul's sorrel, belly deep in the flow parting cold and blue around him. The first line of mules had arrived at the shore already, pressing in, tail to harness, tail to harness. It was a wide riffle with cattails. She'd rebraid tomorrow. The first mules swung heads down to drink and the second pack string passed the paint on the summit, showed him their lowly tails, and descended, then plowed in the riffle now filled with animals and men.

"No room for us," she teased the paint.

The pack train was enormous, ridiculous, no argument. Saul was a hope-for-the-best, expect-the-worst, better-to-have-it-and-not-need-it-than-need-it-and-not-have-it sort. Saul Logic. Everyone has a different sense of the future.

What small men from above. Saul talked to Bowman, Bowman to Saul. The sweat split their shirts in two colors, creek splashing up their legs. *You're not having fun till your boots are wet.* A tired old saying. Someone should say something new? Leave it to the kids.

Saul waved his hat. Hers still hung down her back. She didn't touch it. She would have to burn her diary. Evidence, since she was sure to write about the pit in some weak moment then forget it, like her mule thoughts, telling some future snoop things they had no right to know. How, back at the pit, she'd walked, maybe even *ambled* away from the scene of her sister's escape. She didn't run as a rule, didn't panic, a trait she prized in herself. She'd headed for the herd to think it out. The cows had clattered at the south fence. Dan was blubbering in the corral and everywhere, Saul was making lists in his head. Grannie said *Cows can smell human frenzy.* Ella opened the gate calmly, like ten thousand times before. The cows threaded past her, trotted to the new field, neither rushed nor nervous. The Mormoras stood huge that morning, as now, as usual, reserved, black, and silent. She admired them, but the feeling wasn't mutual.

"Look who's dawdling now!" Saul with his hat waving again.

At the burn barrel, Ella trickled gas and *sauntered* quick to the house. She searched for Ginny's hiding place, where she'd have stashed the DNA evidence, per the cop shows she and Saul liked to watch, some Saul-sperm-smeared panties being a particular threat, checked the back room closet's highest shelf, under the blankets of Grannie's cedar hope chest, in the freezer behind an ice tray. Found no panties at all. She slumped on Grannie's kitchen floor under the table. Her peachy dress later burned with the rest. She'd bumped her head. The table could burn. The four chairs were blue and wooden. It would take a whole day to clean the place, several trips to the dump, which was open on Sunday.

"Saul, check the barn," she'd called and clapped the front door shut. "Close the gate."

Grannie never believed in *trauma*. She'd laughed at the word when it came into style. *The world was made by trauma. Pray you have some or your life is dull.*

After disposing of no DNA, she'd watched the two men *glide* up the hill from Grannie's kitchen window, then the backhoe descend too fast from the oak, a tree not native to these parts anyway, weave and bump over boulders, the mare swinging in her sling, her head dancing crazy. They met at the pit at the bullet hole in the mare's head.

"Life is never dull." Or, "One less thing."

"Took the pistol with her, I gather."

Yes. Ginny had taken the pistol, of course.

(Or was that before the DNA?)

Before and after the DNA, after the pistol, they rolled the mare into the pit. Ella kept her eyes on a ship-shaped cloud off the Saint's Head, the highest jag, and listened to reports from the barn. "The cob is missing—his saddle—headgear." Then she dragged an old blue chair from the kitchen and sat in the shade of the walnut for the backfill. Dan the Baby flung items he'd found in the loft, winged them into sheets of smoke and dirt raining down into the pit from the backhoe's bucket. Old oil can, sheep shears, dyke shovel, rotten oxen yoke, ditching spade. Objects of Dan's misplaced fit.

"Think twice," though Saul wasn't interfering. "Might want it someday."

Dan disappearing into the loft's big open window, reappearing with a scythe, etc. Grannie wasn't big on the concept of irony either. Irony was lower than a snake. Dan found a leghold trap and was dragging it around. He sat with the trap and WD-40 as the pit got filled. Finished the entire can. The chain draped over his thighs. The dirt poured cool and dark. The smoke was blue rising. Later still, he'd insisted on bringing the trap on the trip. Ridden with the chain over his shoulders as far as the quarry, its teeth banging the chestnut's haunches until Maul intervened, took the trap, and (never waste! never abandon anything!) looped it onto the buckskin's load. She was herculean, she could take it, Maul said. Still, Dan's old trap went missing on the first night's campout. The ride's first story, good campfire fare: "The Mystery of the Missing Trap." Some noise in the night, Dan claimed. He'd parted the weeds hunting for it in the a.m., made a mess of the kitchen things too, which slowed Ella's packing. And some bread was missing. Saul pretended to hunt too. This was all fine. Ella would set it all down. She'd remember to *Remember what you want to. Forget what you don't. The key to a good life.*

"Hear the one about the lesbian cowboy?" Bowman asked now, down in the creek.

"No, but I'm guessing that's about to change."

Ella pulled her little book out, unlocked it, tore out the last page and stuffed the mule thought in her back pocket.

They rode on.

The trap would rust, melt, and feed a plant, but the backhoe still hummed in her head. In her head, Saul still (again and again) uncurled himself from the cab, earmuffs down around his neck, the pit full, the pit no longer a pit.

"What we need now," Saul had said, "is a well-trained pack string."

On hard pack, if they were lucky, the cob's tracks were mere dents and scuffs. Ella locked her book. She'd wanted to be a painter once. A nurse. A teacher talking facts. She called the mules names she'd seen in print or on screen. The tall ugly one was Ishmael. She watched the mule when her mind needed quieting, before she thought of the bottle. One red was Ivanhoe, the other Miss Kitty, one little gray was Marlo, the other Zane. Maul had his own names for them, of course. Puck. Lucifer. As though mules care what they get called. A mule is an outsider. Outside the herd, the tribe, the colony. Ella's mind was working fine again. The *town, village, settlement*. The shaggy black was Starbuck. Saul always said this of mules in private: a horse was smart but followed commands without consideration, without employing native wisdom. In her day, Grannie went further: *A horse is ruled by loyalty, love, submissiveness. That's fine. If told to walk off a cliff a horse trots off it. A mule bucks the idiot off.* The red jenny was Ahab, obviously. Then Ella failed completely with the buckskin. *The world can be divided that way. Which are you?*

In Misty Canyon, as dry as bone. Goats with heavy curls moved up cliffs along invisible slants.

Noon again. A shape turned into an elk. Saul glassed it.

"Ginny!" Dan called. The animal disappeared.

The riders took turns with the mules, rope in hand. They turned in the saddle to the shifting lines. The horses could

93

have ridden the Old Swede's Trail blindfolded. They went slow and mostly silent. The wind was too strong for speaking even via cupped hands. The old panniers were canvas. The newest were Kevlar. In the early morning, they'd been braced to the animals, who rolled their eyes. Mules were judgmental as to the skill of the hands working around the frames, tightening buckles and cinches around their bellies, breechings under tails, collars at the throat and down between the front legs, leather, rope, and wood designed over centuries for the containment of the four-legged beasts. The tack was dusty but not neglected. It was Maul's first trip of the year. The sawbucks were sound with the nails in tight. Neat diamond hitches had been slung over last, tightened down and knotted, so the mules had the benefit of snugness. Maul said, "Nothin' worse for a mule than a loose load," as if they didn't know.

The black patch over Dan's eye was some shiny fabric, from an old raincoat maybe, or a taffeta skirt from a back closet. Maybe Ginny's own taffeta. As Ella cut salami in the headlamp at the stone corral their first night, Maul asked her, from behind his hand, if it was true Dan had sewn his right eye shut.

"'Course he didn't."

Maul was a gobbler. To watch the man chew salami was terrible. Bowman was the opposite, a private eater, fastidious and slow, whereas Dan chewed with uncertain deliberation under his patch secured with a fat green rubber band.

Saul noted the elk in a notebook then stuffed it in his breast pocket. The mules invariably veered toward creeks. The ridges cut black against blue serene, like that rubber band into the skin of Dan's face. When allowed to drink, the mules plunged their snouts in, lips waggling. They craned and sloshed big-headed and horse-faced, or small-necked or long-bodied or donkey-like with nonmatching pants, wonders of genetics, unnerving. They rode over bare rock a mile, then gleaming white birch a mile, then east a mile, then uphill six. Maul untangled a red mule from a brown.

"Why the pirate outfit then?" he'd asked.

"He speaks English," Ella said. "Ask him."

Maul did not. They rode on. The air wasn't thinning yet. Home was nearly this same elevation. Ella's nose had stopped bleeding.

Afternoon. A snake stop. "Get me a rope."

Saul tied a knot at the frayed end. He whipped it back and aimed for the head.

"Why does a cowboy wear buttoned jeans?" Bowman said.

Saul took two swings to kill it.

"I don't know," Saul said.

"Because the sheep can hear zippers."

"I've heard that one."

He flipped the snake still rattling off the trail.

"Why do cowboy hats curl up at the side?" Bowman asked.

She watched Saul laugh.

"I'm going on," she said, but her paint stood still. "She's got a twelve-hour jump."

"Tortoise and the hare," Saul said.

Bowman skinned the snake for a hatband. It writhed on with neurological life. He left the pink body in its slender cage of bones, avenging the birds for their stolen eggs.

"She'll cool off," Saul said.

"Let her run with the line," Bowman said. "She'll tire."

More delays, Ella wrote in the beautiful little diary with marbled inside covers, *blowdowns and bottlenecks, new channels made by spring floods, rockslide, detours. When Ginny was a girl she was a pencil in cowboy boots, brand-new black ones (though for Ella it was hand-me-downs from the neighbors (boo hoo)), weeks to break them in, matching holster she said she found in the attic but people knew the truth of the holster.*

Then, *The mules' hips sway.* And then she stopped herself.

Their steps were ginger, never fully trusting the weights on their backs just wide enough for juts and overhangs. They were not overloaded, the Golden Rule, though their burdens were not light. Maul brought the scale and a marker for daily weight, set coffee on a rump, hung bundles from a hook and scale off a branch, pounds and ounces written on tape. When the gusts died down they talked horses vs. donkeys vs. mules vs. other exotic hybrids, zedonks, zonkeys, zorses. The mules had no shoes.

"They're part mustang," Maul said. "Never shoe a wild horse."

"Don't look like mustangs," Bowman said.

There was such a thing as natural affinity, Ella knew. Saul and Bowman, for example.

"For example," Saul was saying, "a snake is not a villain. Just a frail thing hated from the beginning of time."

Maul and mules, for example. There was such a thing as too-complicated-to-pick-apart.

"Eve's refusal of responsibility for the apple," Bowman said.

"To kill a snake," Saul was explaining, "the rope must be aimed perfectly. The knot must hit just behind the snake's head. The spinal cord. When you nail it, there's no wriggling. No suffering. It's over, dead-done."

Sometimes Bowman went ahead with his spotting scope. Ropes were passed, tethers transferred from glove to hand. Saul loathed gloves. He loved a callus. He didn't wash his hands in hot water but scrubbed them in cold and borax. The line looped down from his sorrel's haunches to the red jenny leading the first pack string, two grayish-black behind her, and two big red-browns last, then Maul, his line looping down to the big nameless buckskin jenny leading the second string. She was as tall as Maul's dun leading her. Two browns followed the buckskin. She'd mixed up the names already. The first could pass as a quarter horse. The second brown was the tallest of both strings, gangly and ravenous looking.

"Generally less shapely."

"But not all."

"Smaller, generally."

"But not all."

"They're ugly, all of them."

Maul was silenced. He didn't sulk. He might have said, *I call the tall brown Man-o'-War. A racehorse bloodline. A winner wins. A loser loses.* The black mule was Ella's favorite with his shaggy mane and forelock. She called him Mohammed in her diary.

The chestnut walked close behind the black.

She'd told Dan the chestnut was too old for a trip.

The canyons wound up. The creeks rose with day heat and snowmelt. The mules didn't spook. They plowed under branches just out of reach, missed snags set to take an eye out, single file through creeks dumping onto hard pack. The slipknots were best for quick release at cliffs, ravines. One mule lost was better than the whole string. They walked in the order they'd been unloaded down the aluminum ramp of Maul's trailer where prepayment had been duly made. MULE RENTAL BY THE WEEK, the trailer said. They didn't believe in credit and Grannie always said money was private, but Maul's bib pocket still bulged with Ella's rolled-up bills. In the house he'd picked through the broken china. He'd lifted Grannie's broken English teapot—no spout, no handle.

"What will you do with all these shards?" he said.

"I've got glue." And she took it out of his grubby hands.

The kids would ask someday about their auntie. An earthquake, Ella would tell them, truthfully. Every goblet, every plate, every pretty fragile trinket was smashed to bits. Grannie's figurines and bells with frills, Easter bunnies and crucifixes. Bathwater in the back hall, the toilet kicked off its bolts, a hole in the Sheetrock. Blood. Towels and smears on oak scuffed by spurs. Closets erupting out the back door. Taffeta. A window shattered across a quilt. The clothesline dragged into cottonwoods. Not a frame survived in the parlor. Wires sprung from plaster split and pitted. The fridge door hanging open. Eggs and milk making lakes on linoleum. Paste. Meals of all kinds, corn, oats, rice bloating. The cabinets. Except for salt and cinnamon, no jars survived. The chickens pecked the smorgasbord, bobbed and sipped with pointed tongues. The front door hung wide open. Her scarf that same peachy color as her dress. The pantry: jam, pickles, brine, glass. The barn too. Tack was slashed with some sharp blade, every stirrup, every leather strap, the unions at the fenders. Gratuitous, really. It would take a month to clean it up.

They rode through the hours straight or slumped as their fathers had taught them. Mule ears swizzled when the riders spoke. Ella set the cast iron on buried coals when they made camp. Dough rose inside under lid and mitt.

"It's true about Eve."

"Adam wasn't no catch either."

"Adam would have dropped Eve in a pit too."

Maul grilled onions before the meat. Ella took the spatula from him.

"Why would God dig pits in Eden?" Saul said.

"Pits everywhere," Bowman said.

"Maggots," Maul said. "Putrid."

"Just a story," Bowman said. "Don't worry."

Dan slept by the creek in his tarp, whiskey wafting. He never took his patch off. Bowman took First Watch with his little arsenal then slept with it by a log near his big pretty bay. Saul took Second Watch. He slid out from their small tent and she rolled into the heat he'd left. Maul took Third Watch.

"Why do we need a Watch?" Dan said in the morning. Maul was breaking eggs, brown and pale green shells toted safely in a bin of oats.

"You didn't take no Watch," Bowman said. "Quit complaining."

❧ —— ❧

Grannie had told her Dear Ones: *To miss the buck warns the whole herd. That's bad enough. The Marksman may get no second shot. The herd will run. They know the mountains well and the Marksman will walk and walk in endless overlapping tracks and his hunger will grow. To miss the bear is another thing. The bear won't take it well. He may run and he may not run. If he's injured he may escape to his cave and lick his wounds or he may follow the Marksman. For a bear, boot tracks are big and clumsy, easy as pie. For a bear, the Marksman reeks to high heaven. He doesn't follow the Marksman for tit for tat, my little sluts. He follows out of practicality. If he has an enemy, he must subdue the enemy if he's able. In short, you get one good shot. Make it sing. No time for nerves, self-doubt, or sympathy for the beast. The Marksman must know his target well, his habits, fears, and predilections.*

Their camp huddled in a thick stand of aspen at a three-creek confluence. High above, Ginny wolfed the latest loaf. Her bowels pressed for relief. Why not let them go?

The cliffs were blue-gold in the waxing moon. She crouched on a terrace. The creeks wove around the stand and joined below it. She was cold but had been colder. The trees were scarred by lightning, black gashes that oozed and shone. The posse's gear was a white mountain. Hard to get one good shot through branches. The cob was safe up and over the ridge, tied up at a spring. The saddle had steamed as she'd pulled it off and she'd warmed her hands against the cob's hot back. She'd left the umbrella. Left the red dog tied to the same cottonwood. Muzzled him with a boot string, though she was wrong to, for what if she didn't return?

Her cunt throbbed still, but less. It burned to piss. One knee was sore and both shoulders. Her head. The tent below was cloth zipped up, a closed container, like her cunt, that, like her cunt, opened from time to time. The 30-30 hovered on the tent's top pole. Grannie would have said this of cunts: *Cunts were made for using. The cunt runs everything. Mighty men bow to the mightier cunt.*

It was true and not true.

The three creeks were silver lines joining. The moon faded the stars nearby. A coyote yipped on the ridge. The 30-30 shifted to the coyote then back to the top pole.

Her throat ached. She'd see bruises if she ever found a mirror.

At night, side vision is superior. To say she "saw" movement beyond the far creek would be misleading. Peripheral vision "sees" until the eyeballs shift to center on the object, thereby losing the object in their direct glare. She didn't move her eyeballs. Her one good eye beamed down the barrel through the slot on the sight at the tent. A noise. An ear was aimed too. Conclusion: something large was moving clumsy beyond the far creek, an elk maybe, a bear. Vegetation rippled at the edge of things. Unable to resist, her eyeballs shifted, since humans are devout to direct line of sight. They think eyes belong punched in the front of the head, whereas the horse knows it pays sometimes to be mistress of your periphery. Ginny wasn't a horse yet.

She had time. She was waiting for Ella.

Ella always twisted things: the girl was a berry picker, yes. The women had babies tied to their backs and the bear watched from the ridge. Agreed. But no, she was more than a berry picker. She was other things too, did other jobs in her town, had hobbies. She was valued before this incident. Those matters come into it. The wider things. For some, the moral of the story is *Keep to the Relevant.* As Ella would say,

Don't wander off while telling. Stay in the Clearing so that things are Clear. But the girl, she herself might say, was the daughter of the chief. She had a brother, two brothers, if Ginny remembered right. The brothers come into the story, so put them in, drop them into the landscape of circumstance. That's called the Set-up or Introduction.

Ella's tent was now peripheral. The top pole, the zip, the fly, the mountain of gear, the man on watch, all these objects—all subsumed by the new bigger view: three creeks joining, cliffs. The creature creeping beyond the far creek, if there'd been a creature, had dipped into some depression on the far shoreline, a pit or crack. Ginny listened, glanced at the ridge, as if the cob might be supervising the whole with the red dog, as if standing on that magnificent pit edge.

In the pit the rooster had crowed, the cock. As a girl on the ranch, she'd heard the rooster crow outside her window. And all the boys would come. A few crawled in. That was the girl's decision, in or out, the sill, the panties, the big hairy hole. Reproduction is natural. A cock, cunt, in and out. She felt the space between her legs. Someone before the pit had whispered the word on the ground by the tree. *You cunt how could you?* She felt her cunt. It was a cunt, she felt it. Dan was a good man. Now she knew another side of good. It had taken years to know. *You cunt. You cunt. But what your job is now*, Grannie had said, *what your job is now my little gorgeous cunt is to get out of here. To get to the cob.*

The cob was fine at the spring. Hungry.

The 30-30 went back to the tent. She forgot the creature, the pit. Tore the loaf with her right-side teeth, the rifle butt set in her hip to free one hand, the muzzle on a rock and her jacket as a gunsight. She could've done with another shirt, wool. The loaf was soggy and one of her front teeth was still a little loose, teeth being fragile and poorly designed appliances, a thing she'd never considered. She sucked the bread. It was a wonderful paste now, a love token. Where was Dan? She'd forgotten all about him.

Aspens love a confluence. A hacksaw was propped on the gear. A marmot whistled a warning below. The fire ring was black near the tent not close enough to burn it up. The fly tied out to stones in a half ring. The mules ganged together in deep blue shadow. Not loud for three creeks. Lanterns lit willy-nilly. A cup and spoon on a rock become a table. Her eye was perfect now, the bum eye: seven or eight mules she saw double. Horses picketed and hobbled a little downstream of the mules. She understood this. A horse was better than a mule, that's all. The tent was old. A slender nothing. A small wooden chair stood in no-man's-land between the mules and horses, then was moved away by First Watch. Ginny considered the meaning of the chair and found none. A place to sit. No smoke rose up from the fire ring, but smoke was in her nose, sweat and horses, propane in whiffs, some memory of soup. No movement in the tent. Her face hurt, her left earlobe. The lime had tried to eat her and failed. She saw a shovel. A second pair of socks hanging on a shrub, a shirt. Wool? Ropes lay in proper coils but had been abandoned thoughtlessly on sand where the grains would work in and break the fibers prematurely. She'd spent nights in that old tent. It was tucked deep in scrub. Even in the moon, one shot would likely fail. She was sure her chewing would wake the sleepers. Ella would have pills in the inner pocket of the

103

saddlebag, a small brown bottle, antibiotics. Ginny would wait, a trick learned from her sister.

The 30-30 belonged to Barryman's father. The name was engraved on the stock in gold block letters. Another marmot. The rifle was loaded with six shells when she took it. A box was right there on the mantel by an old clock under a glass dome, not a speck of dust. She left no fingerprints.

        ✑ —— ✐

Day three.

Across a ledge Saul and Bowman led the mules one by one. Ella waited her turn. Saul called. Offered to fetch her horse across. Water makes such noise: a white-storm lullaby. "Can't hear you!"

Saul waited, hands on hips, still a handsome man. Ella grasped the paint's lead and led him over the cliff herself. As she picked along, she told him what she'd someday tell her children, what they'd tell their children, and they their children's children, just as Grannie had told her and Ginny: *The trick with a cliff is that the cliff is not the enemy. The cliff is still. The cliff is helpful, accommodating. It's just a simple plain tipped on its side. Think of your life like the Great Plains. Think of a buffalo roaming at leisure. Let your mind rule the topography.*

And later meadows. "Every meadow was a lake at some point," Maul saying, "Just look. Flat. Even. Green water if you squint." Ella yawned. She was getting older, tired, had slept poorly again.

"Everything was a lake," Saul said. "Everything you see."

Everything was something else once, Ella thought. Sometimes it still was. How did the story go?

Prehistory. A girl on the plains, another berry picker? The women with babies tied to their backs. All picking berries in a clearing just outside their town. Some sorted, some braided each other's hair. It was beautiful and good, but a bear was watching from a ridge. The girl's bucket was empty, a few dried-up berries rolling on the bottom. There must be better berries over there, she thought. The girl wandered from the clearing. This girl was full of mischief, often disobedient. Back in the clearing, her mother was calling, "Come back! Not so far! The bear is watching!" Everyone called, the women and children chiming in, aping the mother's call, but the girl was far. She walked on through the trees toward the bottom of the ridge. Bear scat everywhere, piles fresh and hot, full of berries mixed with fish scales and rabbit fur. She slipped off her shoes and stepped in the scat barefoot. Hot shit slid between her toes, around her heels, up her ankles. She laughed. She'd been warned many times: "Never step in bear shit. It will anger the bear." She laughed again since she was, truth be told, a little arrogant. Her shoes dangled from her fingers. Town was smoke rising from trees. Their voices were tiny now: mouse voices, lizard yowling. Berries up the ridge would be fat and sweet and fill her bucket quickly.

On the ridge, she saw a beautiful man standing in her path. He was tall, handsome, and strong. He wore a beautiful fur coat despite the heat.

He said, "Come with me, marry me, live with me forever."

She agreed. But arriving at his home, his home was a cave.

He peeled off his fur coat, his man-face too, and human-like skin. He was the bear inside the costume, but everyone knows that. Over the years she asked herself, "Did I know too?"

She lived with the bear in the cave forever despite the anguish of her family. They missed her so. She had many children with the bear before she died in some great Invisible War Ella forgot the name of. But when the kids were old enough, the girl sent several back to live with her old family in town. Her parents were appalled at first. Some were frightened, but her brothers were chiefs by then. They welcomed their new nieces and nephews, recognized them as kin, and for this reason, they never hunted bear after that. Something along those lines?

Ella couldn't scold Saul for being testy. She kept her hat tipped down for maximum shadow. Her skin was fragile, pink as a girl, freckled well into her twenties. Burned badly. Her first two kids got the freckles and the burns. Saul's cousin had claimed she could babysit for ten days. Saul's cousin was mostly capable but silly, lacked common sense. She would apply sunscreen, as instructed, would take them to the pool, as instructed, clean towels, canvas bag, as instructed. She'd tuck them in too late, too much TV. This was no crime. She'd be their pal. She'd let them win at cards, a sin Ella would never commit.

The third kid was dark. Saul was fair too and let himself fry. He rode with his hat in his lap now. His sorrel dogged Bowman's bay, passed and was passed. His summer hats were woven about the crown for air flow. Late afternoon Maul shot three red squirrels with snake shot. Roast 'em on a stick on a hot quick fire. Of the joys of life, roasted red squirrels is surely one of them, delicious and rich from the diet of nuts. Bowman shot two dozen more with his pistol, and fifteen shots. Ella poured rice into the Dutch oven. Saul studied maps. Bowman saw to the horses. Dan measured out hay pellets.

"A Dutch oven?" Bowman said.

"That's right," she said and set the lid on.

"I didn't think this was a pleasure trip."

"Talk to Saul," she said.

"*Oh Captain, My Captain*," Maul said.

"Is that all of it you remember?" Ella asked.

Dan washed the dishes later by headlamp. Spoons fanned out in rippling waves.

"Get the chair out of the eddy," she called.

"It's his chair," Saul said.

Night. The changing of the watch, First to Second. Another branch on the fire. Why sleep? The bota passed between scarred-up hands, whiskey, the tent nearby, listening.

"See, Grannie back then paid fifty cents per horseshoe in good condition for her prize wall of horseshoes in the barn. A real bird, a tough one."

"I remember."

"Dan was the new boy in town, finds the shortcut out to her place, past the pasture, sees horse trouble, sets the sack of horseshoes down at the fence post, climbs over. A young chestnut colt is sprawled in knapweed, thrashing in a clump, a front leg wrapped in barbed wire."

"That chestnut he still rides now?"

"Same one."

"Well then."

"Other horses standing by doing nothing, heads up in alert or hanging in resignation, according to affiliation, of course, the mare's ears back, snorting, almost charging him, as he kneels to the colt's bleeding cannon. He talks soft to the chestnut. Meanwhile the two sisters watch him from a tree, seen him in town, wondered about him, the new sweet-faced boy, try to guess what words he's whispering in that chestnut's ear."

"I get the picture."

"Ella would've married him just for that, if I had to guess."

"Well now, would she have."

"I wasn't in the picture yet."

"Ginny behind Ella's back in the tree."

"That's the nutshell."

"Sweet Little Danny cutting the leg free."

"Clip clip."

"Stuffing his Leatherman in his back pocket."

"So it was Ella who found him first, see? She had dibs."

"I see that."

"The *How old are yous*, etc. Same age as her."

"Same as Ella Ella Ella."

"Not Ginny Ginny Ginny. See?"

"I do."

"*Of course I like horses*, et al."

"Ginny spying the whole time."

They drank and passed the bota.

"Ginny always pitied him a little."

"It's clear."

"He was ignorant in the best sense."

Mule Thought #2, a masterpiece (the red jenny, the little gray, and the buckskin): The Kick. Even when the weight was gone, they fretted and mulled over weight, *spoke* (not with words, etc.) and spoke about the weight on their backs, a near obsession, *Yes, but see how the obsession with weight distracts us from more important things*, the red jenny mulled, *from thoughts of freedom, from making constructive plans.* She was always talking like this. *But, ah, what weight on my back*, the little gray fretted, *it is terrible, it is hopeless, I can't conceive of anything else.* She urged him to think past it. *Dream past pain to freedom* was her motto. *There are so many flaws in their system, and anyway we are resting now*, pointing out the obvious (camp, night, Third Watch), but her musings rarely got through to the little gray, or really to any of them. She was a broken record of freedom. They—the mules, the horses, the dog—all blocked out the red jenny's sermons. If some of her seeped in it was only to the unconscious, to be mulled over later, or blamed for their punishment if they let off some kick, a reflex, at an irritant. At Bowman's knee, for example. And even if the kick was reflex, the mule was still beat about the face and neck as a lesson, as punishment, to curb that reflex, to free the riders of the irritant of the mules' reflexes. Yet *Why should they be free of irritants when we have no freedom?* she asked. She found a way to sermonize with every situation. Some admired it, but even they wearied of her *drones about freedom* since they knew they would not go free, not ever, so the thought of freedom was itself an irritant, frustrating (sad), worthy of a kick! And they all knew one kick would accomplish nothing. Ropes had to be dealt with. A kick alone was futile. A kick alone only confirmed the mule's sour, recalcitrant, and vengeful reputation, which was a hurtful stereotype with little truth to it.

The meek shall inherit, the buckskin jenny finally nickered, breaking in, not kicking the thought away, but turning its head by the halter. *The Foals will, and the slavers will burn in Hellfire since slavery is a sin.*

Hear, hear, the other mules trumpeted (all but the red jenny, who was nibbling a knot and worked one bend from under one loop).

The riders got up and searched the shrubs for the source of the ruckus.

The kick did not happen then. The kick could wait, they agreed, for when their target was alone, unguarded or weakened.

Bowman gave off a particular scent, amniotic, they agreed.

They flicked their tails. They tipped their back hooves into the dust, legs bent at the knee.

They were given carrot ends from the bottom of first empty burlap.

Night. Moths rule the night.

By morning the red jenny got her rope untied. Then Maul retied it. He was up the instant she was free.

The red dog was back sniffing dung come morning. It wagged up at a tree where an animal crouched. Porcupine. Raccoon. They lost sight of the dog later. Passed a spine picked clean. A rib cage, also a wet place in sand where someone had pissed, by a pile of horse dung.

"That's the cob's dung," Maul said.

"Genius," Ella yawned.

Later, the little gray jack tried to pass the red jenny. She kicked him in the jaw. The gray carried the blue chair, his only burden, a novice. He tried to pass again. She kicked him in the ribs.

"This red jenny must go first," Maul explained. "She won't tolerate second or third slot." She was the foal of a Clydesdale mother and donkey father. Maul recited the genealogies as the morning passed, which mules were allies of which, which hated males, which females. Which could never be hobbled near this mule or that, or dogs or children, and how the old geezers kicked for fun. Don't walk behind them. Which veterans could be trusted with the most important or fragile items. Which novices showed talent. Which showed none and were heading for the cannery. "Mules are always listening, keeping a dossier." They are shepherds, will stomp a coyote when guarding sheep so keep that dog back. Which were prima donnas. That red jenny must be unsaddled first to prevent a roll or bolt or blow-up twenty miles in, which could crush the sawbucks to smithereens, break necks, lose loads, then it's curtains.

Dan's good eye watered. He'd brought his little magnum but never cleaned or loaded it. Lunch. Peanut butter rolled in bread.

"I hate a mule," Bowman said.

"A mule," Maul said. "He works."

"A horse works. A horse obeys."

"My point is a horse is slavish. A mule can think on his own. A mule is shrewd."

Bowman fed a crust to the big bay. He murmured lovey-dove whisper-talk. "Darling sweet. Wondrous angel."

"Mule's got the most difficult job of any work animal. Gets none of the help a saddle horse gets. No assistance from a rider to shift weight."

"A mule drowns straight-legged," Bowman said. "Flips end-over-end like a cork."

"Navigates difficult trails on his own."

"Your teams look like the cannery crowd."

"No shame in an auction."

"Gelded by nature."

"That eye needs air," Ella said. Dan ignored her. It was a stage of grief and natural.

"It was the left eye yesterday," Bowman said. She tried to remember if it was true.

They rode on.

When Bowman dropped down, the whole pack train stopped as he fingered blades of grass, scoped the ridge, or pawed sand. They waited as he stepped one foot up in the stirrup, kicked the other over, twirled a gloved hand in the air: *Roll out.* She'd speak her mind to Saul that night, curl to his ear about pacing and delay, on whatever coat was rolled-up as pillow. He would tell her again not to worry. Bowman was professional, kept his head down, had been paid well to do so. Their little iron safe was empty now, their bank accounts. Bowman had walked the cash back home before starting. He was not sorry he missed the shindig. He didn't care much for mares in the throes of labor, not much for horses in general, for animals even, though humans were the worst, the shittiest species, and that shindig was another example of "Homo saps run amok." He'd stayed home that night and caught up on his reading.

"Shindig doesn't seem the right word," Maul said. "And you seem to like that bay well enough."

"I like her. But I'd eat her on a desert island."

"On an island," Dan said, "would be fish and roots and quiet."

"Meat is meat," Bowman said. "You eat it."

Another elk. Hawks crisscrossed rim rock. Three rabbits. Bull snake. They passed it. A grouse flew up and dragged her wing behind a cairn as decoy. They all knew that old trick.

"The Old Swede was a man who sure loathed getting lost," Saul said. The trail's cairns were mossed-over yet marched a stubborn line up the drainage.

"Perhaps the Old Swede," Maul said, "was in truth an Old Frenchie."

"A young Brit," Saul said. "Or Russian."

"An Indian with artistic inclinations," guessed Bowman.

"Naw," Maul said. "The Old Swede was a baby in Östersund. His parents were Danish. They met at a goat fair in Belgium. His father found work in his trade in Delft, in Helsingborg. Then Strängnäs and Eslöv."

"Naw is right," Saul said.

"Repeat that last bit," Bowman said and Maul did and Bowman practiced the rolling old sounds in his mouth, asked for spelling.

"It's genetic fact," Bowman said, "some strains of the species are set to wander."

"Berlin. Mainz. Düsseldorf," Maul rattled. "Brielle in Holland, that old walled city famous for its great tower where William of Orange spied on Spanish invaders, signed the manifest in Rotterdam as Cook's Boy on the *Lucinda*."

113

"Now you're just inventing," Bowman said and Maul denied it and they followed the Old Swede's cairns into evening, which stretched each cairn's shadow taller and lankier. The stone heads rolled about in the shifting winds.

"What did the Old Swede mean by that?" Maul said. "Those tiny rolling heads?"

"Self-portraits of a dimwit," Saul offered. "If he had any sense, why would the Old Swede leave the world behind entirely? Why say goodbye to warm home and comforts? Why wander out in this cold and lonely with only mules and traps, flint and knives?"

Lichens knitted the joints so well that the cairns were difficult to kick apart.

"We've all tried knocking them down," Saul said. "All kids have destructive drives. The cycle of living." He glanced at Ella. "Sexual urges, frustrations."

"But lifeless piles of stone?" Maul said. "Why bother them?"

"To destroy is to begin to create," Saul said. "The new overturning the old."

"Cairns are a crutch," Bowman said. He hopped down and kicked it.

"The Old Swede's rolling over," Maul said, disgusted. "Why hurt a thing that's just helping you?"

They marveled at their own energy. They hardly slept. The cob's tracks never seemed farther or closer. They wound up sidehills and cut through marshes. The mules wallowed to their bellies dripping black. The creek disappeared where hidden ducks chorused.

At Ambush Point, Saul went first on foot with his rifle. They startled a young steer on the other side in a thicket. Bowman shouldered his rifle. Saul lifted his hand: no. The steer's eyes rolled. He tossed his big body about in the scrub, cow piles everywhere, liquid mess running down his back legs, lowing, miserable. Bear scat too, dried up piles with old berries. The steer zigzagged up the trail, shot off left and looped back toward Ambush. Where it was thickest, they cut through with a machete. They took turns.

"Where did the cob cut through?" Maul again.

No answer.

"I recognized the brand on the steer."

"We'll let him know soon as we get home," Saul said.

In Ella's book, his head would take a whole page, the horns bleeding across the crease. They'd call it Bull Run for the rest of their lives, as they agreed around the fire later in the flame-tinted somberness of such moments, though the place likely had many names already, back to the Indians who never wrote things down. They were the losers for this simple omission.

Ella turned in her saddle and searched for a posse after their posse, a thing she'd read in a book. She saw the red dog once a day, in front, on a ledge then gone. Saul didn't feel the sun anymore. The nerves in his skin were burnt off. The trail behind pounded powder. Ella wore cotton gloves. The extra pair was leather in her saddlebag with a sewing kit in a clear plastic case. No one needed to know about the scissors. They were hers not theirs. Scissors are lost again and again in innocent but thoughtless ways. Also hers, not theirs: tube of antibiotic cream, the tip uncut. Band-Aids and squares of gauze, ointments, cortisone in syringes. Iodine, tweezers, nail clippers, aspirin to soak beestings, baking soda for wasps, arnica for bruises, cramps, and general soreness. Bluebirds glared royal-ornamental. Four nips of airline gin taped together. It was divine. She'd bring her children here. The little morphine she'd stashed during Grannie's last days helped at times like these.

When a rock broke loose, they touched the horses' shoulder scabbards. Saul wished they'd brought WD-40.

"What in hell for?" Bowman said.

"Everyone needs WD-40."

"Cotton swabs," Bowman said.

"A whetstone," Saul said.

"I have one."

"A bag of mesquite charcoal," Maul said. "Nail clippers. Bubble gum. I don't like the minty types."

"I have all but the charcoal," Saul said.

In a gorge, Bowman said, "I see someone up there." He craned at a fringe of trees.

"You see an umbrella?" Ella said.

"What color?"

The binoculars were an extension of his face. Maul took cover with the mules.

"She doesn't have a rifle," Ella said.

The chestnut waded past. Dan squinted up.

"You don't know what she's got," Bowman said.

Once there was a baby coyote down at Grannie's chicken coop. The eggs already rolled around the bottom of her paper bag. The pup was wary, confused, looking for its mother. Ella set an egg on the ground and backed away. The coyote sniffed the egg, licked the feathered shell, rolled it between its paws to solve the mystery of enamel. It nibbled the narrow end, tried the girth, desperate with hunger and hope. She'd understood it then and now. The pup rolled the egg ever so cleverly toward a rock, where it would have cracked and become food, the baby licking and lapping and living on, if the rifle hadn't cracked from the porch, Grannie standing in blue smoke, the butt in the crease of her shoulder. Ella cried for the coyote. This was before she knew there was no such thing as a good one, wolves either, no good wild dogs of any kind.

Saul and Bowman exchanged binoculars.

"Nah. Nothing up there."

Maul said he once heard of an eagle that picked up a chocolate lab. Flew away with it and Bowman said, "Bull crap."

"I read it in the paper."

Blackflies dove loud at eyes and ears. Noses dripped. Bowman chewed Milk Duds somehow unmelted. He'd cut a small hole in a corner of the baggie and milked them out with his thumb as he rode. He ducked graceful under branches and leaned from rocks just in time. He spoke soft to the bay constantly, loving murmurs. The Old Swede's cairns got rarer but beetles did not. Large armies marched in columns of perfect shiny domes, pinchers gleaming. Some were crushed by hooves. Others lugged dung. The land rose. The canyons closed in. They rode with their rifles out.

"No way she's up to the ridges yet," Saul said. "Not without a magic carpet."

"A Huey," Maul said. "Like I said. I flew one in the war."

"No helicopter could land this tight," Bowman said.

"Depends on the pilot," Saul said. "I've seen it."

"I flew them," Maul said.

"Not here," Bowman said.

Dusk again.

They rubbed their necks at another boulder field, which might as well have been an enormous wall. They unpacked. Maul's hat was nearly swept off a rock when he dunked his head. A clump of sage swept by. They made no fire at first. Too tired and not cold enough anyway. They threw tarps down, rolled out bags where stones were kicked away for easy sleeping. No grasses or flowers would grow there. They were crushed on a regular basis, weekend after weekend, year after year, everyone and their sister and before the buffalo had bedded down there too, and the Natives in teepees or whatever housing the indigenous peoples here really lived in, which would never be known now. They were past. In sleep all creatures want the same things: moss, a bubbling brook for lullaby thoughts, a ring of rocks left by friends for tying out tent flies. She was happy for a minute. *Welcome Ella*, said the blackened rocks of the fire ring. *Welcome Ella*, said the boulder field. The mountains said *Most Welcome Darling Ella* too. The cliffs hung warm in last light. By morning the marmots would see their breath.

They wore headlamps, lit lanterns, poured oats into the nose bags. They ate quickly, cold roast near gone-off, potatoes in stiff foil. Licorice after. They brushed their teeth, spit in the creek. Ella passed aspirin.

The red dog appeared again. It sniffed the saddles and blankets. The mules were hobbled downstream, the bell mares belled. The horses were picketed, all except Bowman's big bay, who needed no picket or hobble. He was brushing her. She shifted in the dark, sighed. His arm swept the starlight slope from shoulder to rump. The brush was soft and old in her flossy mane. Her face shone in rough angles in the moon, bones bulging under hair and hide, encased in the outlandish elongated skull.

"You wouldn't eat her on an island," Maul said.

"I'd eat her," Bowman said. "I'd sell her for glue if the mortgage was late."

"I need a fire," Saul said. He stood from the blue wooden chair. He collected wood. He sat back on the chair with a bottle, a map with the light shining on it. He dropped bits and branches and the fire grew. Dan rolled in his tarp by the creek. "Come on over," Saul said, but Dan didn't.

"What was it like?" Maul said.

"Quit asking," Ella said.

"A shocker," Saul said. "The complex is an average of extremes."

"Fact is falsehood," Dan called from the creek in a clear-sudden voice. "Falsehood is fact."

"Mistakes are rampant," Saul said.

"Should have checked her breathing," Bowman said. "Her pulse."

"I choked her," Dan called. "Like this."

"She wasn't dead," Bowman said.

"I checked her," Saul said.

"You didn't check her pulse," Bowman said.

Ella was cleaning her rifle in the light of a headlamp. She screwed the plunger together. The gun oil and a little cloth.

She set it all down. She switched the light out. The fire was good, jumping high on her hands. Bowman offered his bay the flat of his hand. The paint sniffed the sugar lump, pawed and bit at the sorrel. Ella would gladly take the paint to the island with her. Bowman was repulsive but correct. If she were starving, she would eat him.

"The brain resists a switch like this," Dan said. Saul passed the whiskey to Maul. "The brain is shunted one way. The brain can overheat. All this switching. The brain can explode."

"I'm turning in," Bowman said, but the brush kept brushing.

"See that shooting star?" Maul said.

"I saw it," Saul said.

Maul handed the whiskey back.

"Did you see anything?" Ella said.

"How many times will you ask the man?" Saul said.

"I saw nothing ever," Dan said. "My blindness astounds me."

Inside the tarp he touched the patch on his eye. They could all feel him do it.

"Come out of there," Saul said.

"The barn?" she asked. "A light? A movement?"

"I never saw her once in all my life," Dan said. "She was a ghost to me."

"Must've slipped right past you," Bowman said.

"Some funny cartoon," Dan said.

"I'll look at that eye again."

Ella went over but his hands were out to block her. "You think you will, yes you do," he said. "But you don't run things from here on."

The bay's brush beat down her withers, her leg.

"You're lucky to have us," Ella said.

"Screw you," Dan said. "Lucky?"

"How long have you had that bay?" Maul said.

"A while."

Ella was a black statue over a lump on the ground.

"Come back, Ella," Saul said. When she didn't, he started in on the history of the railroad vs. the highway system. "Many opposed it mightily back in the beginning."

"Now look," Maul said.

"What's that got to do with anything?" asked the statue.

"Highway subsidies," Bowman said. "I hate them."

"I hate them too," Saul said.

"A hoax, all of it, to keep men glued to the tube, to wives, to lawnmowers, banks."

"Goats do a better job," Maul said. "With lawns anyway. More entertaining than TV."

"Who says it's better now?" Bowman said. "I don't."

"But surely a bona fide miracle in other eras. Neanderthal or Bible times, for example, that's what I'm getting at. Miracles."

"I'm going back to get the sheriff now," Dan said, getting up. Wearing the tarp like a cape, he walked to other boulders in the noisy fabric and resettled. Ella didn't follow.

"You go back to the sheriff," she said, "you go to jail."

"I want a firing squad, already decided."

"You don't get to get shot for what you did."

"I guess I need to up the ante then."

"Saul goes to jail too. And we have children."

"So that's the rub."

"That's one of 'em."

"He won't go to jail. I was pleased for him to fuck her."

"You quit that laughing," Ella said at Bowman.

"How 'bout I kill myself," Dan said.

"Saul goes to prison alone then, will take all the blame for selfish you."

"He enjoyed himself well enough that night," Dan said.

"He's a pig like any man."

"Did you enjoy it, Saul?"

Saul set a broken branch on the fire.

"*To see or not to see,*" Maul said. "That is the question."

"You let your life explode on everyone," Ella said.

"Then punishment," Dan said, "is called for."

Bowman was sitting in the blue chair now. When did Saul get up?

"Saul and I in the Pen together."

"I'm not going to the Pen," Maul said.

"You might," Saul said.

"I didn't touch her."

"Accomplices go to jail too," Ella said.

"Then you should hang too," Maul said. "The gallows in the Ladies' Pen."

"I only started a story," she said.

Bowman snorted.

"No law against it," she said. "Others finished it. I barely said a thing. Others stood by."

Bowman snorted.

"This," Dan said, "is proof of God."

"What's proof of God?" Ella said.

"Ginny's dying. Her failure to die."

"Not proof of any such thing," Saul said. "God is good. Nothin' good in this."

Which brought quiet, till Saul talked on: "Think of the Stone Age is all I'm saying. How they would have marveled at these days we're in now, though those brains of theirs were not lesser brains, just brains with less formidable information to consider."

"Stop it," Ella said. "I can't have it now."

"What can you have?" Saul said.

"Saul and me to be butt-fucked in the Pen together." Dan laughed to the sky.

"I'm tired," Saul said.

The fire burned, the mules shifted. The horses were disturbed. Bowman stretched his legs toward the flame. The chair tipped back under him. In time his heels smoked.

"Ginny's not gonna win this," she said.

"*Methinks she does protest very much*," Maul said.

"*Too* much," Bowman said. "Not *very*."

"Don't you ever say her name again," said Dan.

"*I come to bury Caesar not to shoot him*," Maul said.

"The perversions," said Bowman, "that a little schooling permits."

"Ginny can't win this," she said.

"So *that's* the real rub," Dan said.

"Ginny won't win," Ella said. "I promise you that."

"*Out out damn spot*," Bowman asided to Maul.

"I was just thinking that," Maul whispered back.

"*Anon*, what swill," Bowman said.

"You're a mean man," Maul said.

"Sociopath, according to my wife," Bowman said.

Dan held his head and looked at Ella. "You say her name one more time, I swear, my brain will explode."

"Ginny always had an elephantine memory," Saul said.

"Shut up with her name," Dan said. "I'm not kidding."

From the boulders, he winged a rock that whistled past. They ducked.

Saul stood. "No rocks, friend. There's limits."

Another whizzed by and Saul leapt the fire's edge. "Rocks are not a strategy."

"My little son loves rocks," Bowman said. "He's bigger now."

"Ginny should've just died in that pit," Ella said.

A grunt. Another rock. "Don't say it, I said."

Saul backed his way to Dan. "Goddamnit, Ella, quit with *Ginny Ginny Ginny*. The man is agitated out of his mind."

Maul was amused.

"He'll take your head off," Ella said.

"He can't throw straight," Bowman said.

Now Maul was laughing, and Bowman who never laughed a full laugh was laughing full. Dan ran at Saul to meet him halfway and Saul laid him out easy. Saul returned to the fire and Bowman reset the chair.

"Back to railroad tracks," he said in the quiet that came. "Perfect by nature, parallel steel for thousands of miles. Just think of it." His voice was cooling. "Up over every mountain obstacle. Creosote, spikes poured in fire-molds in Boston. The gauge never too wide or too narrow either. Based on Roman chariot tracks. 56.5 inches, the width of two horses. Must have seemed impossible at first."

"Yes," said Dan.

"Gorges. Chasms," Saul said. "Bridges are the answer. Bridges and more bridges."

"Yes," Dan said.

"Invention hatched from the mind of man. A beautiful egg, the shell and the contents both. A crack is damage, but also the glorious beginning."

Dan lay back swaddled in blue crumpled sound.

"Night-night sweet prince," Maul said.

"Damn this lime," Dan said. He rubbed his face, they imagined.

"Lime does what lime will do," Saul said. "Can't stop lime."

Saul took First Watch. They told Dan to sleep on through.

"Why do we need a watch?" Dan carped from a tarp.

"Darkness," Bowman said in a bag by the old dry log. The bay stood over him.

"I love a watch," Saul said. "Like kids again."

"Why rifles?"

"Don't engage with him," Bowman said. "Cut him off."

Saul delivered dental floss to Ella in the tent. Farts and sleepy-time jibber-jabber, the fire nearly out. Saul set the chair in the weeds. He walked around the piles of gear.

Back home, she'd scribbled lists and lists to be ready for anything: A cook tent just in case. A tiny woodstove. A funnel. Screw caps with shiny chains. Glass was too much weight. They were loath to bury trash. *No glass.* It broke in panniers, spills, cuts, a liability. One bottle of cheap champagne just in case.

"Rope," Saul's voice came in the dark. "Rope."

"Hemp, cotton, nylon," Maul was saying. "Singe the ends, prevents more fraying."

"Manila only," said Saul.

"Chuck that nylon. Nothing but heartache."

"Who you barkin' at?" Ella turned in her bag, argued with a memory. "I can bark too." So be it. The nylon rope had been burned with Dan's clothes, Saul's too, after they'd dug in the pit side by side, slicing ears off, snouts.

"I guess she's out," Saul had said to her at pit's edge.

"I guess she is."

Saul laughed with Maul, a rarity of opposites. She blocked them, all, boots and belts, everything. In the Beginning there was fire, earth, water, air. Some knots hook stubborn on the amygdala, rub the hippocampus as truth piles in, an avalanche of shit. Should have worn an apron. Maybe she'd sleep tonight. She prayed for sleep, the little diary lying innocent beside her. Baby booties, paintbrushes for the barn, fucking behind a tree, their peckers tingling, cloth diapers mothballed for grandkids, report cards, book reports, dollar bills, twenties, the loan payment due on Friday. Cowbells, berry bushes. So many dead this year, viruses struck before inoculation. Anthrax. Blackleg. Redwater maybe. $800 a head. There was a hole along the top pole. A satellite trolled across the hole. Finger paint for a birthday three weeks on, party faces blinking in, blinking out. The sky was full of them, berry bushes with shadowy wings, spaceships. The moon was getting round. A very fast shooting star. Small mirrors in leather wallets for ridge-to-ridge communication, since smoke signals were a lie. A first aid kit. Two sticks of dynamite from Saul's days at the mine. Spool of fuse. Compass. Whistle. Through a hole in the tent, Saul shook his head to stay awake. He unzipped his jacket to chill himself.

"Go on to bed," Saul said.

"I'm not sleepy," Maul said.

They talked wire cutters, zip ties, crossties, repellent.

Steer Thought #1 (The itchy steer tells a story with no title.) Bark isn't inert, isn't dead, at all: its remarkable intelligence is active always in protecting its trees from fire, yet if applied to by a humble quadruped, is ever willing to take time out from its duties to collaborate on the destruction of debilitating itches—torture, really, for a mule (or steer) or horse, if the itch is situated under the saddle. Bark is a miracle worker whereby the skin below the itch is freed to breathe, as the oldest and driest mule or horse (or steer) hair is combed away and clumps are left hanging by clinging tendrils from the tree in question, blowing softly there until a storm might sweep the clump off into the air, but until then, the clump from a distance looks like some animal sleeping vertical on the trunk, clinging to it by its tiny teeth or claws, so real-seeming that a hunter might stop and aim.

"Another," Maul said, pointing up.

"A nice one. Make a wish."

The star's tail faded.

"You better sleep," said Saul, then Maul finally did.

When Ella was nearly down for the night she heard a walker by the creek, then a vandal tampering at the pile. She kneeled at the door of the tent. Through the screen, she could see Saul pretending Dan was invisible bent over the bundles, the headlamp off, digging in the bread again. She unzipped the screen, followed him. Saul ignored this too. Dan climbed up into the boulders with a loaf. He was a silver shape in the moon: a child sneaking.

"Bring it back," Ella said. "She wants to eat bread, she'll show herself."

She only heard a splash, no other proof of bread. Could have been anything he threw. Ella looked careful around the rock world for proof of her sister eating bread before she crawled back under the fly. Saul was staring off. His rifle was set across his knees on the chair. He stretched his back when she disappeared, sore from riding. He was an early-to-bed man, a best-work-done-before-dawn man. He wore a jacket he got for Christmas. A cough near the bay. He moved the chair farther behind the mountain of stuff, out of sniper range.

Best get going to the cob.

Ginny lay prone, wide open to the moon.

Her heat reflected off the rock below back into her belly and legs then down into the rock again, a reciprocal arrangement. She considered the bread down at the creek in her boredom. An animal's job was to know the tricks: a wall of weed disguising a net, a bit of worm on a hook, a loaf on a rock. She shook her head. She'd seen First Watch do the same. She was cold. He was cold. She was tired. He was tired. The night air dropped down, colliding with day heat rising. The shifting inversions of chaotic terrain.

Grannie told her Dear Ones: *Consider the freedoms, the benefits of any life you're considering. Keep your minds open. In the mountains, for example, if the Marksman needs to eat, he will eat. The land offers dinner in every bush. Every ridgetop has a bird with a nest and eggs there waiting. Grouse is a fine bird, but a raven would do. A robin was called the King's Thrush for a reason: a delicacy, though small. Every forest has deer ready to turn their sides to you, innumerable smaller animals offering. The mountains aren't fearful places, my darling sluts. They are bountiful. If he is cold, like you are now, my dearest one, the fine Marksman can take a larger animal, that one just over there, for example, the one slipping closer around their camp in the aspens, on the east wall of this boulder field. See it? The Marksman shoots him second. Eats him with his eyes first. Skins him, finds a cave, flings the hide down, wraps himself for many cold winters, naps and dreams of summer.*

But Grannie had lived in town.

Ginny decided she'd fetch the bread but would steal the checkered shirt also, near the dun, but not on First Watch. She'd wait for Third. She'd free a mule. She'd take a pick for the cob's hooves.

Butt of the rifle in the crease of the shoulder. Prone is the most stable position, since earth is more stable than the Marksman. Keep your muscles fresh.

Come out, Ella. Show yourself.

When a rock fell to the east, both rifles shifted. Saul came into the open. The animals smelled her of course, but did he? She reeked enough to register to even the blindest of human nostrils. But the rock was more important. The fallen rock settled itself downhill of her, uphill of Saul, and they three made a triangle. She saw nothing in the rock-sound place. Saul waded toward it through the scrub, his Winchester leading. Saul could be the target of her first shot if need be. A rifle has its own mind.

She aimed at Saul to feel *aiming at Saul*, as in the pit she'd stood on her legs to feel *standing on her legs* and because her legs were fine in the pit. *See, your legs are fine because fucking is natural.* In the pit, the berry picker had dropped the berry comb somewhere in the muck and bent to search for it. The girl was tall, not a woman yet, sunburnt skin, small impatient eyes. In the story, she carried a comb for scouring berries from low thick branches, a cup of hollowed-out wood with graceful fingers arching up from the lip. Her father had carved it, a giant wooden paw. She heard the far-off dogs barking, guarding their patient little town beyond the clearing, moving between humble homes, eating trash, letting the smallest children pet them, howling at shadows of birds circling, since dogs, in all their time on earth, never understood the idea of flying.

The chair was on its side down beside the mountain of gear. She aimed at the chair. She could head down right now. Oats, shirt, a pair of gloves. Saul dipped out of view and reemerged much higher, not far from the rockfall. She'd forgotten him completely but remembered him now and aimed at his hat.

Any animal of size could upset a rock. A bird could. A marmot. Saul stood in the moon for a long time. He called her name as though he expected her to answer.

Still, when Saul's watch was done he climbed in. The sleeping bags were zipped together. He rolled into Ella. He touched her warm skin.

"My fat fingers," he said, working her nightgown.

"Don't tear it," she said. "No more scripture? No sermons?"

"I'm all out."

His hands were cold. The youngest child was only—how old?

Back home her children should be in bed in the two rooms Ella had painted. Saul had dragged tarps in. The children would be rolling in the hot sheets now, summer temperatures. There was no real spring in St. Cecilia. Winter and summer only. The kids would grow into the animals they were. That's all. And Saul's cousin would find blankets if nights got cold. The mothballs smelled like Grannie. If Ella were home, she'd set her nose to their soft bellies: the faintest waft of clove. She'd set their plates in the sink in her kitchen. She'd run water over the edges first, open the window, close it again. She'd fill the sink as hot as she could stand it. Suds. She'd wash the plates carefully. The sponge would be tucked in her small, strong hand since strength and size don't always comport. Her muscles were precise. They would make neat tight circles on the face of the plate and set the plate in the drying rack. She would sweep the floor after, around the kitchen with the wooden broom, out the doorway well into the dining room. She would move the chairs aside. The broom would miss no dust. She would find a small dirty cup on a chair. She would bend to rub a spot from the floor with her finger. She would rub her finger in the suds, dry her hands on a small towel from the bottom right. She would hang the towel over the faucet. The fringe would suck water up. Never rest. Never sleep. Hear a small voice crying for her down the hall.

"The kid will be fine," he said.

She shut her eyes in the heat of the mossy bags. The boulders would be boulders only so long as they could hold off the lichen growing stealthy in the cool spots, the cradles, pits and crotches of things, where moisture is trapped and new life possible, exploding slow over time into a great mat of peat, on and on, in layers, becoming an enormous tongue on the land, green, orange, soft, spilling up the cracks in the Mormoras, filling canyons, plowing up canyon walls, soon eating every bit of the mountains, every peak and valley and goat digested, until it's all only a colorful lumpy blanket on the land, victorious till the ice fields slide back down from the north and freeze out the great lichen fields, the lava spilling in after that, boiling the ice fields, and the jungle taking root when enough dust has settled, shoots breaking pumice to bits, and then the plates will shift deep below all of it, and the mountains will rise again because they must, and snap the jungle's back with new cold, without thought or malice.

$$\approx — \approx$$

FINAL ARBOREAL CENSUS
2179, May 1 (under the arch of blue-tarp sky)
SPECIES: *Callitropsis nootkatensis*
LOCATION: West Sea

Our yeoman truly loved the wing. It wasn't just some mild predisposition. Window cleaning was fine too, for the yeoman. Why complain? Back home there was no need for windows. The views were poor. Their sun was far and cold. The outside was forbidding. Wind was not a word there. Now she could crawl across the wing to touch the waves. Waves were also a non-thing back home. Adventure? Not a word.

A bubble from her sponge dribbled to the sea.

HIS NOTE: *Colt paws the earth with effervescence of desire (joy).*

The crew wondered about the cedar scientist's contribution to "spiritual" publications. Bacteriologists and paleo-ichthyologists whispered behind their hands. What was *effervescence*, really? The yeoman wondered, too, about *desire*.

It was not spoken of but this word had emerged from his pen. He didn't look like a raver. Calm-sad, rather, as his ink meandered like a lost horse in snow.

Not that the yeoman had ever seen snow.

It was known the cedar scientist was forced into cedars. The megafauna arena had been obliterated in the (overdue) advancement of microorganisms. Fungi and lichen were in style, abundant across the galaxies, survivors, some argued "time travelers," clearly holders of great secrets to success. Elephant, anaconda, kangaroo had gotten an overshare of attention for far too long, to the detriment of other worthies. Such emotional favoritism (*desire?*) had caused the deaths of whole worlds. Cedars were the scientist's fifth preference, it was said at mess. His "friends" laughed at his old-fashioned taste, it was said, then shushed for his wife's sake.

The yeoman licked her finger on the wing. She stared through smeared glass at the cedar scientist staring at the horses through smeared glass. Had he wasted his life? She didn't know enough to say. Salt was necessary to the body. She licked her finger again. This shore was nice.

Once she'd sat at mess across from the cedar scientist. He was tall and very thin. He ate only vegetable matter. He didn't look at her plate with its slabs of flesh. He finished quickly, rushed his tray away. Now he finished his report. She stared through the big smear, blurring him in sea mist.

HIS NOTE: *Colt's penis is erect, two feet long.* (It was true.) *The filly's tail whips up and around her swollen parts.*

The yeoman set the bucket down and sat, dangling her boots over the wing. The Resurrected Mule would appear down the off-load ramp at any minute.

The flag flapped onshore.

HIS NOTE: *PIRATE: a thief or hero of the high seas.*

HER NOTE: *A thief or hero.*

❧ —— ❧

The deputy showed up the next morning.

"Good morning, travelers!" he called from atop a yellow horse. A packhorse followed with bedrolls and bags, a dirty-white, flea-bit thing.

The posse's horses were saddled and pack strings nearly loaded. Dan salved sore spots while Maul searched for the spatula. Bowman ate from a bag by his boot. He reached his hand down, his fingers finding boiled eggs already peeled, lifted the eggs to his mouth and chewed. He turned the page in *Last Trackers of the Outback.* Ella had been bathing and dipped among the ferns. Saul studied maps in the chair.

"A bathing beauty! Ready or not!"

The deputy waved a baseball cap. He bounced in the saddle. His badge was sewn with yellow thread. He was center field for the sheriff's team. His brown jacket still had creases. The yellow horse had a sky-blue ribbon braided into her white mane. Her tail blew nearly sideways. She walked with long bobbing strides up the last steep to the toe of the boulder field.

"Never pegged you for late risers. Quite a lot of animals you're packing."

"We travel in style," said Saul. "You're up early."

"I never thought of bringing up a chair before," said the deputy.

"Now you have," Saul said.

134

The cinch was loose. He sagged on the horn. Bowman tilted his head to examine.

"Send a card to your mama yet?" Saul said.

"I did. Brought blanks to write along the trail. Mail later."

"That's nice. We could take 'em now, mail 'em for you. Case we get back sooner."

"Forgot my stamps."

"Oh, we can spare a stamp."

The deputy shook his head. Dan reworked the chestnut's cinches. The deputy watched.

"Where you headed?" Ella called from the ferns, nearly dressed now.

"Where *you* headed?"

"We waited for you Sunday," Ella said. "You said you'd help with the mare."

"Did I?" He was sorry about the mare.

"Rest in peace," Saul said.

"I came over later," said the deputy. "Gate closed. House was dark."

"We closed the gate," Dan said. "Turned the lights out."

"Why the patch?" the deputy said.

"I'm a buccaneer."

"Dropped by your place too," the deputy called to Ella. "Saw your kids. Your sister."

"Saul's cousin," she said, tiptoeing, boots under one arm. "I only have the one sister."

"Had," Dan said and winked at Ella. At which the deputy perked right up.

Saul walked quick to the chestnut. "Let me, friend." He elbowed into the D-ring and Dan's hands dropped. "What

135

in hell are you doing?" Saul whispered, but everyone saw his lips forming the words. Done, he returned to the chair, tipped his hat.

"It's wish fulfillment," Bowman said. "Dan's unconscious is steering the ship now."

"Alright," Ella said, trying to stop them, for all they cared.

"But he's wide awake," Saul said.

"Not how it works," said Bowman. "As I mentioned." They bickered waking or sleeping.

"I know what you're talking about," said the deputy. "I know Sigmund Freud."

"Freud's the wrong one," Bowman said. "Carl Jung's the one."

"I know Carl Jung too," said the deputy.

"A meeting of the minds."

The deputy took a look back the way he came. The way back was a long way.

"Jokers," he said.

"One sister," Ella repeated.

"Sure. Virginia," said the deputy, watching the men.

"Named for our Grannie. The sixth in a line of Ginnys."

"She's older?"

"I'm older."

"Why'd she get the name then?"

"What's her name matter?" Dan said.

"Said it was something in the eyes," Ella said.

"Color?"

"Don't know," Ella said. "Can't ask her."

"Ella's a good name."

"I prefer it."

"Cousin said you were going packing."

"And here we are."

"You didn't mention packing when I saw you."

"Not your business," Dan said.

"He's grieving," Saul said.

"Grieving what?"

"What's not to grieve in this life?"

"The pit's filled in."

Dan switched to the chestnut's shoes.

"That's what's done with pits," said Saul. "You fill them."

"Sorry about breakfast," Ella said. "All packed up." She rubbed her goose-pimpled arms.

"Got the week off. Thought I'd see some new country."

"Real pretty back here," said Saul. "Wonderful choice."

"I'm not good at vacations."

"Use 'em or lose 'em," said Maul.

They all laughed. Ella offered a donut from a crushed oily bag.

"I don't do sugar," said the deputy.

"What do you do?" Bowman said.

"Everything but sugar."

"Can't imagine life without sugar," said Ella.

"Seems sad," Maul said. "Strange."

"Sugar will kill you," Bowman said and winked at the man, set his book down, stepped up for a real look at the yellow horse. They talked of the trail, what to expect up beyond the boulders, how much food, how many days, a week at most, plenty of ammunition. The deputy's teeth were perfectly even, salt and pepper around his ears. Dimples. The yellow horse tossed her head. The deputy pressed his heels down, but did not sit well. The yellow horse moved him to the outskirts of the group. The packhorse followed.

"You're supposed to ride your horse," Dan said. "Not the reverse."

The yellow horse at last obeyed. "I keep asking you, where's your wife? I hear she'll be single soon," said the deputy down at Dan's face, twisted in hate.

"What he wants to say," Ella said, "is we're out here looking for Ginny right now."

The deputy looked to the peaks. "Maybe I'll get lucky then. See her tracks. Find her."

"She took a gray horse," Saul said. "A little cob."

"No note?"

"Ella, did you see a note?"

"We're worried to death," Ella said.

"She can go wherever she wants to," Saul said. "South Dakota. Canada."

"I was once in Canada," said Maul. "Ducks, geese. Very dull."

"Freedom of movement," Saul said. "Makes man Man. We're beasts in cages without it."

"Why'd you fill that pit in?"

"We're all good people," Saul said.

"Why do you care about their pit?" Bowman took the yellow horse's bridle.

"Who cares why he cares?" Dan said.

"People are talking about his pit," said the deputy.

"People love to talk," Bowman said. The yellow horse nuzzled him.

"I'd love to see Ginny," said the deputy, then the wind

blew his cap off and Maul trundled after it, caught it in the ferns, walked back, handed it up.

"Enjoy your vacation," Ella said.

"Those stirrups adjust in a jiffy," Bowman said. "They go up and down, little buckles."

The deputy yanked his horse's head from Bowman. "Much obliged."

"Did you hear that?" Bowman said, with the biggest smile she had ever seen on him. "This lawman here is much obliged to us, fellers!"

"What kind of cap is that?" Dan called. "Can't goddamned ride out in a cap like that."

"He's John Law," Bowman said. "He can wear any kind of headgear."

"Tell her about the mare if you see her," called Ella.

"I'll save the sad news for you," called the deputy. His horses turned at the cairn, up a cut, and disappeared.

"Don't you have," Dan called, "any goddamned better things to do?"

"I guess I goddamned don't," the deputy called back. He appeared above as if his horses were walking on an elephant's back. "If we cross paths, I'll tell your sister you all are hunting all over for her."

"I expect she knows it," Ella called.

⊰ —— ⊱

And, too, here's something relevant. I've told Ella a thousand times: three hundred miles wide, this storm was. Me, just off the ferry out of Haines. I've been through storms. Nightfall up to the border toward Haines Junction. Well beyond that is Destruction Bay. The rig was full and heavy, thank God, ballast. It was a trip gone strange like this one, but quicker. I found out later the Mounties closed the road behind the bumper of the rig behind me, a barricade. ROAD CLOSED. I didn't know it. How can you know the present without it first becoming the past in the future? Can't. How the snow swirled that night. Off the ferry it was only clouds, but at the border snow started. Snow can blind. The road soon wasn't visible at all, no concrete, no lines. Whiteout, blackout. You just had to believe in the road. You had to believe in concrete, in the rig. The rig in front sometimes winked between gusts. Its taillights would flash ten feet out, two feet. I'd punch the brakes. Believed in brakes, my boot pressing them, in deceleration, in diesel fuel, in combustion engines. The rig behind glowed then didn't. This was living, right then, death right there looming. I never hit the bumper of the rig in front. We were sweating, our faces and necks, from the blast of the heaters. Our feet and elbows were frozen from being too far from the vent. Glass was only a sliver between us and Outside, Forty Below. When I say *we* I mean all the drivers in the caravan. It was a pilgrimage, like this one now. *We* in the sense of *us* here in this boulder field now. I don't know their names or faces in other rigs, wouldn't know if they knocked on me and Ella's door. It was a communal experience, brothers born and never known, all orphans now, parted from each other at birth, that storm. The world is full of them, unknown brothers. If we met again by some miracle, we could talk about this storm, how a little kiss between the bumpers might have been comforting, a little

Hi there, friend, then back to the business of not dying, of not freezing in a ditch, of snow not piling on as our fuel ran out, as the caravan went on, lost to us without knowing, as the exhaust pipe clogged, drifting us into monoxide sleeps. I lost the taillights for miles, set the speed with my boot on the pedal, two miles per hour, less, leaned over the steering wheel hunting for my new old friend just there somewhere through the icy slapping windshield, in front of my bumper somewhere. He was not there. He was there. It's hard to explain. We understood. It might have been miles, eons, if your mind shook loose for one split second. No way to stop. We were a train of strangers with no tracks and no knowing who was leading, if the leader was competent, no stopping without getting smashed from behind. No talking the problem out to each other, only trusting, but trusting with no words. As animals do. We were strangers together, family, on this ride, a snow parade in the middle of the night, inching over the black-white earth together, blind, dizzy after an hour, more than dizzy after two, after three or four or ten I was sure I was not on earth anymore. I held my brain in with belief only. My eyeballs were tired from stretching open. The muscles around my eyes in my face. I was flying through black-white space, no beginning and no end to it. Was I moving at all? My friends were gone. It was where I would live forever, in that black-white pulsation, the wind buffeting my rig, me gripping the controls, a ship in swirling fluid, keeping the nose of the ship aimed straight, but what was straight? There is no straight in space like that. Straight is a concept. Muscles in my arms and chest. I was alive and not alive. I would never go home again. Never see Ella or my kid. Only one kid then. The others were later and would never be. There was no home. In time, some amount of time—hours, seconds, years—I was sure it was bits of some celestial explosion I was flying through, a star ignited and cooled off just enough for flying through, and I was flying through it and would never get there, and there was no *there*. I would freeze. I would burn. So I understand what Ginny's feeling now.

❧ —— ❧

"Howdy" Mom—"Here" is little Cowtown under Big Sky—Not there now / "riding" / fill you in later—Can't be same sky as NJ—Not your planet—Bet you're fine—I'm in "The Big Window" —been aching for it—won't die in cubicle—No—Locals ok but "rough around edges"—Outsiders are required to really SEE—Dull coarse men/clever woman—Gotta ride on—

The child mind must be killed off. It was what the postcards meant. Every Revolution requires a Manifesto.

Back in town, two black birds saw him drop the first postcard to her in the mail slot. He'd waited on the corner for a truck to pass and walked back to HQ. Looked both ways just as his mother told him. The opening squeak of the mailbox arrested the birds, as did the whispery slide of the card down the chute and the clanging shut of the metal door. They fluttered on an electric line at these human-only sounds. After the deed was done, he was sure he discerned the titters and tilts of avian editorial. The birds went silent again at his stare. They lifted their wings to catch the sun. Crows maybe. Ravens maybe. Their wings in the morning light were more rightfully *flashes*, blue or purple, a mixture with no word attached, an animal word. *Blackbirds* was a misnomer.

—

Mule Thought #3 (the red jenny and the little gray): Small Birds and Metamorphosis. *What is not a mechanical beast then, the red jenny mulled, if a flock of birds is?* She was lecturing again about respect. *Name one creature that could not be reduced in that way. What rock? What mountain? What wave? What in the universe could not be thus reduced? Is this reduction required by the thinker to feel alive?*

The little gray yawned a big ugly yawn. The noise of the riders clouded his brain, a flaw in concentration that, he was sure, the red jenny did not have.

We must pity them, mulled the red jenny.

The meek shall inherit? fretted the little gray, quoting the buckskin.

I don't know, yawed the curly black. *That might not be us. There are meeker. Small birds are meeker.*

Yes, exactly, mulled the red jenny.

Even smaller, yawed the curly black. *Bugs. How I loathe them.*

So we will be overthrown too then, mulled the red jenny, *by the meeker, by the smaller and smaller, if overthrow is the plan.*

Overthrow is the plan, drawled one of the red twins, who had not a single original idea in their two heads put together. The buckskin jenny was their queen.

It doesn't matter, coughed the tall mule with the strange eye. Morose. Drifting off and out of topical intercourse. He had been robust, once, in general, but now oh so far from robust, and the red twins looked to the buckskin jenny for the final word as Maul checked each and every of all their hooves, one by one, at the next resting place with no shade, no bark, pulling each hoof up between his knees, since nothing could be done about the tall mule's cough.

The red jenny. The red jenny. The red jenny. Who was she?

None of them could really believe her, *since belief depended on understanding and understanding required long quiet thought, over long quiet years without the chitter-chatter of horse sound and cow sound and bird sound and whip sound and there came a time when, if the thinker had not been practicing, the thinker lost the power to think.*

Who had said it? Had he really thought it?

Who cares, nickered the buckskin jenny from the second string. *The meek shall inherit.*

The meek shall inherit, the red twins heehawed.

Later, when the shade dyed her a deeper red, the red jenny told the little gray a story. When she was born, as a foal, she was *gold*, not *red*.

Think on that fact and what it means.

The little gray was thunderstruck. He had no idea how to respond to the story. It was the way she told it, not what she told. As if she'd passed some quiver to him with the mundane datum on pigmentation. What was expected of him? What answer? Why did it matter? He fretted about *gold to red* all afternoon as they were driven up a box canyon. While he knew miracles of color could happen—some foals changed from black to white dappled, some from white to black dappled—he was sure he himself had always been gray.

✄ —— ✄

Another night. Cliffs again. Second Watch looked lean and angular. He had a large scope, also binoculars around his neck. He didn't sit. *Never fall asleep on Watch, that's a Cowboy's greatest sin.*

Why was sleep necessary?

It isn't, Grannie's voice said, papery, from the dead.

Ginny dreamed of roast beef.

Potatoes in foil.

Swiss cheese, turkey chewed on both sides of the mouth.

Pork unsliced, slit open, pepperoni in a bag, salty, hot-sweaty, crushed flat from day packing.

A stick of butter end to end.

Bouillon cubes.

And Ella would have a syringe.

Grannie told her Dear Ones: *Never lean away. Lean into the weight of the rifle, prone, kneeling, or standing. Use your dominant eye if possible. The bolt is forward and down. In stress, check the shell is loaded correctly, right end out. Slide it in. If you fuck it up, don't tell.* A bat flew through.

A Cowboy makes a campfire of whole trees burning.

He owns nothing in the whole world so does not think of waste.

He eats pots of beans with a spoon too big for his mouth, passes the spoon to his friend.

(What friend? What spoon? Poor baby.

It's not self-pity, Grannie.

What is it then? A Cowboy can't afford mercy, the world's most expensive luxury.)

Another movement down at the canyon mouth. She was sure now this movement was an injured animal, a small bear or elk, creeping slow in. She slipped along away from the sound. She'd parked the cob miles off as usual.

Second Watch dipped in and out of shadow. Who cared about Second Watch when cold and running? *You're not running*, Grannie rustled in her head. *You've turned. You're hunting now.*

Turnabout since in the pit, no ladder, no rope. The eastern sky had been full gray leaning toward blue now with the edge of the Mormoras holding the day. An engine had started and she'd dipped down. She'd dragged a calf to her calf and stacked it. She dragged another to make a step. She tottered to the pig and dragged it, its molecules tearing. Barrels stood around the edge. A sawhorse. A stack of pallets. She was hungry. It was another sign she was just a beast. Heat shot up from her cunt to her belly. *You are only a talking animal*, the calf said. The steps she made were beautiful. She crawled up her beautiful steps, her spiral staircase to the crystal chandelier. At the turf, she rolled out of the pit and stared at the sky.

Now where, Grannie?

Oh my little cunt, that's always the question.

When she got Her One Shot at Ella, when she blasted Ella's brain, she'd walk on out to Carlyn over the Mormoras, find the cob a small barn in a meadow with a cat and a goat to keep him company. In the stall each morning she would pitch the flake, no more. He would get fat anyway, fat as a house, her cob. He would soak the hay in his clean water and she would scold him. They would ride. Sometimes they would only walk side by side on the fence line, the goat trailing behind, the cat behind the goat, an animal parade. The red dog would come in time, but not now. The mailbox on the road would be empty and then rust. They would shift and stomp and graze through grass bent in the wind, cut downhill to the creek for more, eat bread in wildflowers tall and thick.

But not yet.

Anger: It's a state of mind.

Nothing real about anger.

A river is real. A creek. A horse. A sister.

Pull yourself together and shoot.

I can't see her, Grannie. She's in the tent.

In some future brain: The view back west.

Faint light on the clouds, maybe a big fire.

Town might have been blown sky-high by some terrorist just like her.

Radioactive, burned up, scoured away.

No way to know.

The curve of the earth blocks line of sight.

Only their camp was clear. The barrels of feed. The tent.

Grannie told her Dear Ones: *Ease in the trigger finger for perfect pressure. Take all slack from the trigger before the shot since the trick with a shot is the shot, it's not the enemy but a simple plain of buffalo turned on its side, roaming topography.* No, that wasn't quite right. Her brain was boxed again. She shook her brain to fix it.

Another rockfall woke her, tumbling down the south wall. The 30-30 had dipped but rose again to the tumble. This was one hell of a clumsy, injured animal. The tent did not unzip in the small ruckus. The mind runs in fatigue, wakes the body. The body is stronger without the mind. Ginny shifted from prone to crouched and back. Second Watch was on alert too, a tiny man, steel pipe to his face, an enormous scope the size of a rocket. Second Watch, her former next-door neighbor, wouldn't sit in the chair. Frailty too was a state of mind. The rifle old and heavy, *a beautiful tool, the most clever and effective invention of man, revolutionary, much debated, it set man above the lesser creatures though man knows he is still one of them. Eats, sleeps, ruts as any goat does.*

Saul and Ella, for example, were rutting in the tent right now.

Second Watch stood listening, ate something with his fingers like a red squirrel.

He is born of a womb, sucks at the tits, dies. In the end, the bugs eat him too. He is equal in all ways to the lower animals, but for that one smart man who forged the first firearm, hammered it, stuck a shell in, passed it around, made man the most successful species this world has known. Who and what else has those kinds of bragging rights?

A shooting star. Refuse of the universe.

The tent puffed. Saul crawled out of the tent to stand, naked and blue, his pecker still slightly stiff, pissed again, arched his misty fountain just downstream of pots washed and upside down, drying. If Ginny set the cob free, would the cob know what to do with freedom? The red jenny had known. The little gray. Run off in opposite directions.

In their new home on the moon, she would slip a finger down inside his ear, root about in the waxy place. He'd press that big bony head into her fist, lips quivering, the drool of bliss, an impossible itch scratched. Waking from not sleeping, she saw a large thing in the aspens now, the Injured Thing. *The Marksman must be willing to endure nearly endless failure. Bones and muscles are faulty. They can't live up to the mind's perfect shots.* But the old lady was dead, wasn't she. Death, the ultimate failure.

Third Watch. Light soon.

Ginny moved downhill easily and slipped among the mules. She took the wool shirt and filled the bread bag with oats, tied it. The mules' shadows stretched and mingled with hers as she moved through. Strider. Punk. Deirdre. May. The buckskin was Millicent. She laughed or almost. Spot was the curly black, no spots. They swung their heads around at Third Watch coming over. Ginny set the bag by a rock and slipped into the creek with the rifle and pistol overhead. She waded behind a boulder as Third Watch smoked a cigarette. He'd set a tin cup with a spoon on the rock, picked it up, ate. It was simple mechanics: molecules escaped through steam as the stew bubbled on propane burners. His hand stirred with wooden spoon. The molecules, thereby, were agitated, had taken flight, were conveyed by updraft to the receptors inside the snout of the beast in the water, not ten feet away. You can die of starvation but not from hunger. Taste and scent are sisters. Hence, the tongue is the most essential *olfactory* organ. Dan had been clear about this. A forgotten organ, much overlooked. It was humanity's last link to the true, animal consciousness of scent it had abandoned, Dan claimed.

The rock was big. Ginny on one side, Third Watch on the other. Third Watch chewed in full rotation. He held his cup to his face, shoveled in. He had a pumpkin head she'd never noted. He reset the rim of his hat as if hearing the thought. She was very cold in the creek and she smelled the impossible distinctively. The sniff of Grannie's old green glowing lampshades, smoking glass dusted, never dusted, a weather vane spinning. A dog sleeping. They were all symptoms of a disease she'd contracted on the tip of her tongue. Her teeth chattered. Hypothermia. Maul smelled her as well as the horses did. His brain simply didn't trust the information. He stared at her scent in the dark and chewed. His tongue was different. Lewd and innocent. His eyes searched for the source of her stink. As he stuffed his face, she shivered and tasted oily cast iron, dried-up and rusty-backed, the water lapping her. Freezing in a creek was a state of mind: Grannie said walnuts were a cure for everything, but she had none and perhaps it was some other nut. Delicious. Evil thoughts creep in. The mare's head was heavy as she'd lifted the pistol to it. The body rocking on the rope.

"I can see you," Maul said, though he couldn't possibly.

The stars shifted overhead in the barely lightening sky, same stars every night, never a new one, yesterday, tomorrow, birthdays, deathdays. Where was the injured animal now?

"Four minutes of cold water is fatal," Maul said. "Kills more people than cancer."

A lie, except perhaps in some twisted, historical count.

He made a move to see and she dipped under. She wished for sun in the night-creek, the very same water the cob was slurping in safety, though the sun was a killer too, bugs and birds, sickly baby rabbits caught out in it, no shade, the mother hauled off by a golden eagle, it smothered old men in waves in crumbling cities, quick as any pillow, dropped them like flies, if you believed the papers, which she didn't. Just words in bubbles. Like till death do us part. Oh, for a little deadly heat now! She rose to breathe. Teeth chattering: the body's attempt to generate kinetic heat. Maul paced the shore. Spontaneous combustion, rays arrived through space that hit a too-wet haystack, the farmer's fault entirely, impatience in teddering, bailing, since all other variables were not variables—sun, oxygen, carbon in grass. They'd discussed it, Dan and she. Ice and sun were the same in the end. They sucked life from wanderers in all desert places. This was a desert, this box canyon, this creek. Eight inches of precipitation a year.

Maul belched beans.

She was swimming in it. The victim crawls toward oasis, just a pile of joints in last locomotion, too tired to stand and walk out from between the dunes. Lost the map, no pockets, never had a map. The map is written in the ancient mind: dragging a line in the sand, a broken leg, a femur: the injured bone snapped in some fall during a battle in the rut, some foolishness, the winning male watching from a crest, chewing his cud, soon to be jerky too, vultures circling. Dan had married her more than willingly. And now the moon fried their separate brains with identical pressure, identical result, since Dan's brain was encased in a black hat of sleep, if she could find his baby-head in the aspen, *show yourself*, an old grass weave plucked from a stack of fingerprinted rims. *Take your hat off*, she might say. *Fan your head with it, cool yourself down*. It was impossible to be a good person. The wool was soaked. She peeled it off. It was what freezing people did.

Third Watch set the cup down. He saw the bag of oats behind the rock, bent and stuffed it in his huge pockets. He lifted his shotgun. He patrolled the edge from mules to horses. She waded ahead, ducked, let him pass, waded the other way. She recognized the chestnut by only his back end. He was too old for pack trips. He leaned his head over the sorrel's neck to look at her.

"Stay away from my mules."

The moon was behind the crowns of the aspens.

"I got nothin' against ya. No dog in this fight."

She slipped out, crept onto shore.

Grannie told the Dear Ones: *Never run. The bear follows a runner. A walker is 50-50.*

She stopped to wring out the wool shirt. She shrugged it on again, walked. She was well up when she turned and there was Ella, the Queen, with her little shiny diary book in her hands and in the wide open too, tearing the pages out. Walking among the mules for just this purpose, perhaps. Too far for the 30-30. She wasn't thinking right. She lifted the rifle anyway. She was a sniper now. The sniper set the bead on the Queen's head. It hovered there and the finger tightened over the trigger but before the squeeze, a confluence of events occurred called "The Creature and the Queen," as follows: Once upon a time, high in a box canyon, the Queen came out, square in the crosshairs, finally, as they say. Then what do you know? The Creature appeared too. Who would believe it? Two targets at the same time. Impossible. The Creature was bigger than she'd thought. The Queen was whiter. She was tearing the page into confetti, bits falling around her. The bead of the rifle stayed on the Queen since she was the most desired target, the most longed for. But 30-30 was entirely unsure now, yes or no, right or left. The rifle moved back and forth between the two. It was the 30-30's fatal flaw. The Creature was much higher in the scree now. She could almost see it clearly. She could almost hear it breathing high thinner air as the Queen crossed toward the mules.

Grannie told her Dear Ones: *For a sure shot, close the eyes before firing.*

Let the rifle find the natural point of aim.

Breathe, reopen eyes. Is the picture sound?

Squeeze. Don't pull it.

Squeeze tender, steady, continue past the point of release, hold after the shot is done.

Relax.

Ginny opened her eyes. Below, the Queen was walking among the mules ripping up the pages of her book into bits then smaller bits then feeding all sizes of bits to the mules. She slipped under bellies and heads to do so, offering palm-fuls of broken paper. Her headlamp beamed through the blotted shadows. Her voice responded to sighs and nickers in and out of view in parts. They ate the paper, chewed it. An arm, a horse neck, a mule's ear bit off on the end. The 30-30 shifted up to the Creature and down then to the Queen in a gown or nighty, pearly buttons. She spoke to Maul, the Keeper of the Mules, then walked to the weeds where the

Priest was sleeping. Bowman. The men were unimportant to the story. The paper bits were falling, eaten. The Creature, too, had pearls up his middle thorax, like fish swimming in a line. In the Creature's hand was a silver tool, wood maybe, then a pair of boots mixed with the Queen's headlamp, a flash of creamy rump, the paint, blended into peripheral sight with the Creature's hands and knees on the rock. How do the eyes mix two scenes? The brain does it all the time. The Creature had a chain with teeth over one of his shoulders, rust rubbing his creature-cape, loose skin or wings held down by chain. The Queen dipped away among the schools of animals. Her lamp submerged and probed reefs of slim legs and hooves and paper fluttering. She was a black submarine beaming plumes of tails, horse heads floating black-plum, ferns and starlight on blue-scaled horse hide, and paper as bubbles through aspens. The Creature was a hovering bird. The Queen stood up. The reef was gone. The paper bits were gone, digesting. Her lamp slid above the surface. Some bird sound had reached her Queenly ears. Ginny turned and ran uphill toward the cob.

She did not think of the rodeo boy as she climbed scree. She did not connect the two. She breathed hard and thought of the cob and this Creature following. The pistol hung in her free hand. The rifle rode over the other shoulder. The scree was difficult and fell away. The sound clinked down, gathered sound, and the Creature shifted out of her wake. He climbed up parallel, spoke something from just below.

"Wait. Wait for me."

She found a rock and flung it. She arrived at the false summit, a grassy edge. The ridge loomed. He climbed fast on all fours. He was a spider, turned out. Another rock. He did not drop his eyes, starving. A light peered from the camp, a lantern. Voices gathered and ran into splashing water. She climbed. She was stronger than whatever it was, the Creature, the spider, the boy. She hated everything and hate was fuel. When her feet slipped, she flung more rocks. She scrambled with bloody hands, exactly what hands were for. Her boot slipped and she looked behind. A huge hat bent down. She lifted the rifle and fired it. Surely a miss, but it was how The Cowboy Got Her One Shot.

Ginny slid down the scree on the other side. No one followed. In the mountains the world begins again and again. At a flat, she let her bowels go. Liberty. She heard voices on the ridge, the Cavalry, Saul and Bowman at the very least. The sun was nearly up.

In the cottonwoods, she explained to the cob about the oats. She opened a can of spiced ham with a sharp rock. She ate ten raisins and gave him twenty. She untied the red dog but unmuzzled later. She cleaned herself by a pool with old grass. She breathed newness in, her dirty insides out. She pulled her pants up. The stars had faded, gave into blue, that strangest and most impossible color. As morning came, she told the cob about the Creature, how even now in the pink light of dawn he tends to his bullet wound since the shoulder damage is ugly. His knife is exquisite, fine old work by the Cutler with an antler grip curved to fit and a very wide blade cut and forged from a saw. Pewter poured nicely at the neck, a leather wrap about the handle, little tassels. To clean the blade he's dropped off the ridge to a new and unknown lava flow. A bush bursts into flame. He turns the blade in blue flicker, thereby the bush cleans the blade. The lava is coming. He slides the tip of the blade into the wound, lifts the bullet out. He sets the bullet on his tongue, swallows it.

He finds a mud wallow. He packs the wound, lies on the ground with the burning land around him as the microbes eat infection gone. The mud dries. The cob listens to every word, tells her she needs rest, more food, an antibiotic. The dog turns a three-sixty in agreement, lies down then rises as she climbs on the cob and they ride on.

> "Howdy" Mom—Yes diamondback (reverse pic)—Snakes are ubiquitous (everywhere)—My broomtails woke a fell'r like this guy just the other day—No one injured but horses do "spook"—Some myths are real—Met a woman—chasin' her—My eyes are opening—Are yours open, mother? The Big Window I'm in it—Effervescent! So long—

Ignorance is not always inherited. The young can rise above beginnings.

He reckoned he smelled breakfast somewhere. Someone cooking it for someone else, not him. He *reckoned*, too, he'd heard a rifle shot.

He'd asked what to call the horses when he borrowed them, but the sheriff said he "didn't believe in naming animals." Why? he asked. Respect or disrespect? The sheriff said names were for people not animals and this shocked the deputy.

The animals knew who they were, said the sheriff. He got no further. It left him in a state of awkward nakedness in relation to his team. He was not a quitter. He tried new names each night, by God. Misty and Clyde. He'd mail the cards back in civilization. His knees ached. His palms rope-burned even through gloves. In truth, rope was frail, just braided grass invented by primitives. Gloves cooked his fingers. He fed the horses apple treats from the flat of his hand. Mandy and Buck. No reaction. What might the sheriff's niece from the city call the horses? No idea. He'd seen palm-feeding on *Gunsmoke.* One thing was sure: the West was the cure for passivity. Neither Cowboys nor Indians were cubicle dwellers. At night in camp, the animals glided toward him for apple treats and his fluids pumped faster, big as ships cutting slushy seas, and he touched his blade.

∽ —— ∾

The rifle smoke was still visible in the dawn light. They were that quick about the chase.

All three Watches rode bareback hard up to the Ridge of the Rifle Shot. Their horses leapt up scree that rolled away beneath their hooves, the men hanging onto manes and necks, their legs gripping the heaving bellies. The horses gasped and seemed to go nowhere but did indeed rise in the end, then rise then rise, growing smaller above the mules that dropped away and away, growing smaller with horses' efforts.

On the ridgetop Maul was too winded to assist the trackers. He parked himself with the horses, talked to them between panting, supervised Saul and Bowman crawling and puzzling over boot prints in the disturbed scree. Blood. He told the horses sweetly how the Old Swede had served out his boyhood on the *Lucinda*, Bristol to Edgartown to Gloucester to Glasgow, Hudson Bay to see the great white bears, deckhand on the *Porpoise*, back to Terneuzen, that sentinel on the sea's brink guarding the ancient heart of Zeelandic Flanders, on foot to Amsterdam when there was no other way, no horse, no cart, and he walked the marshes in the urgent wind, along the dunes it formed, from windmills that harnessed it to stables that hid the horses from it to windmills again, island and marsh to the streets along brick canals, barges moored nose to tail, red lights in the windows at night, fresh round cheeks pressed to the glass, to the Canaries on the *Valentina*, to Morocco to the Cape of Good Hope to the Galápagos on the *Kate* before they were even Darwin's Islands, back to Buenos Aires on the estuary of the Río de la Plata as first mate of the *Sophia*. He had a son who died in Paris, it was whispered. He went to jail in Mainz, it was said for some small theft, a great injustice. Chicago, in time, by way of Great Lakes aboard the *Pearl*, prototype of the first notion of a submarine. The *Eska*, on the Yukon, a decommissioned paddleboat from the Mississippi, south again as a hand on a cattle drive to Calgary. Kalamazoo by a prairie schooner he called the *Gisele* in letters back to Stockholm, then from there, a mule—Rosalyn—to St. Cecilia. He had the best bowl of soup made by the girls in the kitchen at the Mission School.

"They say a human will walk in circles," Maul puffed, "if left in a land with no landmarks."

"The Titanic's route," Saul said and plucked up the spent shell.

The horses frothed, sniffed at the day ahead. Saul handed the shell to Bowman.

"Only roughly," Bowman said. "The Titanic's port was never Glasgow."

"The North Sea is the North Sea," Saul said.

"Those Dan's boot prints?" Bowman asked.

"I was watching him," Maul said. "He was asleep the whole time."

Bowman pocketed the shell. "Maybe you were too."

"Not his caliber," Saul said.

Camp was only a smudge far below. The rising scent of breakfast. They rode on over the ridgetop after one set of tracks.

"Find our gal?"

This from Dan, tipping an imaginary hat, as the men returned from their charge up the slope to the rifle shot and beyond. Fluttering aspen leaves, gunshots. (*They don't call them Quaking Aspen for nothing!* he almost said.) The sorrel and bay drank long after their fruitless chase.

The commotion of the wee hours hadn't woken him. Now, he was eating donut crumbs from the oily bag. The disk covering his socket was dusty. His hat was missing. They'd found a camp of sorts abandoned in a box canyon like this one, tracks from there.

"Too bad," Dan said.

"Should have kept going," Bowman said.

"Why didn't you?"

"Got blood on you?"

"I said he was sleeping," Maul objected. They checked Ella too. Her boots.

Dan turned the bag inside out to pour the crumbs into the flat of his hand. The wind took most. Saul stretched his back on earth again. Dan offered to walk on it, started to pull his boots off. Saul stopped him with one raised hand.

"Looks like sidesaddle," Bowman said.

"Can't tell sidesaddle from the tracks," Dan said.

"Course you can," Bowman said.

"Your horse is favoring her right front," Dan said and moved to the mules, fed them green apple peels. They broke apart in the mules' greedy teeth and fell to the dirt and he picked them up and fed them back to the mouths dirty. He liked the second little gray, and the tallest mule with one strange eye and a beautiful arch of the neck, Arabian somewhere in him. At the creek, the bay drank for a long time and the long neck stretched down and down, the longest neck he'd ever seen, and he called over to Bowman about it, how the bay's neck was like a giraffe's, very like the tall mule's neck.

"Let's go," Bowman said.

"I agree with let's go," Ella said.

Dan found his hat in the bush. He asked if he'd been sleepwalking. Maul searched for two missing mules, another delay. He was calling for the red jenny, whistling for her, also the first little gray. They checked the camp for refuse. Dan told his first Cowboy Joke:

"This cowboy puts on his old gray hat, rides to town picking his teeth. The townsfolk flock him. His horse hates this part, turns a circle in the dust of Main Street, bucks a little to keep them back. *A very bad man has come!* they say. *He has stolen our money, raped our women.*

"Which way did he go? asks the cowboy. What did he look like?

"*You know what he looked like!* they say.

"The townsfolk point vaguely into the rosy distance," Dan said. "Mountains, clouds, a bit of smoke rising. There's many tracks on the road out of town. The whole world out there."

Maul stopped searching trash while Dan finished.

"How's a cowboy to know?" Dan said. "The townsfolk are farmers, or wearing these billowing skirts, pantaloons showing underneath and the men peek as fair hands press the billows down. Ha. Dust swirls up their bodies to rosy cheeks fresh in from farmwork, hands filthy from toil, pulling roots and cutting throats, the pigs in the yard."

"That's it?" Saul said. "That's your cowboy joke?"

They were ready to ride again, a parade, same order as yesterday. The mules lined up with slipknots tied into their tails, double-checked.

"That's right," Dan said. "A joke."

"Giddyap then," Saul said.

✺ —— ✺

Speaking of which, ain't it time for another rip-roaring episode of *The Long Trail of That There Kid*? Today we're proud as heck to bring you an installment we like to call "A Blister Is a State of Mind." (And remember, this play is presented for your complete relaxation—if you feel like hissing the villain, go to it—it's okay with us!)

Starring the kid as THE KID.

161

Ginny, in the role of the Indian Spy, in the role of THE BEAST (hiss!).

And, playing themselves, ELLA (in sheer cloth billowing), THE DEER, THE DEPUTY, THE CAMERA, THE RED DOG, and THE COB.

We find the Kid in a cave at the base of the sister box canyon, shivering, thinner and cold. The wound is in the right shoulder. It's a real gash, open to the air when he cleans out the mud he'd packed in the wound. He eats cornbread he took from the camp. It's what bears do, the mud bit. He lies in the sun to dry the new mud. He is very thin, yes, but still complete. His hat is whiter than ever. His face is ragged but full of the future. The wound on his cheek from the nail healed in two days, a miracle, just a small scar, which bodes well for the bullet. He rises and walks. He walks quickly, quicker somehow than any horse. We see him pass into forests and through rivers. His body shines in the light and water blasts up his slim pant legs. The mud is crusting away. He wears a coat we've seen Maul wearing, too big for him but he has rolled up the sleeves, and at another cave he finds charcoal in some ancient fireplace, smears it on his face for night raids. Montage of switchbacks: the Kid stoops over the creek drinking, gazing back at them from a lookout, some high ridge, the wind whipping—peering down through his spyglass at the cumbersome parade of men, mules, and horses (one female), moving slowly, slowly (why?), up long slopes that never vary in angle, the horses swimming if they must, just the heads of horses bobbing above the surface and one old horse almost swept away. He leaves them to follow the Beast. He has the leghold trap on its chain, teeth crusted with years of neglect.

Until now. He loves the trap. He drags it and swings it over-head. Its whistle is a man-made answer to the wind.

He shuttles between them, follows the Beast's tracks, slipping along cliff walls, hopping barefoot sometimes boulder to boulder. No marks at all. Her eyes are cast down and see nothing. When he feels her about to turn, he slips into creeks and breathes through reeds. He carries his boots and wraps his feet in burlap or sage leaves to fool the tracker. He is alive. There is no person on earth more alive than the Kid. At night, he walks wrapped in a blanket, a crocheted thing from the Grannie's couch. Crochet, he sees, is a weave of holes. Still he's attached to it, loves the blanket, a cape. He changes the dressing on his wound when fever comes. He drops down in their camp every night. He is small and lithe. For a spark, he strikes the back of his hunting knife against flint. In the absence of flint are quartz, jasper, iron pyrite, or native jade. The lid to the barrel of oats is secured by a steel ring, opened by a lever like a thumb pulled back. He digs his hands in, feasts. Mules press in. Ella leaves a saddle blanket unattended by mistake or not. He reminds her of her little son perhaps. He takes the sleeping bag that Dan never uses. It lies right there. The men would not welcome him. He listens to their private talks and critiques them. He hears Dan tell a Cowboy Joke. They sing sometimes, talk about the Beast. The Kid takes hot coals in a large steel spoon and he runs. The Beast who in his head is also on occasion the Indian Spy is beyond him, her orbit the farthest possible to maintain the pull of gravity from their center in the camp. If she goes farther, the string will snap and she will spin off and die in the cold between stars. He dips his hand in saddlebags. He staggers with booty. She is the one who messes with the mules. She's addled. She is quick with knots. Her strategy is liberty over booty, an error. His heart is big and he keeps on going. Sometimes he clamps the ends of the blanket under his chin, a blue and gold zigzag pattern, innocent and yet made with hooks. His uniform is filthy. The piping blends with the fabric now. The bolo is gone. He will travel this way for forty days and forty nights. He shoves one hand then the other in his crotch, or armpits, to warm them. He finds roots to pack in the wound, roots to eat, roots to dream strange dreams. Here's one of them:

THE CAMERA: How did you feel getting shot on the ridge?

THE KID: Only pity for her, the Beast. Only pity. Once she ate a lizard. She looks behind often, believes she's being followed, does not believe it. She carries the rifle sometimes across her lap sidesaddle from her injuries. Her face is yellow from bruising. She feels my presence perfectly yet does not believe in me. This is her great flaw.

THE CAMERA: Almost funny, when you think about it.

THE KID: She limps! She slides off the cob sometimes and pulls her pants down, cools her privates with a sleeve of her stolen flannel. She wrings the sleeve out, re-dips, presses the sleeve to her face, ties the shirt around her waist again. She weighs more than the Kid, but not by much! He would beat her hand to hand. She quarters the lizards, cross saws the abdomens then between the eyes, slits up the tails, a difficult cut on so small a body. I find a variety of weapons in their camp. Knives, shells, and flares, other things I need. She sets the quarter with the front right leg on her tongue in my spyglass. She sucks it. The tiny toes slip out her monster lips.

THE CAMERA: Spyglass?

THE KID: I have one, a toy. A trunk in the loft by an old car under a canvas tarp.

THE CAMERA: How'd they get a car up there?

THE KID: Don't change the subject.

THE CAMERA: (*blushes*)

THE KID: I'm cold. I told you. The going is hard. You savvy?

THE CAMERA: What are you doing for food?

THE KID: Oh, there's plenty of food.

Once the Kid stalks a deer and kills it, knocks it out with a rock, then strangles it. His arm is still stiff from the wound but functional. The deer drags him first through a lake, over a log, over a pit of lava boiling, up a snow slide. He loves his life. He eats part of the animal, heart, liver, drags the carcass to the creek, sets a stone in the slit of the stomach, sinks the deer to keep himself secret. The deer's head nods up as the current takes it. The rock was not sufficient. An honest error. The legs kick. Blood trails behind.

The trees are shorter the higher we go. Five days. Six. The Kid doesn't need a horse yet. Walking is still fine. He tried for the red jenny but mules are wily. Walking is dandy. It builds his strength in body and mind. Simple facts everyone should know. Females tend to be bigger, wider hips, mammary glands. This does not make them stronger but the opposite. Ella's are bigger, fuller, her glands. She bathes every day in the creek. A ritual. As the Beast steals from their camp at night, Ella walks in her nightgown, a flowy thing, nothing. Two women cleaning themselves, thinking secret thoughts, lurking. She appears always on the fat man's watch, the donkey man. The Kid arrives well before, easy stealth on the First Watch, since the man is too confident, the man is a dolt. The Kid creeps among the mules on Saul's watch. He absorbs their heat, eats their grain by the handful as they look on, envious, at his fingers. He will shit whole oats out later until his innards adjust to the fibrous diet.

THE KID (cont'd): In the mountains, for food, the struggle is to learn. The Kid eats *wisdom*. Wisdom drops from the sky, scatters like cake crumbs.

THE CAMERA: Sounds far-fetched. Wisdom does not fill the belly.

THE KID: What's unlikely is this so-called hunt. I scratch my young fresh head.

They're slow. Doesn't seem like any real hunt to the Kid. She's walking that cob. No chases. And the posse walk their horses instead of really riding. Why? They could catch her if they went faster. The mules slow them down but it all seems planned. There's something wrong with the whole thing.

Look at that wide shot, kids! Blue mountains with our injured hero. The toothy chain is wrapped about his waist now. The jaws of its mouth hang like tassels. Then rise! Move, fly, look again! There! Look at the cob grazing by a placid lake on the ridge as she goes to watch the ambush of the sap below, the Deputy, that fool. The sun burns out the last of the world, then drops away when done. The world is gone. Fatigue sets in.

This is the only world: the cob rummaging sweet shoots by the lake.

Also: people at the fire telling stories. The red dog, a sweet companion, but none of that loyalty there that dogs are so famous for. Who is the red dog? He'd find the cob grazing alone at some point, inevitable, since a horse can eat most any plant, a wonderfully adaptive digestive tract.

THE CAMERA: Beautiful.

THE KID: Thank you.

THE CAMERA: What are you after? Why do you keep going? In other words, Kid, what's your motivation?

THE KID: That's easy: the Cowboy is always after the horse and rifle.

THREE

Pioneers

On Plymouth Rock, Bowman said, they knew who was who, and he passed the bota in firelight. They prayed on the shores of the Atlantic crashing, Praise God, Saul said, passing the bota back, for keeping your Chosen Ones Safe across those devilish Icy Waters. Have Mercy on We the Humble. Give us Plenty and Goodness for our Devotion, and He did, Bowman said, plowed His great arm across the land for them, gave them blankets and smallpox and muskets for the heathens, who dropped dead and made way. Convenient and instructive. These pilgrims bowed heads in rough-hewn pews while heathens danced in forest clearings. Who won? Who was given the bountiful rivers? Sweet shores, fish, saltpeter? Follow the punished to wisdom.

They knew who was who on the shores of Africa, Bowman said, as the wooden holds of ships were filled, five hundred in cargo, men, women, children, stacked spoon-fashion below, aimed across the waves to the West Indies. When one of the cargo transgressed, escaped his chains through some devilment, proceeded to slit a good seaman's throat, he was tossed overboard, the loss explained to investors later: another arrogant angel leaving his station. Just as Lucifer had once done, Saul said, to his Father saying,

"I will ascend above the high clouds; I will make myself Most High."

The gods have always used lightning bolts, Bowman said. Plagues and floods have always awaited the arrogant, crossers of red seas and blue mountains that should not have been crossed. Locusts ate Pharaoh's land. He's been warned about the Burning Bush, Bowman said, but Saul held a hand up and corrected him. The Burning Bush was Abraham, before Egyptian captivity, before ten plagues.

"Avalanches then," Bowman said and continued. "They wiped out palaces."

Saul raised the bota. "Yes, they did."

Volcanoes, Bowman went on, incinerate golden cities, as whores scamper to high ground with cheap bundles. Geysers. Swamps. Hurricanes.

"Yes."

They'll be turned to stone for too much beauty, for looking the mayor's wife in the eye.

"It's for our own good," Saul said. "We're faulty goods, ever unable to resist peeking inside forbidden boxes or yielding to the blandishments of serpents bearing fruit."

On the ship, Bowman said, 499 were marched up to the deck in ankle-cuffed tandem to see the daylight, for a lesson in right and wrong as the transgressor sang songs to sharks. The wake boiled red proof. The crews burned their ship on occasion, took to lifeboats, bobbed, awaited another slaver or whaler, and as the screams burned and the ship went down, they repeated the words of the Burning Bush—

I AM WHO I AM, Saul said, rising from an old dry log to piss in a bush.

Most ships arrived in port no trouble, Bowman said, taking a long slow pull. The cargo was sold at auction. Farms prospered humble and God-fearing. The new nation grew up grateful as the heathens made their adieus, trading baubles and ribbons. Some scuffles ensued, sure. Scalpings and baby thefts.

"The path to Destiny is rocky," Saul said.

"The destination and the process both."

Bowman was deep in thought now so Saul finished the whole idea for him, Bowman nodding:

But the seeds in the black fields took root. Weeds and trees shoved off, persuaded by plows and axes. A thief isn't a thief if he's not a thief. The ships' holds were stacked full of cotton, whiskey, and beaver hats and plied east to the old world. A nation was born and moved westward singing out WE ARE WHO WE ARE to blue mountains as buggy paths were bitten into rock by stinking blood and sweat, on through to the Pacific, where we prayed on knees in sand and gave thanks for good fortune and promised more modest clean living.

Dan cut in, uninvited, on their conversation from the desert island of his choice, his tarp by another creek, his patch, his mind: What if Lucifer, Dan said, had an A-bomb in his breast pocket, what if he tossed it through the Pearly Gates as he spun away, punched a hole in a cloud, or if the whore had slipped a bomb from her bundle, rolled it under the mayor's wife's skirts, or if from the waves the shining arm had flung the plum-sized thing that waggled lopsided across the deck?

"What if?" Bowman said.

The trio could have watched the mushroom clouds from Mount Olympus, mother-of-pearl umbrellas on hand for the rain of wings, crowns, and angel parts.

∼ —— ∼

"The stirrups," said the yellow horse. "You look like a stork."

It was a bright sharp day.

The deputy fiddled with buckles. "Much obliged." All his life he had not been anyone and now with buckles on a horse he was someone. "Very much obliged to you."

"That cowboy chatter too," said the yellow horse. "People will laugh."

He loved this talk, though, would not *quit it*—the quaint phrasing of the region spoken with zesty twang and stretch of vowels mixed with leather scent—without a fight. This western phrasing was his now too.

He was a believer in pen and ink. He'd even brought more blank postcards along, a pack in a tight rubber band in his saddlebag: Attractively sunlit bison. Prairie dog families. Wolves. A whole rubber-banded pile of high plains sky-lines by some modern miracle transferred onto three-by-five glossy cardstock, each snapped in a patient moment at the widest of wide angles, rendered with perfect panorama lighting then altered by filters, etc., God knew what, each spectacular natural event thus captured and stored as if *eternal* and not in fact *ephemeral*, as if not pure luck, chance, fate, effort of walking high for the images, as if not blinked by the expansion and contraction of the one of millions of manufactured metallic eyes but rather some divine eye (a lie), though now made available to all forever and whenever by the viewer (the receiver of the card). How revolting. But still he liked stamps. To lick them. The cards were gentle hints. A teaching tool in hopes that the recipient (he sent them only to her) might wake up to modern catastrophe. Though even the tool was necessarily tainted. The miracles of nature on the cards delivered by a vast network of steel-hinged slots and steel-walled rattling and smoky conveyors into the backs of identical left-handed trucks, all undreamed of when those hills back around town were first spotted with cattle. It was lonely to see all this, to be the rare one, by default both a Luddite and a modern man, to partake and grieve that the mass dissemination of the visions (postcards) were only made possible with the very best and most professional cameras, advanced, even futuristic devices, gestated by *the glories* of scientific, philosophical, technological, and therefore man-made mutation (progress) and that these evolutions were *no less profound in effect* than Darwin's type of evolution, though profundity didn't mean it'd turn out well. How could it? There was no comparison. One evolution was divine. The man-made kind—though some argued that man was God-made (as Eve was Adam-made) and therefore it was all one and the same, and this was an interesting point—would rust in the false certainty that evolution always travels in one direction: *for the better.* Buses and trains and food in plastic! How people back home loved them! Delivered as they were by the current gods, the *great inventors*, by the *great tycoons*, the *great factory builders*, the *great men* bestowing all their largesse on the *not-great*, assisted in this bestowing by their multitudes of slaves on

175

the factory floors inhaling ink and steel shavings. The deputy was not a great man, he knew that, but he was no longer a slave. He was free, at least, here, on this yellow horse (with packhorse in tow to boot) on a rescue mission requiring old-fashioned grit and muscle.

Even still. There were ideas stampeding his mind. For example, that despite the *glories* of great human achievement (cures for malaria, etc.), of great human pride (the camera, the right of certain individuals to vote and own property), of great human advancement (spaceships, vast postal networks), of *great progress* (too many to list), it was still the *humble* that people wanted to receive in their mailbox. A *sunset*. A *postcard*. A *picture* from his little camera. And here was another. He had escaped the Great Modern Now. He was in the *Great Rock Eternal* now on his yellow horse with the blue ribbon, the silent packhorse following. How had this miracle occurred? It occurred because it had to. Fate is fact. How else to explain his new bliss on a yellow horse? Deep down people wanted *moonrises* not *postcards of moonrise*, even if they didn't know it. It was better, too, *to be* a deputy, he knew now even after only a few months, than to see a deputy in a book or film or on a paper card. Same too with bison rutting by a fuming boil of geysers. Get into the fumes and breathe! Pride! How easy it would have been to stay at home in Verona. He knew, too (suspected strongly), that no one else knew what he now knew. These locals did not. These people—though born in the most spectacular sunsets and moonsets—were blind to sunsets, moonsets, and bison in fumes, blind though not with the blindness of urban folk, who were blind from *not* seeing sunsets, moonsets, or bison, but, since these things were *ubiquitous* to the locals, though they wouldn't know that word either, blind from overfamiliarity with them, also from too little education. Poor things. Pride and humility! He had the rare, perfect mixture of both. As such, the deputy was one of the few who could *really see* this world: the power of nature, his own fragility and tininess—facts. The facts of this *real life* (not city life, not modern life, not factory-made in New Jersey) were therefore fresh and new to him, therefore visible, therefore more valuable, therefore (indeed) crystal-clear to his baby-eyes: the Wonder, the Devastating Wonder, the devastating improbability that he should exist at all. How did it happen? Humility! As he rode on this pack trip, his first ever, he was nearly overcome with this new world to which he was now newly born. The bare land the engine of the earth had made back in time for forward in time, it made him dizzy, these thoughts, the green beings exploding about him, the horses, the profusion of smaller humbler furred and feathered hidden in the green, prey animals running ahead, predators padding behind at a distance, hiding in cracks as he passed, waiting for their best chance, since the coyote, the bear, the wolf—he was sure—could not tell a good shot from a bad shot in a saddle.

> —Mother, boulder fields more copious than—
> Terrible slopes for even the—This is the Payment
> Part of mountains—Reward is aloft in thinner air
> against the—pelts galore, meat from the back strap,
> if so desired—Quiet of uninterrupted thought—my
> horses are nameless. Here's a picture . . .

When Mother finally asks, he'll say, *We do not name our horses here. The animals know who they are—*

He *found* her small Instamatic camera among his belongings. Had he taken it by mistake? Taken it with purpose but unconsciously? All acts—from birth to the Awakening at the Big Window—are preconscious. Or had she known all the time he was going and dropped the camera amid his underthings? Impossible. There were too many differences between them, child and mother. Only the umbilical cord ever truly connects.

He replaced the sheriffs' team's baseball cap. The cob's tracks hugged the canyon wall, in tight at the base of the cliffs, *needled up* and out onto *tongues of stone*. The Old Swede's cairns were infrequent but reliable. Little stone men walking in a line. It was quite some job, these cairns. No badge but so much care for others, that old man. Who had he been?

The horses swayed on with the smallest tug of leather. He'd never even heard of *a cob* before, cornfields aside. He'd pictured this place in dreams, he on horseback with a packhorse trailing, heels pressed down smartly. The sun sat on the east cliff. A broken antler passed by, a horseshoe with one nail. Thus he wound through cities of rocks, spires, arches, dollops, lava cooled black teetering, lichen holding things in place. He craned his neck uphill for the cob, and then back over his horse's yellow rump for the "search party." They'd brought too many animals. Anyone could see that. They would never catch up to him. It was miscalculation, but they'd not expected him. They were polite, only, as he'd blown by them. He considered the danger often caused by the introduction of the unpredicted. Heart attacks, car wrecks.

He'd passed them two days back. He'd peeled off the Kevlar he'd worn under his new coat that morning. The cob's tracks were all his now.

To drink, he pumped creek water through a filter, a charcoal ring, plastic. Feathers of moss at pools' edges. Clear water magnified color so that the pebbles were more beautiful than any gem. His mother never had one, a ring. As the horses drank he dug the prettiest from the riffles. He'd line them up that evening. When dry, the stones would be chalky and dull, he knew. Moss, near electric green, filled cracks where the sun only dreamed of reaching, if the sun dreamed. Why would it? The sun had everything already: the whole world once a day. The fungi erupted and was throttled by gravity in one hour, melted to filthy slime. He wondered why he felt pity. Fungi may be quite satisfied. Even smug.

The two horses snorted between themselves sometimes, excluding him, and sometimes the mountains themselves made him weep. The Big Window was real. He was in it.

His boots were always wet. He wondered, sometimes, if she was watching him from that cliff up there. *You're not havin' fun 'til your boots are wet*, she'd said once at the Crop and Carrot. Would she remember him? *Howdy, Ginny*, he practiced. *Hello, Ma'am. Fine day.* No woman was perfect, he knew. And he was the kind of person who usually made one mistake too many.

"Heels down," said the yellow horse. "No groaning. Only greenhorns groan."

He passed a fire ring, slid off to investigate the butt ends of old charred cordwood. He sniffed an aluminum can in ash. He kicked a second log away. The can scuttled down a crevasse. No splash. A good rain should wash the site away.

He swung his knee over the saddle, horse's right side.

Now the air thinned. He breathed hard and felt sorry for his lungs. Cigarettes. He turned his back when he smoked, but to what? He'd smoked in Verona at the lake at the bottom of Hathaway Lane. He wondered if anyone was wondering where he was. He saw a dog, once, ahead in the rocks, or a coyote that was very red. He called the dog and it disappeared. His cuffs and socks were soggy as his boots. He stopped to pull his boots off, wring his socks out, and hang them from the packsaddle to dry. He stuffed his bare feet back in. No worry of blisters. He'd packed Band-Aids.

At least he was not over-chatty, the number-one giveaway in a greenhorn.

The trick to Cowboys was Keep to the Literal—

"Does the packhorse ever speak?" The deputy nodded back at it.

"No," said the yellow horse.

The deputy had had a five o'clock shadow when he ran into the posse that morning, but now it was the beginnings of a beard. He turned often to measure progress, altitude, and lateral distance. From a perch above their boulder field, the toe of tumbled rock had been a postage stamp. A society run out of ideas.

The high ridges of the night before were soon, for him, at eye level, then, sure enough, sank below him. He'd made good time. He'd spotted them once that first day. He'd studied them in binoculars. One of them had studied him back, waved up.

Where was Ginny now? What was her line of uninterrupted thought here? What happened on the hill with the mare? He liked the idea: John Law.

He had lied a little on his Sheriff's Deputy application, checked the box for EXPERIENCE IN LAW ENFORCEMENT. We can call ourselves anything, he knew now. Just fill in the blank after checking the box: Lawman. Cowboy. Pirate. Elaborate on the blank line.

His ass hurt. The saddle didn't fit him right. Bowman would know why with a glance, but as for himself, the pain in his ass was a total mystery. Sound carries uphill, he'd always *heard*, but now he *knew*. In these slick rock amphitheaters, he more than understood the nature of sound, and this shift from only hearing to understanding—this seismic shift—caused his body to vibrate in an undetectable way. He'd like to tell some human about the seismic shift. It was, he saw, the only drawback of horses.

"The seismic shift is altitude and fear," said the yellow horse.

They argued.

He'd notched three days on his belt since he passed the posse.

All day after he'd passed them—though it seemed impossible—he was sure he could hear their horses coming. A voice would fade around a cornice, *a crag*, no, *a lookout*. Someone calling out a name. If he was ever murdered— the idea popped into his brain—he would come back and haunt the evildoers as a ghost. Now there were moments he thought only of murder. Ginny was more cowboy than any of them—the next flash of knowing. Still, these mountains were *architectural*, like the city skyline from the bus from Verona into Manhattan, but bigger, better, a thousand times. The distance had swallowed Dan's cries. Why could he not keep his mind on track? The sky looked kind, but was it? At noon, he smeared sunscreen on his cheeks and listened.

He'd lied, too, about the stamps. Of course he had them, a white lie to the posse, *a yarn.*

Worse, possibly, he'd seen one of their mules running free this morning and did nothing. Yesterday, was it? He was confused in general, now, about time in conjunction with location. That red jenny (the correct term for a female mule) had caused his mental muddle, though he had no idea how. Much worse yet, he'd had an *encounter* with the red jenny, along with a lone steer, at dawn. The two strays, the jenny and the steer, had been aimed downhill at the encounter. They'd appeared out of nowhere on the other side of a creek crossing. Silent mountain nights are so entirely full of sound, so deafening, *Mother.* And to be truthful to himself at least, the sight of their eyes, then the huge bodies containing them, had taken his breath. Even divided by a creek, he'd seen that between the mule and the steer had arisen a kind of *kindly interspecies friendship, Mother.* He'd heard of such between horses and other species, goats and sheep, even dogs. In his flashlight the steer had followed the mule, a little to the side, a half pace behind. The steer had been spooked by the flashlight. The steer had snorted and lowed as if in pain at the sight of the yellow horse. He'd lowered his head at the yellow horse even, over there—from the steer's point of view—across the water yet. The yellow horse didn't care. She'd splashed in, straight under a branch, and he, the rider, had had to duck.

The packhorse followed the yellow horse. The packhorse made no decisions. The rope between them decided. The yellow horse had pushed through smaller branches. In time the creek would rise and take the whole tree. The mule was calm as she entered the far shore. Plowed out toward the middle, the steer in her wake. The flashlight prohibited true "eye contact." How opalescent and alien their stares anyhow. He looked away toward the ridges, no comfort there, too dark, confusion of the mind, only to be revived some by *water that poured into my boots!* He felt the shock of cold. He rode, in fact (he thought) with the flashlight under his armpit, the reins in both hands, another sign of a greenhorn. He'd forgotten a headlamp, a rookie error, never to be repeated.

Novice. Plebe. Wet-behind-the-ears.

"Some are late bloomers," said the yellow horse, "to the Big Window."

The western plains were once full of cities, not just towns, not just villages, not just clusters of teepees. The Indigenous Americans had built cities with stone. Stone walls and wooden roofs made of tall trees hauled from God knew where. History books have erased the cities and left only heathens' teepees, but the stone walls stood there and there, and dust filled them in and buried them and affirmed the books' verdict. In the creek, the steer's eyes didn't reflect at all, some anomaly of biology and physics. But in truth, they had, all three, nearly collided in the creek before he could identify which life forms he was sharing the path with: mule and steer. *What are you?* he asked with his mind. The mule had worn only a halter that looked silver in the flashlight. The rope to it had been cut. Hemp. Part of a hobble slapped the water. Would she catch it on something, do herself an injury, in a blowdown or thicket? He considered freeing her of the halter but decided against it. Who knew, at the time, why the mule was there? Halters are necessary and expensive. Why anger the locals? The actual crossing with the mule and steer had taken place on a small island, a sandbar with a single leafless bush, and there he'd pulled his pistol out without conscious thought. He simply found the pistol in his hand. It was an instinct he'd never known was in him, like a mountain in his backyard never seen because of clouds. After this Event, The Crossing with the Red Jenny and the Steer, he'd ridden on to now.

All things considered, even the posse would be a most welcome sight after that encounter, an island of civilization, and he'd be tempted to tell them what had happened: that his horses and the red jenny and the steer had crossed very near each other, nearly brushing shoulders but without eye contact. They'd crossed as if the crossers were not crossing. Then, when back in the water, off the island, having exchanged sides of it, each animal in each party—mule, steer, horses, and man, officer of the law—had stopped dead in the water of their own accord, a delayed reaction of some kind. He could barely look. He had not looked. It had been too much to look back. The yellow horse turned and nickered. The packhorse turned and stared.

He could write this:

> We'd stood midstream looking back at each other's behinds across the island. The water wasn't deep but cold and it rushed around our legs. I could almost

see them all considering, *some kind of communion or mutiny.* I saw the decision. The red jenny and steer turned around, and backtracked. They splashed back through the current, over the island again to get in line behind my horses, now followers. The pair followed my horses out of the creek into trees, up and across several deltas of scree, quite difficult sidehills. A mile. Hard to tell in the dark.

His mother would ask if he had pictures of the encounter. She didn't understand the idea of the sacred. Some events and experiences can only be properly stored in the flesh of the mind, should only be stored there. He'd told her. When he told it again in the future, if he did, he'd say it differently in light of this adventure, this encounter with the mules, steers, and islands: a *picture* fails and worse, he'd say, fades with each examination. The single angle, the single exclusionary choice of light in only one frame. All else cut away. Only that image left. Useless.

That night, the red jenny and the steer dropped back over distance. He lost sight of them. The horses had given no notice. It all made perfect sense now. All lonely creatures love a lonely creature. And all lonely creatures love a leader. But no one likes uphill.

Afternoon after a nap.

Beyond another canyon the trail widened, narrowed, banked, dipped, incline unceasing, hooves reaching, knobby knees near overextending to stone bridges where the horses bunched. Dismount was required. He led the horses, knuckles to pelts. He used kind words, tugged only as needed, gently, promised rest with a view, water, early mountain weeds to chew. He held a willow switch. The animals eyed it. "Show me how to thread the needle. There's a smarty—a brown trout—a baby eel." He remounted.

He loved them.

The stupid ball cap squeezed his head. The creeks flowed in seeming sameness. Nothing could stop them. Boot prints with the cob's tracks. Or were they his own tracks? Another wrong turn. Another unintended double back.

He stared down at rare mud as the horses drank. He marveled at their huge bodies, how water slid silent in hydraulic shivers. The sheriff needed the horses back in a week. His niece was coming from the city. Mr. Bowman had held the bridle face to his face with the yellow horse. He was a vampire in ironed jeans.

Afternoon again. He lost the cob's trail again, kept going. He would find it.

Ferns are confusing. The birds crackled and dissolved into leaves. They thought this rider had some dark plan. They were wrong. He'd lost his way but was not afraid yet. There were no precise words for these new feelings. Liberty. Compassion. Adventure. Wonder. They were insufficient. Bravery. There was no name for him but John Law, a newcomer, an approximation. The ferns and fungi here were new varieties too, explosive, proliferated by mutated spores, parachutes and gliders, hybrids seeking replication as all God's creatures do. He turned back, then back again. *Beautiful* is easy and did not apply to what he saw and felt. A white spiderweb rolled past. He was happy. They would have no Latin labels. New Jersey did not exist. Mother didn't. He was with the anomalies now, singular and unprecedented finally, after all those years of school, strip malls, pop cans, haircuts. His boots were flat bottomed with a heel, since you shouldn't ride Western, Ginny'd told him, except in flat leather soles. He'd seen her always in the market, in boots, muddy, the heels obscured, yellow onions in a bag swinging from her fist. At nearly every creek the animals steered to drink. He submitted. *She would allow the animals to drink*, he told himself. After drinking, the animals revived and resumed their pace and pleasant rhythm. It was right to stop though he lost time. He looked behind him and saw no one. His body shivered in the heat and he realized this was fear. Fear of what? They all drank and drank. Could the horses be teasing? Getting the better of him? If the yellow horse spoke to the packhorse, he knew who was butt of the joke.

Lost.

He'd find the cob's tracks around the next bend. Did horses lie? Did deception require intellect? He soothed himself with thoughts of the female: Ginny headed to the high, cool trees where each trunk would be scorched where lightning had failed to kill it.

Lost is electric in the blood.

He stuffed his water filter away. He drank from the creek on his hands and knees. His eyes, at least, worked miraculously well here. He saw *jagged* for the first time in his life, *slick* and *mossy* and *huge* and *soaring*.

"The West is nostalgia now," said the yellow horse.

"Don't taunt," he said.

"I'm a trinket," she said.

He rejected this. He was too grateful and bitter after decades of pavement for any revision of his notions. It was his mother's fault. She should've taken him to the park more often.

He rode with the compass duct-taped to the horn. It made no difference. He prayed to God. The trees waved down at him, but what exactly did they mean? He wondered if Ginny would save him when he saved her. He consoled himself: this *lostness* said something true about *waiting* and *patience* and *keeping to the path* and *invincibility* that lured only the most *restless but excellent* people. He was thinking in *bits* and *pieces*. Perhaps he lacked salt. He licked some from the top of his fist. *Mother, when I arrive, I'll sit next to this poor lost woman—My spine pressed to rough charred bark—Will comfort her as I never comforted you—How could I? I was just a boy—She will tell me all of it—All the facts of her sad case—A cold spring, fountain of the earth—Dividing place between east and west—*

"Do you have a name?" he said, as he patted his mount's yellow neck.

"You couldn't say it if I told you," said the yellow horse. "You aren't capable."

He found a carcass of a donkey with a leg cut clean off below the knee. A hacksaw maybe. The donkey was fur and bones. Where was the leg? He would never tell anyone.

At each plateau he looked for a woman but saw only more blue vistas, rocks in unlikely poses, ballerinas and ogres with top hats. He held his cap on. He hated the wind. Some people back home said mountains were dull: *no variety in the grand scale.* My God, how the *fear* came *in waves.* He'd never felt fear like this, and he realized the modern world

188

was intent on killing fear off. Other thoughts clarified: only some mistakes are fixable. And Dan was finished. Anyone could see it. He felt pity for the man. The horses sweated along the withers. His pack was full of food and fuel. He would be fine. He would be fine. The packhorse was whitish gray with flecks. He understood the color now. The animals' mouths foamed. They swished flies to no effect. He blotted sweat with the bandana. Their hooves obliterated tracks he made and retraced and would frustrate the trackers in the rear.

"And the packhorse?" he said. "Does he have an unsayable name?"

"I'm sorry," said the yellow horse. "It's out of your league."

The mine shafts were terrifying. Shafts blasted then set upon with picks, propped by rough-cut poles now pick-up sticks in rubble, huge oak beams hauled in for the deeper tunnels. Bones. Two mules had marched the beams in single file, one beam to each side—so heavy—locked together by fate, oak, and ropes. He rolled a cigarette over a stand of miniature pines, his boots brushing the spiked tops. He was a giant in the tiny forest. He smoked another as the horses tore noisily at meager grasses to blunt hunger. A horse is designed to eat almost constantly.

> Mother—here's my address—Maybe you do know—The Great Plains are a vast swath—

"She's forgotten you," said the yellow horse. "You treated her poorly."

"She treated me poorly first."

Bear tracks were everywhere. His own shit was frequent and fluid, what intestines made when terrified. They rode on. Their hooves on stone maintained a monopoly on sound, squeak of leather mixed with sweat and manure. The animals bobbed on, faithful, exactly as he'd seen in movies and in pastures on back road drives with his mother to Amish country, Pennsylvania, the Mennonites, everywhere. She loved to look at them: the women in bonnets in buggies, the girls in ankle-length dresses, blinders on the horses' faces to prevent fear of traffic, the reflective triangles on the buggies' bumpers. The land tilted up forever in his mind. The rock was baking him late in the day, an oven. Ginny had caught him looking down the aisles in the hardware store, a canyon of socks. Absurd life! He'd lost his socks somewhere. No use going back. The world was full of socks, wool and cotton, a planet of socks everlasting, socks without end, Amen. He would bring his grandkids someday, explain to them what we owe to strangers. *Be kind to them. You might be the stranger someday. Everyone needs a helping hand.* That in the highest, coolest, tallest trees, the stands live on no matter the outcome for the individual. They're joined at the roots. The sheriff told him but he already knew. Pine cones roll away from catastrophe. They bear nuts downhill. Seeds open when burned. Chainsaws do not visit such places. He puffed and sweated. He turned to look. *The search party.* A ridiculous attempt at a lie from people who couldn't see the forest for the trees. *The posse.* But they'd marinated in it all their lives. Rednecks.

Sunset with a borrowed one-burner, white gas in a canister, a can of beans.

He had too many gadgets. Too many blinking objects. He removed every battery.

He camped in a meadow half a mile from THE NARROWS on his map. He was fairly sure this was where he was. Made an X. The pen cast crisscrossing shadows. His boots steamed. He glanced into the graying land, the trail he'd made. His pistol was under the book he'd read by firelight.

It was nearly dark. He'd never found the cob's tracks again. It was disappointing. He would backtrack tomorrow. He'd wanted to be a forest ranger. Mother wanted a doctor, a suburb, a cul-de-sac safe for grandkids. He'd handed Ginny the yellow onion. It rolled across the tile floor in the produce section. These people thought—where they were concerned— there was no such thing as foul play.

"What about the mules?" he asked, teeth chattering. "Do they have names?"

"Our names," the horse said, giving in, "are excreted from cells of any orifice."

His mind was altered by altitude, solitude, and fear. It's what mountains did. He sucked another cigarette, steeped his lungs in smoke. He'd learned to roll tobacco from the janitor at the HQ. He stubbed it out on a rock and watched the broken thing smolder. His house had burned down as a boy. They'd moved into an apartment north of the Tappan Zee. He'd slept in the living room with the TV clicker, his mother in the bedroom with—until she'd settled down later—any number of men through the thin walls. Then a comforting thought: he'd find out all from Ginny very soon: *Why are you running? From what? Can I help?* Then another. He'd tell his mother she'd done a *fine job* raising him. He was not disappointed. No one in the whole world was perfect.

"And dogs?" he said. "Do they have names?"

"The tongue," said the yellow horse. "The urine. The anus."

He'd tell his mother what he'd learned here about silence: the earth is only a big rock painted in varieties of browns. A green fringe decoration, blue patches, masterpiece of design, since the repeated patterns suggested variety, multiplicity, where there was none. Earth is just a simple ball. Or, no, he couldn't talk to his mother of such things.

He'd taken, in fact, a self-portrait with his Instamatic of his tent the first night, the peaks behind, the unsaddled horses in the foreground. If he didn't make it out, later they would find the camera. They'd learn nothing from it, though his fingerprints there would convince his mother to accept him as a true missing person, finally. Not Prodigal.

She would frame the image, a figure in landscape, rather dark due to the hour of exposure. They would have to install batteries. He always forgot the camera till too late. Still, it was a classic mountain scene, to be mounted in a rough wood frame from a yard sale. She'd hang it in her tiny kitchen.

❧ — ❧

Horses were erotic for him back then, when they first married and before. He was content with life and she never was. That was always the basic problem. He'd do equine-talk when horny:

"The first horse arose here sixty million years ago, on these very plains."

She'd nipped him like a cat.

"The Dawn Horse was born here."

"Right here?"

He moved her hand where he wanted it. She pawed him like a bear. She didn't know she was a horse yet.

"The Dawn Horse at dawn was the size of a modern fox."

He had a jelly donut on his upper thigh. "The Dawn Horse arose," he said, "same time as the First Primate, and each had five toes. The horse lost his toes one by one, ten million years later had only four, and in twenty only three."

"Where'd they go? The toes?"

"They retreated up the leg." He moved her hand again. "As the leg stretched out. As the grass evolved. The tall grass was farther off and required more walking."

"Ah."

"A longer neck to compensate for the legs."

"Ah."

"To reach and eat."

"You should have been a professor or something." She reached the donut. "Wasting your talent in this cow town."

She mounted him like a horse.

"Don't get sappy."

"Not sappy. Just fact."

She wasn't weak at all back then. Nothing was weak in her.

"The Dawn Horse developed a firm but flexible back to suit the Dawn Primate's round, small, fine little ass."

"All his travel plans."

"Yes."

"The horse obliging him."

"Yes."

"And the tiny man found wide purple leaves."

"What for?" he said. Why ask? He'd lost control of his story now.

"For saddle blankets, of course."

"Of course," he laughed and jelly spewed.

She licked the jelly off his chin, a lizard. "The little primate dug earthworms, cut them down into long strips. Strong material."

"And the saddle?" he said, always giving in.

"Good question."

"For a saddle," he said, retaking the reins, "he slashed a scale from a spotted lizard's wing."

"Pretty nice saddle," she said.

"The best."

"The lizard let him cut his wing?" she said. "Why would he?"

This was the messy part, the bodies making a third thing together, the non-sense of sex, animal collusion.

"He'd been bitten badly before," he gasped. "He could take it."

"Bitten when?"

"A fight to the death with the first bird."

"Ah!" she said and she'd laughed and fucked him and fucked him and that's what she was doing now.

❦ —— ❦

Grannie told her Dear Ones: *When crossing a stout river, a Woodsman finds a calm place, a pool of sorts. Deep and slow is what he's looking for. But mark this: the Woodsman never trusts the pool. He tests it. He flings a stick in to see how it floats, where the current takes it, reads the river. If the stick rolls in the sun, takes its time, lolls and stays, the second stick too, a third also, this last one winged far out as possible, then, by all means, he rolls his cuffs up. But if the stick is spun and tipped or drowned, if it runs off like a tiny canoe, then the Woodsman walks on upstream. He keeps on the shore if terrain and foliage allow it. He wades, if he can, feels the water on his hips or chest depending on depth. He studies the river with all his senses. The river is many things: a trap for land creatures, a place of refuge for the web-footed, a tank for fish, a highway for boats, also a bridge to over there, to freedom, the world's most expensive item. He shades his eyes. How deep? Where are the hidden rocks? The sweepers? He watches the surface movements, marks them, since they indicate killing shifts below. He remembers fish live in the calm currents, but also behind boulders where the water spins endless on itself and finless swimmers cannot get out. Upstream, the Woodsman finds where the river widens. It always does. A place with riffles all the way across, with luck. That's the ticket. He wades in and if the current takes him, that's fine too. He paddles with all his might and exits at the pool downstream he knows already.*

Ginny had veered off the Old Swede's Trail at a broad confluence of river and stream where the mud was baked hard and the cob left no marks for nearly a mile before soft ground again. She'd followed the river upstream. They would miss the turn, go on in confusion to the Old Swede's cabin wondering forever where they lost her trail. Houdini.

Upstream, this river was too big to cross for miles, too fast. She waded in the pool when she came to it, as instructed. She drank at the pool.

The cob drank. The red dog had disappeared. She studied the water from sitting, hands on cheeks. Dozed. The tallest grasses were green and good and he ate greedily. He only lifted his head to stare downstream. He never stopped chewing. His ears pricked.

"What are you looking at?"

No answer. She whistled for the dog. She would get the cob a wife in Canada, some quiet obedient breed from Calgary.

Midafternoon. Very hot.

The pool was enormous, calm and wide, deep green, nearly black where huge rocks submerged. Ragged spruce tipped over the caving banks. The opposite shore was pebbly and wide. Driftwood lay everywhere. She threw a bone-dry branch in. It floated, eddied back to shore. She kicked an old log free of dried mud. She rolled the log out ankle deep, then knee deep over sandy shallows, then chilling her at mid-thigh to the edge of deeper blue. She shoved it parallel to the flow and it rolled. When the current took it, it teetered and spun back end to front, skiffed away out the exit of the pool, leapt a hump of water, seesawed up, dropped away, was gone. She studied the exit. The water flowed over her wrists. Her teeth rattled. The water was blue silt. The cob never stopped watching the downstream trees. She led the cob upstream.

They kicked over forest litter into meadow and sun. She stood in sudden heat and listened, then left the cob, returned through bramble to the pool again. She saw nothing, no follower. She heard nothing. She returned to the cob.

They waded on water's edge when possible. The reins looped down and snagged on snags and she wound the leather around the horn. The land was thick with the ragged and the broken, windows of sun in the trees. They ducked and backtracked. Bramble and thorn. The river dropped out of sight. The Canadians were polite people. Plenty of ranches, plenty of work. The posse could wait for her at Old Swede's cabin till kingdom come. She needed nothing at the Old Swede's now. She'd lost them.

Another half a mile. Horseflies took chunks of skin just hatched. This was the famous ravenous northern jungle. Root balls ten feet tall were sucked clean along the cutbanks but for rodents tangled in the web. Her blisters needed salt. The collar rubbed her neck. She would cut it off with Ella's scissors from the saddlebag. If she didn't lose them at the confluence.

The river widened as predicted by the old lady. Shallow riffles most of the way across with a fast-deep channel in the middle. She dropped the pack on the ground, unpacked it, snapped the duster in the sun, and laid it out like a headless fat man. She set all the contents of the pack on the duster: the gallon Ziploc with hundreds of matches, the map, the sweater, the wool shirt, the snow pants, the last of the beef jerky, black plastic folded, a head of celery turning brown. The measuring tape had been at the bottom of the pack. Nitroglycerin from Grannie's last trip. Nostalgia. The second pair of socks was still damp. Two fifteen-inch flares. Box of shells for the 30-30. The etc. was a blur. She stuffed pine branches into the empty pack. She poured half the matches

197

on the splayed-out map, folded the map around the matches, dropped the map into the Ziploc, folded the plastic down on itself, squeezed out air, zipped the lips, then put the Ziploc in the bag of the alfalfa cubes with the compass, poured all but three remaining matches in with the raisins, bundled this with the walnuts, box of shells, nested all with the Zippo, tied the bag. With her teeth, she ripped a remnant of plastic from above the knot and wrapped the three matches in the remnant and set this precious bundle on the sand with the pistol and one tin of herring. The sun burned her cheeks. She set the large bundle on the wool shirt, tied the arms of the shirt around it, shoved it all into an arm of the duster, then the duster amid the pine branches in the pack, then the canteen, tins, cans of tuna and herring, and the cheese, the sweater then snow pants, but there was no room. She pulled the sweater on and loosed the cob's saddle and stuffed the snow pants under. The apples went in last, nestled with the one-burner stove folded up nested with the partial canister of fuel. She cinched the pack and buckled. She peeled one tin of herring open, ate all and drank the brine, dropped the can. She pulled the sleeping bag over the pack, cinched it at the mouth. She laid the pack on its back and ran the rifle and umbrella along its belly, looped her belt around one end, rope at the other. She stuffed the pocketknife down her pocket last, looped the reins around horn, set the pack on top of the reins, rifle up, stepped her boot up into the stirrup, other leg over. If someone had followed, they were too late now. She pointed the pistol downstream. Flipped the safety off. Nothing. Four shells left in the chamber. She hugged the pack to herself.

"I'm sorry," she said as the cob waded in.

Her boots hung free of the stirrups over the riffles. The cob gazed across the flow to the identical shore, rock walls. A cave. A bird cried out downstream. The pistol was heavy. The cob didn't turn. She saw only birds. Water. She shoved the pistol in her waistband at the edge of the channel. She shoved the three matches in her mouth.

The current was strong but didn't take the cob right away. Then he was floating and her boots had disappeared. He swam as a smooth invisible kicking, his head bobbing, nearly across, but he was jolted as if a hoof found some corner of the far bottom, and he was off. He floated down the narrow channel. On his back, she submerged and rose in the slithering river. The trees whipped by. No one ran along the old shore, not that boy. The new shore was right there. The river narrowed then dipped and the cob dipped under, bobbed up; she slipped off with the pack and let him go.

She swirled in his wake for a very short time only. She pushed the pack out in front of her, kicked and shoved the pack across toward the other side, followed the pack. The water was cold. She breathed shallow and quick. The boots were heavy kicking the pack, shoving it. Her hands gripped the rope and the belt. The river bulged, arched its back, blocked the way to the other side. She shoved the pack. The cob was sideways ahead of her, then the river turned him straight on, his head pumping then gone down the tongue of water between the rocks she was aiming at. She shoved the pack and kicked but was sucked toward the tongue. She followed over the hump as the river narrowed in, a toboggan, knocked something very hard and fast with her shoulder, rolled, went under, tumbled upside down, lost the rope entirely. The pack wagged in the fast water, a horizontal puppet. Her other hand gripped the belt. The pack dove and darted. Someone was pulling it. She jerked the pack and it wouldn't go. The current pulled and the pack shook its head and the sleeping bag bloomed in the water, flapped long and thin, a great fat balloon. The rope was gone. She pulled on the belt. The sun was a water-ball overhead in the bubble-ring expelled from her nose, rising through cold, lacking oxygen. The bubbles slid away downstream.

She scissored to the pack, shook it. Some net still had it, some hook. The rifle was wagging free, ready to break loose. Her hands gripped the rifle and umbrella. She had them both and then she spun away downriver, kicking up to the surface and gulping air before under again in a set of rapids. She got her boots out in front and pinballed through. A small tree ran parallel then dove. She burst out in the pool, kicked across, dragged on an underwater island, stood on her knees, pushed toward the cob dripping on the far shore where the water was almost warm. She spat the plastic out of her mouth.

She stood with the steaming dripping snorting cob.

The matches were damp.

The fire would have been huge. Plenty of pine branches on that beach. She unloaded the shells from the pistol and the 30-30 and counted them on a flat of bark. She stripped and laid her clothes out in the farthest east of the angled rays. They steamed. She pulled the tongues from the boots and turned them over by the saddle and blanket.

She walked upstream first, hunting for the pack. Just like the scissors. She waded in at shadows submerged. They were always rafts of leaves, branches, river refuse. She turned downstream. She found an apple in moss and ate it bruised. She returned to the cob and gave him the core. She sat in the sand. She sorted three matches. Herring in her belly with apple bits. A rifle. An umbrella. A sweater. Snow pants. Coveralls. T-shirt. Pocketknife. Boots. The saddle. The bridle. The cob.

The aspen leaves quaked in the afternoon. She could live here too and in the days ahead she would remember this pool with fondness. She might have built a cabin of sorts there, she'd think later, dug out an earth-bermed home with her paws like a rabbit, flinging sand behind her into the river taking it. She could start chipping a stone knife with rock from rock like an Indian, watch the edge form slowly as if the blade had always been there awaiting the carver. It was a slow craft but a proven one. Or, if luckier, she might search and find an arrowhead already perfect and sharp, tossed away as imperfect by a fussy, dead Indian, or left in the gut pile for the bears, the point of the head impaled in a socket, the facets gray into yellow stone not native to the area but traded with some faraway clan entranced by the red or green of local stone, both sides believing they got the better deal. The current was pulsing well.

They'd never cross this river with the mules so burdened. Safe at least. Freer than ever. But for the matches, she'd beat them. She'd won.

She watched the far shore for the boy, for anyone from her old life. The cob forgave her anything. He was of the

New Life. When she found an arrowhead in the sand, she could carve a fishing hook, braid some grass into string. The Indians had built whole bridges of grass, Dan once told her, strong enough to bear horses and a hundred men into battle with enemy Indians on the other side. *Just run away*, she would have advised the Indians. *Just get out of the way and live. Only shoot if they come too close.* Though what was too close? She slept in peace for once in the late heat. Dry sand, naked, new. The sun dropped. Purple shadows of twisted driftwood crossed her carcass. Her body, like the bark, looked like buckskin. Itched. Ragged and raging, naked, like a sister to her, this dead tree. The wood inside was deep yellow with oily pitch: perfect firewood, like herself. She'd explode and burn well for a long time if touched off by a match right now. She was cured of them, of herself. The river had cured her.

She dreamed the river was purple in shadow. Of the millions of Herds drinking it down, one Herd for every year, the hues of their pelts ever changing, not changing, eruptions again, fish dropping from tower clouds always, an abacus soon, *be patient, lovey,* Richter scales next *brought to you by . . . The Cavemen!* And that tiny Gang of Velvet Foals sniffing steel half buried by a Walnut Tree, a pit again.

She woke. *Black Widows on beaches. Brown Recluses. Scorpions.*

"Go away," she told her Grannie.

Fire is more important than food or water. A fire needs two logs, never one. One log smolders. Fire is a living thing. It climbs to live. Too much smoke will choke it. Every Explorer knows this.

The sun was behind the ridge. One more hour of usable light. The day had nearly passed, was nearly done, another coming with or without her. She watched the far shore. A feeling came and went. When it was done, the residue remained as a thought: perhaps it was a new planet altogether she'd come to. She'd have to name the place.

The red dog swam from the far side as she collected wood. A smooth swimmer. No bobbing just floating, a wooden head in purple flow and he turned his face into gusts pulsing. A tuft was dry on the top of his head. A wave overtook him and flattened the tuft. He fought the current by turning into waves. The river took him too. He disappeared. Then reappeared as she pulled on socks. The cob rolled in last light dust to welcome the dog. The dog's breath smelled of herring. His tongue bled.

Dusk.

The fire in the cave was ignited without a match to the tinder, rather with powder pried from one of the pistol's shells and a bit of the frayed inner pocket of her jeans stuffed in place of the powder, the trigger pulled and cotton ignited and the bit of pocket fell to the tinder—bits of white-dry grass, shredded inner bark, and the powder. The tinder burst into light and heat. She skinned a rabbit she'd stalked and shot. The fur came off as a single coat. The fire lit the cob standing deep in the cave. Behind the cob was a funnel of black. Fire was easy. God burned things down all the time. Catch fire this way. It lives in the coals. Carry the coal with you. Protect it like gold. In your pocket if you must. Between spoons face-to-face.

It was mathematical:

Fire = Life, hence Fire = Matches, ergo, Matches = Canada, therefore A Cabin = x Matches, hence the Old Swede's (cabin) = Matches = Canada = LifeEverAfter, onward onward.

She went shivering to the cave mouth for more wood. This was freedom. She set pine cones in the fire and it flared. She set bark on the fire and it smoked. She went for more pine cones, crawled for pine cones, pawed them to her. She filled the sweater like a basket. The snow pants were old and roomy, pockets in slants for housing the two remaining matches wrapped in dried leaves. She would have liked a cup of tea. She sat watch with the rifle on the saddle blanket and leaned against the saddle behind her. The cob ate rose hips shriveled from last year. She'd gathered them on the new shore during some berry picking she didn't remember now. She'd cut sage for the cob at the cave's webby edge but didn't venture out farther. This is how men became cowards. She offered him pine branches, leaves. He pawed the rock, licked the wall. In the cave, in his loneliness, the bear too waited for the berry picker, painted pictures of stick-figure men on the rock wall in buffalo blood or man's blood and the greeny-grass made of copper dug up from the ground with his big claws. He painted pictures when bored, still waiting for company. She would tell Ella someday. The bear was looking at the moon sometimes and Ginny knew what he was thinking. The bear was longing for something, all and nameless.

A golden cloud needled across the moon. A bat wheeled across the mouth hunting mules. A pop in the rock woke her. A moth flashed in her face. She brushed at it but it was gone. The cob broke wind. Other berry pickers slipped out of such fixes, though many other pickers too had turned back—weak—when they heard their mothers' dwindling calls: "Not too far, my darling child!" There were always those mothers who fretted too much but didn't truly worry at all since they'd never wandered themselves, never considered it, so didn't *believe in* wanderers. These girls were out of earshot when the tether snapped between mother and child, as at rivers. They'd listened for the *snap* when they felt it, heard nothing, were left unsure, listened for aunts and sisters too, but their ears were filled with many other noises: water everywhere falling, rocks, soil moving slow-constant, hawks slicing air, marmots digging, snakes winding in their holes with a soft slither sound that the wind drowned out.

She cooked the rabbit and ate exactly half. She shit out berries and rabbit, returned to the fire. Pissed by the wall. The red dog rose from his curl, stretched. She set more pine cones on.

She didn't think of the boy, any boy. Who was this boy? How did he fit in the circus? The parade? When she knew that much, all would be solved. The Old Swede's cabin would have cans and cans. The fire was dying.

She slept again and dreamed this time of someone in the cave with her. Why not, when the cob has been trained to welcome strangers, and the dog wouldn't bark since the stranger isn't a stranger to him. He slips along the wall, this intruder. The cob lifts his head at the scent of sugar lump. Ginny murmurs to him softly in her sleep. The flat of a hand is offered. The cob shoves his snout around the palm for the sugar lump. The fire is small but still warm and when sure of her state, of deep unconsciousness numbing her brain, the stranger kneels and warms himself. Or is her unconscious-ness more conscious? She is wrapped in a wool sweater. The stranger notices. There is one carcass, a cottontail half eaten. The skin lies beside a drawing of a rabbit on the floor in charcoal, a tiny coat. The half rabbit is frail pink, fetal. The stranger flashes a mirror at her, pure moon at first, then her own face to look at. It's an old Army trick used on Geronimo and his ilk, when smoke signals failed, before phones and walkie-talkies.

She woke. The moon had set. The fire was out. It only smoked a little. The rifle was across her knees and her body was slumped and wrapped about it. The knife and pistol were hidden in the cave where she left them. The rabbit and skin were gone.

In the morning, she walked the shore again hunting for the pack. She reviewed her inventory, swept the river for the losses of the crossing. She was no weeper. She wept in the sand on her knees. To live, she'd need to steal some more. To steal, she'd have to cross back. She'd need the Old Swede's cabin after all.

The river pulsed worse than yesterday, perfect and foul, high and terrible. She nearly shook her fist at the sky, but the gesture was too dramatic. She waded in and aimed at the far shore.

Listen, love. If you fall off a horse, brush off and climb back on. Just so, if a river tries to drown you, you high-step back in.

"Leave me alone," she said to the river.

The key, Dearie, is the breathing. With a lung full the body will float.

"No more, old woman."

A brown snake swam past. A flotilla of ducks held steady in the near current watching the cob plow in. The ducks released themselves to float after the cob in the bright early light and the quickening flow. She carried the rifle. She had no clever scheme for it. The pistol had been shoved under the cob's saddle and cinched down. During this second crossing she would soon break the finger next to the pinky. She would have no recollection of the break occurring. She would bind the two fingers with a strip of burlap at the Old Swede's cabin. The cob would emerge bloody with a gash in his shoulder, the skin cut loose and a flap hanging down. The blood would clot astonishingly quickly but she would not ride him ever again, would walk beside him for the duration of a shortcut to the Old Swede's. She'd heard of it. She'd seen fingers skim the shortcut on maps, a ridge walk above the Narrows, thereby bypassing Elk Valley and the Switchbacks also. She would still reach the cabin first though it would take two hours to find the cob in the brush on the far shore later.

Breathe deeply, my sweet, but as quickly as possible.

"Quiet, please."

Her words were bubbles, fish scales, bark. Dying is easier than living sometimes.

The water took her and she forgot the cob. Sudden losses of love are possible and common. The water was huge and she was a leaf. She tumbled. She gave into *leaf*, to *blade*. Once Grannie's house had been hit by lightning and the pipes under the sink were smoking. The outlets sizzled. Grannie had run to the attic with the extinguisher checked every six months. She, the girl, had been sure the blue light had leapt from the stone chimney to her iron bed frame into her body. It explained everything as she tossed in the river. There was something very wrong with her. There was something inverted, turned the wrong direction as if hot were cold. She rolled in the flow of cold. She bashed and bumped the rocks of yesterday. She choked in the flow of cold. Her lungs were balloons of air. Her eyes opened to rocks passing her boots at great speed, a train track.

The rocks below would never witness the insult of human incursion. Before the river dried up, before the rocks were unearthed and dried in the air, men would have killed themselves and all other fragile things off, and for this Ginny was sorry. She extruded oxygen as slowly as possible. Electric lungs as the bubbles escaped and rolled across her face. There was their mother whom Grannie had nursed in the back bedroom, taken out in a box carried by a man at each end. One man was her daddy, the other man Ella's. That would explain it.

There was the Herd. That would explain it too, like trigonometry.

Listen here, love. Pay attention. The trick to a river is to—

"Shut up, you old dead thing."

—⁂—

FINAL ARBOREAL CENSUS
2179, May 1 (arch of plain old cloudy sky)
SPECIES: *Callitropsis nootkatensis*
LOCATION: West Sea

The ink report was shuttled off by the scribe. The transmission was sent and the crew prepared for lift-off. The yeoman never saw the cedar scientist again.

She lazily fixed an antenna off the hatch. The ship lurked lazily over a sandbar. Mostly she sat on the white-hot wing watching the horses. Mist misted her. Her father had been a sailor too. The colt sniffed a branch on one side of a blow-down. He'd made no progress at all. He might've walked to the trees to find a way to the filly through the thickets. The filly was tired of berries. She might've swum out around the crown of the blowdown. Neither moved.

"Mate already!" called the yeoman. "Go to him! Go to her!"

They glanced at the noise then forgot her, just as the yeoman forgot the hot wing burning her ass, failed to notice the skin of the craft shudder as the off-load ramp slid out from the hold. Without thought, she pulled down the rim of her hat. Her face was burning.

YEOMAN'S NOTE: *Off-load Ramp Invisible to Yeoman on Day One of Adventure.*

What *adventure*? She just sat on the wing as usual.

The Resurrected Mule was much bigger on the off-load ramp than she remembered him in his pen in the hold. Golden-furred, big headed, he blinked and stretched in his first real light. He'd been gestated in a dish, after all, born in a tub with no mother love. The mule scientists had miscalculated, an unsurprising error given all their guesswork. The Mule was nearly twice the size of the native horses on the beach across the blowdown, and he snorted and shook himself and the ramp shook under his enormous shaking weight. His penis was erect and half as tall as the yeoman.

How could that be? She blushed. The filly had not yet seen the Mule but the colt was stiff as a statue, ears back. The Mule waded off the ramp and swam. He never looked back once. The wrench dropped over the edge of the wing, splashed, and settled on sand. Then the kit too. The yeoman didn't notice. The Mule swam toward the crown of the blowdown. The water was crystal clear.

⋘ —— ⋙

They'd all heard of the Throne Room, but none of them had ever seen it. None but Bowman. He'd been there. But he didn't mention it. A branch of cairns led there on the way to the Old Swede's. The Throne Room was a fitting name but no name could prepare you for that place. The height, angles, uniformity of both, black rock only, impressive echo. Old Bloody Europe was popular for naming such places, cobbled Latin derivations with whiffs of queens, serfs, and torture chambers. The aboriginals had preferred simpler nomenclature.

"Mules don't bray," Maul said. "A donkey brays."

"Mules bray in my book," Bowman said. He loathed the fat man. No secret.

He loathed the Cuckold. He loathed the wife of Saul. He preferred to think of them in these terms though called them to their faces what he had to.

He spoke back over the pack string from his biggest prettiest bay. A scabbard down her shoulder housed a .243 Blaser single-shot rifle with a Swarovski scope, variable power from four to twelve, pricey equipment but worth every penny.

Beware of the man with one gun for he likely knows how to use it.
In his gear, in case of mishap, was a Ruger rifle, 7 mm, bolt
action, Leupold scope. *Beware the man with two, because . . .*
Any target under three hundred yards would be down in
one shot. Four hundred fifty yards was not impossible. As
sidearm he carried a Ruger, .22 caliber single six revolver,
good medicine for snakes, rabbits, etc.

He disliked amateurs, but a job was a job. His household
spent and spent. His boy would be out of the nest soon but
was watching Dan's farm for now, fifty dollars per day, so
his household, at least, was gaining from this fiasco. And he
loved it up here. Loved to be away.

Mule one, mule two, mule three, mule four.

The donkey stood high on the slope, wooden legged, head
hanging. Three hundred forty-five yards, an estimate. He
halted the bay, pulled the range finder from its snap case.
Three hundred fifty-one yards to the donkey. He made the
mental adjustment.

Where there was one wild donkey there were a few. There.
Around the crag. The little herd might have been props. He
glassed an elk farther on, an elegant animal. He'd been paid
adequately. He hated town, pitied the people there. There
had been two sets of boot prints in the scree up the ridge
after the rifle shot. He and Saul didn't mention the second
tracks to the others.

Bowman knew the map in his head. Trees did not belong
here. Heroes are born then made. The sun slid regal and
flashed through the ragged crags. The cob's tracks, assuming
they were still following the cob's tracks, had been obliterated
by the tracks of the yellow horse and the packhorse.

At the Throne Room the tracks followed the green carpet up the enormous nave, turned at the transept where one might drop to his knees in shame at the state of things in this world today. The tracks exited at a hidden side door, as if for monks or priests who shuttled books and papers for the King to consider. Through the door and beyond, old mine shafts pocked the walls for several miles, blasted and abandoned to fill coffers, to pay off friends. Only the mule driver stopped to examine the shafts. The others barely looked, since quartz was extremely common and only storekeepers and whores got rich from precious metals.

Dan was useless. The Cuckold. Sulking on the chestnut in the back, an old horse but friendly with a pleasant eye.

Bowman and Saul led by alpine lakes dammed by whole trees chewed down, eviscerated, rolled. Young pines tickled their knees. Side by side round castles for fox and coyotes, raven chicks the size of kittens, beaks gaping. Hundreds of pinyon jays formed a regular convention, the aftermath of mating. Bowman liked these birds. Their gray-blue wasn't flashy or ostentatious but subtle and distinct. Their nests were well hidden from marauders, three eggs, four, though older jays built nests farther out where the sun hit enamel sooner. Those chicks were born first, got more food. Seven years to learn that trick. Pinyons were dead by seven.

"Equipment failure's lethal," said the mule driver, scraping his plate. "Dirty barrel is lethal. Wet ammo. Something will get her."

"Cold will get her," said Saul.

"Anxiety," said the mule driver. "Fear. All lethal."

"She's stubborn," Saul said. "Her biggest danger."

Why did Saul talk to this man?

"Stubborn is lethal," said the mule driver.

"She's impulsive," Saul said.

"Lethal," said the mule driver, as was high water. Injury to the horse. Rockslide. Snakebite.

"Why discuss it?" Ella said. She was with him at least in this.

"Shut him up," Bowman said.

"She'll hit obstructions," said the mule driver. "All I'm saying."

Bowman had owned the yellow horse briefly, won her from a drunk playing twenty-one in Dibbs. He lost her a year later, another drunk. She was later impounded. He'd taught her to count with her hoof. The sheriff didn't know about the counting. The sheriff's niece rode her English on weekends, tight pants, velvet cap, black crop.

Saul's wife wrote IOUs on paper from her little locked notebook. Lined. A tiny rolling three-digit combination. Bowman could tear the lock with one thumb.

One (1) red jenny named _____.

One (1) small gray jack named _____.

She signed it, dated the bottom, tore it out. The mule driver was to fill the names in.

Even for a professional, the cob's tracks posed problems on rock. Bowman asked God for mud and sometimes got it.

They discussed the pit of course, yap yap yap. Broken glass, manure, wheelbarrow turned over. Old lamp fallen in, no cord. Walnuts.

"That deputy," said the mule driver. "Where'd he really come from, his spankin' new duds, who's his family, how long till they come huntin' for him? The man's a fool."

"A week or two," said the mule driver when no one else did.

"A fat man, an endless talker," Bowman said. "Talking is the opposite of walking, and people often swap one for the other and fatten and the blood thickens and death comes sooner."

Quiet. Wind.

"There, a hail cloud is distinct," said the mule driver. "Rows of tits underneath. Black. Full to busting."

"Flood. Swarms. Locusts. Drought kills too."

"Plenty of water," said Saul. "No worry there."

"Hypothermia," said the mule driver.

"True."

"Disorientation."

"Part and parcel with hypothermia."

"Plenty of other causes of disorientation."

"I take your point."

The red dog disappeared. The red dog came back. The dog was important. It moved between.

Saul's wife had a little Derringer in her saddlebag. A mother-of-pearl grip.

"I like your grip," Maul said.

"Thank you," Ella said.

She cleaned it at the fire as they passed spiked Kool-Aid. Maul gave her the look again.

"Ask him yourself," Ella snapped. "I won't repeat myself."

"So, the eye patch." Maul nudged the Cuckold.

"What about it?" he said.

"What's under it?"

"My blasted eye's under it."

"Blasted," Bowman said with pleasure.

"Just tell him," Ella said to Dan.

"What you all want to know," Bowman said.

"And you don't?"

"Did you stitch it shut?" Maul asked. "Or did you not stitch it?"

"He did not," she snapped.

"I've wondered too," Saul mused. "Blood cleans wounds as good as anything."

"True again."

"*Soap's a later invention of man*," Saul said. "Ginny always said that."

"Grannie did." She bent back to the pretty pistol.

"But Grannie was old school," Saul continued, and just as the subject was about to drift off of himself—gone forever—that Cuckold, surprise surprise, grabbed the subject back again, *relented to reveal*, laid it on thick too. Blow by blow now, how the needle when he sewed his eye shut dove under his lashes, swam under the lid.

"No," said the mule driver with pleasure, meaning *yes*.

How Ginny had envied his lashes too, had said so often *long and girlie*, and the needle rose up and out, a red spot, a bulb of blood high on his cheek, and he drew the thread up as far as he dared to, acted it out after a long pull on the Kool-Aid, each stitch with flair, with slow care, as with the bow of a fiddle on the tune's last note (an unnecessary flourish), then the needle rose again and cross-stitched up and over the lashes, no pain at all in firelight now, left just enough thread to dangle free to drink again, and—

"No pain?" Maul said and Dan grinned big and white and spoke of the wedding. Once he was A *pretty blue boy*, whereas Shaw had been the tall, dark-eyed devil, true as true, but how to get past it, and the needle and thread continued on, lashed the lid down, a little tighter each go, repeating across the red and blue bloated tissue, and in this way he put the eye away forever behind zigzag navy thread.

"Liar," Bowman said. "That eye's right as rain."

Hard rain. The sun dried it up and it was parched again.

"Altitude. Anxiety. Terrain is the number one."

The mule driver ate more than his share. The mule driver fell asleep on his watch. Why have a watch then?

"Her mind is the obstruction now," Saul said.

"Food goes rancid," Bowman said.

"She's got ammo."

"Stop repeating."

"Bear. Snake. Mountain lion."

Ella appeared once out walking on his watch, a white getup billowing. She was up to something. She held a finger over her lips, shushed herself, then mumbled to the mules. Spoke to them.

They spoke of the pit only when riding, only at first. Full daylight. Cats in the pit, chicks in the pit due to freezing when the heat lamp failed. Some boot kicked it over. Lamps again. An old fox dead by buckshot.

"I've eaten bugs," said the mule driver.

"'Course you have."

"Prized in China," Saul said. "Taste like lemon."

"She could always eat the cob," Ella said.

"You're funny," Dan said.

"I've never heard I was funny."

"Wonder why," Bowman said.

One must intervene sometimes. It is a hero's job. When the world goes too far, or not far enough, someone responsible must step in. Finish it. Start it.

"It's legal to eat it in forty countries," Maul said. "The taboo is taboo."

"To eat a horse," Saul said. "It's a sin."

"Stringy," Maul said.

Bowman slid down at crushed weeds. If he stopped, they all stopped. They found a strange skull eaten dry and white.

"Sasquatch," Maul said.

Bowman strapped it between the chair legs.

Fresh manure.

"For no food, the cob shits all the time," Maul said.

"It's the yellow horse's shit," Bowman said.

The red dog rolled in it then skedaddled.

"That dog's ugly," Saul said. "Sorta putty colored."

"Excrement colored," said the mule driver.

"Shit," Bowman said.

"But somehow strawberry blond too," said the mule driver.

"Can't be both shit and strawberry blond," Saul said.

"Who made that rule?"

"Some rules preexist," Saul said. "And they outlast us, too."

"I say you're mistaken."

"Say what you want," Saul said.

The mule driver cast about his brain for a comeback. Saul was a winner again, victory after victory. Right or wrong didn't matter. The mule driver would never understand, but started up again.

On second thought, "Naw," Saul said. "Don't."

They debated hue and color blindness. Who names the paint chips at hardware stores? Speculation. Definition. Rods and cones. They entered the Spindle Gorge made of damsels and dwarfs and stone towers of straw. Saul's wife was leading the first pack string now. They debated more to no particular end:

"The red jenny's rope was never cut."

"Yes, it was cut."

"The knot was suspect to begin with."

"It was a perfect knot."

"Ha."

"The knot-tier who does not like women."

"He does. What do you care?"

"I don't."

They didn't discuss the little gray. No one thought of him. It was a fact of the hierarchy of all things living.

"Where'd that dog come from?" Ella said. "Whose dog is it?"

"The shit dog appeared at the shindig on the hill," Saul said. "The shit dog came with some partygoer."

"The partygoer," Dan said, "will be missing the shit dog. Will come looking for his pet."

His first words in hours. The partygoer, the shit dog.

"That's one way to look at it," Saul said.

"Eureka," the mule driver said. "Some partygoer *dumped* the shit dog at the shindig."

"Maybe the shit dog is Shaw's," Bowman said. "Maybe the shit dog came down from some other shit planet. Maybe the shit dog is God. Maybe a shitty mirage."

They did not come to any conclusions.

"But where is it?" Ella said.

"The dog is with the missing shoeing kit," Bowman said.

Another bull snake. Bowman shot it, the Ruger.

"Keep it down," she said.

"It's fine if they hear gunshots," Saul said.

The snake writhed as the horses passed by, eyeing it. The smell was wonderful. Sage. Saul offered gum between the horses, asked for the wrappers back, balled the wrappers into a silver ball, then stuffed it into a pannier. He was leading the buckskin jenny, who was the most like a horse.

"If it was me," said the mule driver, "I'd have taken the Percheron."

"She's not you," Ella said.

"Big horse needs big food." That was Saul.

"You on his side?" Ella said.

"'Twas a neutral comment, dearest."

"Don't tell me to settle down."

"I didn't hear anyone say nothin' about settle down," said Saul.

"The Percheron would be to China by now, is the thing," said the mule driver. "The Percheron would have kicked our butts."

Once Saul told how his father had found a real Roman coin like a dime in an apple grove over in Smarts. "Metal detecting was my old man's hobby."

"It's a popular pastime," said the mule driver.

Bowman's genius was concentration in chaos. Concentration was underrated because invisible. When Saul's wife walked away by herself, which was often, it was with a small bag with a small bottle. She dropped its contents, tiny grains, on her tongue after dinners. Bowman had owned the bay for seven years. He got her from a friend who died. The bay's name was Sara. Saul would get Sara if he died now.

"But really," said the mule driver. "Was the coin Roman as in Caesars? Togas? Gladiators?"

"Togas," Saul said.

"How did he know the coin was genuine? Minted in Rome, Italy?"

"I have the coin."

Once Ella said to that shit dog, "Go find Ginny. Go find your mama."

"A fake?" asked the mule driver.

"It's very old," Saul said. "I can tell you that."

"Old is old. Not the same as Roman."

"I know what I know."

"Let me see it."

"When we reach her," Dan said, "I'm going to talk to her first."

"You're in charge," Saul said.

"She doesn't want to get away," Bowman said. "It's a paradox."

The mule driver asked the meaning of the word, then said they minted fake dimes and nickels in San Francisco. "Saw it in a museum once."

"This isn't one of those."

Hate is fragile. Hate is soft.

Ella always spit her gum only minutes after Saul doled it out.

A rabbit was following them, circling, the same one. Bowman understood the rabbit, the desire to stay with the group, not to stray. If he had the chance, he'd slice a tater, stuff half in the mule driver's mouth, duct tape next, wire from lip to lip. There were plenty of potatoes still. Some wild potatoes seem to fill the belly, but toxins stop the body from absorbing their nutrients. The rabbit skidded into thorns.

That night the Cuckold told another "joke" around the fire. Pink moon. He'd had all day to think of it. He rubbed his hands together before telling it. "This one's hilarious!"

This cowboy rides to town. He wears a white hat. People know just who he is. They flock to him, the townsfolk. They swarm his horse but his horse has been trained. *The Bank foreclosed! Sold to cronies at the railroad. He's in the saloon right now, the papers for all our farms, they've set them on the poker table.* The townsfolk are pretty. They've got flour on their faces from baking bread. "What's he look like?" says the cowboy. The townsfolk exchange glances. *He looks just like us!*

"Ha," the Cuckold said, when no one else laughed.

"Don't you have any funny ones?" the mule driver said.

After Dan's Cowboy Jokes, more talk:

"Everyone thinks they're the hero," Bowman said.

"The correct distinctions have been lost," Saul said.

"The banker used to be the bad man," Bowman said. "Bought up mortgages, ganged up with railroads, squeezed poor farmers even in droughts." Cuckold listened to every word, imagined edging in. "All the old swindlers are the good guys now. Everyone wants to be a banker. Farmers and ranchers eat dirt. Even whores are A-okay. Johns fly out second-floor windows if payment's five minutes late."

"Fact."

"Some whores cry rape now. But rape's not a thing you can say in an animal context. Consent as a concept is reserved for man."

"Fact."

"They don't call it rape when it's seahorses humping. Whales, turtles."

Saul chewed peppermint. "These things are natural," he said. "Though not moral."

There was one time in bed where Bowman lay asleep beside his wife and she turned and really looked at him, the contours of his face, the lines forming in it, and he knew she could see what he looked like as a boy, before she knew him, tender and hopeful, bad clever stupid, wonderful due to the combination, *you stupid boy*, ruined and saved both, but now also the lines of an old man.

"Morality is man-made," he said.

"The term will be understood different in the coming epochs," Saul said.

"The future revises all."

"Hundred percent."

"The lines are fouled irreparably."

Bowman poured water on the fire. "Tell us another from Destruction Bay, another blizzard, lived to tell." And Saul did tell it, passed a little silver flask that had not appeared yet, since the night was done but not done, the fire high, cold nipping at their backs, what delight, an even more harrowing story than the previous, a blizzard like no other blizzard, this time truly unsurvivable, from younger days in the great North American outback, open road, tall passes, money for a new family, a dash of the unexplained, a hint of cosmos, of time outside time, Eternity, Bowman interrupted, since all good stories must include it, a happy ending, cold warmed by sudden, urgent friendship, the moral of trust in men that saves men.

"Can't imagine snow right now," said the mule driver when Saul was finished.

"Then you can't imagine much," snapped Bowman.

He was brushing his bay again though she was brushed well already, not a speck of dust, his back to the fire, a tremble in his hand.

Another grouse dragged her wing. They ate eggs and grouse in fried rice. Nameless gorges. They sat on a pine beached by flood in their grandmothers' days. Termites. It would take ages to pulp completely. The ice dam will burst again. They hobbled about since they were getting older. They were quiet about their pains.

"Do you believe in the devil?" asked the Cuckold. He waded in the creek. The dog dug in sand. He was after a rock, something hidden. Bowman sited in on the dog and Saul said, "Don't bother." Bowman slipped the safety off, and Saul said, "No point in killing him."

"His finger's itching," Maul said.

Ella yawned, watched the dog, then lay back on the sand. The rifle hovered. "That dog will die someday anyway," Bowman said. "No time like the present."

"Most don't like killing," Maul said. "It's simply required by the job of living."

"Some don't practice self-deception," Bowman said. "Everyone likes a kill."

The dog dug faster, sand flying, the illusion of closing in. The rifle did not waver.

"I'm saying not to," Saul said. "That's what I've decided about killing the dog."

"How's this pecking order been decided?" Bowman said.

"I decided that too."

"Noted," Bowman said. "What's the duration of the decision?"

"I haven't decided."

"All decisions have a time frame," Bowman said. "After that, it's free rein."

A bird cried out and the rifle lifted to it. A raven just fledged wobbled in a thermal. When the rifle fired, the dog stopped digging. A squadron of pinyon jays flew up. A semi-automatic reloads on its own. Bowman pegged nearly every one. The blue survivors wheeled upstream. He followed, though he'd lost the element of surprise.

Bang. Bang. He returned a little winded. Ella rummaged in her saddlebag and applied a hanky to her nose that was bleeding again. Dan strode in the water, turning in the sun. He held his hands to an imagined cross. The water slapped up and slapped his hips. "The good are crucified," he said, adding that crucifixions were once very common.

Saul looked away. Spat.

The Cuckold dipped his wrists in, searching the sky with his shiny patch. They ate bread torn off the loaf. Saul tossed it around with cheese in chunks off the dirty block. Dan didn't eat cheese anymore, he said. The shit dog ate the crumbs.

They rubbed their necks.

The Old Swede's cabin had a coffee-can roof. They counted the years since. The cans were red in all sizes, nailed to spans of unpeeled logs. A day or so more ahead.

Bowman peered through his scope at the ridges. Ella trimmed moldy cheese. She was a small-minded creature reliable with a small fat blade. They ate Dan's share. He'd been gone all day, the dog. They studied him licking some riverside clam.

"Any sign of them, Tonto?" said the mule driver.

Bowman didn't look up from the scope. "Screw you."

"Pewter. It can pass for silver."

"They had no pewter in Roman times. So there's your problem."

Ella pulled her boots off. Saul pointed at a flash and she asked him, "What bird?" and he told her. She took his binoculars. She offered Dan a tube of ointment.

"What are you looking at?" said Dan.

Bowman bent to drink like the shit dog.

"Better not," said the mule driver. "Giardia."

Bowman brushed his teeth with a finger.

The mule driver dropped a last iodine pill into his canteen. He would boil their water from then on, he said. They passed crushed corn chips. The horses got the last carrots from the flat of Ella's hand and Saul watched her. The mules gathered in.

"Don't spoil them," said the mule driver.

Ella ate a carrot too, chewed slow circles like a cow.

"But how'd the coin get itself buried in Smarts then?"

Hate is patient. Hate is kind.

"I didn't say I could explain it."

Poor tracking over slick rock. Good tracking through the sandy stretches. Cottonwood seed snowed. No sniper, so they forgot her sometimes, as with electric bills, doorsteps, and the stains inside the toilet bowls, sleeves rolled up hours ago, rolled them down to block light to wrists, Viking camps. Newfoundland.

"No better word in the world than *waterfall*," said the mule driver.

No one debated it.

He talked of red-haired slave girls kidnapped from Iceland by the Vikings, shipped on to Newfoundland since red-headed slave girls went all over. Like coins, beads, and furs in the bellies of Viking ships, beaver pelts later, to the cells of monks in the red-haired villages, uncles to the girls.

"I hate that mare," Dan said. "It's her fault."

Bowman laughed. "You good folks have forgotten all about her."

They found the shoeing kit in the wrong pannier. The favorite hammer was missing still.

"I'd have checked into the motel," said the mule driver. "Called 911."

"She likes a whole pack chasing her," Bowman said.

"Always did," said Ella.

"We're not chasing her," Dan said. "We're finding her."

"I forgot," Bowman said.

"She'll have forgotten something too," said the mule driver.

"Lethal," Bowman said.

"Always forget an item," Saul said.

"Fatigue," said the mule driver. "No firewood on a ridge."

"Guilt," Saul said. "Depression."

"Anger," said the mule driver.

"Self-loathing," Bowman said. "Loss of will to live."

"Loneliness," Saul said.

"Chaos will get her," Bowman said. "Hubris will get her in the end."

"Ha, there's an eagle's nest."

"All that's pertinent is mixed together in the mountains," Saul said. "Every appetite is natural. Must be. Arising as it does from a living natural being."

"Vikings were buried at sea. The red-haired islands were solid rock."

"Heat can cause insanity."

"Lack of sleep."

"The girls traveled west with the North American Indian trade."

"Sea supremacy of Spanish galleons."

"Books, braids, or booty."

"Humans have strange drives."

"Inscrutable inclinations."

"Every appetite is natural," Saul insisted.

"Even murder is natural, incest."

"Must be."

"Strange to think it."

"Think of animals."

"Greed, lying, if that's a natural inclination."

"Bears don't judge."

"Goats don't."

227

"What happened to her note?" Dan called from the back of the pack string.

"What note?" asked the mule driver.

"We missed it," Ella said.

"We'll find it when we get her back," Saul said.

Bowman shook his head. "You people make me sick." And he rode ahead alone.

They scoped a bear, a brown yearling, very high in the scree. They saw him again on his hind legs, sniffing their molecules, dropping to all fours, become a boulder.

Ella's scissors were gone. Her nose was bleeding.

"Epistaxis," Bowman said.

The blood on her face was sandy. Her little bottle was green.

"People die of nosebleeds every day," Maul said. "Clotting issues, elevation."

"Nosebleeds are meaningless," Bowman said. "Don't worry."

"I'm not worried," Ella said.

"They don't mean tumors necessarily," he continued. "Or aneurysms, or dementia eating in at the gray matter right behind the eyes."

"You're a piece of work," Saul said.

Bowman smiled. "I hope so."

Two sticks of dynamite were missing, found, then missing again.

"I wonder where that'll turn up," Bowman said. "This is a professional operation."

The cook sat in the blue wooden chair generally. It was easier on his knees for cooking. The mule driver cut onions and buttered crackers, passed them. Saul washed the cast iron without soap, boiled water, poured it out, slopped the inside with old leaves.

"What did you bring that chair for?" Saul said once.

"None of your business," Dan said.

Saul took it for a gag, slapped his back, but Dan shrugged his hand off.

At the confluence where the yellow horse missed the cob's swerve over hard pack, they argued. They turned upstream first and followed the cob. The foliage was dense. The river was high, probably impassible. They picked on along the cob's swath, tried to cross, lost another mule, another IOU. They turned back and followed the yellow horse instead.

"We know where she's going."

Late afternoon. Mosquitoes were clouds crawling up cuffs and collars. Ella buckled a fly mask on her paint's face. The mule driver complained: Was it right only one animal had a fly mask?

"If you cared for your horse you could lose some weight," she said.

"A human can carry a third of his body weight," Saul said.

"You don't have to carry him."

"A horse's back is parallel to the ground," Bowman said. "The physics is different."

"I don't need your help," she said.

"I'm not helping you."

"It's up to the rider," Saul said. "His own decision how to burden his animal."

"I left my horse's fly mask at home in the rush," Bowman said.

"You were paid well for the rush," she said.

"Too bad those pills don't relieve a female on the rag."

That shut her up and they were able to talk freely: fancy diets from Florida or California on TV, a big money idea, a fraud, $400 just to sign up, my God, my God. They once thought they saw the yellow horse high up over them. But too high. Nothing there.

"Bang. Bang," Bowman said.

Evening. They passed the deputy's tent without stopping. The saddle blankets were stretched out drying, some cheap Native design. A small fire in a rock ring. The man was stretched out. Bare feet. Wool hat instead of the ball cap. A lantern burned beside a book.

"Why does everyone want to be a cowboy now?" Saul said to Bowman. "It's harder than it looks."

"What took you so long?" called the deputy.

"What's the rush?" Saul called back.

"Lost her trail?" Bowman said.

"I did," said the deputy.

"Tracking's an old art."

The line of animals passed slowly.

"Your pack train's shrinking," said the deputy.

"Fewer mouths to feed," said Bowman.

"Keep your eyes peeled, would ya, for two mules on the lam," Maul said and described them.

"Seems you've seen a heap o' trouble," said the deputy. "I got all my horses still."

No one looked at his two steeds grazing.

"Catch the jenny first," Maul said. "She'll fall for a sugar lump. The gray'll follow right along."

"Where's your dog?" said the deputy.

"The bear got him," Saul said.

Ella howdy'ed then toodle-oo'ed. Dan turned in his saddle to watch the last of the deputy float away.

They entered the Narrows that twisted for two more miles, a violet sky dropping as night fell. They followed no tracks now. They flicked their headlamps on. One day's ride to the Old Swede's cabin.

"John Law," Bowman said to Saul ahead of the others. "He's well out of his jurisdiction."

"No jurisdiction here."

"I got dibs on the yellow horse."

Their lights scuttled the ground. The full moon rose.

Through the Narrows they flung their camp things down. The valley was a huge expanse of sand, braided creeks, and occasional stunted trees. The Switchbacks to the cabin wound up the cliffs at the far south end.

She poured rice into the Dutch oven. Pellets to nose bags, etc.

Saul built the fire up, dragged branches of driftwood, and asked his wife, quietly, if it warmed her. She sliced open the last pack of bacon. She fried it on the four-burner. The fire was too hot to get near with cooking tools. Maul unsaddled and chewed tobacco and offered the bag around. Saul tore a plug.

"Poison," Bowman said and shook his head.

Dan refused the bacon or any noodles that touched it. Ella stood over him with the plate.

"I'll eat bread," he said, and she brought some over.

"That's right," Saul said. "Mother him."

She brought a plate to Saul and he ate. He remounted his sorrel. Bowman was up in his saddle already. Dan rose and headed for the chestnut, but the chestnut had been hobbled already. He ran after the men. They'd turned their horses back toward the Narrows.

"I'm coming!" Dan called, running. "This is my show!"

"Help with the mules," Saul called. "Help Ella."

A stone skittered behind them. He'd flung it like the child he was. A tantrum.

"Get back home with the girls," Bowman said. "We're off to park the bus."

And they were. So few of them left to fix things. The next Great Flood was upon them. The last of them was holding the door shut, the water of the dam burst gushing through, no way to stop it forever. The door was bulging, begging to buckle, the last of them with their shoulders to it.

They heard his feet running, no boots.

The creek in the Narrows wound neat and orderly. The west wind pushed sound the other way. Their headlamps made weird shapes until the moon arrived. They flicked them off.

Night passed.

Returning very late, they found the Cuckold sleeping naked on his tarp, fist to face. Sweet dreams were what he wanted. He would die a boy at a very old age, blanket on knee, sipping milkshake from a straw.

"Should stick his thumb in all the way."

They were very hungry but did not elect to wake the others. They didn't rummage or boil water. They unsaddled the sorrel and bay first, the yellow horse and packhorse second.

They washed their hands, squatted at the creek to do it, clutched handfuls of cold sand in the moon in the water. The grains had once lived in glaciers, had a long silent life there. They scrubbed their callused palms, blood from under nails. Millions of grains, granite, silica, a gray cloud. They resided, they knew, in the big picture together. Nothing is perfect. Nothing is guaranteed. Saul was not exactly happy yet. Saul was almost there. He would be. They were sharing this life right now, Bowman told him, at this creek side, at this junction in time. They shared the elation of coincidence if nothing else.

The sun was coming. They stood together.

"A mind can't imagine the truth of the moon," Bowman said, "neither distance nor scale."

It was private and truthful and innocent and intimate. Saul nodded.

"Occasionally there's a glimpse," they agreed.

"The truth must be seen or felt."

If anyone could, it was them.

The yellow horse and the packhorse stood together. The old gang of horses and mules looked on. This first night they were hobbled a little apart, insurance against wandering back while adjusting to the new smells and faces.

Saul would settle into it too.

They did not shake hands but that was the feeling. A very old communion. "Marvel at yourself," Bowman said, and they did. "Think in the Grand Scale," Bowman said, "squint and see the world different."

Saul squinted.

They stripped down and waded out into the stream, hooted

a little. They opened their eyes underwater. They smiled like girls.

"Who invented you?" Saul said, looking shy.

"Who invented *us*?" Bowman clapped Saul on the shoulder in the water.

❧ —— ❧

Mule Thought #4 (the red jenny and the steer): Wondering. *You must calm yourself*, mulled the red jenny. *Panic results in failure.* He did not calm. It was the young steer's nature to be theatrical. *We're free now. Be happy about it. No names pinned on us. We are wild now.*

But oh, this steer was young and heartbroken. Still he rolled his eyes and snorted. His hip still sizzled in memory though the pain of the iron was long gone. He had his own pasture now, a mountain range full of them. He was free *but what was that really*, he wondered. He was one who could not let things be. He had to wonder and wonder and wonder and there is little peace in wondering. *Broken hearts are part of living*, mulled the red jenny. *You aren't alive if you haven't been crushed.*

The steer wondered why. *Must we suffer in this way? We did nothing.*

We are suffering now, even here in freedom, she mulled. *We are happy.*

But why us? wondered the steer. *Explain it to me.*

If you look for logic, you will break your heart again, mulled the red jenny. *Logic is the first and biggest trap.*

All her life, the red jenny was fierce, and she could hit a nerve. The steer wondered, *Why was he big and strong if he*

*had no power of revenge for the pain of iron? the steer wondered.
What kind of trick was that? Who was playing it?*

She tried not to laugh at him, he was so young. Never laugh at babies. The steer wondered if one's character should be measured by one's behavior toward the powerless.

It should, mulled the red jenny. *Nothing is truer.* And she licked him kindly and nibbled his ear.

⁂

Once Grannie told her Dearest One: *When a bear has got the Woodman's scent—I'm talking a brown bear now, a grizzly bear, a black bear is another strategy altogether—the Woodsman must stay perfectly still, play dead if he can.*

The man in the tent below was a stranger. She sat ambush above it, hunched under the old black umbrella though the sky was clear, dry as bone, and stars don't rain. Full moon.

She'd left the cob in the weeds by the little lake atop the Switchbacks. Before the two riders came, she'd sidled up to the stranger. Or his camp, anyway. The man was singing in the tent. Not yet midnight. A nice tenor. The wind took parts of it. She'd dropped down for matches while he crooned, found none, took other things while he sang:

> *When the long, long day is over, and the Big
> Boss gives me my pay,
> I hope that it won't be hell-fire, as some of the
> parsons say—*

The tent flap slapped now below again. Her visit was over. Nylon scented, a fancy new model, likely with the tags still on it. The man inside, she'd seen, tied knots of the most basic type without consideration for the urgent duties of the knot. He was a stranger to rope and leather, some frail flower, though his horses—one yellow especially—were familiar.

The two headlamps swung out the mouth of the Narrows on cue. Flicked off. The horses, however, had pinned themselves to her retinas. Too far to discern breed or color. She squinted for a jawline. Hats are all the same at a distance. *I am made of stone under an umbrella. No breathing.* She could not remember taking the umbrella, the knife either, or the cans of meat, or the matches from the second drawer down. Her mouth had watered at the tent. She saw the flap slither. The moon made a white-blue sculpture of the little construction. She sorted thoughts and concerns for this unknown man, this Damsel:

1. The berries are required, she'd tell him. No mistake. People blame the girl, shaking their finger, but the berries are entirely and completely necessary for the chance meeting of the girl with the bear.
2. The berry picker *must* wander off. There is no story without the wandering.
3. Some bad decision is required. Some terrible transgression. To fuck a bear.

Told him how, in the old days, the men didn't abide clearings at all. Berry pickers watched as the men went off with arrows or rifles, depending on the epoch, from a village or town, depending on the same. The men went. Goodbye. They walked by below the ledge where she crouched. She looked down on them with their noisy gear when all she had was the silent basket. Any man was hunting if young and strong enough, if bearded yet, if anywhere near still able-bodied, if an elk had been spotted in the next valley over or tracks seen in the recent snow. The berry picker ate berries as she watched them, fistfuls. Her lips turned blue, horses and chariots, depending, rickshaws pulled by naked slaves, trucks and mules, bicycles. All berry pickers are the same. She watched them watch for elk. An elk turned a circle far up in a stand of trees, an unreachable perch except on foot. She could follow, therefore, and they could not. This was the price of the adventure. The elk hurried. The elk found the herd, milled among the females, counting. He strutted among calves and yearlings. He herded his herd uphill to the safety of impossible cliffs where they harbored in the sky with their old mothers who were young still, whose tits were heavy with milk again, and the yearlings trying of course to get to their tits. A mother snorted and kicked, causing great confusion among the yearlings. She was still their mother and no longer their mother. She had a new calf now. A yearling watched from a distance the newborns circling under the mother, shy, slipping in close under her chin, circling again on wobbly legs, nuzzling close on a second pass, sucking her. The yearling pushed on. There was plenty to eat. The world was big, everything green, as the men stomped by seeing nothing of them, one fat man on a dun, a king on his sorrel, a fool on his chestnut, the queen on her fine paint, the priest on his bay. The berry picker brushed her frock. She'd killed bugs without thought. The men never saw her. They were deep in their men-thoughts, the women and children, the old men to feed back in town, they prayed on bent knee when the elk finally stopped in range for the projectile spinning toward his rib cage, the pumping organ, to roast, digest, and so live. This stranger in the tent was like an old man, outside the hunt. He counted seeds or dogs too old to follow, or napped under rib-roofed lean-tos, to keep the sun back, to dream of hunts of the past, of the women returning from berry picking, to lie down with them if possible, the woman setting the baby in the cradle or a soft patch of sand, kissing his forehead after letting him mount and fulfill his quick needs, lifting the baby after, returning to roots and berries, to braids, to stripping sinew from hides with spade-shaped knives, or any other things the women did.

She could've told him. Sausages, crackers, matches—hand 'em over.

But now, down in the meadow, the scene was changing: the two riders were coming. Time at their backs, nipping. Most of the stranger's gear was in the tent. Good. The rest was by a log ten feet from it, blocked from the riders by his two horses, all fine obstructions to a successful raid. Fine. She'd meant him no harm. Why fear their intentions? The two riders hugged the far side of the meadow. No clip-clop. As the horses grew their shapes formed. Her irises shoved aside to make room for moonlight pouring in. The 30-30 lay in her lap. Every tent has a back zip, a place to knock and whisper in, to slide in other than the front door. The riders wound closer. Ginny's fingers clutched a stone in her free hand, so the hand wasn't free after all. Stars pricked the black and faded near the moon. Time passed. The pistol was shoved in the waist of her snow pants. Three chambers were full.

The questions are always the same with Damsels. She'd taken a canteen three-quarters full. He could live without it. She'd taken a pencil and a plastic bag with chocolate crushed at the bottom, ate it at the back zipper while he sang:

> *And I hope that it won't be heaven, with some*
> *of the parsons I've met—*
> *All I want is quiet, just to rest and forget.*

She knew it, of course. "The Song of the Wage Slave."
The riders crossed the creek. They knew the poem too.

> *Look at my face, toil-furrowed; look at my*
> *callused hands*
> *Master, I've done Thy bidding, wrought in Thy*
> *many lands—*

The voice was familiar. A voice buying plums. A voice in the line at the fair with some girl, the bumper cars, an unromantic ride. She couldn't summon the face. Faces were fading. She'd taken a lighter. Some books even, *The Spell of the Yukon*, fine old binding, then a little thing called *Disgrace*, though on second thought she cursed her own silliness for flirting with nonessentials, and anyway, why lug around what you already have by heart? Took a bit of string off a loop in the tent, a delicate operation of unknotting the knot, a slow ballet of fingers. She'd lain on her side and worked the knot. String becomes important. Rope is just thick string. She felt his body just inside the tent wall and marveled he didn't feel her too. Most of his food was in the tent, a violation of the cardinal rule: *Find a tree. Hang the food.* She'd smelled it from the back zip. She'd taken his fuel bottle, empty. She'd taken a beer cap.

"Who's there?" said the Damsel.

Ginny waited in cat pose. Coyotes, a gang of them, yipped on the far ridge. The cob was safe in the weeds by the lake at the top of the Switchbacks, half a day's ride to the cabin, no more, but hitting the tent was a better idea. The tent could have saved the day if only the Damsel could've provided matches. She'd skip the cabin, ride north.

(*Spare a few? Much obliged. Surely. Glad to help a neighbor.*)

An owl.

She'd stolen mints. Set one on her tongue as the riders tied their horses at the creek.

> *Wrought for the little masters, big-bellied they*
> *be, and rich;*
> *I've done their desire for a daily hire, and I die*
> *like a dog in a ditch—*

A breeze carried the lines far, and the next.

> *I have used the strength Thou hast given, Thou*
> *knowest I did not shirk—*
> *Threescore years of labor—Thine be the long*
> *day's work—*

A ridge is just a string for the wind to sing on and the crackers had been perfect squares, wheaty, salty, the sausage sliced

in paper wrapper, just sitting under his front fly, waiting for
bugs or thieves. Ginny crawled for an hour—hours maybe—
under the tie-outs to reach them. A lizard. A Snake. She was
rising through the phylum to Horse. The man had stopped
singing by the time she reached her target. He'd come out
into the dark to piss. "Who's there?" And he pissed far off
from the tent to let her break away with the items she'd
gathered, also a pair of rough rubber gloves scooped up last.
There was a rip in one palm. She would forget them on the
ridge later, along with his small leather journal with a snap
and his pencil.

> *And now, Big Master, I'm broken and bent and*
> *twisted and scarred,*
> *But I've held my job, and Thou knowest, and*
> *Thou will not judge me hard—*

Even from this distance, at night, and while injured in the
head, a sniper like her could see the horses. The shape of
them. The stout sorrel. The shapely bay. Dan the Coward
had not come. The chestnut was spared.

When they came on foot across the meadow with their
rifles, the sniper did not call down to the tent. Their boots
were slow and careful, but occasionally kicked stones in error
and the sound skittered up into the umbrella's spokes, clear
as a bell to the sniper, the spy.

Still, the Damsel in the tent was not alerted. Darwin wrote
books on the phenomenon. Animals die on highway center-
lines. Who mourns them? Why cross the road at all? Fools
snore through air-raid sirens, squadrons buzzing. Books and

books on the subject. Such things are not tragedies. It was his fault too. This sleeper.

Nearing the tent, one rider stopped and checked his rifle. The sniper rolled the rock on her leg. The sniper set the rock down and checked the 30-30, set the sight to her puffy eye and then down again. It was hard to know intent. In minutes they will kill this man, or steal his horses, or both, or neither. Maybe ask to borrow a cup of sugar.

Hey you to the tent would be the neighborly thing. The stone in her hand had no fuse. Just normal granite. Why live on as helpless babies?

The riders were two tall beetles walking under hats, though color is nothing at night, a trick, the cones on the retina inventing color for differentiation only, another ploy, Dan had told her. One of his facts: *there is no such thing as color.*

'Course there is.

No sound when a tree falls either. Sound is a wave.

That makes no sense.

What was logic? Were these real men walking with rifles? Or waves? Projections of men? Dan's theory didn't hold. *Shut up,* she'd told him. *I can't think like that.* Why not then contribute your atoms to a more worthy being? An ant. A slug.

With no moon their stealth raid would be stealthy indeed, a bona fide surprise attack, save for the sniper.

> *Thou knowest my sins are many, and often I've*
> *played the fool—*
> *Whiskey and cards and women, they made me*
> *the devil's tool—*

A sniper changes it. They had not *believed in*, had not *planned for* spies with old borrowed saddle rifles on ridges, not even the possibility, and therefore had no Plan B. An umbrella on a ridge at night looks in profile exactly like a rock on a ridge at night. Sage swaddles the umbrella's edges, blends it. A whiff of whiskey too, a flask inside his jacket in the tent. Are they all Damsels? Is that why we save them?

The riders wove closer through sage, stepping quiet slow toward the man's small fire, just embers now. The Damsel should have doused it. The sniper rubbed her purple cheek. Poor, poor thing. The riders made signals, go left, go right.

> *I was just like a child with money; I flung it*
> > *away with a curse,*
> *Feasting a fawning parasite,*
> > *or glutting a harlot's purse;*
> *Then back to the woods repentant, back to the*
> > *mill or the mine,*
> *I, the worker of workers, everything in my line—*

Allergies.

The man in the tent sneezed. He didn't finish the song, and Lo! the riders had now spied the spy. Not pointing, just looking for a very long time.

A cough in the tent.

The yellow horse stood stiff-legged, ears pricked. The packhorse huffed at the riders, a huge guard dog with no fangs. Ginny set the umbrella down and it rolled sideways. She lay prone on her belly. Her rifle found one man's face.

"I hear you again," said the man in the tent.

Saul was wearing the Christmas jacket. They split, Saul toward the horses, Bowman toward the fire ring. The raid was horse theft. That was the answer. The Damsel would see this too through a window, any rip at all. The 30-30 dipped.

The trouble started when Saul stepped among the animals and the packhorse whinnied objection to the raid, exactly what Ginny herself would do if she was the packhorse. The 30-30 lifted again. No word from the Damsel. The Damsel didn't care, perhaps a narcoleptic, didn't want to hear, didn't want to feel the chill of wrongdoing. There were worse things than horse theft maybe, but no, there wasn't anything worse than horse theft.

Wake up, man. Your life is passing you right outside that zipper.

Maybe the man in the tent was always sleeping, that Damsel, as most do most of their lives, sleep. She was sleepy too. Or the man in the tent was sipping that whiskey, or something stronger to fend off sleep, some tincture in a chalice from the palace, as Damsels are wont to carry. Or was he thinking his tomorrow out? Next year? The hero's pin on his breast for saving the day. She would win the pin herself. She would be in this man's dream tonight.

"Answer me," said the Damsel.

The sniper nearly answered but a sniper's work is to never answer.

"I hear you," said the Damsel. "What do you want?"

Saul continued with the horses. Bowman went to the tent, slender and puppetlike, a man on strings. He searched the ground for something. The man's water jug. He motioned with his rifle. Saul and Bowman switched places, a minuet,

Bowman taking charge of the horses and Saul slipping by him, taking the water jug, who knows why. The jug was levered up. Bowman nodded, *yes*, to the jug. They didn't care about the spy now. Or maybe it was all a show for the spy: the water jug was stepped slow as a bear over the coals in the fire ring. The cap was unscrewed, the jug ready to douse the still-glowing coals, which was exactly what the spy herself would do to confuse a Damsel, to block the tent from the view of a sniper-spy.

"You can't have my horses," said the Damsel.

A still life in moonlight with horses, tent, and jug in meadow. A blue-cowboy diorama.

"Because they're not my horses."

The thieves spoke with hands and guns.

Do it now, the rifle said.

Not to worry, said the hand.

Then Bowman reached for the yellow horse's halter as Saul glanced up at the spy: *Don't ruin it.*

"I can't let you take them."

The 30-30 pressed to the crease of her shoulder. The tent was moving.

"I can see you," the Damsel said.

The yellow horse was gathering in behind Bowman going for the packhorse, then a zipper sound, then a first shot came from the tent, then a second from the .270, very close range, then the tent poles fell together and nylon sagged over the man's thrashing shape, then a third shot from the Ruger. Steam and smoke, copious.

Then Saul was climbing the slope. She ran with the rifle and pistol, dropped over the far lip of the ridge into a crack.

At the top, he panted, bent, hands on hips. The red dog had come. He barked at Saul. Saul aimed his rifle at the dog, a reflex, then dropped it and tried to touch him.

"Come here. Easy now."

The dog growled, backed away. Saul held the umbrella under his armpit. He scanned the ridgetop, then set his rifle at his feet.

"We came in peace," he said, hands in the air.

Ginny was curled around her rifle peeping through a crack. Bowman called something.

"We came for the horses," Saul said.

She read the name on the stock of the 30-30, a set of symbols in gold meaning a man. BARRYMAN.

"Couldn't have him skulking around," he said. "Fly in ointment. Just to slow him."

He tipped his hat back, took it off, rubbed an arm across his brow. A tired man.

"He could've walked back," he said. "Very little wear and tear."

The red dog was barking on.

"At some point," he said, "it's only instinct. The trigger finger."

A little breeze. Her finger found its trigger too. She relaxed. Listened to him.

"I'm sorry about this," he said. "The outcome." He opened the umbrella, twirled it.

"Poor man," he said. "Okay?"

The new herd of horses nickered introductions below.

"Life is messy," he said. "Nothing personal. But yes, you're right."

He spotted something moving down the ridge. He lifted the rifle. Too dark.

"He made a mistake down there too," he said. "An error."

He was tall, handsome, and strong. A bear.

"He should have trusted. Goodwill. Just a little." He stood with boots wide apart. The triangle man. "Life is fragile. Life is quick."

Bowman called again.

"I'm talking to her," Saul said, then turned back to the ridge, speaking out over all of it, the whole thing, as if the ridge itself were a huge deaf animal, needing more volume and articulation due to being reclined on its side, slow or temporarily addled.

"You should probably speak now," he said.

"I love your sister," he said. "I'm trying to do what's right for most."

"You could say something right now," he said. "Say, 'I'm coming back in, we'll work it through.'"

He looked at the sky, then at his wrist as if he had a watch.

"Ella's worried about the future," he said. "The kids."

"It's gone too far," he said. "I apologize for what I did at the tree to you."

"Won't get on my knees," he said. "This is the last time I'll say it."

"I said you'd see reason," he said. "Come around."

A rock was stabbing her back. She shifted.

"This ball has to stop rolling," he said. "Only you can stop it now."

"Arrogant," he said. "People have said that about you."

"From here on," he said. "this is your fault."

He javelined the umbrella off the ridge.

Bowman called up to him. "Leave that dog with her!"

Finishing in the meadow was a lengthy procedure. They left the man in the tent. They spoke freely. They wore headlamps again. The devices protruded from their foreheads eclipsed in glow.

"Better get back."

"Drag him."

They cleared the man's camp with care, poured a hat of water on the coals, kicked away the scorched stones. A good rain would wash the camp down into the water table. Snow was always possible. Hail. The site was flattened and bloody. Other travelers would think of hunters, a small elk butchered here. They dragged the tent behind the man's horses, a great imposition on the tired animals.

She watched it all then walked back along the ridge to the cob. The red dog followed, jumping up at her hands, and she swatted his jowls, then forgot to.

The Damsel: She did not know this man, his private matters, his business.

No one stepped in for her.

$\sim$ —— $\sim$

The Long Trail of the Chicago Kid (cont'd). Episode 6: "Humans as Beasts" or "To the Cabin with the Cob," or maybe "Revelation." As you'll remember, our last episode ("The Ambush" or "The Horse-Theft-Gone-Wrong") ended with our hero seeing a pair of dirty horse thieves about their fiendish work. And yet, and yet, those thieves were disappointments to the Kid. Bunglers. Peace seekers.

Our hero is deep in thought as he drops down behind their clean-up in the meadow, takes a few items from their saddlebags, a canteen of liquor, a Tupperware container of leftover noodles, Milk Duds in a baggie, a pair of perfect socks, a sewing kit Bowman took from Ella during the privacy of Second Watch. Yeah, our hero saw him do it. He crosses the meadow near the mouth of the Narrows. No chance they see him in their preoccupation with the current episode of their own long-running serial, "Out-of-the-Frying-Pan."

The Kid doesn't eat a thing yet.

The horse theft was poorly planned, but there's more to it, he feels sure. The Camera follows him, zooms in on his young blue face full of consternation as he climbs that scree that looks like lava cooling, quick up the scree of the opposite ridge, the Indian Spy's ridge, though he is very tired now, depressed by his thoughts, not in the mood for sweating, climbing, or eating. His mind swimming. He is starved and angry. Anger is a state of mind, of course. Life is a state of mind. Death is a state of mind. But now, somehow, his fragile innards have died watching the murder of this stupid man. It is something inside him he never knew.

He arrives on the Indian Spy's ridge just in time to hear Saul's speeches. They were never heroes at all.

The Camera dollies in behind his ridge walk, which you know, kids, is always the fastest way for a hero in these parts to travel, rather than navigating those pesky zigzagging canyons way down there below. The Camera swings around to face him as he runs into the cob in the weeds by the lake at the top of the Switchbacks.

THE CAMERA: So, how much for your story?

THE KID: I want a million bucks.

The cob is injured. An outrage: a raw flap of flesh is hanging from his shoulder. More skin and hair is ripped away all over his body. It is revolting. It is all revolting.

THE CAMERA: That's a lot of money.

THE KID: Take it or leave it.

Not weeping, but almost weeping. A moment of catharsis, perhaps, buckaroos?

He works the knots, frees the injured animal, leads him away along the ridge, downhill toward the Old Swede's cabin. He sits to think, to rest, once, on the slope. Not too long. He thinks of Dan, a man he did not admire much. All is changed now with new ideas. The Deputy and now the cob abandoned and ripped apart. These people are sloppy. These people commit errors one after another. He will never be like them. They are old. The old are soft. Too much weeping. They wear scars and patches they do not deserve.

THE CAMERA: What's wrong with you?

THE KID: I'm tired of your pansy-ass questions.

On the way to the cabin a fox stops at his feet. He drops a Milk Dud for the fox. The fox devours it. In fact, the fox finds here the most wonderful tastes he's ever tasted, knows he will never in his life taste them again. Tragedy. There will be chocolate and caramel only in dreams thereafter. The Kid takes the fox by the scruff. The fox wriggles in his grip as they glide. He pries the fox's jaws open, pulls the Milk Dud out with his third hand. He stares into the fox's eyes. The fox's

250

body goes limp. Once limp, the Kid sets the Milk Dud back on the fox's tongue, closes his jaws. Only then does the fox spit the Milk Dud out.

THE CAMERA: Poor fox.

THE KID: This is what they've done to me. I'm the fox.

At the Old Swede's cabin, he lies on the cot, the cob's saddle blanket over him. He can't rest, planning his next move. He rises and ties the tassels of the saddle blanket to the tassels of the crocheted blanket. He stitches the untasseled sides closed with strips of burlap from the bags in the outhouse.

THE CAMERA: Are you having a breakdown?

THE KID: Call it a metamorphosis.

There is always a road, a highway, and it runs around a mountain range like this one. Before this century it was probably a path, a horse path the Indians made into the high country for hunting, before the explorers came, the settlers, the ancestors of these people here, then the cowboys. When the Kid finds this road, he will take it to catch a flight to Chicago. How, you ask? The ticket will drop from the sky. Or a train, or maybe he'll hitchhike to Chicago, where he will level the playing field between himself and all the rest of them. Once in Chicago, any Chicago you like, he will take a cab to the lake. The water will be blue and big. No one should underestimate water of that size. By then he'll be clean again, with fresh gray pants and a white shirt from a black and wheeled suitcase he will retrieve from the airport's many circulating rings, each run by its own hidden machine, keeping them spinning. He'll steal a bag for suitable outfits, though it'll take several tries to get the right size, the correct

251

cuts to fit his needs, comfortable new shoes that won't pinch his heels. He'll drink water from a bottle he'll find in an ice-filled cooler at a hotdog cart on a sweltering corner, the lake just there across a green expanse. He will sit on grand marble steps between two enormous stone lions. Terrifying is their silent suggestion to these people. These lions are exactly what they want. These people will walk by the lions without looking. They know already. The same people walk by him too. They can't know who he is yet. He will smile at a girl who will smile back. She will be wearing a skirt that shows her knees and her ankles, too thick even now, so young, the shape of two broken pieces of chalk. He will speak to her anyway. If only she were prettier, he will muse on the cot, if only she were prettier. But no. That's no way to think. He's not one of them yet. He is more than them. He is still him and them and her. Anyway, he's pretty sure. He's been hoodwinked before, he knows. But the girl with chalk legs will be carrying a bag in her small right hand. She will pass the lion on the way up the steps to the great glass doors. He doesn't have a ticket. She will stop and say, "You seem exotic," blushing. Perhaps what charms her is the cowboy hat that he still wears with his airport clothes or the arrowhead on leather around his neck. He would have taken it from an airport shop. The TV was blaring and the shopkeeper wasn't paying attention.

There will be grassy expanses along the lake bigger than the Old Swede's Clearing. There will be tall faces of buildings that look like rock cliffs, have been designed that way, he will see now, with pencils and paper, by architects and small, bent city planners. He will never be one of them.

He will slip into the staff room of the enormous lion-guarded building. The outside door will be left open in the back, propped by a worker on the phone in some argument with a friend who stole something from him, a girlfriend or bag of bullion. There will be tanks of fish everywhere in this hollow cliff, along its stairways. The Kid will climb and look at the porpoises and turtles kept in this city building, eels and starfish behind their big mouths, more like gashes with teeth, which look like mistakes, gaps God forgot to fill, but they're really just mouths, a way to feed themselves, to sustain the life provided. He'll find an ill-fitting uniform in a locker. He'll put the costume on, stand inside the big front doors where staff are checking people's bags for weapons, and dip his hands, all day long, in and out at will.

FOUR

Dog

Crucifixions were once very common. Back in the Holier Lands, the damned were nailed to crosses daily as punishment and pedagogy. Back then, the damned hung until dead, unless the spikes were secured improperly, until the limbs ripped free of the iron and the body fell of its own accord to the sand and dogs. The Baker dreamed of it, the Cooper too. But there are always loopholes. Back then, for example, it was known that if the Master of the Mallet was paid enough, three silver coins on his sill on the morning of the execution, he would swing just so, miss the artery. He would shove the spike artfully between the toes or the webbing of the fingers, draw just enough blood to fool amateurs. "Scream when I swing," the Master would instruct as he held your wrist to the crosspiece. "Make me look good." Eyes blinking at the early morning but blazing white sun, the Roman soldiers distracted, digging holes, watching girls. These were robotic men, Bowman explained, with no education, but Saul stopped Bowman in his tracks (again) right there, objecting strenuously to this last characterization of the Roman men-at-arms.

"Alright," Bowman submitted and passed a fresh roasted turkey leg. "*Educated*, but stupid nonetheless," and Saul accepted the addendum wordlessly, his mouth full.

"Brutes," Dan said.

Dan sat awake in the distance, of course, close enough to hear but not to be listened to. They'd not slept. The turkey leg was an enormous appendage, dripping, messy no matter how careful, and Bowman continued. The soldiers were indeed foolish brutes, while the Master of the Mallet was impressive. A big man with big forearms. Tan, rock-ribbed, a black cloth about his head. The kids of the Holy Land never forgot him, ate all their lentils right up without complaint when he walked past their doors at day's end. The alleys were brown with dust. And in fact the stew was hot and good. He was just a man, mothers told their children. Same as they would be, though not so much the girls. He was always tired, like anyone else, hungry too, fast metabolism since a boy, with a thousand chores at home and his wife nagging him about the leak in the palm-frond roof. The wind across the Ridge of Thieves whistled at the town's back, same as any wind through any line of posts. At sunrise, wolves sang. He had wishes like any man, the Master. "A drop of rain? Is it too much?" The Baker wondered the same thing. The Cooper stared up through the desert's roof, chewed roots to help him sleep, bitter and pulpy. If not paid to miss, the Master aimed well, a professional. The feet were most difficult because of their hard shell of bone. He never learned the name of that bone. But if the damned who were saved screamed well enough, it passed for the real thing. Friends came in middle-night with crowbars, a ladder and knife, medicinal herbs too, lavender and frankincense. They hauled the condemned off to a cave outside the city for rehydration and treatment of wounds, tinctures and creams in sticky brown jars, cotton wads dabbed in cool water.

Dogs snored in the caves' corners, angels with tails instead of wings, thumping on stone. When ready, they hurried the rescue to a different city, hidden in a cart of pigs going to market, a pile of straw below snouts disguising legs, then some henna for his hair, trim his beard, a job on a fishing boat. No one noticed net menders. He would work his way up, become captain someday, join the army if he wanted to see the world, one of the Legions, as the dust settled. Most days no one paid to save those thieves and miscreants, though. The Master of the Mallet brought home his meager wages only, a set price per head from the Governor, from the Caesar of the day, which his wife dropped into the pocket of her aproned skirt. Crowds sat on blankets with children and watched the Master work. Mothers tied napkins around their necks, ate goat cheese on chunks of a fresh loaf purchased from a daughter of the Baker who had been sent out with a full satchel that swung across her slim young body. The men watched her pass, thought of cornering her alone in a manger, chatted about her with the Butcher who had run out of meat so took the day off, who cheated everyone. The Butcher was a bad man. The worst bad man in a town of so many. But no one spoke of his crimes for fear of his reprisals.

⁂

In short, as I've told Ella, when your life gets all confused, off-kilter, and you know you've got nothing to be proud of, mistakes were made, well, step back from the small. For example, we think we see the "mountains" around us now, don't we? Those peaks there seem so solid. The most real, most immovable objects we can observe or think about in a lifetime. Well, that notion, I see now, is a lie. Instead of still and solid, those mountains are purest action, crystalline fluid movement. True, they are a visible, solid *surface*, but they're also proof of faults intersecting far below, reflecting only the smallest hint of the tumult, the titanic subsurface battles that dwarf any human action, idea, existence. It's a matter of scale and vision. Bowman is big on this.

What I think is, to God, a mountain is a liquid wave that breaks over ten million years. Not a tenth of one of His seconds.

Can you see the wave now?

Not stone at all.

The trick to peace of mind, to Heaven on earth, to surviving suffering, is to see the mountain as a God would. Molten rock caught in an illusion of stillness by the limits of the human retina.

I'm trying to say to *think big* in times of crisis.

Just as your mind wants to cave in.

Move past what you think you can't move past. Then think bigger. Expand. Look onward to the Grand Scale.

❧ —— ❧

"Maybe we're twins," Little Danny had suggested once to Little Ginny, hooked side by side by heels and small round butts on a pasture fence, knives loose in bloody hands.

A branding.

Little Ella was one post down, miles away, elbows over the top rail, listening, watching three big men tackle a spotted calf in the thick dust and wicked sun.

"No," Ginny'd said, "I'm nothing like you."

That time, Ella climbed over, dropped down, and ran into the fray, a makeshift corral. She held the syringe high and the bucket low, pencil and paper in her back pocket since even then Ella did all the tallying, one slash plus four makes five on torn-off cardboard. Steer or heifer. The men circled in over the calf's small balls. They waved Ginny in for cutting.

"Steer!"

An old man's only job was to sharpen knives. He sat in the shade with the whetstone sipping Coke. Ginny stood over the little bull. The big men held him down, her heel on his hip.

Even in this collective memory, her knife signified something to all.

She slid the knife in not without compassion. This was tradition. These men, after all, invented the procedure, and they had testicles too. The little bull's legs were tied and dragged apart by lassos to straight-legged roping horses. How a workhorse hates a cow! Anyone can see it. Disdain. It had to do with pecking order. Horses worked. Cows did not. Aging horses grazed far fields till their knees went. The bullets came quick and unseen.

After the balls were cut and the waddle sliced free, Dan cauterized the horns. Steam rose and the calf moaned, but not moaning so much as when the brand came. The fire was coal and so very hot. The man rocked the brand in the coals then rocked it in the fur with the same motion. The brand was old and hand-forged, original to the Grannie's line. A squarish V4, same as over the gate coming in.

"Why must it be done?" Ella asked. "Nowadays?"

"Brand's got to be clear or there's no reason for the brand."

Moaning was not the word. Not bellowing either. The calf's skin smoked. His tongue lolled and jumped a foot from his mouth. His mother stood off and considered charging. Her own brand was three times bigger. Years had stretched it across her hide. The men kept their eyes peeled. She was nine hundred pounds or better. Plenty of weight for insurrection. But she was slow and ineffectual, lots of doubt. She must've known too. Seen herself as helpless. How else to explain it. A cow is mighty and can run you right down. But has it happened to you yet?

Why not for love? Why not for her offspring? Why not for any suffering other?

Hard to understand it.

I don't.

Ginny would never have children, whereas this *heifer* lived on and on and the brand went on stretching, since she dropped calves reliably each spring, big strong ones that fattened up well.

She trotted back with the bucket of scrotums floating. Ball sacks softer than velvet. The fur on them was a gorgeous marbled masterpiece even from calves that looked plain from afar. Inside out the sack was white-filmy oyster flesh. The testicles sank out of view in the bloody water. She lifted one out, spun it like a lasso. Ella back on the fence screeched at being splattered. It was long, red, and raw, pulled from deep in the body. Even a girl had to squirm. Ginny tossed a pretty scrotum at Dan. He capped his nose with it to show off then jumped down and chased her. She screamed exactly like a girl.

"Okay, so maybe our *mothers* were twins then!" Dan called.

"No!" Ginny called. "We don't look a thing alike!"

Ella bent for the syringe in the dirt. She'd dropped it at his astounding stupidity. She picked it up along with an old rusted buckle that had lain there for a century. *Stop trying,* she might've told him. *It'll end in tears:* Grannie's line.

The calf bounded up when the lasso loosed. He was surprised to be free, leaped away, wove toward mother to nuzzle and suck. They hate humans, of course.

Grannie bellowed for more coal. She was tall and angular under her black umbrella. She whistled and Ella sprinted, always thinking reward came with goodness and obedience.

All three were recalled to this memory now—each to their own vivid versions of it—Ginny, as she ran the ridge to the Old Swede's cabin, Ella, as she packed up Elk Valley camp breakfast, Dan, as he saddled mules in a separate universe just steps away, hurrying the job to get to the cabin sooner, an error he knew he'd pay for later—and all their lives too, they would recall it, but none knew all but you and me.

Once Grannie told the Dear Ones: *A dog is not wild like a wolf or coyote. He's an invention of man, a long-standing hybrid. No such thing as a purebred dog. He was born of ancient garbage pits. No real wolf would live on shit and rats. The neediest wolves tolerated men, ate from their hands. They guarded the town when the men were gone. The dog does not exist without man though man exists without the dog. It is an uneven arrangement, and the dog has not forgotten the debt. For this reason, the dog can always be trusted. Always listen to the dog.*

She barely heard.

When she found the cob was missing, she spun, forgot the man in the tent. She stared out over the top of the Switchbacks at the morning gray mounds of the world below. Elk Valley, a twist of camp smoke far off. She called to the cob like a dog. When he didn't come, she ran. She followed his hoofprints next to boot prints from the mud at the little lake.

The ridge declined toward the Old Swede's. The roof lay in a hollow of yellow bluffs. She shuffle-ran, then ran, then walked when she couldn't run. In the trees she tripped and tumbled. They'd slept on the shelf in the Old Swede's rafters as children, a frightening-exhilarating coffin space, the rotting wood so near the nose, had been hoisted up on a father's shoulders, or granddad's if fathers were in short supply, uncles, toes in clavicles, ankles to necks, little hands reaching to catch the beam, sweating from the too-hot woodstove.

She zigzagged and tripped. The red dog drank at the creek and she passed him and he passed her. They'd cut messages to the future in the logs. *Rest in Peace* if a bird had cracked its noggin into the single window, buried by creek or stumps with a cross and a name given after death.

GINNY LOVES DAN.

She was no longer hungry. A waste. Always food at the Old Swede's.

She'd fucked Shaw in the back room once. He'd slipped out the back window when Dan came home early calling *What's for dinner*, and for this, she admitted now, she deserved horse theft. She'd sucked his cock. He'd laughed at Dan and pretended not to. For this, she deserved more than horse theft. She was nothing, now, without the cob. She'd laughed with

Shaw only because people laugh when people laugh. Only the oldest and wisest don't laugh at those times. Or the blind.

She stopped short at the edge of the clearing. She could not step into it yet. The porch roof—she knew—was tar paper, while the main pitches were tin pounded flat, a rusty color. She sat by a tree with the red dog beside her. She listened for cabin sounds and thought about sin, a new topic. She could smell the cob but could not look. The blind have an advantage there. The red dog was more brown than red. She didn't love the red dog. She loved the cob. The old, square roof nails—she knew, why look when you know?—were an army marching up, tacking overlapping seams of the tin, up and across, up and across, like fire on a hill. There were other things: only pretty birds got a burial, blue jays or little yellow birds, red. Why? And why would the old trapper have bothered with sills? The red dog had an unpleasant odor. Sills are rampant in our new age, but back then, the old man had to haul the window all the way in, sacrifice a mule's back for this bit of translucent prettiment. Why? The roof nails, when she looked, would be rising out of the roof seams, the result of swollen wood drying and squeezing, of neglect and all-natural processes, rates of expansion vs. contraction of wood, tin, and iron. Starvation of the body is a thing of the past. Starvation of the soul is another matter. She'd fucked him in his barn. She'd fucked him on the rug with blue tassels. She'd fucked him laughing at the world, this trick she was playing on it. There was something missing inside her. For this, a person needs a transplant of some kind, a new soul. Horse theft, she now saw, was only the beginning of the procedure.

265

She crossed the clearing without looking at the cob at the other end, tail swishing, the boy beside him. Under the porch roof in a nest, chicks' small heads bobbed up. Swallows. The door was propped open with a rusted gas can. She lifted it. Five gallons, mostly full. There was a dirty rag stuffed in the spout. The dog barked at the cob and boy. The dog had clearly arrived at some plan. The can had clearly once been kicked by a mule. The scent of gas was very strong despite the rag. There was no floor under the porch, just dirt, bits of eggshell. The bottom logs were rotting. Inside, the floor was wide pine with the huge old table. The cob nickered to her but she was not ready and the human was boss so he'd have to wait. The room was smaller than her mind had made it. The logs were gray. She'd have liked to have known the red dog's plan, the scheme as to the cob and boy. How to get it? The cob nickered again. The red dog barked off the porch. She could hear his hackles up. No need to see the dog at all. The dog's fur had gold too, not just brown.

A raven's nest had fallen behind the woodstove. The nest was huge, a pick-up stick construction of blackened sticks. Its fall, to the raven, must have been catastrophic. Mouse shit was scattered amid the cans knocked over and rolled about below the table. A dog should get tired of barking but, to be fair, it's his only job. The grain of the tabletop was stained from long-dried blood and cabbage heads split by cleavers. She'd fucked someone on a table once. He'd flung his coat down for her. The entrancement of secrets. On this table, a man had lain for stitches, had been horsing around with some slut, his boot run through by a forgotten nail, ripped his foot wide open after he fucked her. The table was pine. A mallet had been used to drive in pegs and left prints at joints. Babies had probably been born on this table. Dan had always wanted babies. Who knew if it was true. No one living could say they saw a baby born here. The red dog was going crazy off the porch now, barking so hard his paws came off the ground.

Relax, she might say to him. *Can't stop the future.*

She took a catnap on the cot as the dog barked at whatever that strange boy was doing with her cob. She blocked the message the red dog was sending her, another sin. *Can't change the world. Accept the world with all its flaws. The world is what it is, take a catnap.*

She rose on the edge of the cot. Plan A had arrived at last. She set the pistol in her mouth, shifted the safety off. When the finger didn't twitch, she waited on the cot for Plan B.

The dog was getting hoarse.

Plan B: She moved the apple crate aside from under the window. Underneath was a square of floor that opened with a rope to a crawl space. She set her valuables inside. The pocketknife and the man in the tent's canteen. She dropped the cover and replaced the apple crate. She set the pistol on the table. Plan C: Sabotage. She unlatched the big gray door to the mother-of-a-woodstove. She propped the door open with the 30-30 standing. She poured ash down the barrel, mashed bits of charred log in small lumps, shoved it all down with the curtain rod. She returned to the apple crate for the canteen, drank, then trickled a little down for a slurry. More char, the man in the tent's bottle cap in her pocket. A tack from between the floorboards. More ash. More char. Repeat. She returned the canteen to the crawl space. The boy was calling.

"Hey! Whatcha doing in there?"

She returned the curtain rod, swept the mess up. A dollop of spit for luck. If the Creature stole her rifle, it would blow his head off.

The dog went quiet. Someone was talking to the red dog. A bird flew past the door to her nest. Her landing on the rim was graceless feathers. Six a.m., no later. She laid the rifle on the table. She checked the pistol's chamber.

The cob was a hundred paces distant and in costume. His mane didn't show. He had a hood on his head that read IDAHO'S BEST. Burlap. Holes were cut for the eyes and ears. The noseband was visible. A stick of dynamite was tied at his mouth to the bit. She thought she'd taken all of it, buried it in a snowfield. The boy pointed to it.

"See?"

The little fuse hung limp. Scissors had been used for the eye- and earholes. The cob was saddled but had no saddle blanket. His pannier hung in a tree at the edge of the clearing. There was a battered tin pot for his water. She would take the pot when finished here.

Ginny skirted the tree edge. The pistol hung at the end of her hand. The boy also wore a costume. Dan's boots, a colorful cape with burlap fringe.

The red dog followed her. She stopped at the edge straight on from the cob.

The cob was ten times bigger than the boy. The boy's hand rested on the cob's shoulder, a friendly gesture. A pile of chain lay at his feet, an old trap.

"Hey there, boy," she called, and the cob lifted his hooded head. She whistled and the cob rolled the bit. The stick of dynamite seesawed. It looked to Ginny just like dusty old paper. She couldn't focus on it. The boy held the cob's reins in one fist and a stick with a big nail under that arm. The stick was the red of Ginny's old red barn.

His cuffs were dirty. Piping. His hat was enormous, filthy. He was taller than she but thin, wiry. She'd never really looked him over before. She wove in and out at the edge of the trees, wanting to see all the cob. He walked the cob to keep her facing him, a show horse. The clearing was made up of hundreds of stumps, a long slender oval emptiness, the cabin at the far end.

"I want my horse," Ginny said.

"He's injured," said the boy. "That's a forfeit."

The flap of skin had dried, a flag of jerky.

Ginny went on dangling, not aiming, the pistol. She saw no other weapons present but the stick and the dynamite. Rusted cans. Dan's boots were an old pair. Why not throw them away? The boy slid around the cob as Ginny slid around the clearing. Now she saw an iron wedge stuck in a stump, the last of a splitting maul.

"I want my horse."

"We all have wants and wishes."

"Some are losers every single time."

"Screw you."

"That's my blanket. My Grannie made it."

"Mine now."

"You've been crying," she noticed.

"So."

"I'll take him now."

"I want to go with you," he said. "I'm done with them." He tipped his head at the ridge. "It's bull crap, their cowboy act."

"You won't be coming with me," Ginny said. "I assure you."

"I'm going to blow your horse sky-high then."

No sudden moves, now. "You can't kill the cob."

"I sure can."

"You can't."

"I will."

"That's not real dynamite you got tied on him. Where would you get dynamite?"

"I stole it from them in the night. Saul stole it from some mine. You know he did."

"No one kills the horse."

"I want to go with you."

Her lips were broken and red and dabbed with spit.

"Those cowboys are pure farce," he said. "I've decided to go pirate now."

"I'm not a pirate."

"Cowboys and Indians are all mixed up. I'm with the pirates now."

Strange to see Grannie's blanket in a clearing, the scalloped edge dragging the ground. The kid lifted the old chain to his shoulder, as if to get going. Ginny let her eyes flick to the ridges.

"They won't arrive for some time," he said.

She'd fucked Shaw in a tent on a hunting trip with many people, a big tent, Dan on one side, Shaw on the other, or not fucking exactly, an animal act, her hand had dropped down inside some flannel or cotton print. These group trips were rare. Only most inclement weather drove them into cook tents. Grannie had been surprised by nothing. She had been ashamed of nothing. She was ashamed of the idea

270

of shame. *Humans are just animals*, she said. *Animals can be forgiven for anything.*

"I'll have my horse," she said, no longer negotiating. "We'll go separate ways."

She stepped slow into the clearing. The stumps were round and gray with time and decline. *Stop*, she said to the thought. *Stop it.*

"Not too close," he said. "Stop there, please." Ten paces away. "I want to travel the world with you. The high seas, what have you. I've decided. I'm with you."

Possibly six feet tall someday, that boy. But not yet. His cape was only stitched burlap to crochet. Ginny's hands shook. Grannie did not believe in breaking down. Breakdown was another of those states of mind. *Do not allow a breakdown. It's weak.* Grannie had said so to the sick cows, to folks dizzy with locoweed. Ginny stumbled and the boy saw. She'd shot a brown bear like a boy would. *Bam. Bam. Bam.* No mercy for the bear. Just an animal. No trouble with killing. No guilt, no blame.

"That dynamite's fake," Ginny said. "But take it off my cob. I don't like it."

"Don't boss me," said the kid.

Ginny never confided in Grannie. Never confided in anyone truly. Truths like: she loved adultery. Arrogance is probably why. This is a confession, Grannie, to save the cob from this boy. Since I am not ashamed. Ella got beauty and I got something else. Arrogance.

"Take the mask off my cob," she said, knees weak for once. "That mask on his face is making me sick."

"I don't care if you're sick," said the kid. "I'll take your rifle and pistol while we're at it." His face was a mess. His arm was in some kind of sling.

"That won't work."

He bent and lifted a pile of burlap she hadn't noticed. He flung it over the cob's back.

"What's on that blanket."

"You can smell it. I dribbled gas on it, an accelerant."

"I know what gas is for."

The cob yawned, opened up his already wide-open mouth, a hideous and undignified gesture.

"Blackmail," she said.

"Blackmail, blood booty, scalawags, all of it," said the kid. "The cob's hostage for the pistol and rifle too. Easier to just let me come with you."

"I'm not going anywhere you want to go."

"Sad about the deputy."

"What deputy?"

"The man in the tent. An officer of the law, yet."

"It's more than sad," Ginny said.

"You sat and watched."

"How do you know?"

He had a box of matches now.

"That's not funny."

The middle of the box slid in and out and his expression got lewd. Ginny lifted the pistol.

"I have things to do."

"I'm young," he said. "But how you all lie and lie." The stick with the nail dropped to one of Dan's boots. The kid dropped the cob's bridle and lit a match. The cob just stood there.

"Last chance," said the kid. "Take it or leave it."

His flame was tiny. The wind blew it out. He lit another at arm's length.

"All right," she said. "I'll trade."

"Where's your stuff?"

"What stuff?"

"Where's your stuff." He waved the match at the cob.

"A hole under the woodbox."

He blew the second match out. Struck another.

"Stop that," Ginny said.

"Don't tell me what to do."

She stepped, stopped herself, two stumps from the cob. The fire barely visible in the morning light. She wound by the stumps behind the cob. He dipped under the cob's legs, hide-and-seek, kept the cob between them, sniffling then weeping only. When his match burned out, he struck the box with another.

"You're stupid. Get back." He blew on his hand. He went back around the cob's rump. He was so thin. His lips were cracked. "You're crazy." The sun was cooking him.

"Maybe I don't want him," she said.

"You like horses better than people."

"I hate everyone."

"You like this cob."

"Horses." She shrugged.

"I shoved a firecracker up a cat's ass once."

"I never did that."

"Liar," he said. "Everyone did."

"I guess you're right."

"Don't try agreeing with me," he said. "I see what you're doing."

"I don't know what you mean."

"Liar liar liar liar."

Her arm was getting tired. She remembered the pistol in her hand when it slipped a little.

"They're coming," she said. "You can go home with them. They'll tend to your wounds."

"What wounds?" he said. "I'm running this thing."

"Okay."

"I'm havin' fun I said." His teeth clenched.

"Okay."

"More tricks," he said. "You should look at yourself."

His face was all screwed up. He sobbed.

"I'll go get the rifle then," Ginny said. The red dog barked at her as she walked, warning about error, the dangers thereof. Don't make one now.

"Be quick," the boy said. "Chop-chop." He was swinging the rusty chain over his head. It clanged at her. His teeth were locked together in a grimace followed by a live snake of iron links that flew at her boots and snapped back harmless. She stared at the familiar thing between them, but had no idea where she'd seen it.

It happened fast after that. It started with her mouth, which said only one small thing to the boy, but said that thing without asking her brain for permission, something like *You prick*, or *Fuck off you little rapist prick*, or *You little fucking rapist cunt motherfucker*. Well, Ginny never was much for control.

So the matchbox slid open. The kid made to strike another one, but didn't; the whole box went up with a flint-white flash. The skirt of the cob's blanket ignited. IDAHO'S BEST started burning around the horse face. The cob reared back and screamed, tossing his hooves at an invisible enemy, since aren't they all? The fire was small at first, a fringe. The cob trotted, then veered disbelieving, then swerved in canter around the stumps and toward trees, jumped and stumbled, dragged himself up, tripped, swerved back. A galloping flame. He could go fast. Ginny never knew. She was running behind him the whole way. His head tossed as his legs kicked at her. Keep back. He bucked and banged, burning brighter across his back, his hood, a horse scream. The sky wheeled. His back, all fire, arched. Things are predictable once the thing begins. Maybe she'd been after death herself, or looking for death both together. None of this was right or real as she tripped and fell after his smoking speed. The boy in his cape escaped to the trees. She heard weeping there. *Stick with the cob*, she thought. The Flaming Horse, plunging into the woods. He tripped in the chaos of brambles. She crawled expecting the explosion, for his head to blow clean off, and she wanted and didn't want to be there when it blasted. She caught him back at the brush at the edge of the clearing. She tried to pull the blanket off but the heat was too much for her girl hands.

"What's wrong with you?" someone called. "What's wrong with you?"

This was the central question. The cob was up again crawling over a downed tree. The burning hair was terrible. The pistol now seemed the only answer. Later, she remembered no explosion, found no evidence of one. The fuse was a zip tie threaded through rolled-up paper. She got as close as she could before the shot. His kick only grazed her.

∞ —— ∞

Before the girl came, the bear sat on a ridge over a great valley. The armies milled below on horses, thousands. They ran at each other. They slashed necks, ran spears through guts. Cannons on wheels blasted bright from muzzles knocking down legions like pins. Flags waved. Flags and flags. The bear had no flags and he felt naked somehow without them, naturally enough. He ran home to his cave. He chewed a buffalo leg. The men he painted after that did the strangest things on the cave wall. He bent down and prayed to the sky, how silly. We feel his confusion and his hope, his longing more intensely, his despair. We consider a bottle of gin. These men, these armies, they were so many. And the bear had no one. His wife had died in the battle somehow, a nurse, some mistake perhaps, but mistakes were natural too, as wars were. He traveled back to the battlefield in the moon a few nights after, tried to catch the meaning, tasted the blood. The dead were fetid and poison, bad food. He found arrowheads and nibbled them. He walked home with the thought of his wife.

❧ —— ❧

She woke in the trees. A metallic green bee buzzed her face, black and yellow stripes on abdomen, copper green head shimmering the thorax, antennae like horns weighing the forehead. This was the Last of Her First Chapters, the First of Her Last. She never liked school much. She liked horses. She liked Dan and the back seat. The berry picker can either stay with her family to the end of time, picking berries, etc., or go with the bear and live in his cave with him. Ginny wanted both. She should have both. She can't have both.

276

When she woke again, lichens. Silk thread on his dog face, the work of spiders. Smoke. Meat burning. She brushed an ant away. She kneeled in the mud. The pool moved clockwise. And, too, if Horse (long dead) had encountered a Richter scale implanted under that walnut tree there amid his Herd the day of that great eruption—ten million years back, twenty million—he'd have turned tail, set hind hooves flying, and bucked the strange invader over, crushing its glass dials and gauges, the needles going crazy inside the machine's glass eyeballs, only finally departing from the broken thing to gallop off, to rein in a mare agitated by the metallic crash, while the foals circled in at his absence, shy, a little velvet gang of them, curious to sniff the steel casing, the riveted corners, quickly retreating on spindle legs when the foreign-smelling object seemed to threaten to pounce. The caveman was not a twinkle in God's eye yet. He was eons away still, as was algebra, steel, and earthquake prediction.

Queen of all dead.

When she woke in the cabin, she made eleven little bombs with cans of peas, gas, and rags. She set the bombs in the apple crate. The grass still burned around the cob. The bullet hole was small and harmless looking. She broke the window for a draft, wrapped several pieces of glass in burlap, set the glass in the apple crate for some unknown, pending use, also the curtain rod and iron wedge. A tooth was broken. She jabbed a finger in. Her hands would shake a little now forever. A ram stood at the bluff top, a stupid animal with a ramrod head. She bellowed at it and the ram bolted and then the sky was all alone again. She wore a new crushed straw hat from a peg. Unless she invented the hat. She never saw it again, anyhow.

There are always more matches in a cabin. They're between the floorboards by the stove. Seven she found. She struck one to a frayed bit of burlap bag. She balled it up when it caught, set the flaming bundle amid the bits of newsprint and pine on the back wall. She, Ginny—the teller now and the audience too—had learned all this in twelfth grade, Mrs. Pilcher speaking from the dead. A beak nose. Pantsuits and a piece of chalk for dividing the story into parts, lines and arrows in chalk like a flaming horse as she torched the cabin.

Pay attention, Virginia. I told you. A swat with a ruler. Fancy seeing you here, Mrs. Pilcher. *But I'm not here, I am in your mind. That's where everyone is. The girl and the bear. Dan is here. Saul is here. Ella is here. Shaw is here. Immortal and incorruptible. You can't kill us off with fire and lead.*

Who's Shaw again?

Shaw is that man you fucked in the tack room.

I don't remember him.

He started all this.

He can't have started it if I don't remember him.

Don't play with matches, Virginia. Burn the cabin down or don't burn it down.

After the cabin came another decision. Maybe the hardest. Should she just go on living in the mountains till she died? And then how to go about that living? Run, or lie in wait?

She watched the fire consume the back wall. Smoke trailed to the window and out. She propped the door open with the gas can still nearly half full. She stood in the clearing with the red dog and the apple crate.

The cabin was smoking well. A few rain clouds were finally coming from the west. The back wall was all but gone before Ginny remembered the chicks. She dragged the table to the door to reach them. She turned the table on its side to drag it, though it had been built in the cabin and would never leave. The chair was already ablaze. The chicks' squeaks were impossible to hear. The mother bird was going crazy in the airspace.

She sat with the cob and was sure she heard voices. *My Darling Horse Killer, My Liar to All, My Thief: fire is a miracle. Burn yourself alive.*

The wind shifted. She drank from a spring. She looked for dragonflies. They were gone. They hate smoke. They'd hate it when the gas can blew.

Before going, she returned to the clearing one more time, cupped her hands around her mouth, called out up into the hollow.

"Don't fire the rifle!"

Bluff and wind bluffing.

"Don't touch the 30-30!"

After the cabin, she trudged after the ram. There is no backpack in the world for an apple crate. She carried it under one arm then switched. Once she set the apple crate down and left it. She went back for it, carried it on her head like a tribal female. She followed the ram all the next day. She exploded a tree with her first bomb and match. She warmed herself at the tree burning. She carried a flaming branch as she followed the ram. Her bombs were wonderful. She wished she could throw farther. The ram watched the tree from a parallel ridge. Or it was a story.

She thought of the boy and Dan and her sister. No plane would see the smoke. She dried her clothes around the tree. She warmed herself naked as Eve on slush since the world had changed all snowy now. God made only Adam in his own image. Eve was made from Adam's rib, but later. God made horses and cows and grain before he made man to farm and ranch. But mules were not made by God at all. Mules were created by horses and donkeys. Was mule then some new freedom? Or sacrilege? Some rebellion?

She wrapped small coals in green leaves, carried fire in the apple crate.

The ram was wily but in snow it was impossible to hide from her. The ram wanted to live. Rams sleep too. She followed him on the ridges and down the rock faces. She wore burlap, drank water. Green beans. Mushroom soup. Succotash in pictures on cans. Once she saw a canine playing with a raven, some kind of war game. The ram was used to her. He made incorrect assumptions about goodwill. She flung rocks and he barely flinched. She followed. She slept in cracks in rocks. It snowed and stopped snowing. A human can live on its own tissue for up to two months, called self-digestion. Ginny self-digested. Velvet antlers are also nourishing, though hardly plentiful. Kill the deer for the antler. Eat the meat, leave the antler. If your knife is gone, simply pound meat to a pulp with a rock. A pounded bird wastes nothing. Elk and rabbit excrement can thicken soup. She herded a rabbit, tackled it. Gall is an excellent spice. Follow deer to salt licks and lick salt with the deer. Blood should never be wasted. It's nearly milk as far as vitamins and absorption. Four sips of blood is equivalent to ten fresh eggs. Keep a jug of it. But also look for eggs. The great explorers were of mixed opinion about the nutritional value of rawhide.

The ram had full curl. She did not eat the red dog. Cannibalism. The red dog slept right beside her. When close enough one match and she tossed the bomb and the ram jumped.

Six bombs left.

The cliff the ram had jumped was only a cliff. When she arrived, the ram reeked. It snowed again. She cut him open with window glass. She retched at the stink of his insides scrambled. She pulled all his innards out, chucked them. The hair on her neck tingled. The bears would be coming soon. The sky was white. She saw breath as she worked. The red dog licked the blood pool.

The branches broke under the weight of freezing sleet as she cut a back leg free. She lugged the leg away. She climbed to a ledge over a low valley into an archway to a cave. The red dog followed. The leg made a bloody line in the snow, zigzagged the path she made climbing up. There was a little pit dug in the ground in the cave and she built a fire with the one ember that had survived the day. Why waste ammo? She watched for bears in the archway. She hauled wood up to the ledge, dried it around the fire before setting it on. She lay on the ground when the smoke got thick. She went back for a second back leg the second day, scared the bears away with growls and fire.

She cut the leg to strips and hung the strips on a lean-to she cut from willow saplings and lashed with soggy reeds. The blood made pools that reflected the fire. She slept under burlap the first night. The second she hacked pine branches down with the wedge, dragged them up to her cave and fanned them around her sleeping place.

Night came more often than it used to. She set stones in the fire. She rolled them out with sticks when hot enough. She slept with the stones under the pine canopy. Her sleeping place, then, was wonderfully warm from their radiance. She woke curled around a stone. She slept in her boots. She ate the ram for three days. She found a painting in the cave, a hand, she set her hand on the hand, stared, then realized it was her own hand the whole time, no painting at all. She packed the ram jerky in the burlap with all her other belongings and went to spy on the bears.

⁂

Consider this too: we are each separate little dinghies, all floating alone but together, all caught in the same currents in the same ocean: a human lifetime. I'm back on the Grand Scale here. We must stick together in the terrible and mighty currents, in calm then storm. In the sun of noon and cold of night we must hold to each other, whatever height of waves or depth of water, whatever creature bumps our hulls, whatever winged beast careens. We must bind together to arrive at the shores we seek together. This is a serious and dangerous duty. In the great struggles of history, many have died for *the good of the many*, for *the right*. We must grip each other's bows and gunwales, make webs of boats, a raft. We must tie stout knots. And if one boat is taken by a wave, if it drifts too far from the raft, we must fling ourselves across the widening gap to it, lean out over the deep, grip its oar. *Haul in, haul in,* and we do, by God. Swim if you must. Ropes, yes, when the distance is too far for swimming or when the sea is rough or swirling with eels. Tender some simple thanks to God it's not you drifting, not yet. It will be someday. Stupidity can be the cause, yes, and laziness too, or selfishness, but drifts are blameless, innocent, and pure, provoked by unseen forces: winds, subsurface events, acts of God we cannot comprehend, unavoidable even given best intentions. We are honor bound to give aid.

But the straying mariner is honor bound also. His duty is to offer an oar across the gap, to catch hold of the rope thrown to him, to pull back to the boats with all his might, to make the greatest effort to save himself, to paddle, to swim, to haul his craft back through the waves. In short, he is honor bound to save himself. His life is a borrowed property, while he lives it, and so must be preserved. The duty of each boat is equal and opposite and reciprocal.

But even assuming all duties are discharged on either side, here is a third case to consider. If the big raft can't reach the wandering dinghy in time, despite its best efforts, if the boat adrift can't be caught, if the vanishing mariner can't haul himself back due to injury or confusion or a rogue wave rolling in, if a terrible fluke of this kind should occur, and there's no changing it, well, then and only then is the raft released from its duty to the departed. There and then the duty shifts, becomes a duty to the safety and survival of the majority. What I mean is there are limited cases that can arise and necessarily alter the laws governing acceptable human behavior. When it's life or death, it's clear as clear.

But Ginny, I see now, is not to be filed under this header. She belongs to the fourth case.

When the unmoored dinghy not only refuses but impairs assistance, imperiling the flotilla so urgently trying to help its captain, well, in that instance, the duty to rescue is inverted. The rules of the Lone Wolf apply.

❧ —— ❧

"Tell me this," Dan said that morning in Elk Valley after the Narrows. He was now saddler to the yellow horse and the packhorse, the newest members of the line, his hands quick about muscles and knots, his sleeves rolled to elbows slick with sweat already though the sun was just peeking behind the peaks in a hide-and-seek of blinding bursts, his shirt a stink of sweat and filth, his eye patch already become obscene, blood and puss and ooze, a living thing clinging to his face—they didn't speak of it—the fabric grafting day by day onto him—attaching whole—to his nose, his jaw. It would never come off. They tried not to look at it. "How can that idiot deputy get by without horses? Way out here?" He grimaced. Tried to laugh.

"Your girth is twisted," Maul said. "Pay attention."

Dan fixed the girth and said—reluctant—"You boys dispatch him?"

He did not look up from his work, the hot yellow breathing swell.

"That packsaddle's crooked," Ella said. "Better redo it."

"I guess the idiot doesn't need horses now," Maul said. "Otherwise they wouldn't be here. Would they."

"It really is," Ella said. "Catawampus."

She asked Dan for another joke. "A joke makes time fly."

"Good ones do," Bowman said.

"Cowboy rides into town in a cloud of dust," Dan said as he sat down heavy on a rock that presented. His legs sprawled. He let the sun cook him as a smallish slog of words unspooled: "The townsfolk come running into dust of their own making, climb their hands up the Cowboy's dirty jeans. *Help us, Help us. A man's robbed our bank. All our savings.*

"Where's the bank? he says. Which way? The townsfolk point him in the correct direction. What's he look like? The devil?

"*Like the devil,* they say. *Yes, that's right!*

"They press their hands to their faces in fright and dismay. They describe the monster, fast on the draw, a face very different from theirs, dark and hairy and dangerous.

"*Actually, he looks a bit like you.*"

Saul checked the knots tying the blue chair to the yellow horse.

"The Cowboy is the Prince of the Land," Dan said.

"Is that right."

"Cowboys wear white hats for a reason."

"Is that right."

On the Switchbacks, the mules walked slowly. The second little gray walked with his mouth open. The tallest mule limped but not bad. The buckskin jenny balked at a hairpin. Maul dragged but she wouldn't budge. He offered handfuls of oats and then she did. The black mule wanted to pass. Maul reasoned with them on ledges without thinking of the

285

nothing behind him. Water jugs were ballast and drummed their ribs. The packhorse carried the deputy's gear. The yellow horse came last with the chair.

At the steepest switches, the underbellies of the animals could be seen from below, the leather circumnavigating their bodies, the stirrups, the heels of boots. They could be identified by scent now: Saul, sharp sour sweat. Bowman, a piney nub, caramel and eggs. Maul, mules and creosote. Ella's braids were new and tight and she smelled like braids, like Ginny at times, looked like her too from certain angles naked in ponds. She'd seen Dan looking, turned her back to his stares, thinking he wanted her maybe, not knowing he was engaged in simple assessment. The hair between her legs was pale brown and not thick at all, which surprised him. Her sister's was thick. Her ass was round and smooth still. "Stop looking," she'd say but then turn and drop her hands. Once offered, he looked away. He himself was greasy with mule balm. Maul had plenty of balm. Dan balmed the mules as Maul commanded.

At the turns, they rested. The horses' mouths dripped green slime that slopped their knees and dried there. Hawks swept by, sped by. They knew the hawk's idea. A rabbit. An old horse. Rabbits were only plan B. Plan A was wait for a stagger. This hawk had seen it all before. The hawk was patient. The hawk would float down. Peck the eyes. Tug the meat, toss it up, swallow: *Come, friends. Eat with me.* The little gray's head hung down. Maul watched him, urged him kindly.

Maul threw a rock. The hawk tipped its wings. The rock fell. The hawk dove.

They wove around a horseshoe ledge under a waterfall. The animals shied, pulled back, and the rumps were pushed from behind. Mist misted their faces. Rocks fell away from hooves. A hoof slipped off but the other three held. Stepping to the ridgetop, they were almost happy, almost real friends. The mountains rippled off. Creeks they'd walked looked foreign and far. At a small lake on top, weeds, and cob tracks everywhere around it. Boots. They all plowed happy into the steaming surface. The hawk ruffled on a rock, lifted his wings to keep steady. Dan gave him the finger. They laughed.

They tasted smoke before they saw flames or smoke. Nearly midday. Clouds.

"Oh, for a bunk," Maul said.

"We were never staying overnight," Saul said.

They rode fast at last. Fire was eating the cabin roof—how copious, how billowing the flames. Downhill they let gravity dictate the tilt of their pelvises, trying to free the horses' backs. The mules got no such help. The loads no longer hung level. They'd been packed too hastily that day. They descended and the slope widened and split and encircled the hollow around the cabin. Bowman split left. Saul split right and the rest followed.

"Where's he going?" Dan asked.

The bay trotted the mossy left shoulder then disappeared into tall straight pines.

"Flanking her," Saul said.

The mules were restless with the smoke coming up.

"Maybe I'll hold them here," Maul said.

"Hold them," Saul said. "Don't hold them. I'm going." They all followed him into straight pines. They saw the bay once, over there, on a jut of rock above the bowl of smoky air. Saul motioned to him. Bowman disappeared again.

The stand was thick and hazy. They coughed and tied bandanas on.

"Why the rifles?" Dan said. "Why the rifles?"

"Yours is out too," Saul said, and it was true, a .24 Magnum aimed roughly at Saul. "Point it elsewhere."

Ella dropped off her paint and walked him through blue haze forest between islands of rotting snow and branches.

"Keep together."

"Over here." Not yelling.

No trail at all. No tracks. They heard a choked call to the left, Bowman. Maul slipped the knots between the mules and packhorses. They spread themselves across the slope, wove downhill, and lost sight of each other. Dan's hand was bleeding. He sucked it leading the chestnut white around the muzzle.

"What kind of thinker wrecks a cabin?" Maul said. "Some kind of selfish. Is there any more crystalline definition? There isn't."

Saul called to Bowman.

"She makes her move," Maul said. "She makes it as she must. Small, injured, scared. Her measly box of matches. Vindictive thoughts. A man is not black inside, not petty. A man would do different. Would leave the cabin with the door wide open for the next visitor-in-need, trespasser even. And if feeling destructive, if so, leave a trip wire to a shotgun's trigger, the butt in the chair."

Saul's hat disappeared ahead of the sorrel. One more call from Bowman.

"Kill the ones you hate," Saul said. "Not the cabin."

"That's right. That's right. That's right."

When the gas can exploded, the light was a quick flash of big roiled yellow. Another surprise. The last of the cabin flamed up as a ball. A tree behind caught from the top, torching up quick, confetti and tree and cabin falling everywhere. The explosion had made its own wind, sparking sticks and igniting rafts of needles. Branches fell, touching off other branches, more smoke, ovations of birds as the horses went crazy, backing and bolting. Their eyes rolled and they reared back and kicked out at mules and men, rope and reins down in their hooves, stomp them if they could, skittering sideways. A blowout on a grand scale. A candlestick pine. More limbs missiled down. The mules scattered back up the slope, or sidehill, or down the rock walls, who knows where a free mule goes, lopsided loads swinging under their bellies, the lashings loose but not loose enough. Dan's hat was really gone and the chestnut bucked for the first time in years. He ran with the mules and Dan waded uphill after him, caught him back up top of the ridge again. He split left this time coming down. No cabin was visible. Only smoke. The bay's foot was caught between a log and stone. The hock was ruined. He arrived leading the chestnut and the tall mule and the yellow horse. Bowman was working the leg and waved him on.

Dan dropped down to his knees anyway. He touched the leg. The bay screamed.

"Get out of here," Bowman said.

Farther down near the clearing he found one sleeping bag, a fry pan, and a bundle of rice hooked on a burl.

The back three sides were nearly gone. The door hung open and burned on. A single pistol shot was heard on Bowman's ridge.

Saul called from somewhere.

The second shot was thirty seconds later. The Ruger.

In the clearing, Saul stared down at the cob for a long time. Bits of burlap flaking off. A mystery, his face said, but no one spoke until Saul started it. He scanned the rock faces of the hollow, lifted his .270, fired off a few rounds. The magazine kept feeding him shells.

"How many?" Saul called.

"Two so far," Maul said.

The little gray mule had returned, and the tallest, a brown. The two reds were missing. The buckskin was seen on the ridge. Bowman was after it last they saw him. Ella was counting pots. The paint appeared with his saddle under his belly. Dan caught his reins. They unsaddled him and he skittered off and cantered a circus ring around the clearing, wild-eyed still. A water jug. A roll of utensils had scattered in foliage. The dun took an hour to come. The yellow horse appeared at the creek with the chestnut. The sorrel would come, Saul said, when the cabin was done burning. The door fell forward halfway. Something crashed and smoked on after. The wind calmed. The smoke rose straight. The two mules were tied together by the creek, no hobbles. Maul inspected their gear. The black mule came to the cockeyed mule, the tallest.

"Three," Maul said. "Only three mules."

"Bowman!" Saul called.

They'd never heard him say the name before.

When Bowman arrived limping with the buckskin jenny, they were still waiting on the sorrel. He sat on a stump near the cob with Saul and studied it. His jeans were ripped at the knee. No asked about the knee but they all looked.

Maul stood at the edge of the trees. He led the buckskin to the creek.

"Four outta ten," Maul said. "Goddamn."

Bowman dragged his leg into the trees again and reappeared lugging the bay's saddle, which rose and fell with his uneven gait. The saddle was fine and heavy. The tack was looped about his neck. The blanket was rolled up on the seat. Metal clanged when he dropped the tack. The afternoon was gray and cooling, fat clouds. He limped to the creek and led the chestnut out, set the bay's blanket on his back.

"What are you doing?" Dan said.

Bowman positioned the blanket.

"You take the yellow horse," Dan said.

Bowman slung the saddle over the blanket.

"Call your horse," Ella said. "Let's go."

"Take a pill," Bowman said.

"He's coming," Saul said. "My horse always comes."

"Everything always works out for you?" Ella said.

"Take two," Bowman said. He tightened the girth.

"What pills?" Saul said.

"Tell him," Bowman said.

"You can't have my horse," Dan said.

"He's mine," Bowman said. "Or he's dead."

Dan dropped the halter. He stepped back. His body went loose but his hands were fists.

"Consider this a warning," Bowman said. He adjusted the stirrups.

Saul turned to the cabin now. He rose from the cob and walked to the smoking face of it. He whistled, listened. He carried the .270. The rifle tipped up and down as he paced. He scanned the hollow. The sun dropped west, just a ball of white. Bowman dug in his saddlebag. Cashews. The window had fallen out. Saul lifted a piece of glass, dropped it.

"I could use some help," Maul said. "Kettle. Spatula, one sleeping bag but very wet." He flung it out. "Dutch oven, no lid. Can I have a nut?"

"No you can't," Bowman said.

The sun slid deeper into cloud. The air cooled. An island of roof had frisbeed across the clearing. Bowman kicked the flame out. Saul stared at the cabin. Ella made a list in her book. Flint striker. Wax cotton balls.

"Get back to the mules," Saul barked, kicked the cockeyed door away. The woodstove was enormous and potbellied, an old army model with a foundry stamp from Dayton: gray, matronly, in an iron skirt. The big table had burned fast. One leg survived. Dan followed Saul but stopped at the doorway.

"Any cans?" Maul called.

"And who would eat soup from an old can?" Bowman said. "A joke."

"You weren't joking, fat man."

"I was."

"Poison," Bowman said. "Those cans."

"I'd smell it," Maul said.

"Botulism has no scent." Bowman winced, bent to his leg. "Buck up, buttercup."

"Time to quit this!" Saul called to the bluffs. Saul's jeans were smoking. "Hey you!" he yelled.

"She's gone," Ella said. "Don't speak to her."

"You hear me?" Saul called. He kicked the stovepipe elbow. "You killed the cob!" he called. "We're coming after you for payment now!"

Echo from yellow bluffs to yellow bluffs.

"Give me some room," he said as if someone were crowding him. "He was never the right speed for her!" he roared.

"The young are stupid," Bowman said. He was brushing the chestnut now, weight on the good leg. "Love is chemicals only. Hormones, regretted later."

"Wrong from the start," Saul said.

"Could go on back," Maul said.

"You all go back," Dan said, watching Saul while everyone else watched him.

"What we need now," Saul called between his hands, "is a mutually agreeable resolution!"

A horse whinnied at the creek. Maul struck off to see about it.

"The pit is the past!" Saul said. "The cob can be too!"

"She's ten miles gone," Ella said, smiled. "You look stupid."

"Stupid."

"To speak like she's listening ever."

"The cob is dead," Saul said. "What are you smiling at?"

"I'm not smiling," Dan said.

Saul's face was very red, very worn out. His hat was hanging from the hand that wasn't clutching the stock of the .270.

"Get out of there," Ella said. "You'll melt your cuffs."

Dan was in the doorway. "Maybe we should split."

"Can't split now," Saul said. "Time for splitting and quitting's done."

Dan was letting the cabin bake him too.

"You'll fry yourself," Ella said. "Just like the other stupid man."

"I don't care if I'm like him," Dan said. "Just another bad man."

Saul turned slow. Dan backed up but Saul kept coming. Dan fell over a stump and Saul stood over him. He shifted the .270 and butted Dan's face with it. The patch stayed right in place. Dan turned the other side of his face to Saul.

"The other cheek," Dan said. "It's all yours."

"Shut up," Saul said. "While I think."

They followed boot tracks out of the hollow up an eastern creek. Only one pack string now. Four mules, one packhorse. Maul led the string and Ella followed it. Dan rode the yellow horse behind the packhorse carting the blue chair and the little gray with no burden at all. He touched the gray's rump sometimes with a stick. They cut up above a ravine. The water stayed low, dropped away. Saul led well ahead on the sorrel, a wide space between him and Bowman on the chestnut, the bum leg hung beside the stirrup. The creek was the only sound. No talking. Some law had been passed against it. Smoke lingered in their clothes, metallic on their tongues. Night came.

The sorrel stopped on a high plateau in the rain. Their ponchos were plastic and flapped like capes. The boot tracks turned steeply uphill south. The horses stood in a line beside the sorrel at the plateau's drop-off. Saul tipped his hat back.

He stared up into black. Water drained down his poncho around the sorrel's rump.

"I love rain," Bowman said to Saul. "This exactly."

"You are an odd man," Saul said. Bowman tipped his hat. His poncho was split in the back to make space.

The chestnut hung his head and Dan watched for complaint but there was none. The plateau was rocky and sloppy. Maul wore no poncho, never did in his life. Ella had only packed four. Maul looked back downhill. There was nothing in the rain, just a beam of light the rain cut across. He gazed back as if in love, as if he'd dropped a poncho somewhere on the trail, as if he'd ever owned a poncho, as if he might find his lost poncho waiting halfway back to the cabin, and he'd say to it, *Ah, there, I see you*, pluck it up, head on down, split with this party, proceed to the cabin, rest under the porch, gather his six mules to the remaining four, up the ridge, down the Switchbacks, through Elk Valley to the Narrows to the box canyons and Throne Room, down boulder fields and out to the world of feed stores and medical clinics and sidewalks and his trailer to the gooseneck hitch on his truck.

They swatted rain. Pricks of sleets, needles, thousands coming down.

"How would Jesse James rob a drive-through bank?" Maul said. "How would he do it?"

"No more stupid talk," Ella said.

"He wouldn't use the drive-through," Saul said. Ella didn't turn but she stared at Saul anyway. The horses drenched, waiting. The mules bit at sleet. "Jesse would go in the lobby to rob a bank."

"No doubt," Bowman said.

"A nasty man," Ella said.

"Coin, bills, or gold?" Maul said.

"Bags of gold," Saul said. "Jesse doubts representations of value."

"Where would he bury the bags of gold?" said Maul.

"He'd eat the gold. Shit it out."

Maul nodded. "How would Ginny do it?" he asked.

"My goodness," Ella said.

"My goodness," Bowman said in falsetto. "He thinks this girl's Calamity Jane."

"She wouldn't bother with drive-through either," Saul said with solemnity.

Dan hadn't bothered with a poncho. He was dripping, shivering. "You and Bowman go south," he said. "Maul and I go north. We split. Ella can go with and where she chooses."

"I know where," Bowman said.

She rubbed the paint's wet neck. She spit past her leg. Saul looked away and erased her.

"Splitting is the topic of the day," Bowman said.

"He talks like a tiny-baby green-parrot practicing," Dan said.

"What did you say?"

"His mind's blocked," Saul said.

"I see that," Bowman said.

"Like any muscle," Saul said. "The mind can seize."

Bowman held his hand out to catch the sleet.

"I have some things to say," Saul said, almost yelling given the racket the sleet made. "I have to get this off my chest."

"Well," said Ella. "Of course you should then. This is a fine time."

The ridges were blurry now with night and moisture filling every space. Saul talked. The sleet was pounding, almost hail. The streams ran down the ponchos, under the animals' bellies and down legs in twisting rivers. The wind whipped plastic around Saul's face and he was yelling his words at the wind now. They caught a word or two. They'd been standing there on the plateau too long and the horses were eyeing each other through dripping lashes. Saul's mouth was moving with energy. The cabin taste on their tongues was food. They extended those tongues, curled, and caught sleet. Not Saul. His lips were twisting as a horse lip twists, showing the band of fragile skin holding the top lip to its inner lining. They heard no complete thought, didn't care. Ella heard nothing at all, but her face changed listening to the purple smudges under Saul's eyes. Perhaps he was talking about the cob or cabin. Neither existed now. The clearing existed but would fill with weeds. They'd brought sticks collected for fires on the ridge when they got there. The sticks were packed in bundles tied with strips of burlap, piled on the tallest, the cockeyed mule. Sleet was the beginnings of snow. It began to snow on Saul as he concluded his speech. Dan was staring at Saul. Saul refused to look. Saul was his own man. Saul lived like he killed snakes, Ginny always said, *all in or all out*. Now his mouth was moving like a dying beetle's pinchers gripped on a lump of pork. Dan smiled at this thought. It was what Grannie might have said. Now the snow was a torrent of blinding flakes swirling white. Another blizzard. When Saul quit talking he respread the poncho. It resettled over the sorrel's rump. Ice was forming on hooves, stirrups. The horses waiting under their riders

in their ponchos could not have been wetter. The next decision was all Saul's. King Saul, this latest revelation, *Eureka!*
The horses waited in a horse-cluster, the mules in a line
of mules, and the men waited too, each swimming in his
own thoughts about what King Saul would do now. God's
great oversight; He'd failed to bestow on men any *unity of
mind* despite being generous with this trait when he was
sketching out His birds and beetles. Each man is kept blind
to all but his own fragments of information. His neighbor
has the other bits and pieces of the puzzle. One neighbor
has a single corner of the map only, another the middle left,
another the middle right edge, but no one has the whole
picture to follow. Each must endure, make the best of his
own paltry material, beg his neighbor for the part he needs
if his neighbor is willing to be begged.

"Well," Ella said, when Saul seemed done. "That was a nice
speech. How long have you been practicing?"

Dan laughed, thinking Saul's thought: that bitch. Unity
after all.

But the moment passed and couldn't be resummoned. His
mouth moving as he talked and talked in the snow was, in
the end, most like a mouse chewing cheese, not a king at all.

⸙ —— ⸙

One day after disaster in North America, Bear and Mouse
descend to a battlefield to feast. They hurry down the trail
from the hilltop overlook. The great fight below is done,
though they know nothing of the reasons or the merits. It is
dinner. Breakfast too, a week at least. All is still and smoky.

Men lie in the fetid muck, most dead and rotting already, some mere boys with stripes down the legs of their filthy uniforms, drumsticks gripped, some still holding pistols. Nearly every eye has been plucked out. Cruel birds wheel. Boys' eyeballs are more tender. Some of the Dead still move though pinned in place, arms grasping for a blade or blade of grass or bottle. The men moan under wagons turned over, run through with oak spokes of wheels, or draped high over cannons. The slope is easy and faster for the long-limbed Bear so he carries brother Mouse on his back, down down, past horses and mules sprawled dead with their masters. A fat man is roped to a chair and he babbles. Death is disorderly, indiscriminate, as always: many varieties of men, every color, uncounted hybrids crying out for mothers, sisters as visions standing just there.

Bear finds a leg and drags it. Mouse finds a bit of cheek and is more than satisfied. A mountain smokes in the distance. They chew and listen to the talk as they eat, become dizzy with food and sleepy contentment. As they curl up in intertwined balls to rest, one big, one small, the sound of the men mixes with sleep, indistinct grunts overlapping, diverse tongues pulsing together in waves of gibberish, accents and dialects all humming as a single hive cacophony.

⚬ —— ⚬

FINAL ARBOREAL CENSUS
2179, May 1 (snow-colored sky)
SPECIES: *Callitropsis nootkatensis*
LOCATION: West Sea

The antenna was the second replacement of the voyage, roughed up (again) by surface wind. The flange that secured the ship's low-altitude antenna was simply a poor design. Another would be procured in the event of a return trip. The siren sounded as the off-load ramp retracted. The Resurrected Mule had been under-the-table add-on freight to make the mission pay. He swam toward the filly's side of the blowdown while the colt charged the waves on the other side. The filly saw the Mule now and pawed the sand, as a seal cow lowed behind her, blinking with her pup, then flopped to surf where the two submerged. Now the Mule waded through the surf along the blowdown and the filly turned circles, waiting. The whole world could smell her in the squirrelly crosswind, sure sign of a storm coming down the coast, and their nostrils flared with her musky scent. Seagulls flew over. Why not a gull census?

The yeoman was floating in the water now, paddling clumsily, and she never knew if she jumped or fell. Who would miss her on the ship? When the filly and the great Mule touched noses, the colt charged the blowdown in outrage, screamed and tried to crawl over it, but quickly caught one front hoof in the tangle. He yanked at his leg but hooves don't operate the same in reverse, given their asymmetrical design, as with *lobster traps* in the time of *lobsters*. An antennaed monster floated in her mind and she thought she'd invented it.

The yeoman gulped salt as she floated and kicked toward shore. She'd never swum before but caught on quick. The New Mule was huge, thirty hands by the ancient measurement, and he approached the filly, who reached up to nuzzle necks. Epoch on epoch since the Great Mule Die-Off, but the idea of *Mule* lingered and the colt thrashed and the yeoman hooked elbows on a branch. The hatch clanged shut and the sun was dropping. The surf boiled around the ship's lift-off vents, engines started, and viewers glanced out as they hurried through their departure checklists, though no one saw the swimmer in the jumpsuit as they rose to the clouds, the antenna turning on the wing. It was working fine now.

FIVE

Mule

They kept the petty criminals as well as some real ones at a small jail outside Mainz on the Rhine. It was an old Roman fort in disrepair. Some of the fine old inner walls were tumbled, broken, had been hauled off and reused. This meant the inside was open and airy, a sort of courtyard, and a few trees grew. The criminals ate bread and gruel and died together in the courtyard. They were friends. They were often thrown in pairs into pits they'd dug side by side with wooden shovels. Outside the fort, the countryside was flat and green. The sky was mostly iron gray, sometimes pale blue with streaks of clouds left by high winds. The mules were harnessed in the courtyard too. They walked in circles at the end of long spokes from a central hub to grind the grain and to lift water from the well. The prisoners built carts to be hauled by mules. The carts were sold at good prices and sent out to haul charred beams salvaged from a governor's house burned down, hinges and iron spikes surviving to build new cells for the prisoners. Every few months a new cell was built. The oldest prisoners drove the carts, a guard behind them. On the way, they passed the smith, who worked his metal in his yard, just off the cobbled center street, hammering shoes for the horses, pounding fleurs-de-lis on shoulder armor, pouring metal into rotten teeth when the doctor was sick or out of town.

They waved. The gate was opened and the cart reentered and the mules were stabled and the prisoners ate lunches of turnips and bread on the steps. They told the others what they'd seen.

Once the guard said to a prisoner, "Come tie my boots. My laces are out of the ribbings."

The criminals made a line in the courtyard. A petty thief was first. He tied the boots and bowed and departed. The guard untied his boots again for the next in line, a forger, who tied the boots. The guard untied his boots again for the next man, the killer of a child. The killer tied the boots up and then it was the same for all the criminals in the line. The last man in line had stolen someone's wife. He bent and kissed the boots when he was done with the laces.

The walls of the fort were made of wood where the stone was gone. One stone tower was perfect. The Romans had built it with greater care and staying power, with a mosaic of a snarling dog in the center of the floor. The woodchucks came in and out under the walls of the fort just as the guards and the warden went in and out the door each day after eight in the morning. At night the door was locked. No guards were wasted with nighttime duty. Budgets were tight in the town due to flooding and plague. They set a stick with a hat in the guardhouse. It made convincing shadows. The criminals might have pushed the walls down together. They never thought of it. They played cards in the sun or snow in blankets.

Once the guard said, "Come give me your blankets," and they all got in a line, one by one, and handed their blankets over to him, all except a man from the tree in the jail yard. They said he had once been a spy. He was young and handsome, tall, blond, and lovesick. They called him the Swede. He sat there all day on a branch, every day, and never played cards. They guessed, at first, he was blind. They admired the way he climbed the tree anyway, felt his way up the trunk and branches with his fingers. He watched the birds that sat on the wall. The other prisoners barely noticed the Swede, thought of him as they thought of the birds, as decoration. When his turn came in line, he gave the guard his blanket, but also his shirt, pants, and rotten stockings, shivered in the tree after, this being November, turned blue and nearly died. They called him the Crazy Swede after that. The guard went home at night to a warm hearth, sent his boys off to work, apprentices for the potters and barrel makers and that newfangled printer. The guard told his boys to learn to read, to keep their faces clean before the master's wives, to stay away from his girls as long as possible, to push boys down if they were provoked in the street. "This is a bad world," he told his sons. "Full of bad men."

A dog came to live in the jail. He walked in one day right through the front door. The criminals slipped him bits of bread, let him lick their bowls. The dog was missing his tail and the pads of his paws has been sliced away. He held one paw up in the cold then another. The Crazy Swede loved the dog more than anyone else. The dog sat with the Crazy Swede, so misplaced, so mutely heartbroken. The dog slept on his pallet at night. The Crazy Swede was a painter. No one asked where he got his paints. He made little river scenes, maybe places he'd seen as a boy. He painted the dog in. He said the dog made him think of purer times. He called the dog by a girl's name. Genevieve. Jezzila. Galinda.

"Whip the dog," that same guard said.

He handed the Crazy Swede his whip. The Crazy Swede hesitated a breath, then he whipped the dog, whipped the dog, and whipped it. When the guard said stop it, "Stop whipping that dog," the Crazy Swede kept whipping.

They left him alone after that. He never tied anyone's boots. The guard never asked anymore, anyway. They dreamed about the Swede all their lives, the other prisoners, said he went to America, somewhere out West, far away from the cruelty of Old Bloody Europe.

❧ —— ❧

The trouble with Dan is he thinks people can't read his face. He thinks he's opaque, that people are too dumb to read the set of his shoulders and his hands in the rain, his back with the rain pouring off it, to read everything about him from a look.

This might sound like a tantrum.

Ella's another one. Ella thinks she knows right all the time, but sometimes not only doesn't she know it, she can't say or do it to save her life. But to get along everyone humors a person like that, gives that person what she wants, and then, in time, she starts thinking this is exactly the way things ought to be. Her way. Say a man goes behind the tree when she tells him to and does what she told him to do behind that tree. She thought she was right at first when she told him to go behind the tree and do what he did. She knows

308

she is right no matter what it might do to the man later, her suggestion or even command to do this thing. But maybe she wasn't right. Or later she changes her mind about what he should've done. She lays that on him too. How can that be right? But she thinks by now the reason everyone does what she says is they see great wisdom oozing out of her, not because they're trying to get along and getting along is more important to them than rightness. It's a vicious cycle.

"Well," Ella might say. "That's a nice speech. How long have you been practicing?"

So here's a good example.

What she means is "I'm going to cut your balls off, Saul, you cross me. I'm going to light a little bomb, saying, 'How long have you been practicing?' meaning 'Whatever you've learned, whatever you say here now way back out on this nowhere plateau in the pouring rain, sleet, and snow, on this fool's mission, whatever idiocy comes to you because of some idea or thought of yours after all this trouble and torment, well, I'm going to belittle it.'" If there's some small complaint from Saul, well, that complaint must be, by definition, some long-suffering grievance; and if Saul has a long-suffering grievance, Saul should've voiced it sooner; and if Saul didn't voice it sooner, Saul should at least have prayed on it and resolved it; and if Saul didn't say it or pray it or resolve it on his own, and didn't write it down in some little journal in his heart and locked it away, secretly hoping Ella would come along and find the little book and pick the lock and read it out, well then, Saul must have been withholding thoughts from her, ideas, notions. Which makes Saul a rotten fucker. A bad man. A poor example of a husband. That's what she means by "How long have you been practicing?" She's not asking. She doesn't understand ideas sometimes arise suddenly. Can't we entertain that possibility? That I, your average man, can have a lightning bolt of insight that maybe no other person in the world has ever had before me? And say it when it comes? Without any lead-in? No practicing at all, no speechifying, just the idea popping into my head and dropping out of my mouth the way a bird lays an egg, like All Creation was made, pure and good? But for Ella, no. She has no ideas come to her like that. So they can't for anyone else, either. Can't see beyond her blinders. Can't see herself, same reason. That's it, the curse of all lower animals: narcissism. Incapable of self-reflection. Far as we've come, the flaw's still in us. Not too much to boast about after a couple million years.

∿ —— ∿

The trouble with Dan is he's weak. Fine in cities, population centers. Nothing a Ruger couldn't fix.

"Some people are alive simply because it's illegal to kill them." I saw that on a bumper sticker.

The trouble with mule drivers is they won't shut up. Nothing a cliff in the clouds couldn't fix. A little fog and slope and good timing. Mule drivers are fat. They have inferiority issues.

Someone must be willing to break the law.

The law is man-made.

The law changes from epoch to epoch. We've canvassed that thoroughly during trailside convo.

The trouble with Ella is she's injured and sentimental and she's married to Saul who is neither. He has a long fuse but when it blows it blows.

The trouble with Saul is his wife.

The trouble with Ginny? I don't have any issues with her. She and I are a lot alike. I'd like to get her in a tack room too.

And as to the Rodeo Kid—if the Theory of Second Tracks is indeed correct—the trouble with him is he's living a fairy tale. He will either die young or live very well at others' expense. Not worth thinking about.

※ —— ※

Dan had explained it once and it was still irrelevant.

He said, "The Horse appears first in the fossil record in this very region of North America."

"I thought the Spanish brought them."

"That's a hideous and unvarnished falsehood!"

"Relax."

"Why are facts ignored?"

"I don't know."

"The horse was not from Europe or *so-called* Asia, not at all, as once thought by kings in their old self-centered world across the sea."

"Amazing." She'd yawned then, but here in the cave she remembered every word.

"The horse is a New World creature," Dan said, "born and bred, on this very ridge maybe, though this ridge was not a ridge at that time, just a meadow really, though a meadow is just a ridge that hasn't been lifted yet."

"Get to the good part so we can fool around."

That almost stopped him, but not quite. He was pure in his flaws.

"There's no animal like a horse," he said. "A most successful species. Why not learn from him right now in this cave."

"I wasn't in the cave when we had this conversation."

"Then let's continue the conversation in the here and now."

"I'm all alone in the here and now."

"I told you then on the bed, the couch, the rock floor, the pickup beds or tents, and just now I told you in the cave."

"Tell me a third time."

"The horse is a miraculous species."

"A sacred animal."

"Yes," he said.

"I don't believe in sacred," she said.

"Maybe reconsider."

"I might someday."

"A nearly invincible species." Dan was so enthusiastic. "The horse can survive anything."

"What's their secret?"

"They keep eating," he said.

"There's nothing to eat in the here and now."

"Keep chewing grass."

"That's all?"

"That's all."

It was technically true. That when the two men were off together, for example, that night for the deputy—Saul and

Bowman, Bowman and Saul—when they left Ella behind with Maul and Dan, Dan and Maul, or when the two men slipped behind trees to discuss maps or manure, galloped off after tracks invariably bearing no fruit, and when Dan wrapped himself in his tarp cocoon to search his troubled private innards, sliding day by day deeper into the blue plastic sheaf of his boy's metamorphosis—thirty-seven years old, better late than never (girls getting no such luxury, at the mercy of first blood on cotton panties you accept the shift to womanhood or kill yourself right then, Ginny had kicked and cried for days, found Grannie's little Derringer, Grannie standing at the girls' door saying sorry, and meaning it, the old lady never having said sorry to Ella for anything, though why sorry at all, since the blood was a prescription of the body not the mind or God or Grannie)—and when poor, poor Dan, blank and petulant, crushed, destroyed, deleted, when even he left her behind for his brooding, abandoned her with the scuttle of cups and dirty pots and mounds of horseshit for stepping in, to stare alone at landmarks that were always the same, another peak, another rockslide, another goat half-buried in the rubble, and then when Maul of all people turned his back on her too, off to the mules with secret sugar hidden in his coveralls, their ugly snouts roving his hand for it with their gloriously grotesquely artic-ulating lips, when the sugar was *right there* before them in his palm, Maul soothing them, *almost got it, almost there*, as if knowing exactly what she needed to hear but saying it to someone else, how cruel, how lonely to be filled with envy for these mules, truly overtaxed and fatigued as they were, stubborn and intelligent, ugly, yes, but a prescription of God,

no fault of their own, while Maul at least was thoughtful to
her, tried to remember her standing there, *ah, yes, Ella*, her
binoculars searching for her sister who was laughing her
head off somewhere, when the paint, of course, too, went off
to graze with the others of his kind (who was Ella's kind?),
treason, like one of her children, who, far off, well come to
think of it, went about their summer joys without thinking
much of their mother, and worst of all, everyone, even those
of them that didn't know it, they were all still thinking of
Ginny, doing for Ginny, standing at Ginny's door banging
on it still, begging her to come out, *Ginny Ginny Ginny*, even
though now it was Ella's turn for her door to be banged on,
to be called to, *Ella! Ella! Ella! Come out to us!* It was at those
times, only then, that she reached in her saddlebag for the
small green bottle of morphine sulfate hypo-tablets, twenty-
one quarter grains.

"What was it really like?" Maul said again and again.
"When you noticed the pit was empty."

"A lightning bolt."

"Anything else?"

"Like the plague," she said, "when you thought it had
passed your town."

"Smart of her to drag the calves. To make steps out of
corpses."

"Any idiot would have dragged those calves."

She took a double dose this time. They understood each
other perfectly. They were not friends. When this search
was done, when Ginny was gone in some permanent way,
no longer empowered to ruin the rest of them, they would all
move to separate towns, separate continents if needed, and

each tell their own facts, never coming in contact. When he asked which child she loved the most, she told her children's middle names, birthdays, and what they were like as infants. She couldn't remember so made the truth up. He asked again and she denied then revised. She wrote the answer in her little locked book: *Yes, there is one, though it's not really more love. More like more affinity.* Her mind came loose with this talk, the proximity. *It looks like more-love to the less-loved. Be careful,* she would tell them. *It's nature's plan to separate mother from children. Heartbreak. Every child is a pioneer.* Maul shot a young bear during "The Night of the Deputy." They never told the others. She wrote it in her mind as a play: Dan in the foreground, sleeping through the bear's death and the deputy's both. Maul caped the bear since the night was young. He rolled the hide up and lugged it far out of camp, leaving the lump of naked meat for Ella's work. He rolled the hide out again to full length and left it, a tiny bear rug on huge sand. It seemed vindictive. She understood it. He wanted a secret too. She'd cut one roast only from a flank. Lavish. They'd rolled the rest of the naked body behind a log together. They saw birds flying eager from the Switchbacks. She'd jerked the roast in a Tupperware of brine. The morphine grains wore off and ran out. She stared into the bear in her dreams, the stomach cut open revealing a pistol, a bottle of baby oil, a perfect rabbit blinking.

The first morning on the ridges Saul banged on the sorrel's shoe and Ella told Maul "The Pit and the Dancers." How once upon a time in a parlor in a farmhouse in a small town by a western river, a personal cyclone had hit.

The TV blared. The cow pit was empty. One man, Dan, was in shock. One woman, Ella, was cooking to soothe and nourish, while Saul, Ella's husband, dialed the sheriff to ask for news of Ella's missing sister.

"Sand in the eyes," Maul said. He waved, Go on.

Dan had aimed the clicker. Sit with him, Ella had said, and Saul sat. They watched a dance show as they ate eggs fried in bacon grease. The final competition, two couples left, one green, one white. The female dancers were slim, bursting bodices, skirts that lifted for lovely legs, dips and knees in air, swirling. The men were fairies. Maul nodded. She meant nothing by it.

"I bet they killed him," Maul said. "The deputy."

"The green pair was clearly superior," Ella said.

"'Course they killed him."

"Which was the better team was obvious. The better team was the green team."

"*How'd* they kill him, though?"

Now, the horseshoe was all metallic echo, whereas *then*, the band had pulsed on for the dancers.

"The sorrel is a horse of a lifetime for Saul," she said. "He'd have waited at the cabin for that horse for a year."

"Don't lose track," he said. "Did they shoot that deputy? Slit his throat?"

"They had grace, the green dancers. That indefinable element," Ella said, the horseshoe *chiming chiming*, sparks flying up for her if she turned to see, which she didn't. She'd watched the dance from the kitchen, making lists. The men had leaned closer to the TV. "I've heard of people falling in love with their captors."

"Stockholm syndrome," Maul said.

"Eat that," Ella had said to Dan, as the music switched from foxtrot to tango. "You could stand to eat a little more."

"But what to do with the body once the deputy's dead?" Maul said. "Lots of places in the mountains to hide a corpse."

"How in hell?" Dan had said when the white team won the enormous trophy, almost weeping over it, half his face shoved on a bag of frozen peas. "How in hell?"

"You aren't listening to what I'm telling you," Ella said.

"You aren't listening," Maul said.

"I wished they'd hurry with the shoe," she said.

"Killin' a deputy," Maul said. "What balls. I ain't got 'em."

White balloons had fallen around the white couple, the green couple having disappeared as if they were never there. The balloons were part of the victory procedure. A true theft of that trophy, Ella said Saul had said, getting up from the couch. He had so many things to do. The dance contest was over. An old dog rose and slinked to the kitchen.

On the ridge, Saul banged steel, the shoe clanged.

"What happened to the green couple?" Maul said.

"You don't care," Ella said.

"You won't tell me anyway."

She did: as the tune crescendoed, a single green balloon drifted down over the dancers. The single green balloon had fallen from a breach in the rigging above the TV box, one of those many secret places. Both green and white balloons were stored separately above the stage in separate cages to be loosed over the victors. The single green balloon had broken free. The commentators said nothing. The single green balloon drifted down to rising music.

"But death is more important," Maul said.

The sorrel's shoe was almost done.

Ella had left the kitchen as the balloon fell to the shiny dance floor, lilted benign in the dancers' breeze. She'd knelt down on Grannie's old braided rug. She'd shoved the dog away as the green balloon slipped under the green girl's skirt and the green man kicked it, thereby scuttling the team's rhythm entirely, thereby losing balance, falling, losing.

Steel succumbed. The sorrel trotted around Saul's lead, testing the new shoe.

"It's too small," Maul said. "I'm sorry to tell you."

"Think," Ella said.

"Think?" He shrugged. "Open your goddamned eyes."

❧ —— ❧

Mule Thought #5 (the red jenny tells a story and is interrupted thrice): The Foal and Coyotes. Once, at night before her escape, they stood together in the dark listening to the red jenny when that woman-thief came in and rummaged the baggage, and then the filthy boy-thief came in and did identical rummaging, and though thirty equine eyes (counting horses) were watching both thieves, each intruding-thief believed *no one* saw them. *A terrible insult, yes,* the red jenny mulled, *to count us all as "zero,"* not incensed, but still interrupting herself to say so, to make this point. Then the boy skulked away in his silly uniform and rags and the red jenny tried to recover the story, attempted to bring the story to its most grievous climax: the arrival of the coyotes. A cruel drooling, yipping pack bunching in close then closer around a poor foal forgotten by the herd, but she was interrupted a second time:

We have sixty hooves between us, nickered the buckskin jenny, countervailing the red jenny's story with her own version of the same complaint about their recent insult in the dark, the three narratives running together, as they do, mules being no strangers to hybridization. *We could've pulverized them each in turn.*

They scrummed and kicked, then came speeches, the third interruption.

The horses too! coughed the tall mule with one gorgeous unearthly eye on the horses. *But horses never miss a chance to humiliate themselves.* The tall mule was tired and sick and lame but still pressed on daily and would die doing so, just like that "Queen" in the billowy getup.

An eye for an eye and a tooth for a tooth, nickered the buckskin jenny. *Go for the knees, the face, the longest slenderest bones.*

They never did hear what happened to the foal.

◆ —— ◆

Dusk.

At a dip in a ridge, Maul led the little gray behind a jagged pumice tower, lava-looking or coral-seeming, maybe a shark inside it, maybe a moray eel frozen in time. This had all been water once. Now it wasn't. Not much use, in times like these, thinking of sharks swimming here, or eels whipping their serpent bodies along a ridge in the sky submerged.

The lead line looped slack. Kind words. The other mules shouldn't see it. Mules could count he'd assured the skeptical.

The three mules watched, the buckskin, the tall mule, the black, all funnel-ears twisted forward to capture every sound for miles, a coyote fart, mice playing checkers, a ghost-deputy shuffling cards. These horse-people were very superior. He and the little gray dropped out of sight. The horses shifted in their saddles and bit flies that weren't there.

They ate mule that night and the next cubed for stew. All but Dan. He looked on in disgust as they filled their bellies.

"*Now is the winter of our discombobulation,*" Maul said, flinging a rib.

They left before dawn.

The boot tracks no longer followed sensible purpose. No cairns. The tracks forked from ridge to ridge, dipped to saddles, postholed through snowfields—sadistic, cruel—only to double back the other way, to a high white peak and around it, skirting immense cracks into ice-blue oblivion, looping around the other way.

Bowman pressed snowballs to his knee sometimes.

"You'd cut it off before complaining," Maul said.

"Where's the coffee?"

Why abide? When Maul spoke, he spoke to the wind. No answer. No answers. He spoke to his mules. They were powerless. They hurt no one. If the mules were made king, what then? It was cold the first few days on the ridges. The ridgetops were snowy or bare though far below somewhere was green. The tracks cut three ways across snow. Which way? The tracks were having fun. Maul pointed this out. Not even a nod. The water jugs gonged on the mules' ribs.

The posse drank tea since there was no coffee. Saul sat in the blue chair. He said his knees were hurting but that wasn't why.

The second evening on the ridges, Dan said, given all, he deserved more potatoes. "If others relish mule flesh," he said, "my percentage of potatoes should rise accordingly."

"A sound argument," Saul said.

Bowman said Dan's meals were his private business. "I, for one, want my due of taters."

Ella tore her potato in two and offered half to Dan. Maul wolfed his quick before the discussion concluded.

"A man's got to live with choices made freely," Bowman said. "No one's forcing him to refuse mule flesh."

"Agreed," Saul said.

"Can't shunt his anti-mule preferences onto innocent others," Bowman said.

"All right," Saul said. "All right."

"Innocent," Dan guffawed, "who's that?" He finished Ella's half.

"It's pro-mule," Maul added. "Not anti-mule."

"Can we stick with taters?" Ella snapped.

Saul watched Dan chew. "I'll tell my decision in the morning." His face said *too tired for such paltries* as he gazed out into the black that was the land they'd traverse tomorrow. He was never one for looking back. "To bed," he said, a rare expression of indecision, but at dawn when the sack was found empty, and when its precious contents were recovered, he was firm.

"Can't hide tubers," Maul said, plucking russets from pockets in Dan's satchel.

"Supplies will not be allocated on a single rider's whim," Saul said. "As for theft, the perpetrator will miss one meal. No food all day on the second offense."

In this case it was breakfast. Bowman fried hash browns. He didn't glance at Dan glaring through cook smoke.

They pitched the tea bags off the ledges like steaming comets. They thanked God for the yellow horse and the packhorse, very handy now. They thanked God for the cook tent, for the wisdom of packing it. They'd dodged a bullet and thanked God.

They slept in a row inside the cook tent, heads or feet to the tiny stove they'd hauled in all this way. The mules and horses stood just on the other side of flapping canvas, heads hanging, resigned, if someone cared to peek through any gap. Maul peeked. Life and pain had not killed his curiosity as it had Saul's and Bowman's. Only Saul and Ella had bedrolls now. Bowman rolled a saddle under his bad leg. The mornings were clear at first on the ridges, but damp and cold, high winds wicking body heat.

"What are we after now?" Maul said. "Why not go home now?"

He was sure no one knew but him. Until now, all his life, he'd been last, generally, to recognize stupidity. Things had changed for him on this trip. The losses were big, but he now saw that he could see some things that others were totally blind to, were crippled by. Maul was not crippled at all. He'd lost weight. He'd made one friend, a real one, maybe two. He thought about devils and what they really were. He left messages of all kinds for rescue. He wanted to live more than ever now.

Sometimes he walked his dun at the front of the whole party. He was their king, and with power comes the *responsibility* to understand the plight of underlings. At night, for his watch, Maul used a trick he'd learned from the Old Swede's prison in Mainz in the Eternal Sweden of the Mind. He set bundles of broken gear on the chair and dropped Dan's poncho over the pile, stuffed the hood to fill the head, no eye patch. He privately referred to this serene replacement of himself for Third Watch as "Poncho Man" and got some shut-eye. Dan had given him the poncho. Dan didn't care about living now. He was thin and angry and the patch was permanent. Ella held a pen and never wrote a word. Poncho Man was fine. No one was coming. It was what the others didn't know. Sometimes they rested in the lee of the many huge jagged pumice towers. He thought of the devil often, how the devil's actions didn't, at first blush, seem devilish. It was part of his trick, his power. Lucifer. Beelzebub. Mr. Scratch.

"Beelzebub was the henchman," Bowman said. "He wasn't the devil himself."

"I dispute you," Maul said.

He loved saying it to that man.

Third day on the ridges Ella offered ham slices from a last and overlooked package. She cut green off. Dan refused meat now, part of his version of "change," of his new "manitude," as Bowman called it.

"How's that leg?" Maul said.

"This leg," Bowman said, "is perfect."

It was Maul's turn for Dan's share. He claimed the green ham and Ella forked green ham and he stuffed green ham in his ever-loving mouth. Saul spat and the spit flew away horizontal. A great blue peak stood off south and someone asked the name. Old Rip. Old Poker. Old Splitfoot, since the devil was a kind of goat.

"Slander to goats," Ella bleated. "Slander to goats."

Tiny spiny split footprints appeared soon after in the snow. A tail dragged behind.

"The Black Spy," Bowman said.

I hate you too, Maul would have liked to say. He would. He would.

The Long Red Twisted Ridge Ride, Maul would call it later, for the rest of his life, meaning this: a Long Ridge, a Red Ridge that was a Gold Ridge at a different time of day. Twisted. And this: the Green and Purple Ranges had backbones of green and purple. They laughed, he and Dan, as the others glowered. Dan's mood swung and swung back. Him and Dan. Dan and him. Ella was a satellite only. They discussed the future as a ridge ever forking, ever T-ing, humping up, dipping down, fractured but not "malformed." A ridge was a Muscle-and-Bone place, the backbone of the world. They were sorry for the lesser mountain places, the low ugly tangled-up gristle places.

"We didn't eat the cob. Why not?"

Dan explained it, though not entirely to Maul's satisfaction. Injustice was rampant. It was no one's fault the way you're born. They were right about him, he admitted to Dan in private. He was a fairy, but in the broadest sense. Dan was fine to confide in. Very troubled. It was part Dan's fault, this mess, but not all, not most. They were both semi-innocent bystanders, caught on the crosswalk at the moment of a terrible car crash. Shrapnel got them and his mules. Wrong place wrong time. But mostly no one listened to anyone. Eyes darted. The sun beat down and cooked men on ridges. It was not hospitable. A carcass. A little naked thing like a deer. He tried to remember what the missing mules looked like. They discussed it. Dan couldn't summon them either. Nature could be very ugly. Saul was on his knees under the stars, but they were just great burning balls of gas. Still, after that, after the most impressive crimes, Saul was back with God again.

Maul lagged frequently. He said he had a big shit coming. All those beans. He slipped down from the dun and built rock piles in threes, the universal number of send help. On his watch he dragged the fire apart into three smaller fires. No one came for them. The explorers brought flags with them. They had no flags. He asked about the map. He should've brought another coat. The villain had taken his. He'd been a scout and could navigate without Polaris or the Big Dipper. The canvas ripped as they struggled to pitch the cook tent. Each watch crouched under the fly with his rifle in the chair. A .270. A .243. His own .22. Snow fell. For Bowman's shift, he rose as if he never slept. Was he a man at all?

"Why doesn't she have a shift?" Bowman asked once, as Ella slid into her sleeping bag. It was no longer zipped to Saul's.

"Why do any of us still bother?" Maul said.

Watch was a sham. Watch was a show.

At lakes on the ridge in snow, the mules bashed through icy crusts. They required thirty gallons a day if working hard, twenty at rest. The buckskin was big-headed and horse-faced.

325

The black was curly-wild, smaller, short-bodied with long legs, more donkey-like, clever and sneaky, as Maul knew himself to be. The buckskin knew it was her last trip. The black mule wouldn't move unless the buckskin did. The tallest mule was called Man-o'-War. He was gigantic with tall socks to fancy boots, statuesque even as weeds dripped from his chewing. He had one strange eye, which Maul had noticed, of course, but never thought about. He and Dan ate dusty raisins a little apart from the others, the last box between them. They were being petrified alive in this inescapable amplifying ridge light. Man-o'-War would be the next to die. He was strong but going lame. His front left knee was the size of a soccer ball. The horses. The paint, a Prima Donna, pawed the ice in frustration, stirred dirt up for all drinkers. Ella slipped off to the dead weeds, always thinkin' someone's watchin'. Watch they did. A woman is, for a man, no matter what kind, a strange thing to look at: her appendages and then the one that's missing. The men washed their faces. They'd forgotten showers. They squatted by the water. Snow clung to their backs. Their eyes were swollen, surrounded by the scaly burn of wind-whipped skin. Scarves were made of summer shirts. More than once Maul asked to see Dan's stitches. Dan promised him yes, okay, but never did show them.

Day Five on the ridges: Fog. No land but peak-shaped islands. The tracks dropped down and they were cloud-dwellers following, gods by definition, since the old green world was truly gone. No iodine. Dan smelled like infection. His patch was stiff and filthy. He turned his back when he washed it.

The skillet was missing. Some claimed Dan was the last to put it away.

"Why don't we just go back?" Maul whispered between raisins.

The mule's loads were light. It was the horses' turn. The buckskin kicked Bowman. He was sure there was glee in the kick. It wasn't a serious injury, a bruise to the hip he didn't show. They would do it again. He'd been warned.

Day Six. Maul saw to their loads, high, tight, and balanced. He'd invented the knots himself, he said. No, couldn't prove it. Bowman had seen knots very much like them in other towns, he said, made by other people good with knots. "Or maybe on TV."

"Could be," Maul said. "Doesn't mean I didn't think the knots up. Knots have ways of spreading. People taking credit."

His knots were intricate, truly expert. His hands moved fast through them, even with eyes closed, see, no eyes required. He pulled the knots tight at the end, opened his eyes again, and winked at Dan. Bowman watched over Maul's shoulder.

"What do you call it?" he said. "That knot?"

No answer. No answer. Screw you. Bowman watched the genius work.

"Thinking up a knot isn't the same as inventing it," Bowman said.

Of course. Of course.

"There's been thousands of knots never recorded," Maul said.

"That's what I mean."

"No," Maul said. "That's what *I* mean."

He had the right way of talking now. He had found it finally, after all those years of laughter behind his back. Bowman limped away, vanquished.

Dan took Bowman's place, resuming his zombie silence as he watched the miracle of the knot turning over and into itself. "Silence does nothing for you," Maul whispered, but Dan, in the end, was a lost cause.

In the mornings, Ella rolled the utensils slowly but fiercely. She sat on the snowy ground with canvas sprawled between her legs very much like a baby blanket. No baby within a hundred miles. Two hundred. The spatula was melted on the tip. Plastic. It was finished forever for pancakes. She tied canvas strips to secure the roll. It seemed to Maul that she was doing fine without her children. For all her hand-wringing. For all her words about beloveds, all her tears at night. She had her paint prancing and stomping, though the brat was not faring well. So many sharp silver things. She counted them daily. Her hands were ripped and chapped. Only her green bottle calmed her down. She would be comical, maybe sympathetic, if all this mess wasn't all her fault.

"We could go," Maul whispered as Dan sat Watch with him. "Let's just go."

The chestnut was old and couldn't carry much. It wasn't the chestnut's fault.

A helicopter was heard the next canyon over. They didn't discuss it. Saul waved them under a wide rock shelf. Dan lingered in the light, even waved his arms up, calling. Bowman darted out and shoved him under. "Goddamn you. Goddamn you." A first, since no one had ever heard Bowman cuss.

The noisy silver thing orbited over flocks orbiting below in wonder at the disturbance, unaware of pilots and searching human eyes since they'd never seen a man.

"*Now is the summer of our discontagion*," Maul said as the silver bird flew away.

Bowman retched up something moldy.

Too heavy on the port side, to starboard. Dan packed, Maul inspected, critiqued as if Dan had never seen a mule before. As if Dan were no longer Dan but a novice cabin boy.

One day on the ridges, the blue chair was tied upright on the yellow horse facing forward. Dan walked behind the chestnut and watched Bowman's hand with a crop.

The fog burned off early. Dan tied a shirt around his head. The clear nights were cold. A quarter moon, a sliver. More snow. Only Saul and Bowman concerned themselves with tracks. They discussed tracks *ad nauseam*. The dog appeared just as they'd lost the tracks. They ate onions, croutons, and molasses from a pot. They passed one spoon between them. They'd built the fire with the last wood hauled up on the pack-horse without permission. Bowman was napping and Saul was out retracing tracks. The three remaining called themselves the Three. Maul, Ella, Dan, in that order. Their socks were frozen. They peeled them off like rotten skin and laid them together close to the meager flame, never touching, in an unintended design of petals. They peeled off underthings and rolled them in snow to wash them. The elastic and straps were stretched wide with age and too much riding. No one teased. Pecker holes had been tucked closed. A gust came and Maul set small rocks on each garment. Bowman turned in his sleep and they held their breaths. The Three took turns sitting in the Chair, "Ginny's Chair," Maul whispered, since it was his job, as the Outsider, to say what was really going on. Ella counted Ziplocs. Three left, she reported, and Maul wondered if there was some sign in this coincidence. From the blue chair they washed the few dishes with snowballs, bending down to the work between their knees. Their voices ran together. Bowman woke up. Saul returned from searching, unsuccessful.

"What's going on here?" Saul said.

The Three laughed. "Yes, it's funny," Maul said. "We think it is. Don't we?"

"You're the new spokesperson?" Bowman said.

"I guess so," Maul said.

That night in the fog, they caught Dan leaving with two mules and the chestnut.

"This is even funnier," Bowman said the next day, when he secured Dan's wrists with duct tape behind his back. He didn't disturb the pirate's patch at all when he wound over Dan's head an entire blindfold of filthy rag. Saul paid no attention as Bowman walked Dan up a ramp of rock and loaded him onto the blue chair atop the yellow horse.

"It's better than walkin'," Bowman said.

"Who could dispute that?" Maul said. In this way, the Three became the Two.

Maul offered to help with the ropes for the chair legs.

They rode on along the ridges like that, the Four plus Dan, the most silent morning of the ride. When the drop-offs to the left or right became particularly dizzy-steep, they held their breaths, looking at Dan swaying in the chair, insensible to his proximity to death. His knees were prim, locked together. His boots had been tied into the packsaddle. They each felt how on a *knife's edge* they were, while looking at Dan, that the wind arrived differently on their skin. The Four realized they had always felt it but never noticed it. *Yes, agreed*, they would have agreed excitedly, if they were ever to discuss it, *the new wind*, which they did not. They would agree, too, on other details: that sure enough the air itself on a *dizzy precipice* rose cooler and damper up from abysses, laden with the slightest scent of moss or lichen rich with chlorophyll, and that the *silence* off a cliff edge echoed with an entirely unique timbre, full of far-off trees and dirt and animal scent, a specific loamy silence, distinct from the pasture-silence of a sloping shoulder. And this would have led, in the end, to an astounding point of agreement the Four would have come to: that the senses, in truth, *mixed* on *an edge*. This was fact. Sight mixed with taste. Taste mixed with sound. Sound mixed with the tingle on skin. The tingle on skin mixed with the pungency of sweat and fungus from some cave where animals dragged dead bodies. Dan spoke sometimes about the Old Swede. How he wished he could've met the man. The Four didn't tell Dan any of their collective sensing, thinking, knowing, or that they would never have noticed any of it, considered it, turned it into wisdom, without Dan's blindfold, without the chair as a prop, without the yellow horse turned circus performer, without the deputy providing the yellow horse, the sheriff further back, this chain of increasingly attenuated helpers, rooted in the shape of the land rising and falling, with cliffs dropping off to instant death.

"Any more cowboy jokes now?" Bowman asked. "Any pleasant humor to share?"

"This ride is the king of jokes," Dan said.

Maul handed pilot bread into Dan's mouth, below the blindfold, for lunch. "Look! I'm your mother bird," Maul said to him. "Here comes!" Dan's wrists, Maul reported, were turning white. The duct tape was very snug. Maul sat on the dun to feed him, reaching up to the chair as Dan's mouth bent down. "He's learned his lesson," Maul said, and also argued for the yellow horse. She deserved a reprieve, he said, since such high-centered balancing required too much energy, enormous and undue concentration for the animal. The yellow horse, after all, had done nothing wrong.

"The cob is dead," Saul repeated as if this answered it. He referred Maul to Bowman as to justice for the wrists, saying, "No more mutiny."

In the afternoon, Dan slumped and seemed to fall asleep. Birds hovered with interest.

Bowman presented a hypothetical to the New Three, who were now his audience, Saul, Ella, Maul, in that order: a man is tied into a blue throne on a horse. There's a cliff. It's a joke on the man. Very funny. The man falls off the cliff or is pushed or flung. Why? The world is crazy. That's why, the world is bad. A long fall with a splash in the creek at the bottom, certain death. The man falls but the man lives. The man lives, but the man capsizes. The chair's legs go bottoms up. The creek takes the man and he's now "A Bobbing Spectacle in Boots."

"Out of the frying pan," Dan called, talking in his sleep.

"Exactly," Bowman said. "You follow me."

Bowman went on: a bear sniffs the Boots from a mile and is curious. The bear comes to the river, runs along it, and follows the Capsized Chair. He's never seen a boot before. He's only smelled Boots. The bear runs the shoreline, pondering the smell of Boots and the meaning of the smell. Here's the thing: for years, Boots have caused endless trouble to the bear's family. His father and sister died on account of Boots.

"*Just leave us alone*." Dan squeaked a poor bear imitation, aiming his voice at Bowman. "*Keep your lead plugs and poison traps to yourself*."

"Yes," Bowman said. "Exactly the quotation."

"The bear's thoughts in a nutshell," Dan said.

"Here's the question," Bowman said. "Which is worse: To drown or to die by bear?"

Saul blew his nose between his fingers and flung the snot.

"To drown is worse," Dan said. "Get it over with."

"A bear can take time killing you," Saul said, his first words in hours. "A bear can toy with you." He reminded the Five of several famous local bear catastrophes.

"Someone should just shoot the poor man," Ella said. "Put him out of his misery."

"Yes," Dan said. "Before something worse happens."

"One person's misery is another person's pleasure," Saul said.

A bank of fog rolled up the cliff. When it arrived and they rode through it, they felt and heard it like a wave. "You're some kind of magician," Dan said, his voice aimed at Bowman.

"I operate at the outer boundaries of human nature," Bowman said. "I study it."

Dan became more natural in riding the chair. The wind swirled and whipped his blindfold. He asked for water and

Saul rode close and tipped up a canteen, said the cob's death had really done something terrible inside him. Dan nodded and gulped. Water ran down his thickening beard.

They finished the story together. The current changed. Rapids arrived just in time. The bear was too slow deciding. Or a man in a chair is too much trouble for a bear. Or the ropes frayed and the man was freed and swam to the opposite shore. Or, no, a sudden wave and the Boots came loose and as the man rolled up for oxygen the bear chased his lost footwear along the shore. Any which way, the man was saved.

Maul helped Dan down from the yellow horse at a lightning-dotted dusk. He unwrapped the tape. "He's learned his lesson."

Dan cooked the last noodles with the last pepper. He wore an apron that Bowman flung at him that he said he'd found at the cabin on a line between trees. Bowman wouldn't eat from the communal pot. Dan sat in the blue chair cooking. The apron had once been white. The ruffles hung off the hem in places. Ella searched for her sewing kit with no success. Saul searched down the trail they'd just arrived on for tracks made by the Thief, the Villain, the Terrorist.

"She's just a woman," Bowman said. "Don't mythologize her. It only makes her stronger."

Bowman brought Ella the spoon when he was done eating. She dropped the spoon. Dan washed the spoon. Bowman: It was hard to forget the man. He was potent. He cast a pall on everything. He came over with a bottle of champagne and the machete. He chopped the top off in one swing. White foam plumed in a cold and sweet fountain.

"Times I feel like dancin'," he said.

They all looked up in amazement at the tall skinny spider waltzing around the fire with Dan in the apron. Levity Returns!

"*Winter of our disingenuation,*" Maul said, flinging a bit of fur. "*The winter of our distress. The winter of our winter. The winter of our disgust and disrepute.*"

Bowman puked, ate nothing.

They left before dawn.

"That leg still good?" Maul asked again.

"This leg is divine," Bowman said. "This leg is delectable."

They saw donkeys sometimes, other shapes. Maul told them the meaning of Three. Ella joined in. She left SOS cairns too. They covered themselves from sun with ponchos. The animals' mouths dripped. A ridge is a backbone of something sleeping. Ella sometimes led the pack string now. Saul rode next to her once or twice and reached across to her. She steered the paint away. Dan volunteered for First Watch and Saul said, "No need. No need." He slapped Dan's back for the first time in days.

"No such thing as a wild donkey," Bowman said. "No one owns it, doesn't make it wild."

"So wrong," Maul said.

It was fun now. He spelled H E L P on a flat top. Morse code could be flashed with mirrors but these were lost at the cabin.

"We're lost too," Maul said. He didn't need their answers anymore.

Only the smallest plants grew on a ridgetop, the micro of the macro, ruling a landscape no one else wanted. Dan was now pedestrian. He kicked every scrub he could reach, which was hardly any. They burned scuttled packsaddle parts, burlap bags. When that was gone, Dan dropped down into cuts to cut more wood with a fat-toothed blade Saul had authorized. Bowman sat above him with a rifle, his bad leg splayed out straight. They drew straws for woodcutting and One-Eyed Dan always lost. Afterward, they confiscated the fat-toothed blade.

A ridge was the humped back of a whale caught in a hole in the ice when it came up to take a breath, and the fire was the air hole, smoking. They looked for coffee-can roofs.

"My kingdom for a roof," Maul said.

No offers.

"Why would the Old Swede stop at building a single cabin?" Maul said. "Why not two?"

"How do we know he did stop?" Maul replied for all.

"The ridges were full of caves," Maul said.

"*Trees, trees everywhere but a not a drop to—*" Maul said.

Dan said "Listen," on all fours, an animal, with his ear to a hole in the ridgetop. He was going out of his mind. Or substitute any name for that *he*, if you like.

Dan staggered. He told stories about the young Old Swede. His girl was a dancer in The Hague when they met, small-boned and frail. They pictured her in their own five ways. On ridges there's so little to think about. One thought can fill the mind for an entire day. Gisele. Gisele. The Old Swede's girl. His parents never liked her. Her parents loved her very much. He met her on a trip south to buy beaver from the New World, to stretch it out with pins, make more hats from each hide, more food on the table, more strength from

336

each beaver to live well on. He met her selling bread in the streets of Stockholm at an execution.

A hanging, Maul thought, but did not chime in. He was boycotting this conversation since he hadn't started it.

No, not bread. Selling chocolate. Gisele, a Belgian girl of great dark beauty. Gisele the German princess. An African princess, a daughter of Eve, and she and the Old Swede, they ran away to Germany. He stole a ring, crawled in an open window on a square off the Leberstrasse. A hot day. A cold day. A ruby, cut a fat rich lady's finger off. Not the finger, rather, her fringed bag. He cut it off the fat lady's arm. He was sent away for ten years. To dig rocks in Siberia, to dig canals in the Orient. They sent him away, anyway, Dan said. And Gisele stood at the city gates weeping, called for him to return to her, and he promised he would, she was running after him there among the marching thieves, murderers, and general evildoers. She called many words of love to him. Her language was a translation but always seemed more meaningful in its errors and slippages.

"Let these horrors roll off the back of your indifference!" she called.

She died, of course, offstage, outside the story, consumption, typhus exacerbated by a broken rib where an officer kicked her down. They'd spoken French as their common language, the lovers. He never learned English in all his years in North America, a few words only. Bread, dog, water. There is no Old Swede's Trail without Gisele's death. The irony of progress.

"No, no, no," Maul said, when he could stand no more. "The Old Swede's mine."

Once at nightfall they found a fire ring in a grotto. The snow caked at the door. Boot prints. They dug the door out with their hands. They kicked ashy slop off the fire ring to coals underneath. They breathed a spark to life. They piled on rats' nests. They led the animals into makeshift crossties. Maybe bandits had lived a winter here and hidden bags of bullion. When the others slept, Maul crawled in as far as he could, ran his hand farther along the floor. He fumbled stone chips that might be gold, jade, or opal. The mules were sad. He understood the mules' sadness. Such high hopes at first: loved by mother from sweet beginnings, full teats of warm milk, then grain from loving hands. So easy to be fooled. Packsaddles were a shock. Hobbles. My God! The whip. Surprise! Bullets for noncompliance. How to live with such losses? Smoke followed stained undulations up hidden chimneys. He found no gold, but pulled out jerky hidden in his shirt. For him, the bear was a fortunate visit by the megafauna. The bear had come in too close that night of the deputy, a newly abandoned adolescent, too young, too hungry, too lonely. There was no other way. The bear was peppery-sweet, divine, nearly too tough to chew, perfect when very hungry. He sucked the bear before tearing off more. He stuffed the pack away. They'd smell it soon. Starving. They turned north the next day. Then east through a pass, turned north toward the Canadian border.

"Why north?" Maul said. "Why not turn around?"

"*The evil men do lives after them*," Bowman opined. "*The good is oft just clear hot drivel.*"

No one heard it.

Saul was watching Ella watch Dan. The couple slept far apart now, no sleep at all, really. They lay inside the tent dreaming awake.

The tallest mule, the brown, was in trouble now. He was full-on limping. Once, at a jagged pumice tower, Maul took the tallest mule's face in his hands. The others averted their eyes. He didn't care. He wanted *to know* what was wrong with this tallest mule. One socket eye was slightly bigger with a spectacular-strange blue-white crystal-marble orb within its bony casing, quite a masterpiece of ocular artistry, a tiny supernova of light and line, woven in jagged color, radiating out from a pupil that was not round. This ragged pupil was a hole light used to enter this mule. It led to a tunnel down into him and gathered up at a pit at the bottom. There it was! Just waiting to receive the big, white, gray-blue tall-mule-world. The mountains and sky in reverse positions mixed with all other things of equal value and no more: rocks, peaks, creeks, bears, rabbits, snakes, villains, masters of mules, men, and women all living inside the tall mule too.

"What's wrong with you?" Maul said. "Tell me."

But the mule wouldn't.

On the last night on the ridges, at dusk, Maul led the tallest mule behind a parapet. The pistol was Bowman's. He'd had trouble with his own, no time to grease it, no grease left. Dan ate crumbs from a plastic bag that blew out with his hand inside it. The lead line drooped slack between him and the mule. The parapet was pumice or coral-looking with blooms of quartz-white worms that broke out as ancient bouquets. The two mules licked snowmelt. The puddle would dry up in a day and leave a muddy shadow. The mule's bones would be found in ten thousand years.

"All will be dead by then," Saul said.

"Our children's children's children," Ella said.

"No more children," Bowman said. "Let's hope."

That night, Bowman hung bells around the chestnut's neck. "No one's taking him."

The blue ribbon was gone from the yellow horse's mane. Bowman took the First Watch, Saul the Last. He said he needed sleep. Maul made a white flag out of the last burlap. The flag was real and brown. He'd hold it out before him. They didn't ask him what the flag meant. He dropped the flag and the pack train flattened it to pulp. One of the symptoms of losing your mind is that you never happen to notice it.

Here's a symptom: In each of their minds that night—the last night of the old world, the first of the new—they were back at the ranch at the beginning of a lightning storm. Rain sprayed sideways. They each stood, alone, looking up through the rain at the crest of a hill, maybe one of the ridges to the south or the foothills of the Mormoras, none of them were sure, the fence careening up the slope and it was dark and fence dissipated into mist until a lightning flash lit the sky and fence and a huge horse on the crest behind it, a real horse, a painted pony too big for this world, so massive and out of proportion for this world it made the herd at its hooves look like long-necked cats. They saw it for only that flash and in the flash the light made its patches purple, blue, and white. There was no tree. The horse was bigger than any tree, legs braced wide, body twisted as it peered down at them, tail and mane whipping then dark again, and none ever telling the others this private but identical vision.

Downhill. Late afternoon. Flat light. Fog.

"See bottom?" Maul called, his voice tinny and contained.

"I'll tell you if I see bottom," Saul called up, his voice small and muffled.

The sun was gray. Their shoulders and knees brushed the rock face. Ripped windows in the fog revealed the marbled distance down. They held their pommels. The slope declined without much variation. No switchbacks. The bottom would be called Low Valley. A fire would be built, hands stretched to it, hot water down the gullet burning the tongue on the way. They'd sleep a little and wake again soggy. Huddle together in Low Valley in ponchos over jackets zipped to necks and knees in a jigsaw of bodies heating each other. They'd hack a tree if needed. They'd torch one off if they still had the flare.

"Do we have the flare?" Maul called.

"We aren't wasting flares," Saul snapped.

The flare was lost with the two browns, maybe. He'd forgotten which and when.

"Lost and free!" The echo was both muffled and booming. A new sound entirely.

He'd have to explain. Lost and free would shock and amaze anyone who truly absorbed the concept.

"My fog is clearing!" He was finally seeing things. "My Fog! My Fog!"

In Low Valley, the cook tent would be too much trouble. Keep going to higher ground. Naw. Tomorrow the cook tent. Tight as a puzzle in the cook tent. Perhaps he'd kiss Bowman in the dark. Bowman would think it was Saul.

"Are you boys in love now?" Maul called down.

No answer.

"Have a little fun with it tonight! Soon!"

No answer.

"My kingdom for a shovel!" He wasn't sure what this meant.

No answer.

"I bet she brought snowshoes! A huge pair, ten feet long!"

No answer.

"She would!"

No answer.

"She's clever!"

No answer.

"I admire her very much now, in fact! The old birch type of snowshoes! The crisscrossed frame! Some kind of webbing. No snow can stop her! Nothing can. She holds all the cards! She's invincible now!"

"How do you know who holds all the cards?" A voice startled Maul. He'd forgotten he was speaking aloud. He was delighted.

"Aha!" he called. "She's not stuck on this moronic trail! She's more lost than we are! She's free!"

No answer.

"No difference but that between us and her! She's alone and free and lost. We're not. Not alone, anyway!"

No answer.

"But what do I know?"

No answer.

"How's that leg? Impeccable, I'll wager."

No answer.

"So what did you do with that deputy?"

A gust.

"Stuff him in some cave in the Narrows?"

A gray bird veering, a seagull, impossible.

"Sure, we dropped him in a cave in the Narrows." That voice at the front.

"Horse goes into a bar." A second voice, too near. "Bartender says, 'Get that thing the fuck out of here.'"

Maul gave out with some spontaneous and sincere ha-has to cover another startle. He patted the dun's neck. There was no light. *What light in yonder window breaks?* He knew the quotations right. It's just that the wrong was more distinctive.

He twisted in his seat to look for snowshoes, for feathers on a beaded headdress. He knew the paint on the Indian's face had some meaning to those people, so too the leather loops around the thick-heathen-upper-thighs, no cover on the callused feet, no horse, never cold, oxygen red if you cut him.

Dan ran down from the fog breathless, startled Maul a third time.

When had he left?

Where had he been, Ella called to him. Henpecking. She was worried. Her complaints were legitimate, but Maul wanted to say to his new friend Ella, *None of your goddamn business*, since such phrasing was the next step in his metamorphosis. He would say it tomorrow. The next day, this next thing.

Dan too was evolving, rebelling. He refused to say what he'd been doing up trail.

Some mischief.

He told one more joke, and in his voice Maul could hear that Dan had supped with the devil, the tone of it like Bowman's voice now: The Prince rides to the village below his castle. He's tired, just back from a battle, another county taken. He's hungry for roasted thrush. The villagers flock him. His steed hates this part, bucks to keep the riffraff off his smithed-with-silver tack. *Bad men have come! They've raided the silos, taken all our grain, raped our women, even took our pot of jam and pig.* Which way did they go? What did they look like? The villagers stare up at him on his Great Steed. The sun is blasting off his doublet. Archers lean down off the parapet aiming.

"I get it now," Maul said.

"No, you don't." Dan ran on.

Maul dropped down to piss off the cliff edge.

"Screw you," Maul said just for fun. He was getting the hang of it. His arc of urine was flying half a mile. "I know what I know."

He was feisty beyond belief now. There was no telling where this was going. He flicked his headlamp on then off and walked the dun. The snow was sloppy concrete. It slapped in his face in a squirrelly, disorienting wind. He swatted snow, walked faster, rubbed raw hands on his windward jaws, pulled an imagined poncho around his face and cinched a cord.

"Good boy." A pat on the dun's neck.

Last words before Low Valley, he thought. The dun was a trusty friend for years, often overlooked given his average but not graceless stature. It was a miracle they were still alive. He was sad now too, like the mules, walking down in fog. When life on earth was over, on Judgment Day, no one in the world would remember some man who got called "Maul" for no particular reason, Maul the modern mule driver, since there was no place in the world, no place in recent history, no relevance anymore for mule drivers, no respect or interest in mules themselves now. Mules were once drivers of history as much as the Percherons, before engines but as much as engines, before wheels but as much as wheels. Mules were engines that walked in eternal rings turning mills, that bored holes deep down for oil to be sucked up iron straws and burned in engines. He will be forgotten, Maul: expert with knots and proud of it. Maul: voyeur and unashamed. Maul: lover of the lowly. Maul: not a brave man. Not a cowboy. Maul: player of cards, pretty good at cards though never able to prove it this trip. A shame since a pack trip is perfect for cards and they might've seen him different when he won at blackjack.

The obituary. Here was a man who liked beef well enough but preferred horse to beef. There was a cannery in Canada he visited once. He bought horses for cheap at auction and trucked them north since canning horse was still illegal here. He crossed the border with a skinny dozen that filled his trailer. The herd thought all was well. The trailer was clean and fitted out, after all, far nicer than the auction, clean water and hay. Horses had never been treated better. They did not accept death in the end. They *did not think* of it. Would their big hearts explode if they saw death before them? He doubted it. Nothing was more natural than death. At the border there was paperwork. A clipboard was passed from the uniformed booth. The horses watched through slats past the light turned green. They chewed in contentment until the very last moments as the trailer backed to the loading dock. None of this will be told in the World of the Future. Or this: that back at his home in St. Cecilia a whole pantry-full of horsemeat awaited him or his descendants. It was a closet he'd converted. Pint jars of palominos, paints, roans, and ponies.

Maybe there was such thing as quicksand.

What's the difference between a closet and a pantry? He turned when he heard a footfall behind. Nothing but snow to be seen. Fog, not fog. Bowman, not Bowman. Trick of the eye. He walked on. Keep walking on! This was the secret to all things. The key to the pantry door would be found on the chain in his coveralls. The jars were stacked in rows, pyramids of jars in the pantry, perfect seals under golden lids, all unlabeled. Not stringy at all.

⚜ —— ⚜

Ginny burned postcards from the book, stamped, in sage pitch.

up-to-my neck—oh Lordy MOTHER—
time and space was—Big Window is—
Moonlit death—airless—
cubicle   effervescent—
scorched

but

sorry
—red dog—

the yellow horse said—

The edges curled up in her heated fingers.

They were a Herd of Two. She petted the red dog's velvet ears and told him, then the silken back of his ragged knees, which caused him to stretch his whole leg out in gratitude, to point his craggy toe toward the cave wall as she worked the question:

(a) dog.

A red dog.

The red dog.

"The Red Dog."

The Red Dog.

Red Dog.

She switched to the ram next.

⁂

They met exactly like this in the fog. It was a mostly silent conversation, the best kind, with hand movements, bodies speaking, and a few words mixed to confuse or pique interest.

"I told you to think."

"We've ruined everything."

"You should have taken the Percheron, not the cob."

They nodded, thoughts meeting and parting. Mules and horses. They danced around each other on the drop-off.

"I didn't want the Percheron." Fog in her face, a waft of it. *A black flash of the below*, she thought. *One could jump.* "He'd gone off with his harem anyway."

"The concept of equine harems has been entirely debunked."

"Is that so." She was bored with this old talk.

"Not a new fact, no. An old fact rediscovered."

"Are there ever new facts?"

"I think we're in one now."

"I think you're wrong."

"That was always the trouble with you."

"Don't start."

Rather, it's now widely suspected that a mare does whatever she wants to in her herd. She nodded, he nodded. Too much territory there. The mare rebuffs stallions as a matter of course, goes off to copulate with satellite studs as well as with desirable males in other bands, out of adaptive necessity. For sixty million years this has been the case.

"People didn't care for the news. Don't want to hear it."

"But who could argue with a man who's done his equine reading?"

"Mocking till the end."

"Why'd you have to choke me?"

"We're beasts."

"You look ragged, like some crazy man."

"Look at yourself."

Her face had changed. Rough and red and the eyes were different, no wonder at all in her eyes now, all wonder. No devil. All devil but subdued: a devil in thought.

"I wish we could fuck." He reached out a hand.

"Why the eye patch?"

He tried to tell her, then gave up.

"Do you have any food?" she asked.

He had never met this woman there chewing jerky stowed just in case. Very ugly, but the chewing made him sure it was real. He tried to summon all the thoughts he'd saved up to tell her when this day came. He couldn't think of one.

"Should have listened to me," she said.

"Stop saying that," he said. "I'm tired of it."

"Why do you stay with them?"

"What am I without my people?"

She barked a laugh.

He tried one last thing to convince her of their twinship: "We were born together in a hailstorm, spit from a cloud, two bear cubs trapped in separate chunks of ice, broke open on impact, tumbled down different slopes, bawling, hungry, bottle-fed by grannies and aunties, reunited later."

"Try all you want," she said. "A nice story doesn't make it true."

"I think you're wrong."

"Goodbye, my friend," she said. The fog in a wave. A strange cape of burlap was wrapped around her.

"How could you ever be sure this is real?" he asked.

"Can't. Assume it is. Or it isn't? No one cares what you decide." She started up the hill with the meat, all of it.

"Come with me?" he said.

"I'm going the other way." She pointed uphill. "To Canada with the horses."

"Change direction with me. The horses are all down there waiting for you."

No answer.

"*Farewell* then," he said.

"Such an old-fashioned word."

"You're so different."

"So are you."

And he walked then ran on down to Ella after that.

Wandering, she caught a talon from above if she needed meat, quick as a mountain cat, big as a bear, brave as a horse, her story almost over. Who would remember her old self? Her spunk, graceful riding, skill with knives? Daughter of the chief. Who cared about brothers? A Bear needs a wife. His cave so quiet and empty down on hands and knees with him through the bushes outside the cave heavy with berries blue and red and black and each a sack of sugar waiting to be sucked and drained and the seeds stowed in her gut to be delivered by her long legs and filthy feet to the next valley over or the next valley over left for the world in a pile of scat, like that oak. She married him over and over and the story was repeated and repeated until it was an object of stone, just like her.

The Herd grazed in the clearing below and she called from the cliff over the Herd's back to the woman who had been her mother.

"It was me who did it all! Not him! Why give the Bear all the credit?"

✿ —— ✿

Mule Thought #6 (the buckskin jenny tells a story): Pestilence. Seas part and close in on the evil ones, and we and the sea drown them all.

Mule Thought #7 (the red jenny tells a story): No Title. The steer kicked her once and she turned the other cheek. The steer wondered if this was masochism. *No*, mulled the red jenny. *Only extremity allows the villain to see his villainy.*

Mule Thought #8 (the buckskin jenny tells a story): Four Mules. The Foal sets them free, one white mule, one red mule, one black mule, one buckskin mule.

Mule Thought #9 (the red jenny tells a story): Love. Water sloshed to their bellies, and they turned their faces to the current, pressing the last of the footing. It had been a small island in a river rising fast at midday. *I've seen worse*, she mulled, before plunging in, the young steer wondering but following, body quaking, his lips dripping green and red from grass and blood.

⸺ ⸺

Saddle up, kiddies, for Episode 5, "Salvation," of *The Long Trail of the Spy!* (That trail is getting so long, in fact, as to be eternal/infinite.) (Ask your parents if you'd like to learn more about infinity.)

Based on a true story!

The Spy doesn't fall for her nasty trick with the 30-30. No sirree! He doesn't fire at the first fat ram he sees, doesn't bleed out in a pond. Not at all.

Rather, as he waits and watches for forty days and forty nights from perches of all kinds, parapets on ubiquitous jagged pumice towers, from under shelves teetering on shelves of snow, in caves a bear has dug—he feels, to his surprise, a spy is spying on him. This Other Spy (that is not the right name yet) is the better spy, compared to himself, with bell-shaped ears for funneling sound. The Superior Spy (still not right, but closer) has eyes superior by magnitudes, both in size (like baskets) and magnification (like electron microscopes) and this Superior Being (yes, that's good) positions himself only on very high peaks. But still this Second Spy's (hold on) superiority is at least within the scale of the Original Spy's understanding. Other Spies aren't. The Spy on the Very High Peak (ah, that's it) is now seated in a tree on a snowy jagged mountain summit (there are so many). When tired of the tree, this spy spreads his wings and drops down to a new and different jagged summit. He stands there for a while, boots wide apart, and surveys the terrain with a spyglass the size of a ship's cannon. He hops ten miles. He watches Our Hero, the Humble Human Spy, with vague curiosity. There are so many other objects to inspect. He can see a thousand miles in all directions. A squirrel rolling a nut at the rim of an enormous nameless canyon to the south. An otter floating at a dock in a great lake eastward by a great city with stone lions blocking its gates to strangers. The moorings are rotten and mostly unmoored. Not that the otter cares about moorings. The otter turns in the water under the dock, dipping toward something deep in its shadow. What is it? Look!

It's a backpack. Torn and waving, empty. An apple floats by, green perfect tumbling fruit, rolling with the current over the line of a stout horse dead on the bottom. It lies broken open, a sunken ship full of water, pony-type, gray, maybe brown, switching, as the apple rolls off the rump, drops to the foal in a pit below. It is nestled with a gang of sleeping chickens and a sleeping man in an eye patch. He holds a broken teapot.

The Spy on the Very High Peak looks too, sees the thing, is amazed.

Meanwhile, back on a very high cloud, the Spy on a Very High Cloud is spying on the Spy on the Very High Peak, and the Spy on the Moon is spying on the Spy on the Very High Cloud, noctilucent pink, altostratus gray, nimbostratus violent-blue-violet, stretched.

Then the helicopter came.

⁂ —— ⁂

The sun was harsh on the eyes in the old days, before modern optometry. Once the Old Swede found a blue bottle and considered making a pair of glasses from it. Some Indian had already made the trail, after all, which left him time for leisure. And it was a good trail! But the bottle came from somewhere else. Outside of history. What was *outside* of it? When would that have been? The world was big, he knew, but nothing compared with the size of Time, that long horizon before Adam and Eve. The bottle was clear deep indigo, not milky at all. A name was scratched on the bottom, a sorry attempt at ownership, at victory over death. The Old Swede smashed the bottle on a very old cairn. *Elizabeth? Margaret?* He tried to recall his old love's name. He gathered in the blue shards. He was clever. He made the world fit his needs. But no, he chucked the shards. He was tired of dreams. He hoisted the shovel. Clucked at his mule. Whistled at the dog, who wagged, spun. They turned uphill into the sun.

He hummed a Swedish tune, *Ma Ma Ma*, to translate a sudden bolt of feeling.

He had to. The best moment of his life had come upon him. Suddenly it was there. *Eureka!* Or not really eureka. He sang out to his companions in a hybrid tongue, a translation of a translation. *Trudging on, hither and yon, alas now, whoa! giddyap, Nelly!* Where were the words that would fit the feeling? Sure of failure, he kept trying anyhow, trying to tell the passing miracle as it passed, this space-time convergence here, this blue-green mountain here, this man-mule-dog alive and moving here, through this *exact* now here, this *exact* stride of trail, *here, here, here.*

⁂

Ella would recall all her life that Lowest Valley seemed very low.

And the horses were restless. Maul would have said "resentful," didn't know how good they'd had it. The snow was done. The fog lay thick and nearly warm. Maul would have added that he, too, could understand the horses' frustrations, since all species had overlaps and intersections of sympathies with other species, and Bowman would've snapped that anthropomorphizing was the worst kind of self-obsession.

"Where's Maul," Dan said.

The two mules stood side by side. The buckskin with her exceptionally beautiful musculature—he'd never noticed—and the black with lush curly waves over his eyes, thicker and wilder. They were wild mules now.

Bowman limped to the old chestnut and spoke into one huge chestnut eye. He tied him to a branch that hung from nowhere into the cone of headlamp light. When Bowman turned, the cone sliced across his barrel chest, his knee, a buckle, a brass loop, into the fog until the fog turned the light back as if it hit a wall where the light balled in swirl and probed no further, hovered until Bowman bent to tasks again, whereby lit the root of a tail, a steel jug with fingers gripping it, etc. Dan looped the yellow horse's rope around a separate branch. The buds were very late. The crown would not be full in August. The two branches had no relationship. They were disconnected intersecting props dropped down from some man-made rigging. A tug on one would not matter to the other. Why not? No way to know what this valley actually contained. A cabin, maybe. A silent and lightless city. A set of cliffs just behind the branches: be careful where you step! Anything was possible.

Saul pulled bags from packsaddles. Ella stood and counted horses, mules, and men, a slow-thinking-girl, a cartoon-girl. The cones of their four headlamps flew about and clashed and banked in the fog in separate and intersecting radii. Lowest Valley, therefore, was entirely a guess, as all things are, an *apparent* valley only. Tomorrow, in the sun, there might be no cliffs, no flat, no branches in a new kind of land they'd never seen.

"I said, where's Maul?"

The mules were unpacked and now the four cones of light made the little room for them to work in, to sleep in, a manger of light and fog, a very small private and dripping place, snow becoming slush becoming mud already by hooves and boots and the concussion of bags and bundles falling, getting soggy. Parts of faces, a knee in soggy pants, a hat, a spoon on canvas rolled out. Unfinished leaves appeared still curled up, tender green things built for snow in May. They disappeared when a head turned a fraction. This is fact: the effect of a fraction. And it was always true!

Their manger was made of fog walls and paler reverberating reflections of light on snow. At the bump of a head or the shove of a mule's shoulder, even the darkest places were sometimes light. A boulder was a wing chair, then stone again, then nothing. An animal's hide or sleeve was doubled by triple shadow when two cones of light swung together, then a third. All the lights flew off at sharp sounds. A true *plunk* then *splash* caused the animals to prick their ears, to turn, but the *plunk* and *splash* was not repeated. Ella tried to light a lantern but the fuel was gone. A wick could do nothing alone. She lit a candle and set it on the rock and it made its own small room of light.

"Where's the dun?" Dan said.

"Maybe he turned back," said Bowman. "He was aimin' to."

Ella had tied her paint to a branch. Brown patches of his hide floated in the fog, independent. She stared. He wasn't a horse anymore but a puzzle with half the pieces gone. She tipped her head. The room was smooth white, an ever-moving ceiling with branches in it. This was spring. She'd never have guessed it. Fat roots dove under snow.

"What's for dinner?" Ella asked, sitting so still.

"Bread and water," Dan said.

"Bed for me," Saul said. "Too tired for food. Too cold." He was chewing something hard to chew.

"What are you eating?" she said.

"Jerky."

"What kind of jerky?"

"Bed, bread, dead," said Bowman.

"It's a famous verse," Saul said. "Old Testament."

"It's Shakespeare," said Bowman.

"What kind of jerky?" Ella said. "I asked you."

"You know what kind of jerky it is."

"How would I know?"

"You brined it, smoked it."

"I'd never imagined the ending of this," Dan said. He was sitting against the tree, his filthy knees before his face. The patch in shadow. His light on Bowman's face.

"No," Saul said. "A surprise."

"There're no laws here," Dan said.

"There's no law anywhere," Saul said. "The law is just lines on paper, words."

"There are no words here in this valley," Dan said.

"I can't even think the word 'laws' here."

"I can."

"But you still only think in words," Saul said. "I got back to something deeper. I'll keep to animal thought, myself, from now on. You try it. Go back to it. All else is translation. All translation is never right, all approximation."

"Where's Maul?" said Dan.

"The wall tent," Ella said.

"What about it?" Saul said.

"I'm very tired," she said.

She stood when no one stood. She found a tarp in a sack by the yellow horse. She flung the tarp out but found no poles, found the blue chair in a black hole. She found a cooking pot. Bowman went for wood, foot dragging but not much.

357

Ella scooped snow into the pot, cut poles with a knife and flung the ripped tarp over the top pole. Dan stood. He leaned on the tree. He watched Ella work, a blue flame produced by the flint striker and waxed cotton balls and a dial on the one-burner, one canister of white gas that had been the deputy's. The flame rose weak, hesitating. Dan took the .270 from the sorrel's scabbard. He lifted it to his shoulder, left the headlamp on. His thumb moved on the safety, and Saul stood up, his headlamp aimed into Dan.

"Whatcha doin'?"

"I'm aiming a rifle at you."

"I'm asking a deeper question."

"This world is bothering me."

"I've got the very same feeling."

Ella crouched over the one-burner now, not cooking or stirring the pot of snow. The horses rustled in some bumper-dance. Juniper was getting crushed. She could smell it.

"Put it down, darlin'," she said.

"Shut up," Saul said. "Stay out of this."

"I'm not your darlin'," Dan said.

"Ah," she said. "Saul is."

"My expectations are too high," Dan said, forgetting her.

"Let's clear this up," she said, but listless, no one heard it, waiting for her blood to rise and engage, waiting for someone new to interrupt. Always waiting. She stared into the dark over Dan's shoulder. The blue-ring flame hissed and warmed her hands, a crown of heat on the little stove. "We'll work on fixing it," she said without saying it.

"Sit down," Dan said and Saul crouched. "This will be a kind of suicide."

"Okay," Saul said.

Ella touched the pot and her hand sprang back. A tiny sea was foaming between aluminum shores, an island was made of snow, then submerged, subsumed.

"Little Danny won't do it anyway," she said, searching for the lost island at the bottom of the pot. "He let Shaw fuck her in the ass in the bedroom. You'll live to be a hundred."

It was a new tactic. Dan turned the rifle on her for a moment, but Saul was the main event. "Ginny's coming," he said. "I saw her today coming down."

"Good to know," Saul said.

"We forgave each other."

"Wonderful news," Saul said. "Let's all go home then."

"Put the rifle down," Ella laughed. "No need for it."

"Maybe this was the last night of the world," Dan said.

"That would be okay with me," Saul said. "The world could stop spinning here and now. But, you know, it probably won't."

"If it stops spinning right now," Dan said, "it'll be night forever from here on out."

"I follow you," Saul said.

"No more sunrise and sunset. Dark stays dark. Light stays light."

"Yes," Saul said. "I know. I can see that."

"Ready or not, we'd be nocturnal creatures overnight."

"I can see your logic. Makes perfect sense."

"Can you put that rifle down to discuss this," Ella said.

"Our eyes will be nearly blind at first in the dark," Dan said. "They'll grow bigger with each generation to compensate for the new scenario of permanent darkness."

"I got it," Saul said. "Evolution. Improving as needs change. The dark descending."

"I need to understand this now."

"That's what every person feels."

"This darkness," Dan said. "I can't take it anymore."

"I know what you mean."

They might have hugged in the dark as their headlamps spun, but that cannot be reported here. Rather, Saul was cross-legged on the snow, then he stretched his legs out in front of him, crossed his boots at his ankles, slouched a little.

"I'm not the same as you," Dan said.

"Men are all the same," Saul said. "Like all wolves are the same. All wolves kill sheep. One way to handle them."

"There's all kinds of differences in wolves," said Dan, and then they were going on about wolves.

"Why argue?" Ella wondered.

"Okay," Saul said. "Agreed. There's differences. But go for the big picture here. We've been friends a long time. It doesn't have to end this way."

"How do you know this is an ending?"

"You're pointing my rifle at me. As you noted."

"Bowman's out there somewhere."

"'Course he is."

"Ginny is behind him in a cave with a knife."

"Poor Bowman," Saul said. "A dead man."

"I don't care that much about dying," Dan said. "I want my life again."

Ella's face was blue in the flame. The little sea in the pot was blue light boiling. She turned to look at Saul and the sea went dark as his legs lit up and then the flat side of his big face. She grabbed the pot's edge with her bare hands and flung it at Dan.

Dan fired the .270. Saul was flung back. He lay on the snow as if pinned to the ground with a steel stake. His hand reached up to touch his middle. Dan had done it, put a hole in Saul. An eye for an eye. Dan let the rifle fall in front of him, looking at a dead man. Ella leaned over Saul, seeing him in a new way. She had a few moments in blue smoke and sulfur to consider who Saul would be now. This new man: Saul the Victim. He licked his lips as if he would speak to her one last time, to apologize or analyze, surely not to complain. She didn't look when Dan lifted the rifle again, shouldered it, and turned to kill someone else. He searched the dark behind him. But the dark is big and hard to sight in.

"Where's Maul!" Dan called.

"Dead," Bowman's voice said from somewhere out there.

Dan swung around. The headlamp beaconed out.

"Kill that goddamned light," Ella snapped and wiped her splattered temple.

He never had time to. The second and third shots flashed from the dark, the semiautomatic. It was done. Dan's neck spouted red. Dan stood the shot well then dropped to his knees, then dropped forward, his arms catching his fall, since this new Dan would not fall on his face. His arms gave out and slid, fingers tunneling the muddy snow. More blood had splattered Ella's stunned face. She roused herself. She frisked Saul's hips for a gun as, from the darkness, she heard Bowman's uneven footsteps coming. He never arrived. She heard the sound of cracking as someone smashed him with wood on bone. Next the clatter of steel to stone. The Ruger had fallen. Bowman grunted. The Indian Spy had intervened in their lives again.

The horses and mules were upset for a while. Then they settled.

She lived alone in the room of light and fog now. The snow was nearly boiled away. She lay down to curl into Saul. He was still very warm, always a furnace of a man.

Then she sat up.

"Bowman!" she called. "Bowman! Bowman!"

~ —— ~

Mule Thought #10 (the buckskin jenny tells a story): Genesis. *And I saw when the Foal opened one of the gates, and I heard thunder, one of the four great mules saying, Come and see. And I saw, and beheld a white mule with a bow and a crown and she went forth conquering. Then the Foal opened the second gate, and I heard the second mule say, Come and see. This mule was red with a great sword entrusted to take peace from the earth, and that men should kill one another and all other creatures too, all and all and all. Then the third gate, and I heard the third mule say, Come and see. And I beheld, and lo a black mule with a pair of balances on her back, and I heard a voice in the midst of the four mules say, A measure of wheat for a penny, and three measures of barley for a penny; and see thou hurt not the oil and the wine. Then the fourth gate, and I heard the voice of the fourth mule say, Come and see. And I looked, and beheld a buckskin mule and her name was Death.* (The remnants of the pack huddled close now.) *Hell followed her with the power to kill with sword, with hunger, and with the beasts of the earth, kicking, stomping to pulp, biting, and when she opened the fifth gate, I saw under the altar the souls of the slain crying, etc., Please please please! Those men who had no mercy, never once, did not even know they lacked it, a great earthquake, and the sun became black and the moon became as blood and the stars of heaven fell unto the earth, even as a fig tree cast her figs away shaken of a mighty wind, and every mountain and island was moved out from their places and the kings of the earth, "great" men, rich men, yes, chief captains, mighty men, so called, and every enslaved man and every free man hid himself in dens and caves in the mountains, and they said to the mountains and rocks, Fall on us, and hide us from the wrath of the Foal: The great day of Mule Wrath is come.*

❧ —— ❦

When she entered the light, Ginny looked the dead men over. She had the Ruger in a makeshift belt. She bent over Dan for a long time. She shoved wet from her cheeks. She rolled Dan off the .270. Her fourth finger in the trigger, others bound together. She raised the rifle at Ella. Ella held her hands up.

"No words?" Ginny said.

She bent first to peel the headlamp from around Dan's head. She stuffed it into her strange rags of clothing. The light glowed from some nether space inside. The .270 was tipped from the crook of her arm. She went to the chestnut next. She shifted the blanket forward on his withers, spoke to him, lifted the saddle on. The bridles were never taken off, the bits. She bent and checked his legs. She stepped to the sorrel, the blanket, the saddle, then the paint next, then the yellow horse, then the packhorse, then the two mules last. The dun walked in and she checked him over.

She tied them together in no order, tail to harness, tail to harness. When Ella leaned toward a coil of rope, Ginny aimed and fired at the coil. She stuffed the rope in a satchel. She added snow to the pot when she found it. It melted at once.

Ginny leaned over Ella and dug in Saul's pockets, found his knife, two sticks of gum, unwrapped both, stuffed them in her mouth, breathed, chewed slowly. She gathered panniers and rifled through them, dropping items out, stuffing others, small bags, crumbs, a ripped-up poncho, a lighter on the ground, a blue tin cup, a fork with a tine bent back. She wore Saul's headlamp. She turned it on and off. The light was very weak. She tapped the light and the beam doubled. She poured the hot water into the tin cup and drank it. She adjusted the headlamp strap and wound the light back onto her head. She bent once again to Dan and looked at him for a long time. She pulled his poncho back from his face.

She let the chestnut sniff her down.

She bent over Ella, shut off the one-burner. It cooled and she unscrewed the white gas canister. Gloves, several pairs. She stuffed these in the pannier. A pencil, a book. She lifted a water jug, shook it, shook a canteen, a cartridge for the magnum. She slid Dan's belt from his belt loops. He was still and cooling. She wrapped the belt around her middle, with the knife cut a new hole.

"Where's Maul?" Ginny said.

"Over there somewhere. Below the cliff."

An empty ammo can. Another pannier.

"Where's Bowman?" Ella said.

"Over there," Ginny said. "Groggy. He'll get himself loose after we go," and Ella thought *he doesn't deserve to live*, but

364

didn't say it. It was the end of that time in her, and the beginning of something else. Continents inside her were breaking past each other. She had never believed in it. Change. Evolution of the self.

Rope. A bit of string, a spatula.

"Get his shirt," Ginny said. "His coat. Socks."

Ella undressed Saul down to his bloody T-shirt. Ginny did the same with Dan and disappeared again. She wore Bowman's gloves.

"Put it on," Ginny said as she wound up rope, made neat loops over her arm. Ella stuffed her arms into Saul's coat.

Ginny studied the map in the headlamp for a long time.

"Get up," she said.

"I'm cold," Ella said.

"Get up."

They dragged Saul and Dan to the tree. They didn't pray. Bowman was making noise by the creek. They got walking.

Ella led the mules and horses. Ginny walked behind. The red dog trotted beside her.

They spoke very little, and then only about the girl and the bear. Think of it like landscape, Ella said, the anthropological tradition in her clan yes showing type of people separation of the sexes duties of the womenfolk also character berry picking tearing her apart the only soothing being the out-reaches of the—

"Stop," Ginny said.

"The bear, he's sad. He sees the world all new and we're crushed with him."

"Enough."

They slept on both sides of burning trees. They burned a tree every night. There were plenty of trees and sacks full of matches.

When they reached the road, it was nearly dark again. It was a small road with local traffic, no cars for some time. The sisters walked north on the road, Ginny trailing behind with the little cavvy—horses, mules, and dog—trailing her. When a vehicle came it was a pickup driving south. It slowed, passed them, accelerated then slowed before a bend. Ginny cut Ella free, shoved her into the road when she didn't move. She clicked her tongue at the animals, turned them swiftly north again, steered into a ditch, the steam of bodies swirling as they disappeared back into trees.

Ella was not fast. She limped and listed. In the pickup's flashers she turned ruby red. A door handle. She climbed in.

The inside of the truck was green light beaming on the steering wheel, fingers gripped around it, and some music playing. There was a rearview mirror, a dial for heat, an arch from blue to orange to red to explain it all to idiots. The mirror, like all such mirrors, had a swivel neck. She twisted it, avoiding her face, looking out through to the road behind, all last year's leaves turned red and tumbling across the red pavement.

The driver nodded and sipped a Coke.

"Let's go back," she said, and as always, the vehicle did exactly what she said.

Some kind of four-point turn. Pointing north at a standstill, the driver opened the glove box for tissues. She peered up the road from where she'd just come.

"Is someone out there?" said the driver.

Her explanation was truncated due to the lateness of the hour, the dryness of her mouth, her shaking hands. "Yes."

The driver offered her a bag of nuts and a Coke from a cooler in the jump seat. How did he know she was starving? There was beer in it too. She drank it by sips. The shadows in the headlights were only shadows. The pickup stood for a long time. High beams. The road was narrow and pocked—marked from poor engineering and cheaters in the construction phase. So many small country roads this far north were built over ice lenses, unwittingly or just typical cheap planning. The lenses lifted the pavement first, the elastic action of a great inhale. In time, the rock exhaled and the ribbon slumped as the heated cement melted itself.

"Mm," said the driver.

She was tired. She was making no sense. She was filthy, too thin, and wild looking.

"My children are in St. Cecilia," she said and the driver turned the heat up a notch. She told him, "Everything's gone." Her name first was stolen years ago, a real soap opera. All she wanted was scrambled eggs. The driver had snack food and told her not to wolf it.

"It was really all Grannie's fault," she told the man.

He offered her aspirin. The cotton was still jammed under the cap. He dug with his fingers.

"Cat got your tongue?" she said.

The pills spilled into the chasm of the footwell.

"Never mind," she said. "Could you take me there? To St. Cecilia. I'll pay you for gas. Every penny."

She looked around for a purse. The town was a small one. The driver nodded. All the way around the mountains. The driver knew the place. She turned the heat dial down the same notch the driver had recently raised. Though shivering, she wasn't exactly cold. It was some other kind of shiver, crackling from inside like the road did, breaking out, since cement was not meant to bend at all. She was like that.

"Hurry," she said.

The driver stepped on the gas.

She looked at him, kindly. "Is there something wrong with you too?"

The ice lenses were only the beginning, she told him, added to lifting and slumping, even greater aggravation brought on by the tiniest of ongoing seasonal effects, moisture filling tiny cracks, forming holes, pits, freezing, thawing, requiring, in the end, always a big machine with a bucket. She blinked. Oh, she was tired of buckets.

The pickup had turned again, speeding south, and in a few miles she found herself kneeling on the bench seat, facing back, hands on the cold rear glass of the cab.

"All my things," she concluded. "I've lost them," and she went through the list of the missing for the driver, and how she and her sister had once been close but now were hardly speaking. Now when they spoke, they spoke only of the girl and the bear. The girl and the bear were *a code*: a way to communicate when speech was impossible. The driver understood fine. Ella could see that fine. The way he nodded, his hands on the steering wheel saying and asking her without asking (another code) to *Please go on, tell me more.* And she did: When the bear was young. Ambitions. Rate of copulation. Slid snow on his belly, a toboggan. Yes, Joy, he was full of it, and grief too. Was *necessity* to him. The propensity. Outside and inside, Ella explained. Implication of thrusts, of fires, of cave paintings duly changed.

The driver lit a match and smoked. She took the cigarette from his mouth and smoked it down, set it back in his lips.

"The end," she said.

The pickup rolled forward to the curve and around it. It drove for miles, very slowly. She talked of Eve next, since it was not the end yet, mother of all the world, since every woman can trace her line back to this apple eater, friend of snakes, birther of birth and death both.

The truck pulled over. The hazards blinked in indecision.

"Let me out," she said as if she'd planned it.

The door swung open. She was out. A deer in the road. A piece of chalk. The End. The End.

The truck inched forward to go on about its life without her. He would tell a few people who would tell a few what he'd seen and heard this night. All would be well if he told enough of them. The owls watched in the branches, the separate plane of birds, their clock-faced faces following Ella trotting north now, their heads ticking degree by degree with Ella's strobe of movement in taillights, then none when the truck skidded off. The owls invented Ella just as she had invented owls in her busy life, tawny and vivid, wise or wall-eyed, neat tucked feathers as a rule, wings reaching as needed to hoist the owl into the air—a flying owl, a swooping owl—and the owls made Ella vivid and tawny, more round-legged than themselves, taller, with slender pathetic wings pumping as she ran toward takeoff. She ran better with only owls watching. She ran over the center line, swerving reckless, a new trait in herself she would prize.

"Where are you?" Ella called into a slice of sky. "Take care of all those lovely critters for me, sister dear. I did my very best to catch you, you know!"

The red dog dipped under from the dark leaves, departing with his new herd, not all red at all but in the sun tomorrow flecks of gray and black, peppered effects.

Ginny called out to the herd she led north. She was breathing hard, sweating in the cool. She called out to the herd with no need to but to be neighborly, and only to those in the small slice of the universe she could see, her own three-sixty, that private computation, that proportion men could calculate, give name to, boys in white jackets, slide rules in pockets and telescopes, boys like Dan before he was turned into Dan, the potential of Dan lost by herding cows and men herding him, or Ella, or perhaps even Saul if he wasn't Saul, a country boy. These people.

No matter now. To see into the universe, to measure it, to run *into it alone*, to say anything about it, for *Ella Ella Ella*—for anyone at this late date—it was nearly impossible. Far-fetched.

She hurried on calling into the impossible, calling out up the trunks of trees and owls' downy fronts into the black curtain that stretched out between the fringe of needles solid as cliffs. She tried to pierce it, the sky, to part the curtain with her body: the projectile of living. She tried to run off the edge of the earth's carpet into infinity. It was hard to do. The horses were tired, the mules, the dog. She hurried on, out *to* and *between* starlight, which, she could see now, even from there, was just skeins of bright shiny seaweed stretched up from the bottom of the sea-night-toward-earth, around earth, vines whipping beyond humble earth in graceful waves in the waves of space, wagging and snagging from roots in the sandy cold soil of the beginning. In the beginning was Ella and Ginny.

The universe was scented in her own sweat. Black-bruised-purple of prune skin, the pores broken open to disbelief and cold night air. Life was done. It was starting. She began *to see* for a millisecond into the flat of color behind the curtain down the roots of the entrance of on-and-on-beyond for a fraction of a millisecond. She ran into the terror of knowing all she saw. To be blind is so tempting! Where, if entered, she would never return fully, innocence lost.

SIX

Tree

MULE CENSUS
Day One, Yeoman's Calendar (dawn-sunset)
SPECIES: *Equus asinus* × *Equus caballus*
LOCATION: Yeoman Sea

The yeoman didn't near the colt as she swam past him by the blowdown. The shore was just there and still very nice. Dry. The colt was enormous and sad. He snorted at the yeoman as if she were an enemy. Night came and she listened to his bellows. Three eons since barbed wire but the colt knew it still, memory of rust, ripped flesh, wolves. The wolves were thick on the West Sea but slept daytimes and when storms came. It was a dull name: West Sea.

What was an eon? Who decided?

The tide came in and swept the blowdown out. Behind the storm the moon glowed through in breaks in clouds. She crouched in the seagrass. Gulls nested safe in holes on cliffs. Nothing could reach them. There was a whole herd, the huge Mule in their midst. She saw them in retreating flashes of lightning.

On the West Sea—she'd heard at mess—the cedars were *truly worth study.*

Silly thought. It was better to smell them. Sit.

Several varieties were mixed with redwoods and sequoia all the way north to the chilly wide expanses, *ha ha ha*, where the New Mules would await another Heat Event to restore grasses to the great flat plains that arched to the East Sea where trees grew to more modest height since winds whipped the biggest off cliffs to jam the shores of archipelagos beginning the next great land bridge.

She laughed and laughed. There was plenty of food for all. Seaweed. Snails. The berries were every color. Red. Purple. Blue gone waxy-pink, dried, crushed, smeared on ferns. She needed no fire. The worst thing about berries: they got dull.

At mess, they would have eaten the last pie. This was her last thought of them.

Rain all night. Sun all day. She kept the herd in view or within her sharpened earshot.

It was warm enough for no coat mostly. No winter. It was the eternal time of the unwitnessed.

HER NOTE: The Mule is "Adam," a mythological reference. The Filly is "Eve."

Storms were famous. In the mornings, green needles edged the beaches for miles—she walked in the herd's tracks—turned yellow or rotted, washed out again to deep sea places—she could envision this—to blanket rocks and feed strange fishes down below—she could not envision them. The wrench and kit eluded her at first. The bucket washed up in a net of seaweed braided with balloon-shaped fishes that stung and she gave wide berth to. Whole trees fell across the shore leaving enormous gashes at tree line, balls of roots towering, and the gashes filled with starfish at high tides. She ate the starfish. She looked at the sea and the clouds. A whole life could be passed this way. Cliffs broke free, killed by water seepage and tree roots creeping, new cliffs appearing behind, taking turns at sunlight. Destruction, she saw in time, was the essential work of trees. She lay in the seagrass and calculated. How big a tree to split a mountain? How to split continent from continent? To split a yeoman from a wing?

She was a shaving, a fleck, with ever-red lips. A flag.

She stepped out of her jumpsuit and waded into the water. Sea sloshed around her legs. There was only the sea and her and that colt somewhere. She could marry him and live at sea. Only three hooves are needed for swimming. A colt should be easy to spot. She shaded her eyes. She dove. She called to him, *Romeo!* There was a pencil in the kit at ten fathoms. A stick of sodden gum. She ate berries three meals a day. It took weeks for her bowels to regulate. She patted bricks from the huge piles of mule dung, baked them in the sun, stacked them for a tiny dwelling. She dreamed of a wall with a window. Where was that Mule and his herd of shitters? She called to them each by name. There were many foals.

She whistled. No answer. She had not seen them all day.

The sun was very warm.

Her sun.

Time accrued like coral. Time passed and her coral accrued. Thoughts sharpened with variation and repetition. She named herself captain. She lay on the shore by her empty jumpsuit. She would replace it with mule skin. Impossible to be together (sea and shore). Impossible to be apart (sea and shore).

ACKNOWLEDGMENTS

Thank you:

Stephanie Steiker, for your couch, for the Old Swede, for your patience and spitfire genius. The wizardly Jeremy Davies, who hung on and kaleidoscoped the book into focus through a global pandemic. And Other Stories—Tom Flynn, Javerya Iqbal, Nicky Smalley, Stefan Tobler, Tara Tobler, Emma Warhurst, the authors, board, translators, subscribers and readers—all who support books with their lives.

Karen Shepard and the women of the 2013 Tin House Summer Novel Workshop. Sandra Jensen, Nancy Foley, Tim Sutton, and Margaret Eagleton. Lynn Grant, Cheryl Niemuller, Devon Ronner and Barbara Turner. Melinda Haas. John Vinduska and Sherri Jackson, who gave me the mare and Percheron. All my friends who put up with me. Thank you.

Wendy Williams for *The Horse*, and Joe Back for *Horses, Hitches and Rocky Trails*. Robert Service for "The Song of the Wage Slave."

Experts and technical consultants: Letha Robertson, Justin Elkins, Kevin and Kylen Ulrey, the Wayne and Yelena Hage family, Dave Gudelauski, Oz Wichman, Betsy, Ella and Arthur Vielhaber, Sharon Weisenbaum, Ella Cummings. The Indigenous American storytellers of North America over eons on whose land I live and learn. The UMass

Amherst Program for Poets and Writers, Sirenland Writers Conference, Tin House and BOA Editions.

My thanks to my mother and father, who never told me to stop. To my family. To Jerry Elkins, who gave me a desert home and his vast knowledge of the wild in which to write this.

To Pearl.

To all the beasts.

Dear readers,

As well as relying on bookshop sales, And Other Stories relies on subscriptions from people like you for many of our books, whose stories other publishers often consider too risky to take on.

Our subscribers don't just make the books physically happen. They also help us approach booksellers, because we can demonstrate that our books already have readers and fans. And they give us the security to publish in line with our values, which are collaborative, imaginative and 'shamelessly literary'.

All of our subscribers:

- receive a first-edition copy of each of the books they subscribe to
- are thanked by name at the end of our subscriber-supported books
- receive little extras from us by way of thank you, for example: postcards created by our authors

BECOME A SUBSCRIBER, OR GIVE A SUBSCRIPTION TO A FRIEND

Visit andotherstories.org/subscriptions to help make our books happen. You can subscribe to books we're in the process of making. To purchase books we have already published, we urge you to support your local or favourite bookshop and order directly from them – the often unsung heroes of publishing.

OTHER WAYS TO GET INVOLVED

If you'd like to know about upcoming events and reading groups (our foreign-language reading groups help us choose books to publish, for example) you can:

- join our mailing list at: andotherstories.org
- follow us on Twitter: @andothertweets
- join us on Facebook: facebook.com/AndOtherStoriesBooks
- admire our books on Instagram: @andotherpics
- follow our blog: andotherstories.org/ampersand